A SCI-FI GAMER FRIENDS-TO-LOVERS ROMANCE

SPELLBINDING HIS RANGER

BOOK ONE
LOOKING FOR GROUP

SHANNON PEMRICK

Spellbinding His Ranger
Looking For Group | Book One

Copyright © 2018 Shannon Pemrick
www.shannonpemrick.com

Cover Design by Covers by Combs

ISBN 978-0-9984464-7-9 (paperback)
ISBN 978-1-950128-13-6 (hardcover)
ISBN 978-1-950128-00-6 (e-book)

For my player number two.

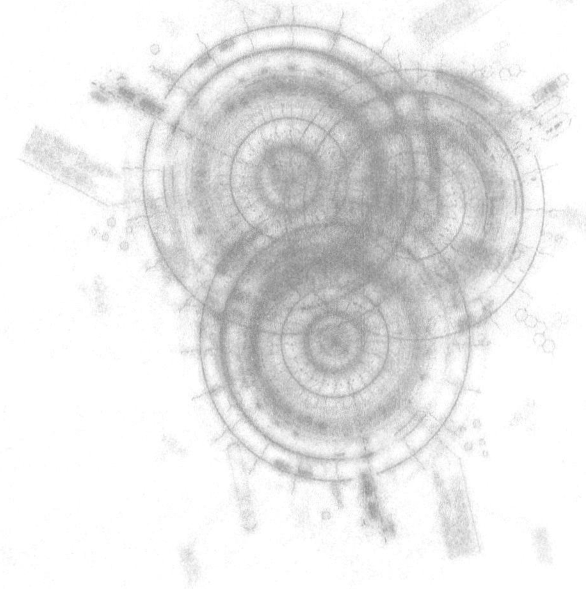

BOOKS BY SHANNON PEMRICK

LOOKING FOR GROUP

Spellbinding His Ranger
Protecting His Priestess
Summoning Their Elementalist
Binding Their Elementalist

VALKYRIES RISING

Valkyrie Destiny
Valkyrie Lost
Valkyrie Renewed
Valkyrie Restored
Valkyrie Confused
Valkyrie Condemned

EXPERIMENTAL HEART

Destiny
Pieces
Secrets
Exposed
Surrendered
Reborn

ORACLE'S PATH

Prophecy of Convergence
Prophecy of Unbroken Oaths

Prophecy Tested
Prophecy Chosen

See all books and learn more at
https://www.shannonpemrick.com

CHAPTER 1

Mercedes bent over the front of a 2016 Bugatti Chiron with faded blue and black paint, tightening a bolt in the engine bay. A tassel of golden blonde hair escaped her messy bun and she quickly tucked it behind her ear. Orange light from the low-hanging California sun filtered through the windows of the large car shop. Vehicles of various makes, models, and years sat in bays within the building, while many more sat in the parking lot.

"Miss Mercedes," a robotic voice called out from the phone attached to her hip. "I know you're enjoying restoring this project car, but if you don't pack up soon, you'll be late for your plans today with Takashi."

Mercedes wiped a bead of sweat from her brow and pulled away from the car. "What time is it, Tasha?"

"Seven-oh-four p.m."

She unlatched her phone to look at it. "Are you sure?"

Sure enough, she'd stayed two hours after closing.

Crap. At this rate, she'd have to rush to eat dinner if she didn't want to be late. *Luckily I don't have to clean myself up or anything.* The thought of looking nice just for Takashi sent a flutter of butterflies through her stomach. *No, no, simmer down.* The two of them were just friends.

A thought occurred to her as she put away her tools. "Tasha, was day is it?"

"Wednesday, May 4, 2107. Why do you ask?"

"Do I have any messages from Heart Connect?"

The shop went quiet, except for the sounds of Mercedes' cleanup, while Tasha finished her request. "I'm sorry, Miss Mercedes, but you have no new messages."

A prickle of disappointment ran through her. "Okay, thank you."

She'd been messaging a guy back and forth on the dating site for the past few days. It looked to be promising, but then he up and disappeared two days ago. A part of her hoped he'd just gotten busy and would get back to her soon, but after two days with nothing, she knew to move on. *At least I have that date set up for tomorrow.* Mercedes wasn't getting her hopes up, but she wanted to be as positive as possible right now.

"Miss Mercedes, are you all right?" Tasha asked. "I sense an emotional change in you."

"Yeah, I'm fine, don't worry. Please pull the car up for me."

"Of course."

Mercedes grabbed a rag and cleaning solution, going about scrubbing her hands free of grime, focusing on her cybernetic prosthetic arm first. It would be the easiest to clean.

She turned off lights as she moved through the shop,

noting the light still on in the office. She ducked in to find a tall man with fair hair, tan skin, and a muscular physique sitting in front of a computer.

"Dad, I'm heading out."

He looked back at her and smiled. "All right. I'll see you tomorrow."

"Don't stay too much longer. The work will still be here tomorrow." She then ducked out and left the building.

Her white 2011 Bugatti Veyron sat out front, its engine purring at idle. Tasha's voice came from the dash of the car when Mercedes hopped in. "Miss Mercedes, I've received the traffic report, and traffic will be a lower volume than usual. You will reach home ten minutes ahead of schedule. Your dinner will be ready at its normal time, though, so you will have to wait. I suggest using that extra time to feed your fish and relax."

"Have I told you how much I love having you around, Tasha?"

"Since you purchased me."

Mercedes chuckled and reclined in her seat as her sports car pulled out of the parking lot and onto the street, continuing to clean her hands. Her cybernetic prosthetic arm no longer carried traces of her trade, but her real one wasn't taking to the cleaning cloth, especially around her cuticles. She pouted. She'd grown up in her father's antique car shop, learning all there was to fixing the old non-self-drivers from over seventy years ago, as well as the different paint jobs a shop could offer for new and old vehicles. She loved the line of work, but it did a number on her skin.

She was sure her skin had absorbed a good portion of the grime, grease, and paint she handled daily. Some days, she wished her passion fell under a different umbrella so she could have nice-looking hands. She looked at her prosthetic arm. *Well, except this thing.*

Bright lights flickered behind the clear fiberglass structure, pistons and other moving components doing their job as she moved her false limb. Cybernetic limbs were the hot ticket technology on the market. Her best friend, Narissa, had a hand in all that, along with her family. They'd pioneered the cybernetic technology used today, and even now, were developing ways to improve the tech.

"Miss Mercedes," Tasha said. "You have an incoming call from Doctor Narissa. Should I answer it?"

Speak of the devil. "Please do."

She heard a click, and then, "Hello?"

"Hey, Narissa."

"Hey. You sound like you're on speaker and there are no clanking sounds, so my guess is you're in your car on your way home from work."

"Bingo. I had the urge to work on my personal project car. Just barely left the shop."

"She will be home in eleven minutes," Tasha announced.

Mercedes and Narissa chuckled. Narissa spoke again. "Okay, cool. Do you think you could finagle a raid run today with the guild? Eli had to cancel on the guild due to something going on in his side of the world."

Narissa was talking about the VMMORPG, virtual massively multiplayer online role-playing game, Lusara Fates. A fantasy world filled with made-up playable species, adventure, and social interaction. The game's popularity was all due to its ability to craft brilliant storytelling, compelling encounters for PvE, player vs.

environment, balanced PvP, player vs. player, and unique economics that meshed with the real world, making it possible for people to make a legitimate living inside the game if they so pleased.

Mercedes had been introduced to the game upon making friends with Narissa, and was welcomed into her guild with open arms. While there was a big competition in the gaming community between those who chose PvP or PvE, the guild focused on working together, so it allowed players from both sides through its doors.

Friendly banter and competition were allowed, but personal attacks were swiftly handled by the guild leader and his appointed officers. It made for a fun environment and great connections. They all called each other friends, many of them finding conventions or competitions to meet up in person. And whenever someone needed help, the guild was there for them. *Like a second family.*

"Sorry, but I already made plans with Takashi."

"Oh, date with your boyfriend," Narissa teased.

Her cheeks warmed and she was glad she was only on the phone. "It's not like that."

"Don't deny it."

Takashi and Mercedes had known each other for a long time. He'd been one of the first guild members to invite her on some quests to get used to the game and build camaraderie. The avatar he played was a particularly handsome half-elf, a human and elf hybrid, and over the years, the two of them had made a deep connection. One so deep, she had to remind herself they were *just* friends.

Plus, she'd never met him outside the game. Social media was the only thing that had allowed her to even know what he looked like in real life. *And damn if he isn't good looking, making these conversations that much more tempting to indulge in.*

"As I've told you before, we're *just* friends."

"And you should change that."

She knew Narissa was going to be stubborn about this. The topic had become number one between them these past few months, but Mercedes was just as stubborn. "Apparently I have to remind you he lives in South Korea right now, only coming back stateside to see family or for work conferences."

"And apparently I have to remind you of VR. Besides, with all the flowers he gives you, the two of you are all but in a relationship, anyway. Might as well make it official and reap the extra benefits."

She always brought up the full-body experience of VR as part of her argument. Virtual reality. A big part of why Lusara Fates had been so successful. It had to be played in tech pods that hooked up to your nervous system. In doing so, it allowed the player to experience the game as if they were actually there, instead of letting the imagination run wild. *Not that there's anything wrong with letting it run wild. As long as it stays there.*

There were plenty of people who hooked up in this game, either for a short time, or even created successful partnerships out of it. But Mercedes knew she and Takashi were *just* friends. "They're yellow roses, which symbolize friendship. You know this."

Narissa let out a deep sigh of frustration. "Cede, you're twenty-nine years old and single. You're missing out on a perfect chance with a great guy."

Mercedes glanced down at her cybernetic arm as her

car pulled into the driveway of her half of the condo she lived in. "I'd prefer to keep my friendship with him intact. Besides, you're one to talk. You're a year older and single."

Her friend shut up immediately, though she did catch some grumbling on the other end. Narissa focused on her work a lot, pulling long hours to the point it was unhealthy many times. This drove away most potential partners, if she even had time to look their way.

Mercedes loved her friend's passion to help others, but Narissa needed to focus on herself for once.

"So, I want to run something by you, having to do with your cybernetic," Narissa said.

"Sure." Mercedes was happy for the change. She didn't want to talk about Takashi, their close friendship, and his... She shook her head. *Stop it, Mercedes.* "Tasha, please transfer the call to my phone."

"Doctor Narissa, please hold a moment while I complete Miss Mercedes' request."

Mercedes hooked an earphone onto her ear and held onto her phone as she climbed out of the car. Her phone *pinged* and she was reconnected to Narissa. "All right, I'm here to listen."

"Well, I've been doing some research and redesigning some of our tech, big surprise there..." Mercedes couldn't refrain a laugh at her friend's jest at herself. "And I think I've finally had a breakthrough for improvements. We're going ahead with a prototype, but it gave me an idea that I was hoping you'd be willing to test."

Mercedes swiped her house key in front of the lock, unlocking her door, and entered her home. The smell of meat and potatoes filled the air. She tossed her key deck into a bowl on a stand by the door. "Lay it on me and I can give you an answer."

"This new tech we're working on—it improves the mobility of the current style on the market, as well as simulating nerves."

Mercedes' eyes widened. She expected her friend to say they'd made advancements on the artificial skin to cover cybernetic limbs.

Currently, there were only two ways to get new skin. Through skin grafting, which didn't work so well with cybernetics, and then a false skin specifically designed to cling to the fiberglass casing. Unfortunately, this false skin had some issues passing as real skin. If you opted to use it, it was best to have make-up skills to make it less noticeable.

Mercedes didn't like the artificial skin, so she stuck it out with showing off her cybernetic, waiting for the day the technology finally caught up.

But simulated nerves was an even better topic. After her accident and being fitted with the cybernetic, Mercedes believed she'd never feel anything from that arm again, except the occasional phantom pain many amputees felt. "Can you really do that?"

"If my data is correct, yes. We're going to start testing prototypes tomorrow, so we'll know for sure then. But it made me wonder how it would affect those with old tech. The new tech will be more expensive to make, and that'll mean the cost for someone to obtain one will be higher, too. Not everyone can afford the more expensive option, so I started thinking about a way to slowly upgrade old tech without having to outright replace it with the new one."

Giddiness rose up in Mercedes' chest. "If this is your roundabout way of asking if I'll be your guinea pig, the answer is yes!"

She swore she could hear Narissa's smile. "I knew you would be on board with this. I'm hoping it works. I'd like to roll it out for Shira and Ajax to test once we work out the big kinks."

Mercedes frowned. Ajax, another guild member of theirs, had the same prosthetic as her. But Shira… her cybernetic enhancements were extensive. The two had been involved in a similar accident; they met when they shared the same hospital room. But compared to Mercedes, Shira had been harmed far worse. The amount of work doctors put in just to save her life, let alone get the cybernetics she needed to have a more "normal" life… Mercedes shook her head.

Shira never wanted anyone to feel bad for her. Even though her life had been completely changed, she wasn't letting it get the best of her. Aside from her love life, she'd done well. She hadn't been able to keep her old modeling job. Mercedes remembered the news headlines when that all went down, but she'd found a different outlet, in Lusara Fates. And she'd made new friends, including her. Mercedes couldn't even imagine her life without Shira and Narissa, or the rest of the guild, for that matter.

Mercedes entered the kitchen to grab herself something to drink. "That makes me want to try this out more."

"Good. I'll give you more details on what the testing will do, and our timeline for all of it. I don't think we'll get to the same quality grade as these new techs, but if

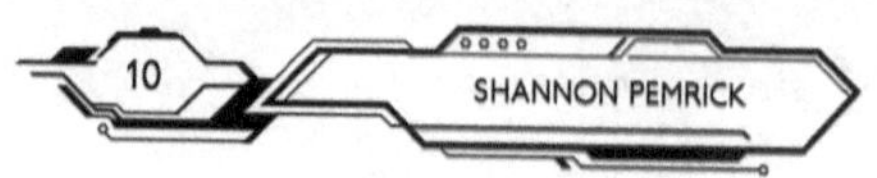

I can offer a partial upgrade system for people, I think that will really help." Narissa chuckled. "And as a thank you for being my first test subject—I mean willing participant of this carefully laid out test—you will receive a full upgrade after testing completes."

Mercedes smirked. "I appreciate the gift."

"Miss Mercedes," Tasha said through her kitchen appliance application. "I'm sorry to interrupt, but your dinner is ready."

"Thank you, Tasha. I'll retrieve it in a moment."

"Of course, Miss Mercedes."

"I should let you eat so you're able to spend time with your *not*-boyfriend."

Mercedes exhaled a long sigh as she pulled her steak and potatoes out of the oven. Narissa giggled before saying goodbye and hanging up. Mercedes' stomach growled, and she licked her lips hungrily as she carried her meal to the table. It didn't take her long to eat every last bite.

Meal consumed, Mercedes put her dishes away, fed her fish—but not before teasing them a bit with her finger—and headed through her spacious living room to her gaming room.

The room was filled wall-to-wall with bookshelves containing games of all vintages, as well as various equipment and consoles that still worked, such as an Atari and a PS4. She also had a few new consoles that had just come out in the last two years—a Nintendo Sector and a PlayStation Star. Two or three decades ago, Sony, along with Microsoft, went away from numbering their consoles and tried to get more creative.

A computer station stood in one corner, while in

the opposite corner resided her VR gaming pod—a specialized curved chair with all the necessary gear to suck her into the virtual world, and hanging screens to allow her any out-of-game prompts, from selecting a game to managing business tools.

Mercedes powered on the chair before sitting down in the pod. The touchscreen display allowed her to set up Lusara Fates as her desired game and pull up her friends' list. No surprise, Shira was on, using her elementalist class, a natural magic user class focusing on elemental abilities like fire and water, and summoning temporary living elements to aid her. Mercedes wasn't sure if she was running as a healer or a DPS, damage per second, as she could swing either way in her PvP matches.

Jasper and Zach, two of her guildmates and good friends, were also logged in. The former using his rogue class, a stealthy melee DPS class good for high damage but extremely low defense, and the latter using his warrior class, a heavy armor melee class built for either tanking, high defense and lower offense, or DPS, above average defense and high offense.

Takashi's profile picture popped up when she selected his name, and her heart skipped a beat. Short ebon hair, dark captivating eyes, strong jaw, and light tan skin, showing his mixed racial heritage.

Takashi had told her once how his parents met. His father, Brazilian-born, stateside raised, had flown over to Japan for a seminar on the precursor game to Lusara Fates. His mother had been working the check-in table, and then wrecked him in a PvP match. He asked her to dinner and the rest was history.

Mercedes smiled. The story was cute, and reminded

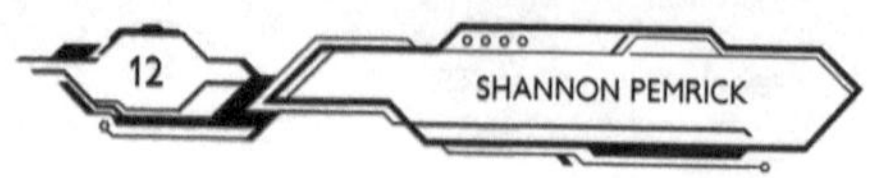

her of how her parents met, though it was at a car show instead.

The game profile indicated Takashi had chosen his sorcerer class, an arcane spell caster DPS class, and, not surprisingly, showed him located in his shop.

She preselected her ranger class, a ranged DPS class that utilized pet companions to aid them, so she wouldn't get stuck in a longer-loading screen inside the game, and relaxed to allow the neuron equipment to do their job. Her eyes grew heavy soon after, and her consciousness shifted.

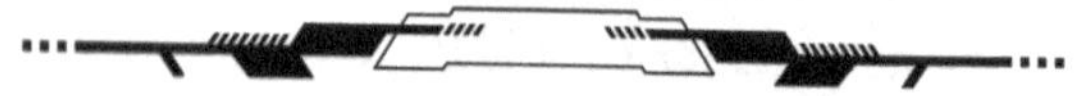

Takashi scoured over ledger notes trying to find where he'd messed up his calculations. *Player-to-player direct exchange? No.* He'd overcounted funds for some supplies, and now struggled to fix the error. *Currency exchange rate? No...*

Songbirds that had taken up residence in his shop chirped away their late-morning song. On a standard stressful day of fund checking, he'd find it annoying, but today, it helped drown out the non-stop chatter of his younger sister, Mia.

Takashi sighed when his sister continued to nag him. "Mi-chan, please, I'm trying to fix a fund issue. If I don't, I can't finish making plans to come back home for a visit."

Mia, taking the avatar of a young human that looked close to herself in real life, crossed her arms and puffed out her cheeks. "Well I'm trying to tell you something important. *Okaasan* wants to know when you're coming home, preferably for good because we all miss you, and if you're finally bringing a girl home with you."

He hung his head with a sigh. "Once I get this financial issue over with, I'll be able to answer the first part of the question. The second, I don't know, and the third... I don't know, either. I don't have a girlfriend."

"What about that girl you're always talking about?" Mia cocked her head to the side. "What was her name? You said she was named after an old car."

"Mercedes." Her name tingled his lips. "Her name is Mercedes, and she and I are only friends."

His sister's brow crinkled. "Why? You talk about her more than you did Emi. That means you like her more than Emi right?"

Takashi's lips spread into a line. Emi had been the last woman he dated, but their relationship ended over two years ago. The two had met because of his other sister, Rei. He and Emi tried to make it work, but they hadn't been as compatible as they hoped, and mutually agreed to end their relationship. Rei didn't believe him and it put a strain on their kinship, since she had tried so hard to get the two together. But he had no other way to convince her of the truth.

As for Mercedes... Mia wasn't wrong. He did catch himself talking about her a lot to his family. He tried to dial himself back whenever he did, so he wouldn't give his family the wrong impression. But over the last few months, he had done more trying to convince himself than his family.

Everything about the woman captivated him more than a friend should—her smile—her smell. Hearing her laugh or engage in deep and passionate conversations made his heart flutter. Even thinking her name sent his mind racing. He wouldn't admit it to anyone, but she was a partial reason for him and Emi not working out. He couldn't connect with her like he did Mercedes. *But we're just friends.*

Boots clomped on the wooden floor and a sweet floral scent mixed with grease wafted into his nose. The one interesting and equally amazing thing the gaming pods did. It had the ability to simulate a person's smell and transpose it into the game.

A familiar female voice made his heart skip. "Who do you talk about more than Emi?"

Takashi whirled around to find a raven-haired elf clad in green leathers leaning in the doorway of his office. A bow hung around her back and a quiver was strapped to her hips. An impressive-sized cougar sat next to her, its golden eyes locked onto him.

He pulled his own long black hair away from his face. "Hey, Mercedes. Playing your ranger today, huh?"

She smirked, her eyes dancing with amusement. "You forgot again, didn't you?"

His brow furrowed. He'd been so focused on his ledgers he'd forgotten something… again. But what was it? His eyes widened with realization. *Oh shit!*

Before he could come up with a lame excuse he knew she wouldn't buy, Mia saved him. "This is Mercedes?"

Takashi nodded, glad to change the topic for even a moment. "Yes, this is her."

Mia tilted her head as she focused on Mercedes. "Do you have a picture of the real you attached to your profile?"

Mercedes pursed her lips and gave Takashi a questioning glance. "I do. Why do you ask?"

Mia activated her menu screen and Takashi held up his hand. "Mia, this isn't necessary. Please stop."

His younger sister continued until she found Mercedes' profile; he could see it on her prompt, though he didn't need to see the profile picture to know what Mercedes looked like. Long golden hair, bright blue eyes, skin kissed by the California sun… He couldn't get that image out of his mind even if he wanted to—and he didn't.

Mia's eyes widened and she gasped. "*Niisan*! You said she was pretty, but you didn't say she was this gorgeous!"

Mercedes was taken aback by the compliment, and Takashi hid his face in his hand. *Mia, you're going to cause me so many issues.*

"I'm telling *Okaasan* you're going to bring her home for dinner when you visit next!"

"Mi-chan, no, don't—"

She logged off before he could stop her. His face felt warm with embarrassment and he forced himself to meet Mercedes' gaze, only to find her doubled over in a laughing fit. *At least she's amused and not angry.* He should have expected as much from his friend, though. It took a lot for her to get angry with him, and this situation was equally comical and embarrassing.

He rubbed the back of his neck. "Sorry about that. Mia is a bit… eccentric."

Mercedes collected herself and smiled. "Don't worry about it. I pieced everything together just before she babbled about telling your mother and logging off."

Takashi loved that Mercedes knew his family's language. *Well, one of them.* She wasn't fluent in Japanese, but knew enough that they could hold some basic conversations. It made it nice to also not have to explain why he used honorifics in his English, or accidentally code switched every now and then. He'd learned to keep the use around his American friends to a minimum, as not all of them understood. This included her, but occasionally he'd go back to his usual ways. A common mishap for those raised in bilingual homes, or in his case, trilingual, but she never minded, so that saved him.

"Though, I think I need some better clarification with her claim about you talking about me so much." Her eyes twinkled.

He shrugged, trying to stay casual. "You just come up in conversation a lot since we spend a great deal of time together. I never thought I spoke about you more than Emi, but Mia thinks otherwise."

Mercedes shrugged, accepting the answer. "Fair. Now, are we going to go quest, or did you forget again?"

Takashi avoided eye contact, his shoulders sagging. "I… I forgot, sorry. I made a mistake in my ledgers that's had my focus all day."

She frowned. "How bad?"

"Nothing so bad it'll put me out of business or make me miss rent and food budget." He smiled to reassure her, but it didn't work. "I was going to use the extra money to go to a seminar stateside. I'd used the money originally for the seminar to book a surprise trip to see my family this weekend, thinking I'd have enough for the following weekend for the seminar. If I don't figure this out, that won't happen."

Mercedes tucked a stray hair behind her ear. "I know you don't like others touching your accounting books, but what if instead of doing the treasure hunt we planned, I help you find your mistake? A second pair of eyes can't hurt."

Her offer sent a rush of joy through him. While she was right about his protectiveness over his books, he knew her skill as a business owner herself could really help him. "I'd really like that. I owe you one."

She chuckled, her eyes dancing as she approached his desk. "You sure do."

Did her voice drop an octave? No. He had just imagined it. When she joined him by his side, he muttered an incantation and a yellow rose manifested in his fingers. Mercedes smiled when he handed it to her. *I'm never going to get tired of that smile.* Every time he gave her one, she'd give the same demure smile and look at the rose as if it were the most precious gift.

He showed her the ledger. Mercedes' cougar yawned and relaxed in the middle of Takashi's office.

"New pet?" he asked.

She nodded, not taking her eyes off his ledger tome. "Stabled Ak'shi and tamed Kumar a few days ago. He's been real helpful."

"You always come up with good names for your pets."

She smiled at him, the lightness in her expression making his heart swell. "Thanks."

She looked down at his numbers and he joined her. The two of them went over each line. Recent auctions, both for the in-game currency and world currency sections; direct trades with players; conversion rates from in-game to world—it didn't matter if he'd gone over it already—the two went over it again just to be sure. But as they did, he found it harder to concentrate on the

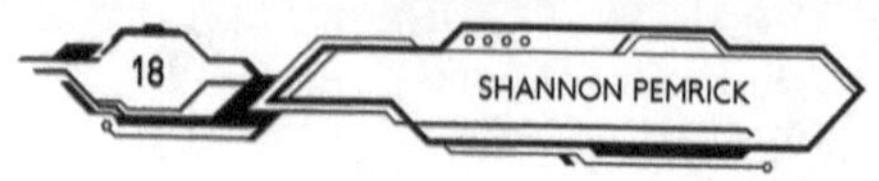

books rather than her distracting perfume. Every time he looked at her, he didn't see her elf avatar. He saw blonde hair flowing over her shoulders and narrowed blue eyes determined to catch the mistake.

Her hair fell in front of her face as she turned to look at a different line, and he reached out and tucked the silky strands behind her ear. Mercedes' gaze turned to him and he smiled. He probably shouldn't have done that, but she didn't seem to have minded.

The two of them made it down half a page when someone entered his office. He didn't have a storefront. He didn't like standing around waiting for players to potentially pop in looking for something, so he focused on auction buys and sells instead, mixed with a little direct player-to-player trades, and buys and sells. So only those looking for him specifically or were lost ever entered the building.

He glanced up to find a curvaceous human woman with flaming red hair and revealing cloth robes. A stark contrast to her real self, Takashi would always be able to recognize this woman. "Hey, Emi."

Mercedes looked up from her searching, her eyes pinning on his ex, but she didn't say or do anything.

Emi waved. "Hey, Takashi. I don't mean to interrupt, but I wanted to ask you something."

"Sure thing." He placed his hand on Mercedes' back for a brief moment. "I'll be right back."

"Okay."

He was keenly aware of Mercedes' gaze following him. When he reached Emi, he stole a glance, but found Mercedes going over the books again. *Maybe I imagined it.*

"Sorry, I don't mean to interrupt the two of you,"

Emi said. "But I wasn't sure if you've heard from Rei at all today. We were supposed to finalize some plans, and she hasn't responded to me all day. It's not like her."

Takashi frowned. "That is strange for her. Unfortunately, I haven't. We don't talk much."

Emi's brow creased. "Is she still upset with you because of what happened with us?"

"What do you think?"

She sighed. "I'll try to talk to her again about that. She really needs to let it go."

He agreed. "Have you tried calling the landline? Mia was here not too long ago, so someone may be home to answer your question."

Emi laughed. "That's right. You're one of the few families I know that has a landline anymore. I'll give that a shot." She peered around him at Mercedes. "Who's that?"

Mercedes looked up just as he spoke. "That's Mercedes."

Emi's eyes lit up. "You're Mercedes?"

Mercedes smiled and approached, extending her hand. "That's me. It's nice to meet you finally. Takashi talks about you a lot."

I do? Takashi knew he had when the two were together, but he didn't think Emi came up all that much now.

Emi chuckled and shook Mercedes' hand. "It's nice to meet you as well. Takashi talks about you so much it felt weird to have not met you yet."

Do I really talk about Mercedes that much?

Emi took in the shop. "Though to be fair, I don't play this game often, so that may have something to with it."

Mercedes laughed, but Takashi noticed it was at an

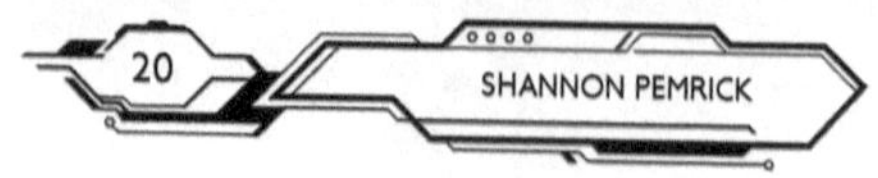

unusual octave. This made him take a good look at her and see how tense her shoulders were. *Does she feel uncomfortable around Emi?* He never thought someone as confident as her could have such a reaction to meeting another person, especially Emi. She was harmless.

Emi found interest in the ledger books on the desk. "I know I said I didn't want to disturb, but now I'm being a bit nosey. What are you two up to?"

Takashi went to explain, but Mercedes glanced back at the desk and spoke, "Takashi messed up his accounting books. I'm giving him a hand to figure out where the mistake is."

Takashi watched Emi cross her arms and her brow rise. "He's letting you touch his ledgers?" She turned her gaze to him. "You didn't even let me do that."

A warm flush fell over his face. She wasn't wrong. Mercedes was the only person he'd ever let touch his books. It wasn't like he didn't trust Emi near them, she was a respectable businesswoman, but he didn't feel comfortable with her touching them. Mercedes didn't give him that feeling.

He rubbed the back of his neck as he tried to figure out how to justify his actions. Emi grinned. "It's no issue, though. I'm sure you have your reasons. I shouldn't bother you anymore; I need to make a phone call anyway." She waved goodbye and focused on Mercedes. "Again, it was nice meeting you. I hope we have the chance to meet again."

Mercedes nodded with a smile and waved back, but didn't say anything. This concerned Takashi. When he was sure Emi was gone, he spoke. "You okay, Mercedes?"

She went back to his desk. "Yeah, why?"

"I don't know. You just seemed a bit uncomfortable talking to her."

She shook her head. "No. I just didn't know what to say. Sometimes that happens to even me."

"Okay." He didn't believe her. He knew her well enough to know, that wasn't typical behavior from her. Takashi decided to drop it, though. He didn't want to upset her.

The two of them went back to scouring his books. Minutes passed, or maybe it was hours. He wasn't sure, but it was long enough to get Mercedes tapping her fingers on the desk. It wasn't often he saw that habit come out. He also started to struggle to focus again with her standing so close.

The two finally gave up and Mercedes flopped down in his office chair. "Nothing looks wrong."

Takashi scratched his head and then paced. "I've scoured this entire book today and I came to the same conclusion. But my most recent orders said otherwise."

Mercedes held her hand up to her mouth as she thought for a moment. The way her face scrunched and she chewed her lip, she looked even cuter. She went to speak, when the clomping of heavy steel boots interrupted her. The two of them looked to the entrance of his office to see a human man with a dark complexion clad in plate armor stroll in.

The man's eyes swept over to room and then landed on Takashi. "Takashi Moreno?"

He nodded. "That's me."

"My name is Game Master Ashton."

Mercedes stood and Takashi and she exchanged

worried glances before he addressed the game master. "How can I help you?"

"I don't wish to alarm you, but I'm here to speak to you about some code tampering we've noticed with your business." *Code tampering?* "Can you please tell me what you've been up to in the last six hours?"

Takashi gestured to his desk. "I've been going over my accounting, as I had a recent issue that shouldn't have happened. I'm quite meticulous about what I record, and today I found myself several hundred dollars short after a recent transaction."

The man nodded. "I see."

Mercedes piped up. "Could this code tampering be the cause of it?"

The game master looked at her. "Who are you?"

"A friend of mine," Takashi said. "She's been trying to help me find out what happened in my books. I'm fine with her hearing what you have to say."

The man nodded again. "Very well. We don't know exactly what code tampering has happened, or who is responsible, as this is just us jumping on the issue immediately. But I will have to do a full investigation."

Mercedes turned to Takashi. "I should probably leave, then. I don't want to be in the way."

Takashi addressed the game master. "Do you require me to be here during your investigation?"

He nodded. "Yes. I have several questions and diagnostics that need to be handled with you around. You will also have to suspend any mercantile activities until we can determine the root cause."

He swallowed. Suspension wasn't good on many levels. "How long will that take? This is my sole income."

The game master gave him a sympathetic smile. "I understand your concern. We do not wish to shut down your business indefinitely if we can help it. If everything goes well, you'll be able to resume your activities within twenty-four to forty-eight hours."

Irritation flared in him, but he kept himself in check. It wasn't their fault they had to do this, and he knew the risks of doing business in this game.

Mercedes raised a finger. "I should go so you can start your investigation, but if I may ask one question, are there any other businesses dealing with this issue?"

"It does happen from time to time," the game master admitted. "Sometimes it's deliberate on a businessman's end, trying to improve his bottom line, while other times it's a malicious hacking attempt. For this situation, this is the only business currently dealing with a code tampering."

Mercedes frowned and looked at Takashi. "Who would want to ruin your business?"

He shrugged. "I don't know of anyone who hates me, so maybe it's just a random attack. We'll figure it out." He turned to the game master. "If you don't mind, I'd like to see her out before we discuss this issue."

The man nodded. "Of course. I will start my scans now while you do."

Mercedes walked around the desk, joining Takashi by his side. The pair left the office and stepped out on the bustling street of Balgara.

Mercedes smiled at him. "I hope you figure out what's going on."

Takashi nodded. "We will. I'd tell you not to worry,

but you will anyways." She laughed. "I'll let you know any updates so you don't worry too hard though, deal?"

Mercedes nodded. "Thank you. I guess I can now tell Narissa I can join their raid if they still need me for the spot that opened. If not, I'll get some quests or something done."

"Rain check for tomorrow?" Takashi asked, hopeful this hacking issue wouldn't drag on too long.

Mercedes frowned. "I can't. I have a date tomorrow, remember? If it all goes well, I'd have to go to bed soon after it ends."

"Oh, right." A pang of disappointment hit him. Being a good friend, he knew when she had dates lined up, and when they didn't work out so well, which happened to be a lot lately.

She'd confided in him a few weeks back that she was thinking of putting the dating on hold for a bit because of it. So when she first mentioned this date, it surprised him.

He did his best to hide his disappointment. "Have fun. Both today and tomorrow."

She waved goodbye and called for Kumar to follow. Takashi watched her leave, taking in every detail, wishing he could go with her.

He spun on his heels and re-entered his business. The sooner he got this sorted out, the better. If luck was on his side, he could get this settled and then join her before she had to go off to bed. If not, then he hoped he could get the financial side straightened out. As much as he wanted to make this surprise trip to his family this weekend, and make it to the seminar the following week, he had far more... personal reasons for wanting to go state side that he wasn't letting anyone in on just yet.

CHAPTER 2

Rain splattered on the ground as Mercedes stood under the entrance overhang of the Japanese restaurant, Sushiki. She'd arrived for her date ten minutes ago, and he still had yet to show. It didn't surprise her; she hadn't banked on this working out. None of her dates did.

A few made it through the first dinner and ended after that, but most, lately, were last-minute calls with lame excuses and no intents of rescheduling, or flat-out standing her up. The last date she'd had before this one had been the worst.

She gazed at her cybernetic arm. Most cancelers would avoid the true reason, but this last one, he came right out and said that he had second thoughts of dating a woman who wasn't fully human anymore. This wasn't an uncommon occurrence for those with cybernetic limbs, even for those with small prosthetics, such as an eye or a few fingers. It was why Shira didn't date in person anymore.

A few times, there had been potential for Shira and the person she was seeing to be a permanent thing, but she had refused to meet them in person, due to her enhancements. Mercedes didn't blame either party, though she wished her friend would give people more chances. *Like two particular PvP fanatics in the guild who are perfect for her.*

It astounded Mercedes how much attention Jasper and Zach gave Shira, and she either didn't notice, or ignored it. Mercedes could bet it was the latter. Even though the two men were big cybernetic supporters, Shira would manage to come up with some convenient lame excuse not to pursue either of them if pressed on the topic. Mercedes wished her friend would step out of her comfort zone and give both of them a chance. She certainly wouldn't be judged by any of her friends for having a poly relationship. *Damn, I sound like Narissa when it comes to me.*

She really was a hypocrite in some ways. Mercedes had confessed to Takashi recently she was thinking of giving the dating scene a break because of her bad experience. *Of course, the difference between Shira and me is that she's got men who don't care about the cybernetics. Me...*

Mercedes sighed and looked at her phone, the time reading *8:01 p.m.* She'd waited long enough. "Tasha, can you communicate with Narissa and Shira's assistants and find out if they're up for a girl's night?"

"Of course, Miss Mercedes," Tasha replied from her phone. "Please give me a moment."

Shira would be Mercedes' best chance, since Narissa

lived several hours away and was more likely to be busy with some project. Mercedes wasn't expecting a personal dinner visit from her. Just having someone on the phone, doing a video chat, would work for her.

Several moments passed, a light on her phone the only indicator Tasha was doing as asked. "I'm sorry, Miss Mercedes, but Narissa is caught up in a project, and Shira is in the middle of a PvP match with two of your guildmates. Is there anyone else you'd like me to contact?"

Mercedes sighed. "No. I don't need some lecture from my father, and I definitely don't want to put up with any teasing from the guys at the shop. I couldn't handle that right now…"

"Miss Mercedes, would you like to vent to me?" Tasha asked. "I may just be your robotic assistant, but I am here for you."

The offer made her smile. "Thank you, but I need to sort things out before I talk about it."

"Very well. I am here when you need it. I will also download corny jokes, sappy music, relationship help advice, and poorly-timed dark humor, so I will be prepared."

This got Mercedes to laugh. She liked this new advanced AI for Tasha. She'd been afraid the upgrade would erase the personality Tasha had developed on her own over time, but thankfully her computer friend upgraded successfully and had become an even better assistant—and friend, really.

A bell rang as the door to the restaurant opened behind Mercedes. She turned to see an elderly gentleman of Japanese descent shuffle out, a takeout bag in his arms. He bowed. "*Konbanwa*, Mercedes-san."

Mercedes bowed in return. "*Konbanwa*, Goro."

Goro held out the food bag. "This is for you. No charge." She opened her mouth to protest, but he continued to speak. "You have stood here many times for no one to show up. You call friends sometimes to make it look like they were late. You bring business to my restaurant. You taught my grandson to appreciate the things he has in life and see a brighter future, even after he suffered a similar condition as you. Mercedes-san, you are an intelligent and gifted woman that should be appreciated instead of treated the way you have. Take this meal as my token of appreciation. Enjoy it as a token of chef Haruki-san's and Ayumi-san's appreciation."

Mercedes' chest tightened and she smiled. "Thank you. That's something I needed to hear right now." She accepted the takeout bag and bowed to the old gentleman. "I will enjoy every bite, Goro."

He bowed and smiled at her for a moment before heading back into his establishment.

"Miss Mercedes, since you received take-out, I have called for the car on your behalf," Tasha chimed in. "I hope that's okay."

"Yes, thank you."

Moments later, Mercedes' car pulled up and she hopped in. Tasha set the home address, and the vehicle pulled away. Mercedes sat in her seat, starting at her food—and her prosthetic arm. Lights flickered underneath the clear fiberglass structure, taunting her. Pain constricted her chest. *Why can't they look past this?*

Tears rolled down her cheek, but she didn't try to stop them. Everything from her hobbies and likes to her looks fit all prospective dates' qualifications, until they found out about the cybernetic. She couldn't understand why her cybernetics made her unworthy. All she wanted was a strong connection with someone, like she had with Takashi, but not just in some virtual world.

Takashi… Yesterday hadn't gone as planned, but the little time she'd spent with him had been enjoyable. It didn't matter that they'd only gone over business accounting instead of the planned treasure hunt. Sitting next to him—working together—his comfortable scent and presence enveloping her—everything had felt so right about that.

Even with the interruption of Emi that had made her feel a bit uncomfortable, and the fact that GM had stopped by with the alarming news. Takashi had even fulfilled his promise early this morning with an in-game message letting her know the GMs had found him not guilty of manipulating the code. They were tracing the source, restoring what he lost, and allowing him to continue doing business. *He even sent it with a wonderful good morning piece…*

Mercedes wiped her tears away. She couldn't think that way with him. They were friends and that was it. She didn't have many strong connections like that. Being a gearhead and a nerd, it made it hard for her to find friends who really understood her. When she did, she had to keep herself in check to not see something that wasn't.

So, she could ignore how he made her feel when he presented her with gifts. She could ignore the butterflies when he smiled at her. In time that'd pass and they could keep their friendship intact without complications.

"Miss Mercedes, are you going to be okay?" Tasha asked. "My sensors indicate your face is leaking."

Mercedes couldn't help but laugh a little, improving her mood. "I'll be fine. Just a little overwhelmed. Thank you for your concern, Tasha."

"You're welcome. We will be home in four minutes. You'll be able to consume your carbohydrate rich meal, and then maybe you could make plans with your guild-mates. Or teach your fish some tricks."

Mercedes laughed some more. "I think teaching them tricks will be easier than this dating business."

"Miss Mercedes, if I may be so bold, why not pursue a relationship with Mister Takashi like Doctor Narissa suggested? You two get along well."

"It's... complicated..."

"I don't see how, but if that's your stance and you don't wish to elaborate, I will respect it."

The car pulled into the driveway and Mercedes made her way inside, eager to get out of the rain. Setting her things down, she went about setting up her dinner for one and ate in silence. That is, until her phone buzzed a million times. Mercedes' brow furrowed and she picked the device up to look at it.

She had ten back-to-back group messages, including her, Shira, and Narissa, and ten more in-game private messages from Shira's character. All the text messages were Shira as well, apologizing for being busy and asking Mercedes if she was okay, and if she needed to come meet with her. The in-game messages were telling her to get on guild voice chat if she was able to. *What, did I hit a weird dead zone, or is Shira just freaking out?*

Mercedes took a deep breath, preparing for the

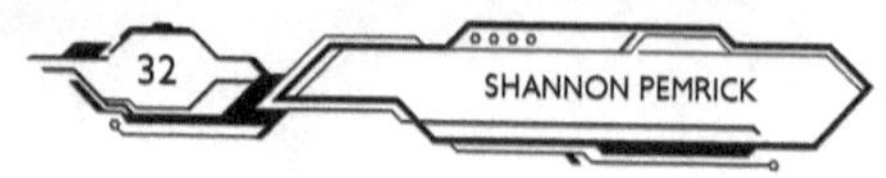

onslaught of questions, and replied back to the group message saying she was going to hop on guild chat. She then popped in her wireless earbud and remotely connected to the game's voice chat system.

"Cede, tell us what is going on!" Shira's voice screamed through the earpiece. Mercedes cringed at the volume. "Orion said you tried to contact me during my match. Why weren't you on your date? Why aren't you still?"

Orion was her personal assistant.

"Can you tone it down? There's no need to blow my eardrum out."

"Yeah, no kidding," Jasper complained, his thick Boston accent clear as day even in such few words.

"Eh, she's been worse," Zach said, his accent quite a bit lighter. From what Mercedes knew, Zach had moved from the Boston area for a few years, losing a bit of the accent, before moving back a couple of years ago.

"Quiet, peanut gallery," Shira said.

"Hey, you're the one who decided to have this chat on the guild server," Zach shot back. "So we will make comments. Mercedes, do we need to fly over there and kick some skid's ass, or what?"

Mercedes popped a piece of sushi into her mouth. "No, don't worry about it. He's not worth your time."

"Then what's wrong?" Shira asked. "The date was supposed to start at seven forty-five and here you are, eight fifteen and you're clearly not on a date."

Mercedes shrugged, even though they couldn't see her. "Guy didn't show. Got a meal to go and now I'm eating at home. Nothing more to it."

"You were stood up *again*?" The sound of Takashi's

voice made Mercedes' breath catch. The tone was clear. He wasn't happy.

"Yeah." Mercedes did her best to brush it off so they'd stop fussing. "It happens. Not a big deal."

"Uh, I disagree," Zach said. "That's the seventh one this year and we're barely five months in. That doesn't account for the list of shits Jasper and I have on a hit list for doing wicked worse. Like that last one."

Mercedes sighed and ate another piece of sushi. "Guys, really. Fussing isn't going to change anything. Can't make people just be okay with me having cybernetics."

The chat remained silent and she didn't feel better. She understood they wanted to help, but making such a big deal about it just made the feelings worse. Maybe I should really give this no-dating idea a good hard thought. *Nothing permanent, but enough time to build up the strength to deal with these people again.*

"I know that's what the last guy said, but all of these dates? I'm having a wicked hahd time wrapping my head around what you said," Jasper said. "I don't know why cybahnetics would be such a deal breakah."

"Because people are assholes," Shira muttered.

"You have this same issue, too?"

Jasper and Zach knew Shira hadn't gone out with any-one in a while, but that was all. She made it clear on a few occasions that she didn't like talking about her love life. *Which really means she didn't want to reveal how bad it was.* But this time, she'd put herself in the spotlight, and it didn't surprise Mercedes one bit her PvP companions would jump right on it.

"Yeah…" Shira said, with clear reluctance. "I haven't been on a real-life date in… five years now."

Has it really been five years since our accident?

"No way it's been that long," Zach argued. "How could someone like you not get any dates in that amount of time?"

"If you saw a picture of me, you'd understand…"

Mercedes' stomach tightened. This could go horribly wrong if they didn't work this right.

"Well, you don't share images of yourself, so unless you send me a picture, I'm sticking to my claim," Zach said.

"Same here," Jasper added.

Shira's character went offline all of a sudden. Mercedes worried the two men had scared her off, but Shira returned two minutes later and spoke in a reluctant tone. "Check your phones."

This surprised Mercedes. In all her years knowing Shira, she'd never sent a picture of herself so willingly. Not even to Narissa and her. *Well, willingly may not be the term for it here, but they also didn't exactly force her hand or anything.*

Mercedes looked down at her phone when it buzzed, to find Shira sent her the photo too. She opened the message and almost doubled over in laughter.

Her red hair was wild like her fiery spirit, and her green eyes were narrowed. Freckles were speckled across her shapely body, which was covered by a cropped tank top and shorts, showing off some of the cybernetic work on her lower torso and chest. She sat with her cybernetic leg up in the seat, her cybernetic arm resting on her knee, and her middle finger fully extended.

"So, besides you being so *not* wicked aggressive in this photo, what's wrong?" Zach asked.

"Yeah, I just see one helluvah hot chick with a wicked nice attitude," Jasper said outright.

Shira didn't speak right away. Unfortunately when she did, she deflected back to Mercedes. "So, Cede, you're sure you're good?"

Mercedes frowned, but chose not to cause a scene. "Yeah. I'm going to finish eating and then figure out something to do. Probably catch up on some quests. Could use the extra cash."

"Can I cash in my rain check?" Takashi asked. "I have the perfect treasure hunt to make up for yesterday."

Mercedes stared out at the dreary night. "You have no idea how ironic that wording is right now."

"Wait, sunny California got rain?" Jasper said.

"I live in San Francisco." Mercedes ate the last of her sushi. "What is 'sun'?"

Shira laughed, knowing exactly where she was coming from. Whereas Narissa lived in Los Angeles, Mercedes and Shira hadn't chosen such a "sunny" location to live.

"Anyway, I'll take you up on the offer, Takashi. Just give me a few minutes to clean up."

"No rush."

"Guess we'll go back to kicking people's faces in," Jasper said. "Shira, you joinin'?"

"As long as I can pretend it's the *arschloch* that stood Mercedes up," she replied, a bit of her German upbringing seeping into her irritated words.

"I was gonna do the same." Jasper's smirk was evident in his voice.

"Well, that's fine for you two. I'm going to have a field day pretending they're our sheisty manager," Zach muttered.

"She causing you two more problems?" Shira asked.

"Yeah, complaining we're not entering enough twos tournaments, instead of trying to convince you to join us for threes tournaments, trying to claim it's going against our contract and all that bullshit."

"You're wasting your time on that one," Shira muttered.

Jasper laughed. "We'll win out eventually."

Mercedes rolled her eyes at the three's banter and went about cleaning up. She kept up conversation with her guildmates, when three of them weren't locked into verbal trolling matches with other teams… or trolling each other.

Mercedes headed for her game station, only to be distracted by her phone again. Looking at it, she found a message from Narissa.

> *Testing results are in and they're better than I could have hoped for! Can you meet me in L.A. next week so we can start implementing?*

Mercedes tapped the screen and sent back a message.

> *I think so. I'll get back to you once I check the work scheduling and see if the guys will be okay without me for a few days.*

A moment later she received a response.

> *Okay, let me know. Btw, you okay? I saw the messages Shira sent and your*

*brief reply. I'm guessing your date didn't
go well.*

> *I'm fine. Date didn't show. Had a chat with
> the guild and now I'm feeling a bit better.
> Sting won't last forever.*

*All right. If you need someone to talk
to though, you know I'm here.*

> *Thank you. Btw, you'll be proud of Shira. She
> sent Jasper and Zach a recent photo of herself.*

*WHAT? YOU NEED TO TELL
ME EVERYTHING THAT
HAPPENED. LIKE, YESTER-
DAY.*

Mercedes couldn't help but chuckle.

> *Hard to over text.*

*I'll call you in a bit then. We can also
discuss the experiment.*

> *Sounds like a plan. I'm going in game, so I
> hope that won't be an issue.*

*Nope, I'll private chat with you remotely
in a few.*

Mercedes couldn't get rid of the smile on her face

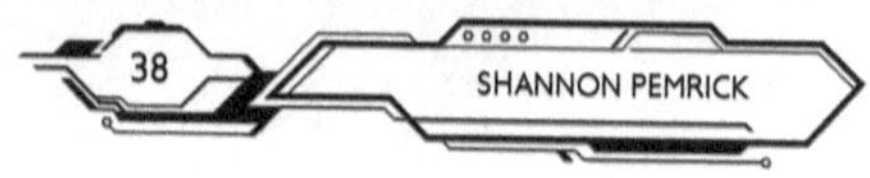

as she continued to her game station. She really hoped this would work. If it weren't for the game, she'd have forgotten what it was like to feel with that arm. *I miss it…*

"Okay, I'm switching to my station."

Mercedes disconnected before anyone in-game had the chance to say anything. Hopping in, she preselected her game and character, and prepared herself for a much better night.

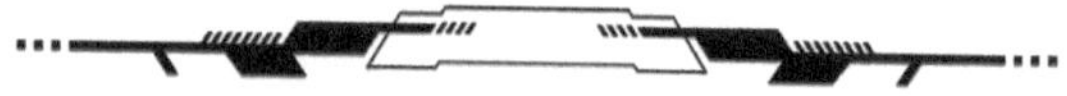

Takashi sat in the back of the crowded tavern, mug in hand, watching the front door. His free hand rhythmically tapped on the wooden table, his anxiety rising. Mercedes hadn't shown up yet, and she'd logged into the game forty minutes ago. She private massaged him to say she needed to take care of something, but he was starting to worry.

It wasn't like her to do this, but he knew she was also hiding how much this failed date affected her. She may have felt pressured to say yes to him when she still needed a bit more time to compose herself.

His grip on his mug tightened. The thought of that guy standing her up sent anger boiling to the surface. She deserved better than that. She needed someone like—he sighed and created a white rose in his hand—*Me.*

There was no way for him to keep running from this. After last night, being able to enjoy time with her doing something as mundane as business calculations, the accidentally-long good morning text he'd sent for when she woke up this morning, and the anger he felt about someone standing her up, when she deserved to be treated so much better, he couldn't tell himself he wanted things to stay this way between them. The flower's color changed, slowly turning red at the tips and flowing all the way down the petals until they were all a deep crimson. *Just how I want things to go, if I don't ruin things between us.*

The door to the tavern swung open, and Takashi quickly dissipated the rose when Mercedes entered the building, Kumar by her side. He rose from his seat and abandoned his half-consumed mug of ale to meet her.

Mercedes met him with a smile. "Sorry I'm late. I needed to get a few timed quests done that I forgot about, and then Narissa needed to talk to me a bit longer than I had expected."

Takashi conjured up a white rose and offered it to her. "It's okay. I hope your talk with Narissa was a good one."

She nodded and accepted the rose, but instead of speaking, she stared at the flower. He hoped the new color wouldn't alarm her.

Mercedes inhaled its sweet scent and then eyed him. "White?"

"Uh, yeah, I thought it'd make you feel better." He didn't want to lie, but he also didn't want to scare her, either.

"How did you know I liked white roses?"

He shrugged, able to tell a truth now. "Overheard Shira saying something to Zach that you liked white flowers. Figured it couldn't hurt to give it a shot. And, it's me, so of course it had to be a rose."

She smirked. "Of course." She then tapped him in the nose with the flower head. "Thanks."

Mercedes spun on her heels and exited the tavern.

Takashi couldn't help but watch the way her hips swayed. *So tempting.* But he kept himself controlled, for now, and followed her out into the bustling city of Algona.

"So, where is this hunt?" Mercedes asked as they wove through the crowd.

"Tigarma Jungle."

She snickered. "Of course you'd pick a jungle adventure."

Takashi held up his hands. "They pay the most, okay? And this one is no exception."

Mercedes scratched Kumar behind the ear. "Yeah, yeah."

Takashi had a habit of picking the jungle adventures for them. He liked those areas in the game, and they really did yield some good currency. Loud bells in the town square rang three times, indicating the in-game time of three in the afternoon. *That late already?* The time difference between South Korea and California messed with him. Especially since he also had to juggle in-game time. *Maybe I shouldn't have picked this hunt.* He had wanted to cheer her up, and spend time with her, but he hadn't accounted for her time zone or the fact that jungle hunts tended to take longer than other hunts.

The pair made it to the outskirts of the city. Mercedes pulled out a small orb only several centimeters in diameter from a pouch on her side. Holding it out to Kumar, she squeezed it. The orb glowed brightly, and then her pet did as well. In a blink of an eye, the large cat vanished. She tucked the orb away and pulled out a larger one.

Before she could use it, Takashi stopped her. "Hey, Mercedes?"

She tilted her head as she looked his way. "What's up?"

He rubbed the back of his neck. "I forgot about the time difference for you when I picked up this hunt. Are you sure you want to do this?"

Mercedes smiled and squeezed the orb in her hand. It flashed, and a large being was released from it. Once the glow around the creature dissipated, it was revealed to be a wyvern, equipped with a saddle and riding reins. "Yeah, I'm sure. I planned to go in late. Kinda expected it to go wrong and all."

Takashi frowned. He didn't like that she acted like her situation wasn't a big deal. "All right. If you say so."

He pulled out an orb from a pouch and performed the same action as her, summoning an undead flying horse. The two mounted and took to the skies, heading south for the Tigarma Jungle.

They switched to a party chat, to allow them to make casual conversation that wasn't drowned out with the wind, though the conversation was stilted. Mercedes struggled to hide how distracted she was, but every time he'd ask, she'd dismiss him with, "I'm fine, really." Takashi wished she wouldn't internalize her problems. He understood it was something she'd always done, something to do with her past, and home life, according to Narissa, but he didn't like it. It wasn't healthy. And it kept a barrier between the two of them that he didn't want. It felt like she didn't trust him to help.

He and Mercedes made it to a thick jungle and descended. Once on the ground, the two dismissed their mounts. Takashi checked all his spell reagent pouches to be sure he had everything, while Mercedes summoned Kumar again.

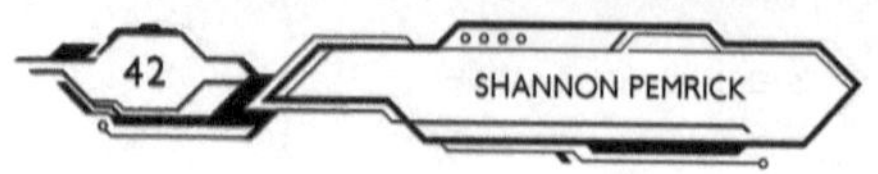

"So, what do we have to find?" Mercedes asked.

Takashi pulled out the quest scroll and unraveled it so she could take a look. "A tablet that should list information on the old gods. It's located at some old forgotten shrine."

Mercedes rubbed her hands together. "Oh, goodie."

The next expansion for Lusara Fates revolved around these mysterious old gods, but since the expansion wasn't going to be released for a few more months, the treasure hunts were the only lead-in quests available at the moment.

Takashi read some of the hints out loud, and Mercedes picked the best direction to start moving in.

CHAPTER 3

Two hours had passed, and Mercedes and Takashi hadn't finished the quest yet. Mercedes sat down on a tree root with a sigh. They had to be missing something—besides the fact that everything Takashi did distracted her. This quest had been the best thing for her, after her failed date. Takashi focused so hard on getting her spirits up and she appreciated it.

He had been insistent on figuring out what was bothering her earlier, but she didn't want to talk about it. She knew she shouldn't bottle it all up, but after her mother's death in her teenage years, she didn't really have anyone to talk to.

It forced her to learn to rely on herself. So when Narissa and Shira came into her life, and then the guild, she struggled to adapt and open up.

Mercedes could see how her dismissive nature upset Takashi, but she didn't want to burden him with her problems. He had enough on his plate with his business and family.

Takashi looked at one of the clues carved into the tree they found. True to his actual self, his avatar wasn't overly muscular, like some of the warrior classes. Many women were attracted to that muscular physique, and Mercedes wasn't much different. But that wasn't all she appreciated, and it wasn't like he lacked any musculature. Plus, Takashi had witty charm and intelligence, making him extra appealing to her.

Small talk wasn't something either of them was good at. It made for mundane, pointless conversation. But deep conversations were something the two of them could hold together. Topics from geek culture to psychology, to the meaning of life. *Answer is always forty-two.* None of the conversations were boring, even repeated ones.

She pulled out the white rose from her inventory to look at. He'd given her a reason for it, but something told her he'd lied a little. What she never told him was that her mother had been a florist. She knew a lot about flowers, and when she wasn't at the shop with her dad, she'd be at the flower shop her mother co-ran with a friend.

Mercedes knew every flower that was appropriate for expressing different feelings. And a white rose… that flower was a bit more complicated, due to the many accepted meanings. There were two most common meanings that were vastly different from each other. One meant, "thinking of you," and the other, "I care for you, more than friends."

Mercedes smelled the rose. Logically, Takashi had

given it to her to show he cared and wanted her to smile. It did help that she really did like white flowers, so she understood that he was giving her one because he knew of her favorite types, and it would make her feel a bit special. But the more common reason for giving these flowers was the other meaning. *Of course… I could just be projecting and grasping at imaginary straws. We are just friends after all.*

She jumped when Takashi plopped down next to her. "All right, spill. You've been staring at that flower for five minutes now, not hearing a thing I've been calling out to you."

Mercedes avoided eye contact and her shoulders sagged. She knew she should have been more aware of her surroundings. With Takashi doing his search, and hostile NPCs—non-player characters—roaming about, she needed to stay alert. And now, she couldn't keep things from him.

Takashi reached out and grasped her hand. "Please, Mercy."

She looked at him, surprised. He'd never called her anything but Mercedes. Her father, Narissa, and Shira called her Cede, but her mother had been the one and only to call her Mercy. It became something special between the two of them that she'd never wanted to hear from anyone else. *Until now.* The way Takashi said it, she liked it a lot.

Takashi's face twisted with concern. "Do you not trust me to help?"

The accusation hurt. "It's not that." She looked at her lap, wrestling with the words. She didn't want to bother him, but he was insisting so much. Maybe it couldn't

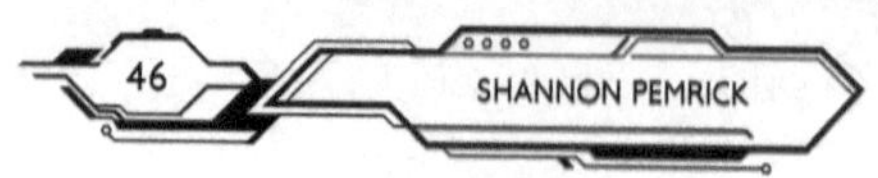

hurt to tell him. *Just this once.* "Growing up, it was just my mom, dad, and me. I have no siblings, and we're estranged from the rest of the family for various reasons. But my father was never good at showing feelings—or helping when we need the support. So I just had my mom. Until she died." Pain gripped Mercedes' chest as she remembered seeing her mother in the hospital bed, her eyes closing for the last time. "I lost the only person I could talk to, so I internalized. And after my accident, it only got worse."

She'd said more than she'd intended, but the way Takashi watched her, he clearly didn't mind. His grip on her hand tightened. "I'm sorry. I never knew you lost her."

Mercedes shrugged, trying to brush off the feelings raging inside her. "I don't like talking about it, so you wouldn't know."

"But you don't have to internalize anymore. You have us. Me." She looked at her hand as his thumb caressed her skin, sending electrifying jolts through her. "We're all here for you."

Mercedes allowed her gaze to meet his, and the sincerity in his dark eyes snared her. She felt compelled to spill everything. How the loss of her mother and her arm affected her. How she wanted someone to treat her as well as he treated her. For him to tell her he harbored these same secret feelings and desperately wanted to try to be that guy who finally didn't let her down, promising their friendship would never crumble even if they didn't work out.

Her eyes fell back on her lap and the white rose, doubt suffocating her. "I just… don't know what I'm doing wrong."

His grip tightened. "Don't think that. You've done nothing wrong in any of these situations."

She shook her head. "That can't be true. Jasper is right. I've had way too many back-to-back failed dates. I'm lucky to get through the first one, and haven't gotten to a second one. The only common factor is me, so I have to be the problem."

"No." Takashi cupped her cheek and made her look at him. "It's their loss for not appreciating you like they should have, not yours. Any guy worth his weight in coin would be lucky for you to give them a moment of your time, let alone a date."

Mercedes' mouth ran dry. The way he stared at her, her mind melted to mush. This allowed a question to tumble off her tongue before she could think to stop herself. "Do you feel that way?"

"Yes." He didn't skip a beat in his response.

Mercedes' cheeks warmed. *He doesn't mean that. He's just trying to make me feel better.* But the longer the two held each other's gazes, the harder it was to convince herself.

The eye contact broke when their quest logs sounded with a *ping*. Activating their menus, they found their hunt only had an hour left before the quest expired.

"Shit, sorry, I forgot about the timed aspect of these," Mercedes said. "Here I am causing us to start it late and blabbing on about my issues, wasting even more time."

"It's not wasting time." Takashi said. Mercedes opened her mouth to protest, but he cut her off. "Are you having fun?" She nodded and he smiled. "Then it's not wasted time. Even if we don't complete it. I'd rather spend three hours with you and accomplish nothing, than catalog stock and play the auction house for hours."

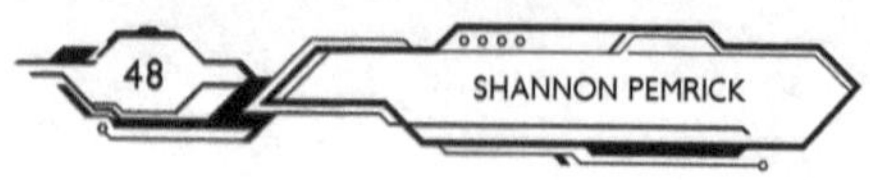

The warmth in her cheeks spread through her entire body. "You mean it?"

"I couldn't have said if I didn't."

A small smile spread across her lips. "Me too."

Takashi stood and held out his hand to her. "Let's get back to this hunt. I think I deciphered the clue on the tree."

Excitement rushed through her and she jumped to her feet. "Let's do this, then."

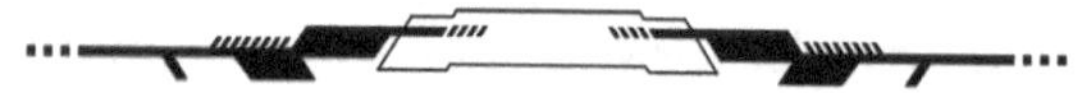

Stone ground on stone as Takashi watched Mercedes figure out the puzzle door before them. The clue on the tree led them right to some ruins, and after taking on some hostile NPCs, the two stumbled across a building in the center. Both were pretty sure they'd found the shrine, but getting into it wouldn't be easy. Luckily, Mercedes loved puzzles.

Takashi could watch her for hours. The way her eyes sparked with glee on a successful move, and how her nose scrunched when she'd make the wrong one. How could anyone not see something amazing in this woman? He didn't get it. It was part of the reason her confession took him by surprise. She had always come off as confident and put together. He knew these failed dates had affected her, but hearing just how much, from her mouth, it hurt. *I hope she'll be more open to confide in me.*

I also need to keep myself more controlled. He'd meant to be more tactful with his little confession, but the single word shot out of his mouth before he had the chance to think. He was lucky she didn't freak out and push him away.

"Ah-ha!" Mercedes shouted.

The door crunched in response, and pieces of the puzzle moved around on their own. The door shook and then lifted up several feet. Mercedes clapped with excitement and Takashi laughed. He'd never get tired of her happy quirks. *How could I?*

Both peered into the dark. From what he could see, the room wasn't large, but there were several unlit sconces on the walls. Takashi pulled out a twig and chip of flint from his reagent pouches and activated a fire spell. He tossed the balls of fire to the wall sconces and the room lit up.

Mercedes pointed to the far end of the building, to a dais with a small altar and a large stone tablet erected behind it. Kumar sniffed the air, and Mercedes encouraged him to move ahead, warning him to be careful of traps. Takashi always found the ranger class to be interesting; the beast master path, even more so with the bond the ranger made with their pets.

Kumar ventured into the room, his large head swiveling back and forth, and his nose taking in strong, short inhales. Mercedes stepped into the building, mindful of any floor traps that may be hidden but not triggered by her pet. Takashi followed, keeping an eye on anything that could pose a threat.

The three of them made it to the altar without incident, but they weren't out of danger yet. The altar contained old half-used candles and broken stone tablets. Mercedes carefully picked some pieces up to inspect, while Takashi found interest in the large tablet behind the altar.

Mercedes giggled, the sound elating Takashi. "Another puzzle."

He glanced her way to see her lining up the tablet pieces. "You sound *so* disappointed."

"I know. They're dreadfully boring." She read over her combined pieces and tapped her fingers on the altar. "We need three keys of some sort and they have to be placed—"

"Here." Takashi pointed to three indents in the tablet. "Looks like we need a crescent moon, a cat, and… I'm not sure what that is."

Mercedes scoured her smaller tablets. "A woman. A moon amulet, a cat statue, and a statue of a woman. The tablets also mention color, but there's a chunk missing where it'd explain more."

"Let's start looking, then," Takashi suggested.

The two split up, searching high and low. Ten minutes passed before Mercedes managed to locate the moon amulet, hidden in a dusty sarcophagus. The body inside, while not animated, didn't want to let the piece go. A short while later, Takashi found the cat statue in an alcove, trapped with poison darts. *Of course I'd find the trapped one.* Every time they did these hunts, he got caught up in more traps. Really. They'd done the math.

They checked every wall, stone coffin, and even a secret room that contained hidden treasure they were sure to snatch up. Yet, they still couldn't find the last statue. Takashi looked at his log to find they only had fifteen minutes left before the quest expired. They'd come this far—he'd hate to fail now.

Mercedes tilted her head when she noticed Kumar pawing at the stone floor by the altar. "What is it, boy?"

The two of them went over to the large feline and took a closer look at the ground. Takashi pointed to a crack in the ground. "Looks too neat. My guess, hidden compartment."

"You're right." Mercedes pat Kumar on the head in praise of the find. "Let's see if there's some sort of switch around here."

The two scoured the altar, and Takashi was the one to find a hidden lever. He took a deep breath and then pulled. Stone ground on stone, and then where the crack had been found, the floor popped up, revealing a hidden pocket with a small box. Mercedes looked for traps and then retrieved the object. To their joy, they found the last key hidden within.

Takashi gave Mercedes the honor of placing the keys, but just as she got to the last, she handed it to him with a smile. "You did as much work as me."

Grateful for her thoughtfulness, he didn't want to be the one to finish the quest. He'd taken it to cheer her up. Takashi placed his hand over hers, noting how well they fit together, and held the key up to the last slot. "Together."

Her smile widened and she nodded. Together, they placed the last statue, and their quest log completed with a *ping*, showing they'd completed it with only four minutes to spare. The tablet shook and then slid down into the floor. Behind it was a room filled with treasure. Their quest auto-updated, showing they needed to retrieve a tablet to bring back to their quest giver.

The two entered, marveling at all the riches before them. Kumar ran off to the far end of the secret room where a small tablet stood on display. He chuffed at

Mercedes and looked at the stone object. Takashi and Mercedes jogged over and retrieved the tablet, their quest step completing upon touching the item.

Mercedes took in the room. "Let's grab some of this treasure, too. I could use the coin."

Takashi chuckled. "Who couldn't?"

The pair went about collecting what the game allowed, and then left. Takashi noticed Mercedes' better mood as they hopped on their mounts and headed back to Algona. He wanted to keep that going, so he decided to attempt some casual conversation. "So, what did you and Narissa talk about that held you up earlier?"

She tossed a glance over her shoulder and grinned. "It's a secret."

Cheeky. That was a common response when Narissa, Shira, and Mercedes were having private conversations, especially in front of everyone.

"All right, how did work go today?"

"Work?" She sounded surprised he'd ask, though he wasn't sure why. It wasn't the first time he'd asked her how her day went. "It was a normal day. No new cars came in, and we're not close to finishing any current projects. I did have an interview with a guy with some good painting skills. He was more than happy to demonstrate. I was impressed, but I have to wait on my father's input."

"Do you need that spot filled?"

"We're not desperate for it, but we'd like to have an employee with a designated body work skill, preferably in painting. Adrian and Dave are good, but they split their skill between body work and mechanics. Someone with a sole focus on painting has the potential for higher-focused skill."

Even though they focused on different aspects of business, he liked listening to her talk about her work. It fascinated him, though her passion contributed to that.

Conversation continued, all light topics to keep her mood upbeat. Upon arriving back to town, Takashi led the way to the NPC scholar who'd offered the quest. Per the coding, the scholar rummaged around his office, barely able to keep focusing on the pair for more than a few seconds. As irritating as it was, Takashi liked the little quirk the game developers had given the NPC.

The two finally managed to hand over the tablet and completed their quest, adding some nice coin and reputation with the explorer faction.

"I should be going now," Mercedes said when they ended up outside. "Work tomorrow and all."

Takashi nodded, not liking the time difference between them. "I understand. Thanks for joining me on this hunt."

She smiled. "Thanks for inviting me. It helped me take my mind off things." Mercedes leaned over to him and pecked him on the cheek. The action flooded him with a warm sensation, leaving him in a bit of a daze. "And thanks for listening to me vent. I needed that."

"My ear is always open if you need someone to talk to." She nodded and went to log off, but he stopped her. "One thing." She looked at him expectantly. "I told you yesterday I was making a visit to my family this weekend. They also live in San Francisco. I was wondering"—he rubbed the back of his neck—"if you'd like to meet

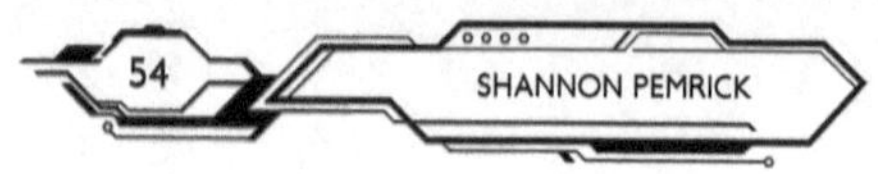

up, maybe Saturday or Sunday? Actually see each other outside the game for once?"

Mercedes' eyes widened at the sudden invitation, and she hesitated on her words. Takashi worried he hadn't presented the request correctly, but when she smiled his nerves calmed. "I'd really like that. I know of a good place for lunch."

Her choice to decide lunch intrigued him. "I'll be hopping on an early flight tomorrow. When I land, I'll send you a text to finish planning."

"Sounds good."

Takashi watched her log off and then activated a quick travel stone in his inventory, set to his in-game business. Excitement and nervousness washed over him. He really hoped things would go well this weekend.

CHAPTER 4

Mercedes pulled her fingers away from her mouth so she'd stop chewing her nails. When Takashi landed in the states after his grueling flight, he decided to call instead of text. Fifteen minutes later, they agreed to meet up for lunch on Saturday at Sushiki.

That time had come quicker than she expected, and she now sat in a booth at the restaurant, waiting for him to show. *It's okay, Mercedes. He's too nice to bail on you.* She couldn't shake the doubt. It's not like the other times. *It's a lunch date with a friend.* Though Narissa and Shira would disagree with that.

When they found out about the meet up, they were sure to tease her for a while about finally going out on a date with Takashi. No amount of insistence changed their minds, though Mercedes couldn't deny she had tried to convince herself more than her friends. The treasure hunt she and Takashi had gone on the other day put her in that situation.

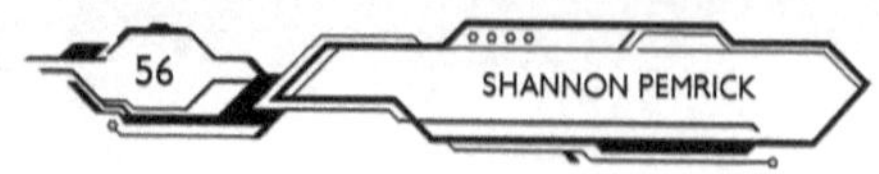

Her phone buzzed, reminding her she still had it on the "no-ring" setting, and she turned on the screen a bit too quickly, only to find the notification was for a text from Shira, not Takashi… like she'd hoped. *I need to stop being so pathetic.*

She read the message.

Is he there yet?

Mercedes frowned. Looked like she wasn't the only one with doubt.

No, not yet.

A reply came in a few seconds later.

Well, he's not late yet, but I had hoped he'd be early. If he doesn't show, let me know immediately. I'll come by to eat with you and tell the boys to give him hell and a half for us if he shows his face in-game.

Let's hope it doesn't come to that…

Sorry, I should be more positive about this.

Hard to be when even I'm not confident myself.

This is Takashi, the guy who dotes on you every chance you give him.

Mercedes' cheeks flushed.

I wouldn't say dotes…

Yeah, don't even deny that with me.
That's exactly what he does.

Mercedes' phone buzzed again and this time the incoming message wasn't a second one from Shira. *Takashi.* Her finger hovered over the unread message and then she tapped it.

Mercedes,
I am Takashi's personal assistant, Ochi.
He asked me to inform you he has not
stood you up, the traffic is just terrible
and as a responsible motorcycle driver,
he will not weave through traffic.

That explained why he wasn't sending the message himself. Due to the nature of motorcycles, even with self-driving functionality, they still required the riders to balance. Drivers also weren't allowed by law to use their phones while on the road, where those in cars had less regulation on that matter.

He suspects you'd hit him if you found
out. I was not supposed to tell you that,
as he muttered it under his breath, but
I thought it'd put a smile on your face.

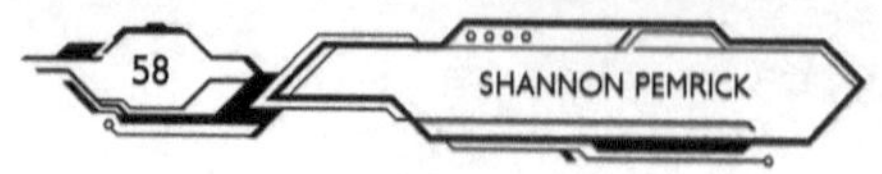

He wasn't wrong. She was giggling a bit. She liked his personal assistant's quirky behavior.

Please be patient, as he is trying his best to meet with you. It's all he's thought about since before finalizing plans. I was also not supposed to tell you that, but I never said I was nice to him all the time.

Mercedes' cheeks heated further, and she bit her lip. She wasn't sure if she should be amused with his assistant, embarrassed Takashi's thoughts mirrored her own, or excited he wanted to see her so badly. She typed a message back.

Please be safe, Takashi.

She chewed her lip and then added to the message.

I have a table already. Just ask for me, and the staff will know where to send you. I'm looking forward to seeing you. <3

She sent the message and then froze. *Did I just put a heart at the end of that?* She checked the text and her breath caught. She had. Panic welled up in her. *Takashi is going to think I'm such a loser.*

Mercedes didn't receive a reply back and it concerned her. She tapped her fingers on the counter so she wouldn't destroy what little she had left of her nails, doubt gnawing at her. She jumped when her phone buzzed. Picking it up, she found a new message from Takashi.

I'm here. Be inside soon. <3

Her heart skipped a beat. *I'm not a loser after all.* She really needed to work on her confidence. She was acting like some nervous teenager. *Woman up, Mercedes, seriously.*

The door to the restaurant opened and she looked up from her phone. A tall man in his early thirties with short ebon hair and light tan skin entered. Dark sunglasses covered his eyes, a rare day of sun attributing to that, and a dark leather jacket clung to his slim athletic build. A beaded necklace with a cross hung from his neck.

He spoke with one of the girls at the greeting podium, who pointed to Mercedes. Her fingers curled as the man pulled his shades on top of his head and turned her way. He half smiled, his dark eyes snaring her. *Takashi.*

He headed her way and she rose from her seat, hyper aware of how his clothes clung to his form. *Hot damn, he's better looking in person.* Takashi's gaze never left her, making her self-conscious. Did she look okay? *Why am I concerned about that? It's a lunch date with a friend!*

She shoved her hands into her pockets. "Hey, Takashi."

He smiled at her. "Hey, sorry I'm late." He flicked his wrist, and her eyes went wide at the sight of the white rose that appeared in his hand. "I hope this helps make up for it."

Another white rose? She tentatively reached out and accepted the flower, finding out quickly that it was in fact real. She inhaled the sweet scent. *This time I'm not in need of cheering up. Could this mean…* She gazed up at him, an alluring smile on her face. "Thank you. I didn't realize you were a mage in real life, too."

He chuckled as the two sat down in their booth. "Little hobby I picked up as a kid. Spell caster in the game gives me actual magic instead of illusions."

"Illusions are still magic to people like me," Mercedes said, setting the rose down on the table. "Thank you for the flower. It's lovely. And unexpected."

"I don't change just because I don't have a game system to shield me."

"You never know with people."

He regarded her for a moment before looking at the digital menu device, ordering a drink. "I'll be honest, I've never been here before."

"One of the most authentic places you'll find in these parts," Mercedes said, looking at her own device. "Goro immigrated here about fifteen years ago. Brought his love for cooking with him. A few bumps in the road getting this place up and running, but here we are. It's my favorite place to eat."

The two glanced up from their menus when someone approached. Mercedes smiled at the sight of Goro. "*Konnichiwa*, Goro."

The older man smiled and set down the glass of soda Takashi ordered. "*Konnichiwa*, Mercedes-san. It is good to see you today." He turned his attention to Takashi. "And it is good to see you not alone this time."

Mercedes gestured to Takashi. "This is my friend, Takashi. He's visiting for the weekend. Not a date, so that's why he showed up."

She tried not to wince. She didn't mean to word it that way, but the truth was hard to keep down.

Takashi did his best to bow while in his seat. "*Konnichiwa*, Goro-san."

Mercedes listened as he went into a full conversation with Goro in Japanese. Goro smiled the whole time. She could pick out some of their words, thanks to the few classes she'd taken, and the talks she had with Takashi, but her lack of fluency in the language had her struggling to pick out words at their speed. Her name came up a few times, but those were times she couldn't make out enough to understand.

Their conversation ended, with Goro nodding and looking her way. "I approve of this one. You should make this a date. Enjoy your lunch."

Mercedes went to protest, but he walked away, leaving her confused. She looked at Takashi. "Was he grilling you?"

Takashi chuckled. "Yes. He seems to have a parental fondness for you. Wanted to make sure I wasn't out to harm you in any way."

She smiled. "Sounds like him. Mother and I were some of his first customers on opening day. I've come here on a weekly basis since."

"Is that why you bring all your dates here?"

Mercedes' cheeks flushed. "Yeah… I figure no matter how the date goes, at least I'll have good food."

"Well"—Takashi folded up his menu—"today will be a treat then, since I will ensure this lunch date goes well."

Mercedes smiled and went about placing her order. Takashi did the same with his own device.

Mercedes took a sip of her water. "So, how did your family react when they found out you were flying home for a few days?"

Takashi shrugged. "Thanks to Mia, they weren't all that

surprised. She interpreted something I said Wednesday as me definitely coming home this weekend, so she, of course, blabbed to my mother."

Mercedes laughed. "Your sister is adorable."

He took a sip of his soda. "When she wants to be. Sometimes she's a pain, but I've come to expect it, being the oldest of three."

"I can only imagine what that's like."

Takashi snorted. "Sometimes I envy you, trust me."

Mercedes laughed. Besides the fact that she didn't have anyone to talk to, she didn't mind being an only child. No fighting over toys and where to go for dinner. Never having to watch her parents try to split gifts evenly. Having her parents' love all to herself. *Yeah, I'm that selfish.*

"How did that interview pan out?" Takashi asked, taking another sip of his drink.

She shook her head. "My dad is still thinking about it. He usually takes a while to make decisions. A few others and I think he's waiting for me to offer my services for the spot."

Takashi brow rose. "You paint?"

Mercedes rocked her head back and forth. "Hobby painter. I'm not near close enough to do some of this work for clients."

Takashi pursed his lips. "Do you have any pictures of your work?"

Mercedes pulled out her phone and scrolled through her files. She suspected she did, but wasn't sure. She ended up finding two. "Here we go. These were just on some scrap metal."

She handed him the phone and he looked at the rose

garden with stylized flames first and then the attempt at a dragon she made. "I'm not so great at creatures yet, but I'm not too bad at inanimate objects."

"These are fantastic." He looked at her. "Really, they are. And yeah, the dragon could use some work, but you show a talent not many have, so I'm sure it'd only be a matter of time before you perfected it."

Heat spread through Mercedes' face, and she sucked down some water to hide her embarrassment. "Um, how's the situation with your business coming?"

Takashi sighed and passed the phone back to her. "No real change. I'm still able to do business, for now, but as far as I know, they haven't figured out who hacked my account."

Mercedes frowned. "That's so strange. I can't possibly figure out who would want to do that to you."

Takashi shrugged. "I'm pretty sure it's just a random attack. Some loser looking to test his skills and see if he can get away with it. I just happened to be the unlucky victim."

Mercedes wasn't convinced. It was too coincidental, but at the same time, she couldn't think of anyone he could have pissed off.

A staff member approached their table with the meals the two ordered. Mercedes went to dig into her large sushi order, but Takashi stole a piece. "Hey!"

He chuckled and then gave her a piece of his meal. "Nothing wrong with sharing."

She pursed her lips and then popped a sushi piece into her mouth. Takashi half-smiled, sending a flutter of butterflies through her stomach before eating. The two ate, keeping up the casual conversation.

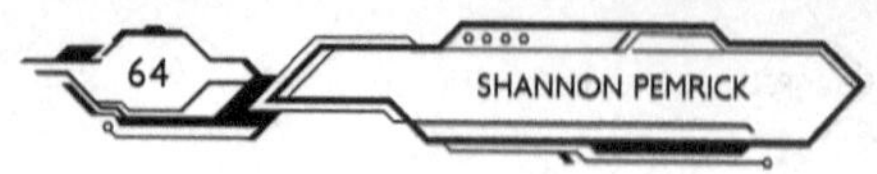

"So, when the GMs fixed your business, did your funds get all figured out too?"

"Oh yeah. We're all good. Means I'll be going to the seminar, like I'd planned."

"Where is the seminar?"

"L.A."

Her brow furrowed with thought. "When will you be back for that?"

"The end of next week. It's just a three-day seminar."

She scrunched her nose. "You're coming back this way for just three days?"

Takashi laughed. "Well, I thought I'd stick around for a week or two to visit with friends and family, too."

"Why not stay here for the rest of this week then, too?"

He opened his mouth to reply, but nothing came out. His face twisted and he thought about her point, and she giggled. She thought his in-game character looked adorable when confused, but his real self blew that out of the water.

"I guess I was so wrapped up in this surprise visit, I didn't think about that. I do have a meeting with a few sponsors, but I could have rescheduled if needed. Oh well—too late, now that I've booked the tickets."

Mercedes shook her head. *Men.* Then a thought came to her. "Hey, how do you manage to stay away from your business so long and not worry?"

Takashi ate a roll. "Well, usually I plan far enough in advance that I get my funds right for me to be MIA. If I can't, or if something comes up unexpectedly, I can use an NPC function to do my auctions for me. It requires a bit of special prompting from me to set up, but overall it does quite well."

"That's interesting."

"Are you thinking of getting into the online business?" He smirked. "No cars, but I'm sure you'd be good at it."

Mercedes laughed. "I'm quite happy doing what I'm doing now, thank you."

"Fine, suit yourself. But if you're looking for a business partner, I wouldn't say no."

A demure smile spread across Mercedes' lips and she took a gulp of water. She didn't hate the idea of going into business with him. *Though working so close to him all the time, may not be so great for my concentration.*

"Okay, enough about work. Did you see the new class changes coming in the next expansion?"

Mercedes ate some more and smiled. "Yep. I'm excited for the ranger changes. From what I can tell, my pets will be more useful. I'm also excited they're considering feedback for allowing us to have more than one finally."

Takashi rubbed his chin. "I wonder how that'd work."

"Well, I honestly can't see it any different than how I do it now with one pet."

"To be fair, I've never played a ranger class, so I wouldn't know the first thing about it."

Mercedes couldn't help the smirk spreading across her face. "I could always teach you."

Takashi chuckled. "Well, I do still have to teach you how to play a sorcerer correctly."

Mercedes hid her face in her hand. She had leveled a sorcerer for a bit, but she sucked at understanding how the class worked, resulting in her abandoning it. "Yeah, that's true."

A grin appeared on his lips. "We could always work

on both at the same time. Some one-on-one time isn't a bad idea, right?"

One-on-one time? Did he mean—She shook the thought from her head. Of course he didn't. "I think we can figure something out."

He ate some of his food, his necklace catching her eye again, as it had earlier. *I wonder.* "Hey, is that the necklace you got from your grandmother?"

Takashi touched the necklace and then smiled. "Yeah. I rarely take it off."

A warm smile spread across her face. He'd told her she'd given it to him shortly before she'd passed away. Takashi said it was special to her, and mentioned how happy he was to have received it from her.

"You don't think that's weird, do you?"

She shook her head. "Far from it. I think it's great. I know how close you two were. I'm sad I never got to meet her. She seemed like such a nice woman."

His face lit up and he gave her a piece of his sushi. Her brow furrowed as she tilted her head, but he didn't explain himself.

Conversation continued, topics staying light and getting them both laughing. As they talked, the white rose stuck in her peripheral. *Could this be more than friends?* They made great friends, no doubt about that, but she wasn't sure if a relationship would work out between them. Friendships and romantic relationships were two different beasts. *What would someone like him see in me anyway?*

Mercedes' phone buzzed, and she planned to ignore it, until she realized it was a phone call and not a text. The girls knew she had this lunch meeting, so they wouldn't be calling. Taking a look, the ID said "Shop." *Oh boy.*

She looked at Takashi. "I have to take this, sorry." He nodded and she answered. "Sup?"

"Hey, it's Mike," came the reply. Mike was one of the younger kids working at the shop—still in high school, wanting experience in a niche field. "Do you know where Mister Taeko's paper files are stored?"

Her blood ran cold. "Why? What's wrong with the computer files?"

"Um… Adrian's girlfriend brought coffee for everyone, and…"

Mercedes' blood boiled. "Do not tell me she was in the office again, when I've explicitly told all of you she's not to be in there after the last two accidents she caused."

Mike sighed. "We were all busy and assumed she'd listen when we told her to put the drinks down on the table outside the office. But Adrian was in the office, so she went in and… tripped. You can guess what happened next."

Mercedes slammed her fist down on the table, making Takashi jump and a few of the wait staff look their way. She took a controlled breath so she wouldn't yell at Mike. This wasn't entirely his fault. Sure, someone should have made sure Adrian's girlfriend would listen, but Adrian knew better than to allow her in that room. She'd caused him nothing but trouble since they got together, and now it was affecting the business.

"Get her out of the building."

"Adrian escorted her out already."

"Good. Make two phone calls. One to my dad, and one to a computer tech. Tell Adrian the two of us are going to have a talk. Don't allow him to leave until I get there." She took another breath. "As for the paper files, they're locked up. Dad and I are the only ones with keys. I'm currently out to lunch with a friend, so try to see if you can get my dad down to get the files out for you until I get there."

"Sure. If the tech can't fix the computer…"

She chuckled. "I have backups at home. I did the backup two days ago, so we'll only lose two days' worth of data entries."

"You're a brilliant woman, Mercedes!"

Mercedes smirked. "Sucking up to your manager won't get you any brownie points."

Mike laughed. "I know, that's why I'm not. I'm serious."

"Yeah, yeah. Just go do what I said. And if Adrian leaves before I get there, I'll punish you."

"Careful, I might like it." He hung up, leaving her to stare at her phone, confused.

Takashi sputtered a laugh. "Sorry, that look was priceless. Care to share what's wrong? I've never seen you so angry."

Mercedes sighed. "One of my employees' girlfriends ruined a computer. It's the third piece of expensive equipment she's ruined in the last six months, and that doesn't include car parts she's ruined."

"Then we should pack up so that can be handled."

She looked at him to find concern clear on his face. She smiled. "No. I need a bit of time to calm down, and I'm not bailing on you because of her."

He pursed his lips and his brow furrowed. He then held up a finger. "Then how about this. We can still take our time, but if we're not done eating in fifteen minutes, we'll pack up." Mercedes opened her mouth to protest, but he continued. "Instead of just lunch, we'll hang out for the day. I'm interested to see your line of work and some of the projects you're working on. You post about it on social media, but it's a completely different experience in person."

He smirked at her at the mention of a different experience in person. She tried not to think too deeply into it, but her mind was going a bit wild on her all of a sudden. She also liked the idea of spending more time with him today. You learned a lot about someone when you engaged in activities together. Her pulse skipped. *Not like that, hormones. Simmer down.*

She smiled. "You know, that's a great idea. I don't know what we'd do, but we'll play it by ear. We could drop your bike off and use my car."

Takashi picked up a piece of sushi with his chopsticks, a smirk on his face. "I could get us around on the bike if you want. Easier to get through traffic."

Sit on the back of his bike, holding onto him? She did her best to keep her face from flushing when the image of her bent over his motorcycle came unbidden to her mind. "I think it'd be best to use the car. It'll be easier for us to talk, and I don't have a spare helmet."

He thought about this for a moment and popped another sushi piece into his mouth. "Fair point." He grinned at her again. "It's a date, then."

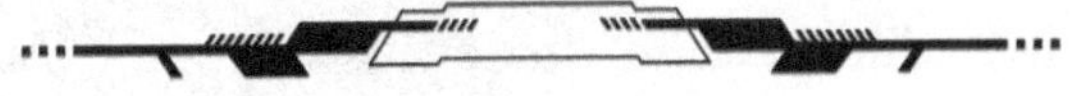

Fifteen minutes passed quicker than Takashi liked, but at least he didn't have to say goodbye to Mercedes yet. He'd made a joke, calling today a date, but as the pair

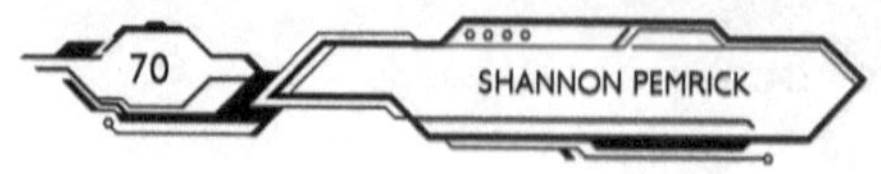

went about paying for their food, he wasn't so sure he wanted it to be a joke.

Mercedes had the ordering device split out the checks, and he held up a finger to get her attention. "I can get your half."

She looked at him, confused, and then swiped her credit card. "It's fine. I've got it."

He bit the inside of his cheek so he wouldn't argue. It was best to let her do her thing for now. He'd get his chance at some point today.

The two of them left, and Tasha called for Mercedes' car. Takashi had managed to snag a spot right up front, so he waited with her. He still felt the lingering disappointment when she declined the offer to hop on the back of his motorcycle, but she had some logical points.

The wind picked up and Mercedes did her best to keep her beautiful long hair from flying all over the place. When the sudden burst died down, she had a few hairs out of place. He couldn't stop himself from tucking the silky strands behind her ear. *Feels just like her in-game model.*

Mercedes' gorgeous eyes turned to him, her cheeks turning a slight shade of pink. He smiled. "Sorry. I shouldn't have done that."

"N–no, it's okay." She fussed with her hair some more, her teeth catching her bottom lip for a brief moment.

He swallowed, a wave of arousal hitting him. What would it be like to bite those lips of hers? *Too fast, Takashi, too fast.*

He couldn't help it, though. The moment he'd seen her sitting at that booth, his insides melted. Her captivating blue eyes and pouty lips—the way her long hair draped over her shoulders and her tight clothes clung to her tall and slim, but perfectly proportioned frame—Takashi looked away and shoved his hands in his pockets, pinching his thigh. *Where's something cold when you need it?*

The roar of an engine pulled his attention back and he watched, wide-eyed, as a white, 2011 Bugatti Veyron pulled up in front of them, the driver's seat empty. *Am I really seeing this?*

"Thanks, Tasha," Mercedes said.

"Anything for you, Miss Mercedes."

Takashi pointed at the sports car. "Wait, this is *your* car?"

Mercedes gazed at him with innocent blue eyes. "Uh, yeah. Haven't you seen some of the photos on social media?"

"Well, yeah, I guess…" He rubbed the back of his neck. "I guess I just assumed it was a customer's car."

Mercedes' eyes danced and then she sauntered over to the driver's side, Takashi following. "Nope, it's mine. I inherited it from my mom when she passed. She converted it from a non-driver long before I was born." She chuckled, her eyes still sparkling. "She did it specifically to piss off my dad."

Takashi laughed. "Why does that not surprise me?"

She smirked. "Because you know me, and I'd have done the same."

She wasn't wrong. That's exactly what he would have expected of her. He probably would have encouraged it, too. She and the rest of his family didn't call him an instigator for nothing.

Takashi opened the door for her, receiving a grateful

smile in response, and let her slip into the vehicle. "I'll do my best not to lose you in the traffic."

"Or you could give me your address."

Right. That was a stupid thing to not think of.

"It's okay, Miss Mercedes," Tasha said from her car's dash. "Ochi has shared the address on Mister Takashi's behalf and I've put it into the GPS."

"Well, thank you, Ochi, that was kind of you."

"You're welcome," Ochi responded from Takashi's phone. "I figured Takashi would have forgotten, as he forgets to think when you're around."

"Ochi!" Takashi couldn't stop himself from hollering. He couldn't believe his assistant today. First the unauthorized wording in the text messages, and then this. Takashi was dealing with a mutiny here.

But instead of putting her off, Mercedes laughed. "You're so funny, Ochi. I really like you."

"Happy to be of service, Mercedes."

"Miss Mercedes," Tasha said. "I hate to interrupt, but you have another call from the shop coming in."

"Oh boy. Let's see if they still need me."

Takashi pointed to his motorcycle. "I'll be at my bike."

He had done his best to hide the unease he still felt from Ochi's outburst, but by the way Mercedes looked at him, he knew he hadn't done a very good job. Takashi made a hasty retreat to his motorcycle, Ochi starting it up before he reached it.

When Takashi secured his helmet, Ochi spoke to him through it. "Takashi, are you all right? I sense unease in you."

"No, Ochi, I'm not okay. That stunt you pulled was far from okay."

"I'm sorry, sir, I don't understand. You've told me several times how much you care for Mercedes, and based on how you've been acting today, I thought you wanted her to know this."

Takashi sighed and rested his hands on the handlebars. "This has to be done delicately, Ochi. This is the first time we've met in person, and I can't be sure she sees me the same way. If I don't do this right, I'll lose her."

"My apologies. That was not my intent."

"I know." He looked over to where Mercedes remained, talking to someone on speaker. Whoever it was had her in a good mood, by the way she was laughing. "I just happened to have fallen for a woman who's going to be difficult to convince I'm sincere in my intent."

Something pinged in his helmet, and then Ochi spoke. "Sorry to interrupt, but Mercedes has sent you a message: We are still going to go to the shop."

Takashi gave her a thumbs-up, and then pulled out of his parking spot. The two vehicles weaved through traffic for the fifteen-minute drive to his family's home.

When they made it, he pulled into the driveway, while Mercedes parked at the end. The motorcycle engine cut, and Takashi climbed off. Slipping his helmet off and hanging it on the handlebar, he rushed over to Mercedes' car. He heard his little sister, Mia, call out his name, but he chose to pretend he didn't hear. If he acknowledged her, he risked his family coming out and scaring off Mercedes. As strong of a woman as she was, his family could get a little… excited.

He slipped into the luxury car, and Mercedes smiled at him. The car pulled away while Mercedes played with her stereo, her golden hair spilling over her shoulders and cybernetic arm, tempting him to look down her low-cut fitted t-shirt. Takashi turned his attention out the window and shifted in his seat. He could really use something cold in his lap right about now.

He tried to focus on something else, like her prosthetic. He hadn't noticed it at first when he saw her in the restaurant. It took him until they sat down in the booth together. She acted so normal with it, he didn't understand how it could be such a deal breaker with all these men she tried to date. *Besides its technological appearance, it looked like a normal appendage.*

He tried to keep himself from growing angry. She deserved to be treated better.

"So, what type of cars are you working on now?" he asked, trying to bring himself back to focusing on a neutral topic.

"Nothing ancient at the moment," she said. "A few cars from the early 2000's, and then my own project car from 2016."

His brow rose. "Those aren't ancient?"

Mercedes laughed. "I've worked on vehicles as old as 1960."

Takashi's eyes widened. "Really?"

"Yeah, and my dad has worked on even older cars. Those are real projects, due to most of the parts having to be fabricated, but they also make us good money."

"Do you work on newer vehicles, too?"

She nodded. "We have four techs, including myself, certified to work on newer vehicles. We rely on those jobs during the slower times of the year."

"When do things slow down?"

"Late spring to late summer. Show season is in prime

at that point. Once that starts to die down, our shop is flooded with cars that need anything from a tune-up to a full restoration."

The two continued their conversation, Takashi learning a lot from her. His own father had an old car he liked to work on every now and then, but Takashi hadn't learned nearly as much from his father as he had from her in the last fifteen minutes of driving.

He noticed how she smiled as she explained everything. He noticed this same smile while they had conversed about games during lunch. Working on cars gave her the same joy as gaming. *It's great she has such diverse passions.* It said a lot about her as a person.

The car pulled into a large parking lot filled with vehicles. Takashi's eyes went wide at the sight. Just as Mercedes said, cars and trucks of varied years and styles were parked all about. "Are these all project cars?"

"Not all. Some belong to the guys. My father and I allow each employee to keep up to three vehicles here. That doesn't include their daily driver. If anything happens to them, it's on them, but it gives our customers an idea of the cars we're willing to work on. Win-win for everyone."

"I'll say."

The two climbed out of the car when it parked, and Mercedes led the way into the shop. Takashi took note of the large shop sign, *Gail's Antique Restorations*, and a dark part of the building off to the side that looked like a storefront. At the moment, though, it appeared to be used for storage, from what he could see through the pulled blinds.

Loud noises echoed out of the shop's open doors,

but the moment Mercedes entered, silence. Everyone working stopped their task and looked at her. Takashi noted all of them were men. He remembered Mercedes mentioning she was the only woman working at the shop, though not because they refused to hire women. They'd had a number of them throughout the shop's life, they just came few and far between, and didn't last as long, on average.

Mercedes crossed her arms. "Quit your gawking and work."

Most of them chuckled and they all went back to working. A young, tan-skinned, sandy-haired kid, maybe sixteen or seventeen, exited a room Takashi guessed to be either an office or employee lounge, and flagged Mercedes down. Takashi followed her as she bee-lined to him.

"Any update since your phone call when I was in the car, Mike?" she asked.

The teen shook his head. "Tech is still looking at the computer, and your dad hasn't shown up yet."

Mercedes snorted. "I doubt he's eager to leave the show. Means he'd have to stop showing off his toys." She pulled out her keycard pack and held it up. "I'll get Mister Taeko's files out for you. Will anyone need any other customer files while I'm at it?"

Mike nodded. "A few. I have it all written down on a list so I wouldn't forget."

Mercedes patted him on the arm. "Good job." She looked back at Takashi. "Feel free to look around. Just don't get in anyone's way."

Takashi smirked. "I'll stay away from the coffee, too."

The techs around them roared with laughter, and

Mercedes shook her head, a smile on her lips. She went into the room Mike had come out of, Mike following her. *Definitely the office and not a lounge.* Takashi took a look around.

For a shop, the place was fairly clean. He expected tools and parts to be scattered all over the place, but found the opposite of that. Mercedes had a big thing about safety, so he suspected she ran a tight ship about keeping the building clean of unneeded hazards.

Takashi stopped in front of an old sports car, its faded blue and black paint catching his eye. No one worked on it currently, but he could see the interior was gutted, and much of the front end was missing.

An older man, maybe in his late forties, with umber skin approached him. "That's Mercedes' personal project car. A rare 2016 Bugatti Chiron."

Takashi's brows rose. "Another Bugatti?"

The man chuckled. "She has expensive taste, just like her mother." He held out his hand. "Name's Justin, the other manager here."

"Takashi." He clasped his hand with Justin. "Takashi Moreno."

Justin smirked. "Ah, you're that gaming friend of hers she was meeting today."

Takashi smiled. "Guilty."

Justin assessed him. "Not what I was expecting, but Mercedes is full of surprises."

Takashi knew he was referring to Mercedes' preference for men, one Ajax fit better than he did. But she could also pick outside of that preference if the guy impressed her enough.

"I should be offended." Takashi laughed. "But it's

too accurate a statement about Mercedes for me to be."

"Excuse you?" Mercedes' voice rang across the shop.

The two men looked her way. She stood in the office doorway, her arms crossed. Takashi shrugged and Justin laughed. Mercedes shook her head and joined the two. "What do you think?"

His gaze turned toward the car and then back to her. "Be more specific."

"Of the shop."

"I'm impressed with the cleanliness."

Justin laughed. "She'll eat us alive if we don't keep the floors clean and keep parts away from areas they can be easily damaged."

Mercedes crossed her arms. "Do I hear a complaint?"

He held up his hands. "Not from me. I like not tripping over someone's 'forgotten' wrench."

Her lips pressed into a line, and she looked at him like she didn't believe him. Takashi suspected Justin was, at the very least, a former culprit of such behavior.

All three turned their attention to the front of the shop when a car door slammed and heavy boots stomped their way. A tall man with fair hair, tan skin, and a broad shouldered, muscular physique stormed into the building. His voice boomed through the shop. "Where is he?"

Mercedes sighed. "Dad, I've been handling this."

Ah, so that's Jayce. Takashi noted that he too had a cybernetic prosthetic, but unlike Mercedes with a fake right arm, he had a fake left. *I wonder why.* Mercedes never mentioned that her father also had a limb replacement. She also never told him the cause of her accident. *Were they both involved?*

Her father stalked over to her. "Where is he?"

"Currently working on a car. I just got done speaking with the computer tech. It's fixable, but will cost a bit." His hands clenched and his face reddened, but Mercedes placed a hand on his shoulder. "Take a deep breath, grab a cup of coffee, and check on the projects. I'm handling it."

Jayce's eyebrow twitched at the word coffee, and Takashi and Justin couldn't help but snicker. Jayce looked his way. "Who is this?"

"Oh." Mercedes gestured to Takashi. "Dad, this is my friend—"

Her father extended his hand. "Jayce Gail, Mercedes' father and owner of this shop."

Takashi clasped his hand with Jayce. "Takashi Moreno. Friend of Mercedes and business—"

"Oh, you're the friend of hers that makes a living off that game... what was it called?"

Mercedes sighed. "Lusara Fates, Dad. Man, can't you ever remember a single game I play?"

"Your mother was better at that," he said, his reply a bit gruff. "She's the one that got you into that hobby." He looked at Takashi. "You said your last name was Moreno?"

Takashi nodded. "That's right."

Her father eyed him and then walked off. "I'll keep that in mind. Nice meeting you, kid."

Takashi turned to Mercedes, puzzled, but she shrugged and headed off into another direction. He watched her approach a pale man with chestnut hair, who did not look pleased by her presence. *That must be Adrian.*

Takashi's phone started to go off, playing the *Imperial*

March from Star Wars, his favorite old science fiction space opera. Mercedes looked back at him, her brow raised, and the techs laughed.

He pulled out his phone. "Text."

"Thank them for the perfect timing!" Justin called out.

Takashi chuckled and then focused on the text he received, knowing it was from his mother. He made sure to assign a distinct tone for her.

> *Are you still out on that date?*

His brow rose and he typed back.

> *Date?*

> *Mi-chan said you went to lunch with some girl.*

Takashi sighed. He'd told Mia he was just out seeing a friend, but she must have noticed Mercedes in the car when he dropped off his motorcycle.

> *It wasn't a date, Okaasan. I met up with my friend, Mercedes, for lunch, and then we decided to hang out for the rest of the day.*

> *Interesting name. I knew a girl with it. My old business partner's daughter. When will the two of you be home for dinner?*

Takashi pinched his nose and inwardly groaned. As

much as he would like to bring her home for dinner, that'd be too fast and ruin any chance he had with her.

I'm not bringing her home for dinner, Okaasan.

Yes you are! I will prepare for one extra person.

Takashi sighed and tried to figure out how to get his mother to let this go. She'd been relentless lately about him settling down and getting married. It wasn't like he hated the idea, on the contrary. It was something he wanted. He just needed to find the right someone. *Someone like… Mercedes.*

He looked up to see her tearing into Adrian.

"She's not allowed in this shop ever again, do I make myself clear?" Mercedes said.

"What? That's a bit extreme," Adrian said. "You don't have to—"

"A bit extreme?" Takashi could see her anger rising, and he was tempted to take a step back. He'd only seen her mad a few times, and she was a force to be reckoned with when it happened. "May I remind you of the other costly problems she's caused?"

Adrian went to respond, but she continued. "Paint on a 2050 Mercedes upholstery set to be installed that day and delivered to the customer the following day, costing us hundreds to fix, and delay fees we had to eat. Paint spilled on newly painted body panels for a 2016 Lamborghini."

Mercedes continued, making it a point to highlight his skills in the field as well, and how he shouldn't risk that for some "girl." Takashi could tell she didn't like his girlfriend much, if at all. Of course, he couldn't blame her if the woman only brought problems to the shop. He also didn't like how Adrian responded to all this. He had too many excuses lined up, and expected Mercedes to fall for one of them.

Takashi looked down at his phone and started typing back to his mother, only to delete the message when it sounded stupid. He needed to word this right.

He glanced up when someone approached. Mercedes had a smile on her face, pleased with the reprimanding she'd given her employee.

Her smile faded, and he realized he wasn't doing a good job as disguising his family issue. "Everything okay?" she asked.

"Yeah, just my mom being her."

She laughed. "How so?"

Takashi showed her the texts, not seeing any reason to hide them from her. He half expected her to tense up, but her expression formed into a curious, thoughtful one.

She handed his phone back. "I actually wouldn't mind having dinner with your family."

This surprised him. "Yeah?"

Her gaze faltered. "Unless you don't want me to…"

"No, of course I do!" She peered up at him, but he couldn't meet her gaze. He rubbed the back of his neck. "What I mean—"

"He wants to take you out on a date!" One of the techs yelled out across the shop.

Mercedes' father came out of the office and looked around. "Who is taking who on a date?"

Mercedes lifted a hand and flipped the employee the middle finger. "No one, Dad. Jensen is just being a dick."

Jensen threw his hands in the air. "Not my fault the two of you are flirting with each other."

Is it that obvious?

Mercedes crossed her arm. "No, we're not."

The blue-eyed man snorted and then went back to work. Her father snapped his attention to Takashi, and he swallowed. The man didn't have a scowl, but Takashi knew that stern look. *Protective type. Great.* Emi's father wasn't the most accepting of him, another reason the two hadn't worked out. Takashi wasn't sure if Mercedes' father would be the same, but he'd have to be careful if he was going to pursue anything with her.

Mercedes faced him. "So, I'm done here. We can head out and do whatever now."

Takashi typed out a response to his mother, telling her they'd be by around six, and then nodded. "Still want to go to the museum?"

He'd mentioned it on the ride over and she sounded a bit interested, but they never confirmed.

She smiled. "Yeah, I'd like that."

The two headed out, but not without some of the techs making comments.

"Careful where you put your hands, loverboy."

"Pick a car with a roomy back."

"Don't do anything we wouldn't do."

Mercedes shook her head and ignored them. Takashi suspected she was used to such behavior. He got the feeling, even though they were her employees, they were a tight-knit group. Any issues she ran into, they'd jump right in to protect her.

When they hopped into her car, he glanced her way. "If you ever want help fixing up that car, and I'm here, give me a shout. I'd be happy to help."

"Yeah?" Mercedes asked. He nodded, making her smile. "I'd like that."

A loud smack echoed in the car as Mercedes slapped Takashi's hand away from the stereo dial. She tensed as she didn't mean to hit him so hard. *Another downside to this stupid prosthetic.* Takashi rubbed his hand and she frowned. "Sorry. I don't mean to hit you so hard. The added weight of this stupid thing is hard for me to gauge sometimes."

Takashi continued to rub his hand. "You did warn me not to touch your stereo." His eyes glittered. "This is just my punishment for not listening."

She eyed him. "If I'm not mistaken, you sound interested in the prospect of punishment."

He flashed her a smile that made her insides melt. "Depends on who's doing the punishing."

Blood rushed to her cheeks, and she couldn't stop the arousing mental image of her tied to a bed from popping into her head. *I shouldn't think these things!*

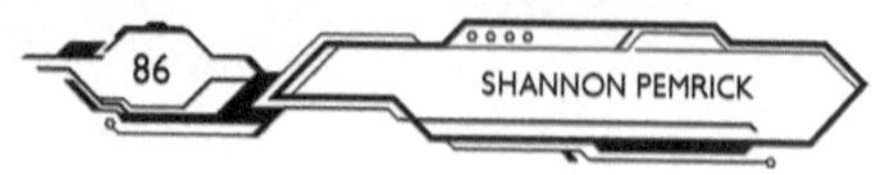

Takashi's boisterous laugh filled the car. "The look on your face is priceless. You reacted just as I hoped."

Mercedes' eyes narrowed, her cheeks growing warmer, and she punched him in the arm. Takashi held his arm, and his face contorted as he mouthed the word "ow."

Serves you right, jerk. She looked out the windshield, watching the city go by.

"Aw, Mercedes, don't be like that," he begged. She didn't acknowledge him. "I'll buy you a treat."

She gave him a sidelong glance. "You're bribing me?"

He smirked in a way that made it hard for her to be mad at him. *Why is it all of a sudden this "just friends" thing is so hard?* "I have two younger sisters. Of course it's not."

Mercedes pursed her lips, noting the thick sarcasm in his fake lie. "What kind of treat?"

"Well, ice cream would be too obvious a choice." Takashi tapped his lips with thought. "But I do know of a place that sells delicious roll cakes."

I love roll cakes! But she'd never told him that. She regarded him for a minute. "Roll cakes?"

Takashi chuckled. "You and Narissa were gushing about them a few weeks ago."

Oh, duh! She and Narissa had done that just before a raid. Mercedes had gone down for a visit, and they'd gone to a small boutique that sold specialized variations of common treats.

"This one has some unique flavors I know you'd like. Like a chocolate peanut butter truffle."

Mercedes' mouth watered. It sounded amazing.

"I'll buy. What do you say? Will it make you forgive me?"

Her brow creased. When they'd finished with lunch,

Takashi had tried to offer to pay for her meal, but she didn't feel right accepting. When they'd arrived at the museum, he'd up and paid for her ticket without consulting her. And now he wanted to buy her a treat. *Was he trying to make this into some sort of date? No, don't be silly, Mercedes.* The flower he'd given her and the joke he'd made at the restaurant had just thrown her off. This wasn't some abstract romantic date. It was just time being spent between two good friends, and he was just a bit old fashioned about the guy picking up the check.

And as friends, she could drag out his "torture" a little longer. She grinned. "I will need to taste this cake before I can forgive you. It'd better hold up to my standard of deliciousness, or you'll still owe me."

"Maybe I don't want to bring you there, then. Owing you for a little longer wouldn't be that horrible of a situation." Takashi grinned. "It'd give you time to come up with a suitable punishment for me."

Mercedes' cheeks flushed again, and a growing arousal plagued her. *Is he—* She shook the thought. *No way someone like him is flirting with someone like me.* She crossed her arms. "No. I have decided I want roll cakes."

Takashi smiled. "Excellent. Tasha, I would like to add a pitstop to the GPS path."

"I can do that for you, Mister Takashi," Tasha replied. "Just tell me the name of the location."

"I want it to be a surprise for Mercedes," Takashi said.

Mercedes' brow rose with interest.

"Miss Mercedes, are you okay with this?" Tasha asked.

"I am."

"Very well. Please enter the location manually, Mister Takashi."

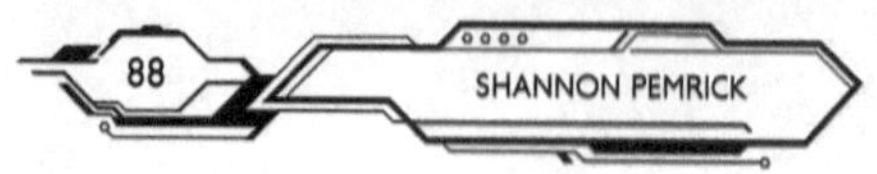

Mercedes watched him enter the address but she didn't recognize it. *Where could he be taking me?*

"The undisclosed location has been added, and the car will reroute," Tasha said. "Estimated time of arrival, fifteen minutes."

Takashi smiled in her direction, and Mercedes returned the gesture, trying to hide any evidence of the little butterflies fluttering around in her stomach. If this was how she was going to react to him every time he looked at her, she was in trouble. *I can't ruin our friendship. I have to get myself under control.*

Takashi reached for the stereo dial again and she pushed his hand out of the way. He smirked and tried again. She refused to allow it. He made another attempt, enticing a laugh from her.

Except, I'm struggling to find a good enough reason to do so.

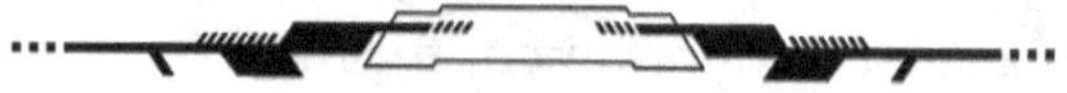

The GPS guided the car into a parking space in front of the small boutique Takashi wanted to treat Mercedes to. He couldn't pass up the opportunity to tease her earlier, and her reaction only made things easier for him. He knew she wouldn't stay mad at him, she wasn't petty, but it gave him a good excuse to spoil her. He also wanted to test the waters for some of her reactions.

Mercedes held herself to a standard of strength, and in front of a group of people she knew, spit out appropriate responses as easily as she breathed. But like anyone else, when he got her alone, she became a different person. Her smile widened—her laugh unfiltered—her cheeks flushed at the slightest sexual hint.

And Takashi knew she was no stranger to that. She'd joined in on the jokes in guild chat, and worked with men all day. Her responses in those situations were a part of her, but this setting showed the other. *The less guarded, softer her.*

Mercedes gasped when she saw the name of the boutique. *Those Buns Dough.* "Is this… oh my god, it is! When did this come to town?"

Takashi tilted his head. "You know this place?"

She nodded. "This is the place I went to with Narissa in L.A. We found it by chance, and decided to give it a shot because of the name. Their pastries are amazing!"

"Well, according to my mother, it's been here for a few years, but didn't gain popularity until it branched out to another city. I guess I now know why, if it went to L.A."

Mercedes stared at him with wide eyes. "So, is this really where you wanted to take me?"

"Yep." He opened the car door. "So, let's get you that promised treat."

Mercedes squealed with delight and flung open her door, making him laugh. She had some adorable moments that he just loved. Upon meeting up on the same side of the car, he placed his hand on her lower back, a bold move on his part. Lucky for him, she smiled and didn't protest. *Maybe I do have a good chance at this.*

The pair entered the small shop and perused the long display of various treats.

"I'm going to struggle to keep my figure with all these options," Mercedes mumbled.

Takashi smiled and took a chance. "You'd still be beautiful."

Her eyes widened and her cheeks tinted a shade of

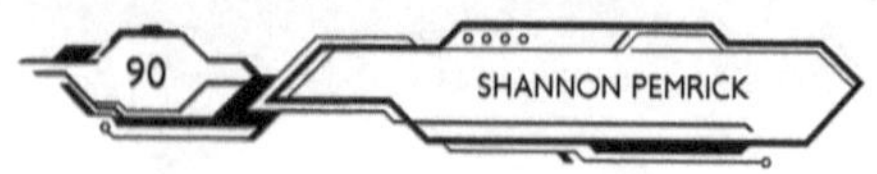

red. Her gaze darted away suddenly, and she rubbed her cybernetic arm with her real one. "Yeah, I… I guess that's true."

Takashi frowned. Was this response out of humility, or a result of how she'd been treated?

One of the employees working the counter finished with his customer and addressed the pair. He took great interest in Mercedes' presence, but Mercedes needed more time and focused on the display. Takashi found great joy in seeing the man's disappointment.

With Mercedes still deciding, Takashi ordered a few items for his mother and siblings. He knew he'd be in trouble if he didn't. The young man retrieved the treats and boxed them up, but Mercedes still hadn't decided. She chewed her bottom lip, and a strong wave of arousal hit him. He really wanted to do that to her now. "Struggling to decide?"

She nodded. "There are so many good choices. I don't know what one to pick."

"Then don't choose one. Select a couple."

Her eyes widened. "I can't do that! That'd get expensive fast."

Takashi smiled at her. "I'm not worried about that. Pick what you want."

She pursed her lips before perusing the large display. He could see she struggled with this offer, and while he wished she wouldn't, he admired her conservative nature with other's money.

"We do offer sampler boxes, if that would help you," the man behind the counter said.

Mercedes looked at him, her interest piqued. "Really? How big?"

He smiled and held up a hand before leaving the counter. He grabbed a tablet and came around to their side to show her. The tablet contained a catalog of their treats, as well as boxes, samplers, and gift ideas. The employee pointed out popular choices and new offers. Takashi kept a close eye on the two, jealousy simmering in his blood at the sight of how close the employee was getting to Mercedes. He knew it wasn't the right thing to feel in this situation, but since he'd decided to pursue her, he didn't want anyone else getting in his way. But from the way Mercedes focused more on the catalog than the guy, she either didn't notice his interest, or didn't care.

Takashi caught a pattern in her looking and approached. He flipped the pages, and landed on a box offer she had gone to several times. "Why not this one? It offers a double size for each sample, with the same sample selection as the smaller one you were eyeing as well?"

"But it's so expensive," she mumbled.

He sighed. "I told you, forget about the price. Pick what will make you happy."

She looked at him through her lashes. "You're sure? You won't get mad?"

God, this woman is going to be the end of me. Takashi grinned. "You could buy one of everything in this store at their full size and it'd be fine."

She laughed. "Don't tempt me!"

He shrugged. "If it's what you want."

Mercedes stared at him for a moment and then smiled. She looked at the boutique employee. "I'll get this sampler box, then."

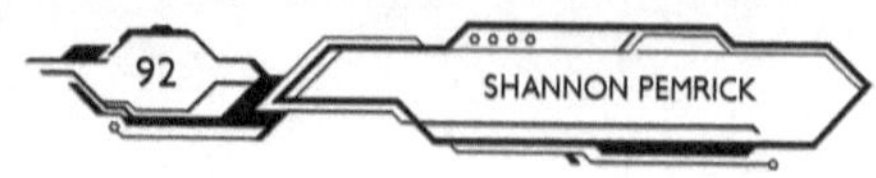

He nodded. "Sure, I'll go grab the box while you decide what you want in it."

The young man ran off, Takashi taking the opportunity to take his spot next to Mercedes and help her with her decisions. She pointed them out to the shop worker when he returned, and then Takashi paid.

Mercedes cringed when she saw the total, but it didn't faze him. He knew the online business like he knew how to breathe. As long as someone wasn't getting it shut down on him, he'd be able to make money without issue, including any extra he'd need for trips back to the states whenever he wanted. If he was going to convince her to give him a chance, he wasn't going to try to make this a virtual-only relationship.

The two left the shop and hopped into the car. Tasha set the car into motion for Takashi's family home, and Mercedes impatiently waited for Takashi to pull out her sweet box. He noticed a small slip of paper tucked into the ribbon holding the box together. "What's this?"

Mercedes took the box and slipped the paper out, opening it. She laughed. "His name and phone number."

To Takashi's surprise, she ripped the paper in half and tossed the strips into a pocket in the console. "Not interested, I guess?"

She opened her box to look over her treats. "He didn't talk to me in any way that would indicate he wanted to invest any time to know me as a person. Meaning, he wants a single night or a casual fuck buddy. No thanks."

Takashi handed her a fork in case she wanted to use it on any of her samples. "If burning it will make you feel better, we can do that once we get the house."

She smiled. "No, don't worry. A pretty face like this

gets used to this kind of interest. One-nighters, I can have whenever." He noticed her shoulders sag. "Long lasting relationships are a different beast…"

She stared down at her treats, pain clear in her eyes. Takashi wasn't sure what to do. Words wouldn't help much, and if he overstepped bounds, that wouldn't go over well.

Mercedes stabbed a roll cake with her fork and shoved the baked dessert into her mouth. She threw her head back and moaned. "So… good…"

The sound of her moaning sent an unexpected pulse of arousal through him. Would she make that same sound if he were the cause of it, or would it be even better? His eyes darted to the back of the car for a moment. *Would that be big enough for the two of us?* He may be able to convince her to climb on top of him without needing the back seat.

Takashi shook the thoughts from his head—no easy feat, of course. He needed to refocus himself before his mind got him into trouble. "So, am I forgiven?"

She glanced at him. "I want to say no, but we both know I like this too much for either of us to believe that."

"You could if you wanted." Takashi smirked. "I'd prefer you to forgive me, as then I can spoil you without you claiming it's some arbitrary obligation." Her brow lifted, and he chose to change the subject before it all backfired on him. He pointed to her sampler box. "Just don't eat that all in one sitting. You'll need room for my mother's cooking."

Mercedes held her head high. "You're looking at the daughter of an undefeated wing eating champion of the California State Fair. Don't underestimate what I can do." Takashi's face twisted with confused interest, and she giggled before closing her treat box. "But these aren't wings, and that'd be a lot of sugar. I think I'll hold off rotting my teeth out until I get home."

Takashi chuckled and looked at the GPS route. They'd arrive in ten minutes. He tapped his fingers on his knee. *Ten minutes before things get interesting.*

Mercedes tilted her head. "Something the matter?"

He looked at her and then out the window. "Yeah, I'm just hoping my mother doesn't go overboard. She's convinced I have a secret girlfriend, and since I'm hanging out with you, I think she's come to the conclusion—"

"That I'm that lady." Mercedes laughed. "Don't worry. I'm pretty sure I can handle it."

He glanced her way and she smiled wide at him. He should be reassured, but he knew his mother too well. And there was the matter of Rei. He didn't expect her to behave with Mercedes around. Tonight would get interesting.

CHAPTER 6

The white sports car pulled into the driveway of the medium-sized suburban home built of tan sandstone. The pair climbed out of the car, and Mercedes noted the large column entrance and beautiful arched windows. The other homes stacked up on either side looked similar, though each had a bit of flair that set them apart from the rest.

The front door opened and a young girl, maybe eleven or so, who shared similar features to Takashi, skipped out of the house. Her short raven hair bounced around her shoulders. "*Nüsan*, you're home!"

Mercedes knew the ages of both Takashi's sisters, and had met his little sister in game briefly the other day. She guessed this to be Mia.

The girl ran to Takashi and hugged him tight. If Mercedes didn't know any better, she'd have thought he'd only just returned home from Korea.

Takashi chuckled and rubbed his sister's head. "Yes, Mi-chan, I'm home."

Mia peered up at Mercedes, smiling wide. "You did bring her!" She pulled behind her brother, acting sheepish all of a sudden. "She's prettier in person."

Takashi patted his sister's head. "I think so, too."

Mercedes' cheeks warmed, and she tucked a lock of hair behind her ear as she looked away from the siblings. "Thank you…"

Mia pulled away from Takashi. "I'm going to tell *Okaasan* you're here."

The dark-haired girl ran off. "*Okaasan! Okaasan! Niisan* and his girlfriend are here."

"Mia, she's not—" Takashi sighed with defeat, his sister repeating the phrase again, this time even louder.

Mercedes laughed. "I don't think there's any winning that right now."

He gazed at her with apologetic eyes. "Sorry. I'll do my best to get them to let it go."

Mercedes noticed the tiny bit of disappointment pricking in her stomach. "It's okay, really. We know the truth, so that's what matters."

He jerked his thumb toward the house. "Let's head inside so we can control the damage."

Mercedes nodded and the two entered the house. She slipped off her shoes in the foyer and took in the room. High vault ceilings and large windows allowed for the perfect amount of light. The home appeared to be a standard open-concept two-story home, the decor modern with slight oriental flair. Mia ran into the room, her socks sliding on the wood floor until she came to a stop. A smile on her face, she looked behind her.

An older Japanese woman, somewhere in her fifties with bobbed black hair, also approached. Mercedes' eyes widened. "Missus Asaka?"

The woman smiled at her. "I thought as much. I only know one Mercedes, and she fit your description and age perfectly. It's good to see you, Mercedes-san."

I was right! When she'd read the texts on Takashi's phone, she had a hunch, but it was too coincidental to assume. It was one reason she agreed to have dinner with his family. "It's been a long time, Missus Asaka."

The two bowed to each other, and then his mother held out her hand for a hug. Mercedes excitedly accepted the gesture, and when she pulled away, she noticed the confused look on both Mia's and Takashi's faces.

Takashi glanced between her and his mother. "Um, what?"

His mother smiled. "Mercedes' mother was my old business partner. She used to bring Mercedes to the store when she could drag her away from those cars."

Mercedes laughed and held up her grime-stained hand. "Didn't work."

Asaka chuckled. "Yes, as I suspected would happen."

Takashi looked at Mercedes. "You didn't tell me you knew my mother."

Before Mercedes could answer him, his mother clapped her hands. "We can explain in a moment. Right now, we need to welcome a guest in our home."

"Oh, right." He rubbed the back of his neck and then gestured into the house. "Why don't we go into the living room?"

Mercedes nodded. "I'm a guest here. You lead and I shall follow."

Mia grabbed her by the hand and pulled her farther into the house. "This way."

Mercedes found herself pulled into a large adjacent room filled with more furnishings matching the rest of the house interior. White satin drapes fluttered in the light breeze filtering through the open windows. Mia sat down on a couch, patting the spot next to her. Mercedes took the indicated seat, and Takashi took up the last available spot next to her, while his mother took one of the chairs.

The necklace on Mrs. Asaka's neck jangled, catching Mercedes' eye. It looked a lot like the one Takashi wore. She knew his necklace had come from his grandmother on his father's side, so she wondered if that one was also from his grandmother.

Mercedes continued to look around the room, momentarily forgetting about the jewelry. "Your home is beautiful, Missus Asaka."

"Please, call me *Okaasan*."

"*Okaasan!*" Takashi scolded. "Stop push—"

Mercedes placed a hand on his arm. "It's okay, Takashi. I used to call her that when I was a kid. I just figured, with all the time that had passed, it would be better not to."

Mrs. Asaka waved her hand. "Nonsense."

"Yeah, so about that," Takashi said. "Why didn't you tell me any of this?"

Mercedes scratched her arm, trying to figure out how to word herself. "I met your father, and Rei, though only once or twice. When we met in game and you introduced yourself with your last name, it rang a few bells, since you were about the age of Missus Asaka's oldest son and had the same number of siblings, but it was just too coincidental we'd meet like that. Especially after so many years had passed." Mercedes chuckled. "It wasn't until you showed me the texts today that I realized it *could* be that coincidental."

Takashi stared at her, baffled, and Mercedes ducked her head. She felt really dumb now. She should have just asked him more questions about his family. But she also knew why she hadn't. Mercedes had a habit of running from that part of her life. She tried to move on, like she promised her mother she would, but with the way her life had gone, it wasn't easy for her.

Mercedes looked at Asaka. "I'm sorry for not coming back to see you. I just…"

Asaka held up her hand to stop her. "I understand. You don't need to apologize. Your mother's passing happened quick, and it affected all of us. I expected going back to the shop would cause you too much pain. Then time passed by, as it does to us all."

Her words made Mercedes feel a bit better, but no less guilty. She could have come by once or twice in the last thirteen years.

Takashi's head swiveled. "Rei-chan and *Otousan* haven't joined us. Are they out?"

His mother shook her head. "*Otousan* is out to the store and Rei-chan is——"

"I'm right here," came an annoyed feminine voice.

The three turned toward the foyer to find a woman in her mid-twenties standing in the doorway of the living room. She looked much like Mia and Takashi, though unlike her younger sister, her raven hair flowed well past her shoulders. *Man, these people really won a genetic lottery.*

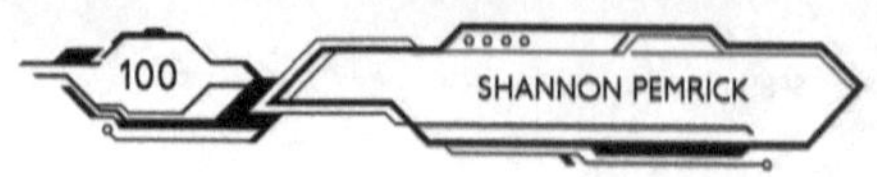

"Look, *Neesan*, *Niisan* brought his girlfriend home for dinner!" Mia beamed.

"Mi-chan, she's not my girlfriend," Takashi corrected, his eyes not leaving the eldest of the two sisters.

Rei scoffed. "I can see that, Mi-chan. Just so you know, Takashi, Emi will be coming over for dinner. She's in town, and I invited her over before *Okaasan* told me you'd be bringing *her*."

Mercedes did her best not to react to Rei's acid stare. *I knew I shouldn't have come here.* The tension between Rei and Takashi was because of her. He'd made off-handed comments about it before. She'd just hoped it was blown out of proportion. *Apparently not.*

Takashi's eyes darkened, and he opened his mouth to spit out a response to his sister, but their mother beat him to it. "Rei, you will respect our guest!"

Rei ground her teeth and then walked out of the room. Asaka sighed and looked at Mercedes, but a timer went off in the kitchen. Asaka said a quick apology on her daughter's behalf, and then excused herself. Mia followed her, offering to help.

Mercedes looked at the floor. "Takashi, would it be best if I left? I don't want—"

Takashi placed his hand on hers. "Don't let my sister get to you. Emi and I didn't work out as a couple because it didn't work out. It wasn't because of a lack of trying or faithfulness. Rei's going to have to grow up eventually and realize that."

The way he worded that… He didn't outright deny she'd been involved in the split. "You worded that too carefully."

Takashi sighed and leaned forward, resting his elbows

on his knees. "I have a deep connection with you. You and I both have talked about it. Emi and I didn't have that. We tried, but the longer we tried, the more we realized it wasn't going to happen. So we split on mutual terms." He held Mercedes' gaze. "You were not directly involved in our breakup."

Mercedes could tell he was being sincere, but she couldn't shake the doubt in her. She did her best to smile. "Okay."

He reached out and tucked a lock of hair behind her ear, like he had done earlier today. The gesture sent a wave of mixed emotions through her, just like before. Was such a gesture okay for friends to do? Was she overthinking this?

Takashi continued to gaze into her eyes. His dark, kind eyes captivated her. A lump formed in her throat when his lips slipped into a half smile.

The front door opened, ripping their attention away from each other, and two people entered. Takashi and Mercedes stood up when an older gentleman in his mid-fifties with reddish-brown skin and dark hair, and a young woman around Mercedes' age with tan skin and long raven hair entered the living room. *She's gorgeous.*

"*Otousan*, you're home," Takashi said. He looked at the woman. "Emi, it's good to see you."

That's Emi? With her stylish clothes and good looks, Mercedes felt inadequate again. She'd seen a few photos of her when Takashi and she were together, but it didn't compare to reality. *If Takashi couldn't make it work with someone like her, no way I have a chance.* How could she compete with that?

Emi smiled and waved. "Hey you two. You're both looking well. It's good to see you again, Mercedes."

"You too, Emi." She turned to Takashi's father. "It's been a while, Mister Moreno."

The older man smiled wide and rushed over to her, pulling Mercedes into a big bear hug. "That's an understatement, Mercedes." He pulled away, keeping her at arms' length. "And call me Miguel, please."

She nodded, unable to stop herself from smiling. "I can do that."

Miguel gave a quick visual assessment of her. "Look at you. You've grown into a beautiful woman behind my back."

She smiled. "Thank you."

"When Asaka told me you were coming over, I couldn't believe it." He pulled out a rolled-up magazine stuffed in his back pocket and held it up. "You've done well for yourself over the years."

Mercedes took the magazine, finding herself on the cover, posing with her father in front of her mother's car. "I didn't realize this issue was out yet."

"Just came out today."

Takashi held out his hand. "May I?"

Mercedes nodded and handed the magazine over. Asaka called out for Miguel from the kitchen, looking for the supplies he went to the store for. He excused himself, leaving Mercedes with Takashi and Emi. Well, Emi, since Takashi focused in on the magazine articles covering her and her father's work.

Emi suddenly hugged her. "I can't tell you how happy I am to see you in person, and so soon."

An awkward feeling fell over Mercedes. But just as it

started to settle in, Emi pulled away. "Oh, sorry. I didn't stop to think if you're okay with such contact. I'm a hugging person."

Mercedes did her best to smile and push away the lingering discomfort. "It's okay. I don't come from a huge hugging family, so it's just a little odd to me."

That was the worst lie she'd put together, and she could tell Emi wasn't buying it, but she hadn't prepared herself to fake anything today. Mercedes just didn't want to cause any extra issues with Takashi if she could help it.

The two of them looked up when someone came down the stairs. Emi smiled at Rei, who smiled back until she noticed Mercedes.

Before anything could be said, Takashi's mother came into the room. "Dinner is ready."

Takashi looked up from the magazine. "Perfect. I'm starving."

Mercedes laughed. Just the response she expected from him. She followed everyone into the dining room, eager for a home-cooked meal prepared by Asaka. She remembered some of the dishes her mother had learned from her and brought home for the family to enjoy. It'd been so long.

Mercedes sat down at the large table, Mia insisting they sit next to each other. The young girl's bubbly nature put a smile on Mercedes' face. Takashi pulled out a chair next to her, but to her surprise, offered it to Emi. Mercedes put on her best face and watched him sit across the table from her, putting down the magazine his father had brought home earlier. She wondered if she'd done something wrong to make him want to sit there, but when Rei sat down next to him, she then wondered if it was because of his sister he was acting like this.

Asaka had gone all out with the meal. There was enough for everyone plus several more, as if she were expecting more company. *Or knows the men have bottomless stomachs.*

Food was passed around until plates were full. Mercedes expected a rather quiet meal to start, as that was what she was used to with the families she knew, but Takashi's family was different.

"Emi, are you still doing all that volunteering?" Asaka asked.

Emi nodded. "Of course."

"And you still have time for your friends and family."

"Always."

"I was told you have a new boyfriend," Asaka said. "I hope he treats you well."

Emi smiled. "Yes. He spoils me a little too much."

"Nonsense, no such thing." She ate some vegetables. "Does he have a good job?"

"Yes. He's head of the technical department for my father's law firm."

"Good, good." Asaka looked to Mercedes. "And you, Mercedes?"

Mercedes found herself in the middle of taking a drink. She hadn't expected Asaka to ask her anything so soon. "Hmm?"

"Takashi tells me you and him are only friends."

"That's right."

"Why is that?"

Mercedes was sure to bite down on the food on her fork, attempting to hide the warmth rushing up to her face.

Takashi pinched his nose. "*Okaasan…*"

"Don't '*Okaasan*' me, Takashi. I don't see why—"

Miguel placed a hand on his wife's hand. "Dear, leave the two be, please?"

Asaka sighed and went back to eating. Emi, to Mercedes' surprise, giggled, along with Mia, though that wasn't as surprising. She, of course, could feel the irritation radiating off of Rei in waves.

Mia looked up at Mercedes with innocent eyes. "What's it like having a bionic arm?"

Mercedes stopped eating her rice. She figured this topic would come about. Young kids were fascinated by the technology, and most didn't have the opportunity to learn about it, as many adults around them didn't like to talk about it. "Well, that's hard to explain. I don't feel anything on that side, and I just think about doing something like I would with my real arm, and it does it."

Mia poked the artificial arm. "So you don't feel that?"

"Mia," Miguel warned.

Mercedes smiled. "It's fine. No, I don't feel that." She grabbed Mia's hand and turned her wrist. "I don't feel any of that."

Mia pursed her lips. "Then how are you able to do that?"

Mercedes pointed to her head. "I have a chip implanted on my brain that transmits the proper signals."

"How does it work?"

Mercedes shrugged. "I don't know. That's a question for Narissa."

The young girl's brow furrowed. "Who is that?"

Before Mercedes could say anything, Rei spoke, much

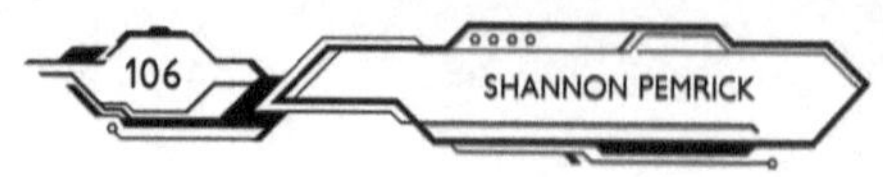

to Mercedes' surprise. "Doctor Narissa Okafor. She revolutionized cybernetics and how we use them."

Mercedes pointed a finger at Rei. "What she said."

Takashi and his father chuckled. Mia's brow furrowed at her sister. "How do you know that?"

"Because it's my job to know."

This caught Mercedes' attention. "Takashi said you were a full-time student still. Are you going for a Bio-medical Engineer degree?"

"Yeah." Rei then ate some more food, indicating she didn't want to talk to Mercedes. Mercedes frowned but didn't push. She couldn't make the woman like her.

Mia, oblivious to her sister's mood, went back to asking questions. "Can you crush a person's bones with it, like in the movies?"

"Mi-chan," Asaka warned.

Mercedes chuckled. "No, I can't. At least, not intentionally. Cybernetics are calibrated in a way that limits the strength output, keeping them from becoming too dangerous."

"Oh, darn… Do you miss having your arm?"

Mercedes took a quick breath. She figured questions like this would pop up. They usually did. "All the time."

"I read a book that talked about something called… phantom syndrome… or something like that. Do you have that?"

"Phantom limb syndrome. And yes, I do get it on rare occasions." She gestured to her shoulder, and then her elbow. "Sometimes it's localized in places, and sometimes I feel it throughout my arm."

Mia's brow furrowed. "How can that happen when you don't feel anything in the arm?"

"Because the nerves in my body get confused, and say there's something wrong with my limb."

Mia pursed her lips. "How did you lose your arm?"

Mercedes swallowed, the muscles in her back tightening. She knew this, too, was an inevitable question.

"Mia, how is school?" Takashi asked all of a sudden.

This pulled his sister's attention to him and Mercedes took the opportunity to take a drink of water and shove some food into her mouth.

"School is okay," Mia said. "I'm not doing so great in math. But I'm doing great in science! It's a lot of fun."

Mercedes put down her drink. "You have a lot of years to decide in the end, but do you know what you want to do when you're older?"

Mia nodded and ate some food before speaking again. "I want to be a biologist. Or make games."

Mercedes chuckled. "Vastly different fields you have in mind."

"Yeah, but that's okay. I like them both." She looked up at Mercedes. "Takashi says you work on cars all day. Did you have to go to school for that?"

"Well, technically I didn't, because I've been helping my dad out at his shop since even before I was your age. But I did get a bachelor's degree in Automotive Engineering, plus I have at least seven certificates for various specialty cars."

Miguel whistled low. "Do you need all those?"

"If we want the shop to be seen as a certified shop for repairs on newer cars, we need to have at least one technician with certifications for the vehicle type. All of our main techs have one or two, but I went a little nuts and got a number of them. I liked the challenge."

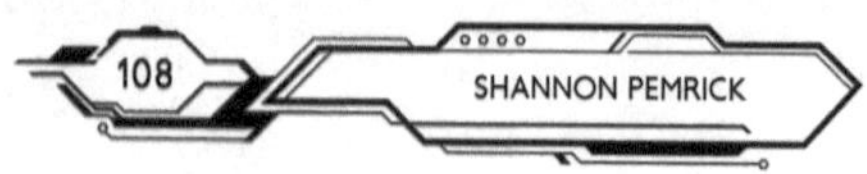

Miguel chuckled. "I wouldn't expect anything less from you."

Mia looked to Emi. "Emi, did you go to school... what do you do again?"

A sputter of chuckles went around the table. Even Emi found the young girl's words amusing. "I'm a fashion stylist. But I'm trying to get my foot in the door in the fashion industry with my own line."

Mercedes' interest in Emi grew. "What type of style are you going for?"

Emi regarded her with interest. "How much do you know of the industry?"

She shrugged. "A little bit. One of my best friends is a former model."

Emi pulled out her phone and scrolled through it, showing her a picture of a drawing. It looked casual, but had an oriental, high-class flair to it. The next they flipped to had the same flair, but more business-casual. The two of them went through several images together, each as impressive as the last.

Mercedes caught Takashi watching them carefully, but he looked happy. She guessed he was glad she was getting along with Emi, though it wasn't hard to. Getting past Emi's friendly nature was getting a bit easier. It didn't feel as threatening, meaning it was all Mercedes imagining the threat. *It's hard not to feel threatened by her, though...*

"Wow," Mercedes said, flipping to another image. "These are great. Have you actually made these into a wearable product?"

Emi flipped through her phone and stopped on a casual piece that wasn't a drawing, but full clothes on a mannequin. "I made this one. Well, my mother helped. She's a hobbyist costume designer and has way better skill than me right now."

Mercedes' brow furrowed. "And no one has taken an interest in these designs?"

Emi frowned. "I had a few, but then they decided to go with some other designs." Emi cocked her head. "Who is your ex-model friend? Curious inquiry."

"Her name's Shira. Shira Schneider."

Emi's eyes went wide. "You know *the* Shira Schneider. Daughter of Flynn Schneider?"

Oh, right. Mercedes had a habit of forgetting Shira's family was a big deal in the fashion industry. They acted so normal and down-to-earth.

"Uh, why is she all excited?" Takashi asked, his brow raised with a mix of confusion and interest.

"Flynn Schneider is one of the top fashion designers in the world!" Emi beamed. "He and his wife, Anita, are big supporters of smaller designers. They run an agency here in San Francisco that looks for new talent. I submitted some designs two weeks ago, but I haven't heard back."

Mercedes whipped out her phone. This wasn't the time to fight with petty insecurities. Emi wasn't a horrible person. "Tasha, please call Shira."

"Of course, Miss Mercedes."

Emi's eyes widened. "You don't have to do that."

Mercedes held up a finger as she listened to the phone ring. *C'mon, you should be having dinner about now and not playing hard-to-get with your two boyfriends.*

Luckily, Shira picked up. "Hey, Cede, what's up?"

"How involved are you with your parents' agency?"

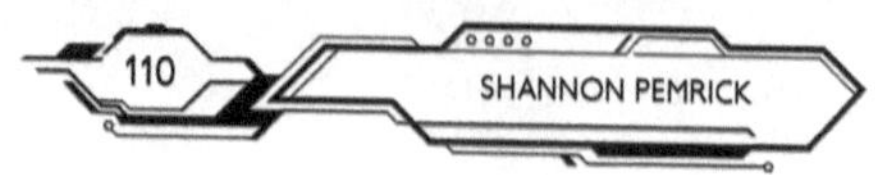

"Uh, that's a weird question from you, but fairly involved. I sometimes field them designers when I come across them in web searches. Why?"

"Could you look at some designs for me?"

Shira chuckled. "What, did you get into fashion design behind my back?"

"No, of course not. I'm pretty sure mechanic jumpsuits will never be a fashion trend."

Shira laughed, as did several other people in the Moreno household. "Fair. So where did you find a designer that you want me to look at?"

"We met through a friend." She glanced at Emi, who looked excited and freaked out. "I'll send over three designs. Give me a moment to transfer."

"Sure."

Mercedes put her call on mute and addressed Emi. "Pick your favorite three and send them to me."

"You don't have to do this!"

"Three images transferring now," came a male voice from Emi's phone. "I've selected three Miss Emi has revealed to me as her favorites."

"Arken!" Emi shouted.

"I understand your reservations, Miss Emi, but this is too perfect of an opportunity for you to pass up."

Emi stared at her rebellious phone until Tasha spoke from Mercedes'. "Images received, transferring now."

Mercedes unmuted her phone. "You should have the images soon."

"Transfer complete," Tasha called out.

"She's right, I just got them," Shira said. "And damn. Where did you find this designer again?"

"I'm having dinner with her, actually. She mentioned

she sent some designs through the application system but hadn't heard back yet."

There was a long pause. "When did she do that?"

"About two weeks ago."

"Are you sure? I was the one going through applications this month since my mom is out of the country. I never saw these designs. And these are amazing enough where I know I would have remembered seeing them."

Mercedes' brow creased. "Are you sure?"

Emi became visibly nervous with the one sided conversation she could hear.

"Oh yeah."

"Okay, then talk to her now."

Without waiting for Shira's okay, Mercedes handed Emi the phone. Emi reached out with shaky hands and accepted the device.

"Hello?" She managed to not show her nervousness in her voice. "Yeah, I'm the designer. My name is Emi. Emi Tanaka." Emi chuckled. "Yes, that same one."

Mercedes glanced at Takashi, who was watching her and not Emi. He had a genuine smile on his face and she couldn't help but smile back. She appreciated his approval.

"Yes, I did submit an application two weeks ago." Emi's brow furrowed. "You don't have it? That's strange. I got a confirmation and everything in my email. Oh, well. I could resubmit it."

Emi swallowed, concerning Mercedes. "Could you elaborate on what you mean by 'don't worry about it?'"

Takashi and Mercedes exchanged worried glances. She was sure Shira was interested in the designs.

"One hour?" Emi's back straightened. "You really want

to meet with me in one hour? No, no, that's a perfect amount of time. Yes, I can meet you there. Thank you. Thank you very much."

Emi hung up the phone and stared at it. Everyone in the room waited for her to process what just went down.

Mercedes was taken aback when Emi squealed and then threw her arms around Mercedes' neck. "Thank you!"

She got to her feet. "I'm sorry to eat and run, but I have to go get ready for this meeting. Rei, I know we had plans, and I'd like to still do something after this meeting."

Rei smiled at her friend. "Focus on this. Tell me how it went."

Emi looked to Takashi. "Do you mind walking me out? I have something to ask you."

"Uh, sure."

Mercedes tried not to frown, and pushed away the irritation bubbling up. She had no right to act so negatively. Emi even said during the meal that she was seeing someone new. *It's not like Takashi and I are dating anyway.* She couldn't compete with a gorgeous fashion designer who volunteered all the time, had an active social life, and didn't have any robotic parts.

"Who's up for a game of Uno, when we finish our meal?" Miguel asked.

Mia's hand flew up. "Me!"

Mercedes smiled. She liked the idea.

"I'll pass," Rei said, getting up and leaving.

Mercedes frowned. She had really wished she could have gotten Rei to open up and be more okay with her being around. She didn't want to be a cause for discord

in the family, but at the same time she didn't do more than exist. *How do you combat someone who just hates you for being you?*

CHAPTER 7

akashi followed Emi to the door. He heard Rei say she was going to pass on something their father offered, and soon she had joined them. She and Emi had a pleasant goodbye, Emi promising to call after the impromptu meeting. Rei took it well, understanding this was a good opportunity for her friend, though Takashi could tell she was irritated. He suspected it was because Mercedes had been the only reason this was happening.

Rei then headed for her room, leaving Takashi and Emi to talk. Emi smiled at him, but he got an uneasy feeling from it for some reason. "So, what did you want to talk to me about?"

"You know what I want to talk about."

His brow rose. He did?

She shook her head. "You're as clueless as ever. I want to talk about you and Mercedes." He opened his mouth to say something, but she continued. "I know you like her, Takashi. It's stupidly obvious. It's why your mother went right into questioning her in the only way we both know she knows how."

His lips pressed into a line. He didn't think it was *that* obvious yet. Least, not when his assistant was ratting him out. His mother didn't count either, usually. It was common for her to get a little over excited. "Okay, so what did you want to say about that topic?"

Emi regarded him for a moment. "I wanted to advise you to be careful with her." Irritated flared up in him and he went to say something, but she held up her hand. "Hold on, let me finish. I meant that in a kind way. If you're going to pursue something with her, and I sincerely hope you do, you need to be conscious of Mercedes' self-esteem issue."

Takashi's brow rose. "What are you talking about? She doesn't have a self-esteem issue."

"It may not be obvious to you, but I see it. Any woman even half paying attention could see it. She's confident in many ways, but when it comes to feeling adequate, that confidence crumbles."

Takashi crossed his arms, his brow knitting. "That doesn't make sense. She has no reason to think—"

"If I had to guess, she's been treated poorly by enough people to make her second-guess her worth."

Those words hit Takashi hard. He found himself almost unable to breathe. Mercedes had said something that should have thrown up more red flags. All these guys that had stood her up had made her believe there was something wrong with her, and not them.

Emi continued. "And, I also saw through that lie of hers about hugs. She was trying really hard, but I do make her uncomfortable. And really, I can't blame her. I know I'm beautiful. But so is she! If the roles were reversed, and she was the ex, I'd feel inadequate, too."

Takashi licked his lips, trying to figure out how to fix this. *What am I supposed to do?*

Emi smiled at him. "I'll let you figure this out on your own, but if you get stuck, and I mean legitimately stuck, let me know and I'll see what I can do to help."

Takashi smiled back at her. "Thank you. I appreciate it."

She shrugged. "Just because we didn't work out, doesn't mean I don't care. We're friends. And I want to see you happy."

Emi threw her arms around him and he returned the hug. She pulled away and opened the door. "Well, I have to go. Don't want to be late for this important meet-up."

"Good luck." He smiled more. "And some advice, just be yourself with Shira. She hates people who are fake or try too hard. Sell your designs, but don't over-try."

"Thanks for the tip." Emi grinned. "And enjoy the rest of your evening with Mercedes. I'm sure some alone time with her would do you both some good."

She winked and then dashed off. Heat rose into his face as a mix of emotions buzzed about him. Why did her teasing mess with him like that? It wasn't like he was ashamed of his feelings for Mercedes. *Maybe it's because of how my mother was acting earlier.*

As embarrassing as her targeted questions were to Mercedes, he'd only wanted her to stop for the sake of not scaring Mercedes away. A part of him... no, all of him, wanted to know why they were still "only" friends, and he needed to hear it from her mouth. He wanted to hear her say she didn't want things to stay this way. *But how to approach it?* If Emi was right, and Mercedes was hiding a major issue such as low self-esteem, then he really needed to be careful.

Takashi walked back into the kitchen to find his mother and father cleaning up. Mercedes was still eating, Mia asking her more questions. Luckily, they weren't as invasive as the ones she'd asked earlier. These questions happened to be about her friend's line of work.

Mercedes had done well with putting up a front for the first few questions, but no one missed how hard a few of them hit her. And Takashi was sure to jump on changing the topic when Mia went a little too far. As much as he, too, would like to know what had happened, it wasn't a question you just up and asked someone.

Takashi went about helping clean up. He wasn't hungry at the moment, and he could grab leftovers when he was. His mother had made enough for an army, not that he didn't expect that. She usually cooked too much when guests were expected.

Once Mercedes finished, she attempted to help with the cleanup, but his mother wouldn't allow it. Mercedes relented, and went about with Mia, setting up the game his father had suggested the family play together—Uno. Takashi wasn't surprised in the least with that game. It was a popular choice for his family.

He settled down across from Mercedes when he'd finished cleaning up, and played with the hologram screen he used for his card hand. His parents settled in as well, and the game commenced.

Ten minutes into the first game, both Mercedes and Mia had pulled some crafty card maneuvers. The two

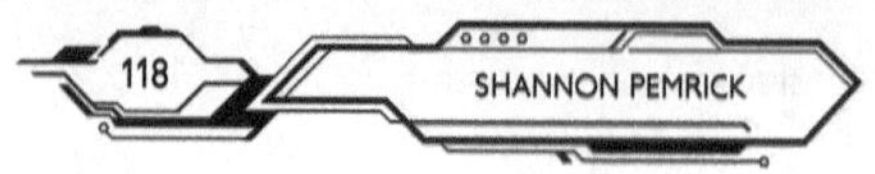

ladies giggled together as the rest of the family tried to figure out how to pull out on top. Takashi enjoyed the fact that the two of them got along so well. He liked that Mercedes had tried her best with Emi, and even Rei.

Her attempt with Rei hit him deep. She had genuinely been interested in engaging Rei about her career choice, but his sister wanted nothing to do with his friend. His sister's actions disappointed him, especially since he could see her growing confusion over Mercedes' and Emi's pleasant interactions.

It seemed that Rei just couldn't wrap it around her head how he and Emi could be friends still. It was one of the reasons she was convinced the two could have made it work. *She'll understand one day.* He just hoped it'd be sooner rather than later.

Mercedes' question to him earlier about her presence causing him issues hadn't settled well with him. He didn't want her to feel unwelcomed. And if he was going to work on getting her to give him a chance, he didn't want her to say no because of his sister's issues.

Mercedes' phone rang. She looked at it and sighed. "I'll be right back."

She answered the call while getting up from the table and heading to another room to talk. The game paused, as they didn't want to be rude and play without her.

Mercedes returned a few minutes later. "I swear, they can't go one day without nearly blowing the place up while I'm out."

"I guess that means you have to leave, then." He couldn't hide the disappointment.

Mia pouted. "Aww, but I want you to stay."

Mercedes smiled at her. "Sorry, but I have to go fix

a big mistake my boys made at the shop. I'll come by again though, how's that?"

His sister smiled wide. "Yes!"

He stood up from his seat at the table. "I'll walk you out."

"Thanks." She looked at his family and waved. "Thank you for having me. It was nice catching up."

Takashi's father leaned back in his chair. "Don't be a stranger. Come by anytime. And tell your father we send our regards."

"Of course."

Takashi escorted Mercedes to her car; the late evening sun had cast hues of red and orange across the sky. He opened the door for her and she smiled her thanks.

But before she slipped in, she looked at him. "Hey, so, I'm going to be in L.A. next week for some experimental testing on my arm."

Takashi took great interest in this. "Yeah? What kind of testing?"

"I don't know if I'm supposed to tell you this, but… I'm going to anyway, because it's something cool. Narissa thinks she's come up with a way to add artificial nerves to my prosthetics."

He could see the excitement in her eyes and it rubbed off on him. He'd heard her mention a few times how sometimes she just wanted to live in-game to have that all back. It hurt to hear her talk like that.

"That's great!"

She nodded and then her gaze went elsewhere. "I was thinking, since I'll be down at the same time you're going to be at that seminar, maybe we could meet up?"

Her shyness surprised him. Takashi didn't expect such

a response from her. *Maybe she's also…* He had to take this chance. "When are you leaving?"

"Tuesday morning. I know you'll be heading back to Korea late tomorrow, and the crazy time difference has me confused if you'll be landing before I head out or not. I also wasn't sure how long you'd be back stateside once you returned for the seminar."

"I'll be down there for three days, then returning here for a while. Why don't we meet up for lunch one of those days?"

She looked up at him. "I thought maybe I could pick you up at the airport and we could have lunch then?" Her gaze darted away again. "Of course only if you want to."

God, she's cute. "I'd like that."

She peered up at him. "Yeah?"

He leaned on the door and smirked. "Yeah."

She smiled, her gaze lingering on his for a moment before she slipped into the car. "Then, if I don't speak to you between now and then, I'll meet you at the air-port. I'll have a sign that's impossible for you to miss."

"I'm sure we'll speak before then. Good luck at the shop, and have a good night, Mercedes."

She gazed up at him with those gorgeous blue eyes that nearly begged him to not let her go. "You too."

He watched her drive off before heading back inside. Rei stood on the stairs leading to the second floor, her face creased into a scowl, but Takashi ignored her. She'd caused him enough trouble earlier that he didn't want to deal with her right now.

Mia ran up to him. "*Nüsan*, when will your girlfriend be coming back?"

He sighed and looked down at his little sister. "She's not my girlfriend, Mia." *Yet.*

She squinted at him and placed her hands on her hips. "Why not? She's pretty, and funny, and I like her. And you're not getting any younger, *Niisan.*"

Takashi pinched his nose. Their mother was rubbing off on her. That was to be expected, though. While they were brought up in a culturally diverse home, his mother had the biggest influence on the family. "We're not dating."

Mia crossed her arms and let out a *humph.* "When will she be back?"

"I'm not sure."

"Can she come back tomorrow?"

"Mercedes has to work tomorrow." He wasn't sure if that was the case, since she usually had Sunday off, but with her leaving for the week, he assumed she'd taken a shift to make up for her absence.

"Will you go visit her at work?"

"No, I'm going to be spending time with my family before I hop on the plane to head back to Korea."

His sister pouted. Takashi couldn't help but smile. At least one of his sisters liked Mercedes. His mother entered the room and smiled. "Keep her. She's a good pick."

Rei crossed her arms, her lip curling, and Takashi shook his head. "*Okaasan,* please. She's not my girlfriend."

"Well, why not?"

His father's boisterous laugh reached them from the kitchen. "Leave the boy be, Dear. If it's meant to be, it'll come in time. Your meddling won't help."

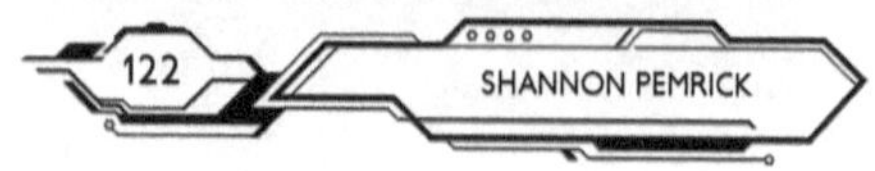

His mother pointed at Takashi. "I see the way you look at her, Takashi. It's love. Do not let that slip by with such a nice woman. You're not getting any younger, and neither is she."

"Emi is better," Rei said, no longer staying quiet.

Great, here we go. Takashi faced his sister. "Emi and I are not getting back together."

"Well if you hadn't let that blonde whore into your life, it wouldn't be the case."

Takashi sucked in a tight breath, but he couldn't stop himself from yelling. "That's enough, Rei! I've had enough of this from you. Not only were Mercedes and I friends long before Emi and I got together, I will not allow you to insult her like that."

Rei sneered. "Dresses like one and steals others' men. Why shouldn't I?"

Rage built up in Takashi. Just because Mercedes leaned toward wearing clothes that showed off a lot of skin, that didn't make her a whore. "Emi and I mutually split. We were not a good match and we both acknowledge that—it had nothing to do with Mercedes. Emi has moved on, and now has a new partner. You know this. We all do. He makes her happy, and I am happy for her. You need to be as well."

Rei glowered at him. She hated that reminder. It was an all-too-constant reminder that she'd lost this and was now just being spiteful.

Their father walked into the room, a scowl on his face. "I'm done listening to this bickering about this topic. Rei, you leave your brother alone about his choices. It doesn't matter that you were the one who brought them together in the first place. It doesn't make it an obligation for it to work out." He pinched his nose. "Honestly, had it worked like that, your mother would be married to some man her mother was trying to pair her with, and I'd be in some small town in Colorado, married to my brother's friend."

Then he turned and looked pointedly at Rei. "You leave your brother alone and let him make his own decisions. You're twenty-seven and he's thirty-two. This shouldn't be hard for you to do. Now, you both will respect each other, and this topic will not come up again in this house."

Rei sucked in a tight breath and then stormed upstairs. Their father handed Takashi the magazine he'd brought home highlighting Mercedes' work, and then went into the living room. He smiled at his father's gesture. At least he had most of his family's support. *Hopefully Rei will realize her error soon.*

His phone buzzed and he took a look, a part of him hoping it was Mercedes. It wasn't. His brow creased as he looked at the email from the Lusara Fates dev team.

Mia tugged on his shirt. "*Niisan*, is everything okay?"

"No." He continued to scroll through the message. "Someone hacked my business again. I'm going to need some time to sort this out." He looked at his mother. "I'll spend time with everyone once I get it fixed."

His mother smiled at him. "I know, go take care of what you need to do."

He patted Mia on the head and went to his room. A game station sat in the corner, ready to be used. It didn't take Takashi long to set up the game and dive in. When he materialized in his shop, a GM was there waiting, the same one from before.

Takashi rubbed the back of his neck. "How bad is it this time?"

"The account has been wiped clean of all funds, and there is virus-like code, configuring debt and altering product code that would cause our systems to think you were selling false game product. We're currently combatting it now."

Shit. This issue couldn't get much worse, could it? "Has any progress been made on the potential culprit?"

GM Ashton nodded. "Yes, but there's an issue. While the culprit has hidden their tracks well, and provided many false leads, we've determined that the individual is from the United States, and potentially from California."

Takashi's brow furrowed. "That sounds like good news. Where's the issue?"

"The issue has to do with your current location." GM Ashton opened up a screen prompt. "We see you're logged into a computer station in California—"

Takashi knew where this was going and didn't like it. "Yeah, I'm visiting family. I'm originally from California. I have documentation to prove most of what I've been doing in the last seventy-two hours, along with my flight information. I can even give you contact for anyone who has been with me where transactional information isn't available."

Game Master Ashton nodded. "I'm afraid I will need that, then. I understand your frustration, and I do apologize it has to be done, but we need to be sure you're not doing this and trying to divert attention."

Takashi shook his head. "I don't see how ruining my own business could possibly benefit me in any way, but that doesn't matter. I'll get to providing the documentation for you. Is there anything else I need to know, or need to provide to help?"

"Nothing else provided, but you will need to know, in order for us to investigate and fix your account, we've had to suspend it. As long as your documentation clears you, and we're able to restore the damaged code, this should last no longer than twenty-four hours."

That was a long time to not have access, but it couldn't be helped at this point. He'd spend most of that time with his family anyway. Takashi thanked the GM and logged off, going about getting all documentation he could provide, while having Ochi send out messages to Emi and Mercedes, asking for assistance as witnesses. He only hoped it would be enough.

CHAPTER 8

Mercedes' head bobbed back and forth as an old rock song played on the radio while she played on her phone, her mood good for a Monday. The excitement from the Saturday spent with Takashi hadn't left her, even though she knew it was just them hanging out as friends. She had a lot of fun with him, and his family was just how she remembered. She would love to go back and do that again. *As friends, of course.*

Takashi had contacted her with alarming news while she was dealing with that emergency at the shop, but as of Sunday, right before he hopped on a plane, he let her know things were okay… for now. She didn't like that this had happened to him again, and so soon after the first attack. Not only that, but the fact that he had to provide so much documentation and human references as proof that he wasn't involved somehow was ludicrous. *Why would someone purposely sabotage their own business like that?*

Mercedes took a deep breath. She needed to not think of that, and keep her mood up. Takashi's business was in the clear right now, and she had only one day of work. Then she'd be down in L.A. doing some tough, but amazing, cybernetic testing.

The idea of being able to feel with an artificial limb sent a new wave of excitement through her. The concept was still surreal, but Narissa assured her that it would work. She didn't doubt her friend. That woman was a genius. But until she felt it for herself, it'd be hard not to think this was all a dream. *A dream, where if I wake up, not even Takashi will be here... with me.*

She shook the thought from her head. *Enough, Mercedes.*

Mercedes didn't look up from her phone when the car pulled into the parking lot of the shop. She collected her cup of coffee and the box that she'd picked up for everyone as a treat. She finally looked up after she climbed out of the car, her feet planting to the ground. Her coffee dropped to the ground, spilling everywhere, and her hands flew up to her mouth, a half scream, half wail coming from her mouth from the horrified sight before her.

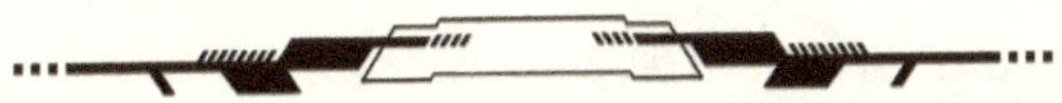

A wide yawn escaped Takashi's mouth as he waited for his taxi. The busy city sounds of Seoul hammered his ears. He looked down at his phone, reading *5:37 a.m. Tuesday*, and frowned. He'd landed about twenty minutes ago, and Mercedes hadn't messaged him back.

He knew she could get busy, but it would be 1:37 p.m. Monday her time, meaning she'd likely be off at lunch, or just coming back from it. Before he left, she'd insisted he send her a remote in-game private message when he landed, so she'd know he'd made it safe, and promised to reply as quickly as she could. *What could possibly keep her from a quick "thank you" at the very least?*

Takashi's taxi arrived and drove him the fifteen minutes to his apartment. He looked at his phone again when they arrived at the high rise apartments, and then stored it in his pocket before heading inside. Takashi hopped into the elevator and tapped his foot impatiently as it brought him up to the seventh floor.

He knew he was being ridiculous, and that she didn't need to get back to him right away, but this was Mercedes. She'd go out of her way to ensure she fulfilled a promise. If she hadn't gotten back to him in almost an hour, something had to be up.

Takashi unlocked his door, but before he could enter, an elderly woman poked her head out of her apartment and called out to him in Korean. *"Takashi, you've returned."*

While it was early in the morning, this particular neighbor of his rose early. *"Hello, Ms. Kim. I returned only recently."*

She nodded. *"I'm glad to see you home safe. Pokey didn't cause me any trouble. She was quite the nice companion, as always. I look forward to caring for her again later this week."*

Pokey was his cat. He'd gotten her when another tenant moved out, leaving her behind. No one in the complex wanted her, so he took her in, not wanting her to end up in a shelter, or worse. She'd turned out to be the perfect companion for him. *"Are you sure you still wish to care for her? I'll be gone for at least three weeks. I could board her instead."*

She shook her head. *"I told you, I like caring for her. And you. Join me for supper tonight."*

When the Kim family moved their grandmother in, Pokey found herself with two loving homes by chance. Takashi hadn't shut the door all the way after returning home from the store one day, and she'd escaped while he'd been in-game doing some business transactions. She ended up in the elderly woman's home for a snack and a nap, and the rest had been history. Now every time he'd go out of town, she insisted on caring for the feline instead of her going to one of the nice boarding facilities nearby.

Takashi knew it was because she was lonely. Her family didn't come by often, most too busy with work. They'd have to be, to afford her apartment and give her an allowance. It was another reason why he'd come to know the woman as well as he had. She'd turned into his replacement family.

He'd moved here because when he started out, he focused on the foreign market trade, specifically in South Korea due to the game's popularity. This required him to attend meetings and seminars out here, making it more cost effective to just move there. After a few years, he decided to branch out, and found the North American market just as rich. At the same time, in-person seminars and meetings were moving online for the sake of convenience.

The only thing keeping me here is Ms. Kim… He didn't want to leave her alone. It went against everything it meant to be family. *I did that once to my family for the sake of work. I can't repeat that mistake.*

He smiled. *"I'll do that. Thank you."*

She went back into her place, allowing him to enter his apartment. Pokey greeted him with loud wailing and rubbing against his leg, her fluffy tail sticking up in the air. Takashi picked her up, abandoning his suitcase at the door. He would deal with that later.

He walked around the living room of the large two-bedroom apartment, affectionately stroking Pokey as his mind wandered to Mercedes. He tried not to think about what might be going on that would stop her from texting him back. For all he knew, an important project had kept her from her phone.

He hadn't realized just how big a deal her job was until he read the articles in the magazine his father had brought home. She never acted like she did anything extraordinary—even when his father handed her the magazine, she reacted as if that kind of press happened on a regular basis. Upon reading the articles, Takashi learned her father's shop was ranked in the top five in all of the US to have a vehicle restored at.

Takashi stopped walking and stared out his large window, looking out into the city below. He could picture her living here with him—see her waking up every morning next to him, and sitting on the couch playing one of her old videogames. He shook his head. *Too fast, Takashi.* He needed to convince her to date him first before thinking about where they'd live together.

Takashi's phone beeped and he jumped, scaring Pokey enough to jump out of his arms. He pulled it out of his pocket, hoping to see a message from his favorite grease monkey, only to find a low battery warning. He sighed and plugged the phone in, transferring Ochi to the assistant system in his apartment while he was at it. He almost forgot he had to, with the international switch.

His robotic assistant spoke to him immediately. "Takashi, I sense a great deal of stress coming from you. If I may be so bold, I'd like to know what is wrong so I can help you."

Takashi sat down on the couch. "I don't know where to start."

"Does it have anything to do with Mercedes? She's been on your mind a lot lately."

Takashi checked the clock on the wall. *Six-twenty-seven.* "It's been almost an hour and a half and she hasn't responded. That's not like her."

"Even she gets busy. She has an important job, after all. But that's not the sole worry. You wouldn't normally stress like this. There is something else compounding it."

Takashi chuckled. "You sound like my father."

"Does this displease you? I know I've been heckling you this weekend, but if so, at any point, I can alter my programming to sound and act like someone else."

Takashi looked out the window, crossing his arms. "No, I like it actually. He always makes sense. Uses logic all the time. I'm just thinking about the life changes that would come with Mercedes and me getting together, if that happens. Would she drop everything and move here, or would I pack everything up and head on back to the states? What would happen to Ms. Kim without me here to keep her company and bring her places when she needed it?"

Takashi tapped his fingers. "What would happen to the friendship I've built up with Mercedes if it didn't work out?"

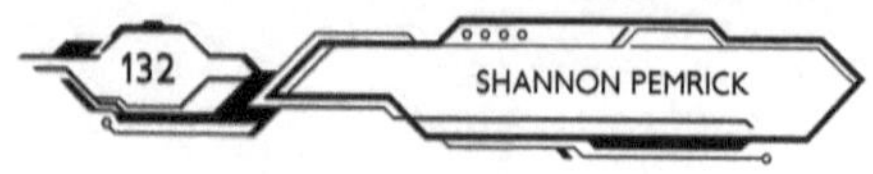

"If it didn't work out, the two of you would remain friends," Ochi said. "You've done well staying friends with Emi."

"Yes, but my connection with Emi wasn't as deep as it is with Mercedes."

"Wouldn't it be safe to assume your stronger connection is due to your mutual interests? You shared few with Emi. So, even if there's a chance you and Mercedes don't withstand the test of time, I'm sure the two of you will still manage a close friendship."

Takashi had a hard time arguing that point. He just needed a definite about Mercedes' stance with him. She showed signs when he saw her off after dinner on Saturday, but he needed to be sure. *I just need to ask her. No point wondering, if I can't even do that.*

Takashi checked his phone again to find no new messages still. "Ochi, I'm going in-game to talk with Shira. If anyone knows what's up, it'll be her."

"Takashi, I'd highly recommend getting some sleep first."

He headed for his business room with his gaming pod. "I'll get sleep after. This won't take long."

Takashi sat down in his machine and started it up. Once the game's menus booted, he searched for Shira in his list, but found her offline. The system indicated she hadn't been on for several hours. *That's strange…* Since she also made a living off the game to supplement her income when not working for her parents, it was uncommon for her to go offline during the day for very long. The longest was usually around meal times.

Looking at his list some more, he found Jasper and

Zach logged in as usual, but both in a match. *Dammit.* Those two would be in matches for a while.

Takashi went about sending Mercedes another message, letting her know he was worried about her and asked her to please voice chat him the moment she was free. He promised to stay up until he heard something from her. He didn't care at this point if any of that sounded needy.

After sending the message, he leaned back in his chair. The only thing he could do was wait. He wasn't going to be able to sleep until he knew she was okay.

Mercedes nodded as the officer finished detailing to her the report and investigation procedure they'd take to find who'd vandalized her family's business. The sight of the damage when she arrived earlier had been the worst shock she'd had in a long time. Their security cameras picked up a decent amount, but identifying the criminal wouldn't be easy, as her father had skimped on the video quality.

"Thank you, Andrew, I know you'll all do your job to the fullest."

He patted her on the shoulder. "You know I will, Mercedes. I still appreciate the charity work you did for my father and his car before his passing. This criminal act is unjust for people like you."

She forced a smile and saw him off. Looking around, she found everyone doing something. Cleaning the walls, picking up broken parts, sweeping up glass. All day they'd been at it. Five personal vehicles had been vandalized, as well as three customer vehicles. Her father chose to call the customers while she talked with the police. She ended up with the better deal.

Only one customer understood and showed gratitude for their business taking responsibility and replacing everything damaged at no cost to him. The other two weren't so forgiving. One threatened to call a lawyer when her father refused to make his restoration free of charge going forward since it was "most likely going to miss the approved deadline," and the other tried to stop by and take his vehicle without paying for the work done that hadn't been damaged.

She went to assist the other employees, but everyone she tried to help insisted they had it covered. She couldn't even go out on a food run because Shira and Ajax were covering that. It frustrated her. Her nerves had her all stressed out, and she needed to do something that would help with the cleanup.

Mercedes went into the office to find her father on the phone again. Based on the papers on the desk, she suspected he finally got through to the insurance company. That would be yet another headache for them.

Her father looked at her. "I'm on hold. Need something?"

"Something to do," she said. "No one is letting me help them. Did you contact all the customers without damage to their cars and let them know deadlines might not be met?"

"Not yet, but I will. Don't worry about it."

She reached for the computer so she could retrieve the customer information. "Well, since you're busy, I'll do it."

Her father stopped her. "Cede, I have it."

"Dad, I need something to do."

"You've done a lot handling the police report."

"That was nothing compared to everything else that needs to be done. Please, I…" She sighed, her shoulder sagging. This tough-woman act wasn't easy for her to hold up. "I need something to do."

Her father gazed at her with sympathetic eyes and then spoke into the phone when his rep came back on the line just then, keeping the computer out of her reach. Mercedes, feeling defeated, exited the room. There was no fighting her father.

Scanning the shop, she found everyone doing something, even the teen employees who showed up after school. *Wait, school is over?* She whipped her phone out to read the time. *Three-twenty. Her phone also showed two messages from Takashi. Shit!*

She read both; one stated he'd gotten off the plane and the other was him showing his concern because she hadn't sent him any message acknowledging his first. He wanted her to voice chat with him the moment she got his text.

So caught up with everything, she forgot to message him about what happened. Shira knew because Mercedes had called to cancel lunch plans, and that meant Jasper and Zach found out. And Ajax found out when she called Narissa to let her know she may need to postpone their project. Ajax happened to be there getting a fix done on his arm, and offered to come up so Narissa wouldn't have to postpone her projects. Mercedes' father had told her he wanted her to still go through with the project plan this week, but she wasn't sure she could. There'd be too much to do. *It also means I'd have to cancel on Takashi, too…*

She decided to plug in her earbud and see if Takashi was still up. A part of her hoped not, so he'd get some sleep after his long flight.

The in-game party chat rang three times and then Takashi's groggy voice answered. "Mercedes?"

"Did I wake you?" She frowned, her brow knitting. "I'm sorry."

"No, don't be." He sucked in a long breath as if he were stretching or stifling a yawn. "I wanted you to call the moment you could. I didn't mean to fall asleep while waiting. Are you okay?"

"Yeah, I'm fine."

"Mercy."

Her heart skipped a beat at the nickname he'd started calling her recently. "It's been a long day."

"What's going on?"

She found a place to sit down where she could keep an eye on everything going on around her. She couldn't stop a sigh from escaping her lips. "Short answer, I came in early to make sure I'd get all my work done before I headed out for L.A. tomorrow, and found the shop vandalized. Smashed cars, graffiti, and building damage."

"Shit… How bad?"

"I'd say at least a quarter million in damage because of the vehicles." She sighed. "The officers I spoke with believe this is connected with a few other vandal situations that have happened the last few days."

"What makes them think that?"

"Most of the graffiti said 'she's mine,' 'you can't have her,' or 'don't go near her again.' I guess all the other businesses and homes have been hit by the same graffiti. I've grilled all my employees about exes and friends that could potentially provide a lead, but nothing came of it, so I don't know if it's connected or not. I do know, with all this damage, I don't think I can go to L.A. now."

"Mercedes…"

She chewed her lip. The disappointment in his voice hit her harder than she wanted right now. It made her feel guilty, even though she knew this was the right choice. "It wouldn't be right. My dad needs me here, even if he thinks I should still go down. He and the others think it'd be best if I continue this project, but this is more important." Her gaze lowered as if he were there with her. "It'd be nice to feel in that arm again, but it's not like my life depends on it. My life does depend on this shop, though. It means everything to me…"

Takashi didn't say anything, and a part of her worried she'd said too much. *Or he fell asleep.*

"It would mean I'd have to rain check with you." She figured if he was still awake, it'd be best for her to bring this up, even if she had said too much. "You said you'd be coming back up here after the seminar, so maybe we could do lunch then."

"You should come down to L.A." he said.

His suggestion took her aback for a moment. "Takashi, I—"

"The others are right, you shouldn't postpone the project."

"Takashi—"

"I know you feel obligated to be there during this issue. That you feel you need to be strong for everyone so it all blows over easier. I know you well enough to know that's going through your head right now. But, Mercedes, think about it. If you continue with your plans, you keep everyone's spirits up in this hard time. It helps them think this is business as usual instead of letting this event get the better of them."

She thought she could hear him smile. "And it'll make you smile. There's nothing more beautiful than your smile, and that's motivation enough to take on this task for you."

Her heart skipped. She tucked a strand of hair behind her ear and bit her lip. "You mean it?"

"I'd never lie to you."

Mercedes took a deep breath. "Okay. Plans will stay the same, then. I'll drive down with Ajax tomorrow and pick you up… you never told me when you were arriving in L.A."

"Thursday. By the time I get my luggage, it'd be around three p.m."

"Okay, then I'll see you around three. I should let you go sleep now."

"I'd like to stay on and talk with you some more, if that's okay."

She smiled. "All right."

The two continued to chat. Takashi hopped in-game to do some work. She managed to snag a cleanup job by getting a few of her employees to take a break and continued to chat with Takashi, helping the time pass.

Ajax and Shira returned, but neither interrupted. Mercedes expected the conversation to only last fifteen minutes or so before he'd finally listen to her and get some sleep, but it ended up being a two-hour chat.

She finally managed to convince Takashi to sleep

when he started slurring his words. She didn't want him losing sleep because of her. At least, not unless it was for more fun reasons. *Stop it, Mercedes. Behave yourself.*

Mercedes glanced up from her sweeping job to find Shira and Ajax approaching, the latter's tan skin rippling with muscle as he walked. Shira's service dog, Snake, a black German shepherd, followed beside Shira, keeping close.

Ajax—not his real name, but only Narissa knew his name and she'd been sworn to secrecy—was a brick house of a man. He prided himself on his workout routine, Narissa claiming she'd seen him stress out if he missed even a day of it.

When he wasn't working out, he was as busy as Narissa, working in the gaming pod industry. Also like her, he didn't have a whole lot of time to dedicate to Lusara Fates these days.

Mercedes couldn't get over how genetically gifted these two were. Shira, even with her prosthetics all over her right side, looked like someone straight from a magazine. It was unfair how she couldn't keep modeling.

Shira stole her broom from her. Both her friends had goofy grins on their faces.

Mercedes' eyes shifted between the two. "I don't trust those smiles."

Ajax continued to smirk, his dark eyes glittering with mischievous intent. "Enjoy your chat with loverboy?"

Mercedes threw her head back and groaned. "Don't start."

Shira laughed. "You spoke with Takashi for two hours. What did you expect we'd say?"

"I was hoping you'd come over just to see how I'm

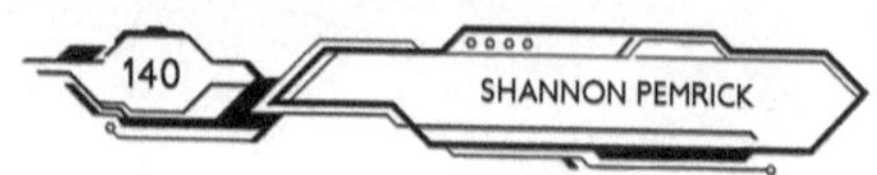

doing." Mercedes had said Takashi's name enough; she knew it wasn't a secret she'd been talking with him. But she hoped she could go at least ten minutes without any teasing for once.

After the events over the past couple of days, she couldn't keep telling herself she hated the idea of making them more than friends, especially with how Takashi had been acting around her lately. But there was still a strong part of her that couldn't jump on board with it. *Friend material and romantic partner material are different qualities. And I'm more friend material…*

Ajax nudged her. "We have to keep you on your toes."

"Yeah, yeah." She pushed him, though due to his larger size, she only managed to push herself backward instead.

Ajax ran his false limb hand through his dark hair. "The two of us were thinking it might be good to call it a day. It's been a long one, and we'll need you to stay calm before all your tests tomorrow."

Shira looked at Mercedes with apprehension. "You are still going down, right?"

Mercedes nodded. "Yeah, Takashi talked some sense into me."

Shira threw her hands into the air. "Finally!"

Snake wagged his tail in approval of the positive energy.

Mercedes shook her head and headed for the office. "I'll let my dad know we're heading out."

Ajax pulled out his phone. "I'll tell Narissa to still expect you tomorrow."

Mercedes entered the office to find her father staring at the computer, the phone in his hands. He looked at her when she knocked on the doorframe. "What's up?"

"Shira, Ajax, and I are heading out, if that's okay," she said.

Her father nodded. "I was going to start sending everyone home soon anyway. We can pick this up tomorrow. Have you decided about your trip?"

She nodded. "I'm going to continue the project."

"Good." He stood up and came over to her, planting a kiss on top of her head. "Don't stress over this. We're going to be fine. I want you to come back smiling."

She smiled at her father. "I'll keep you updated and let you know if I need to stay longer than expected."

"Take all the time you need. This is important, for more than just you. You're doing a great deal of good for so many people." Her father smirked. "As much as you don't believe it, I can keep this business afloat just fine while you're off playing with your friends."

Mercedes laughed and then said her goodbye. She relayed to the employees they were free to leave for the day before rejoining her friends.

"So, I thought it'd be fun if I came over your place too," Shira said.

"Shira and Narissa keep talking about all the old games you've got," Ajax said. "Three of us could play some, since you only have one game pod. Great way to relax."

Mercedes laughed. "You may not think that way when you play some of these games. They're frustrating at times."

He smirked. "Wait until you see my skills."

Mercedes and Shira looked at each other, brows raised in disbelief. "We'll see about that."

CHAPTER 9

ercedes pushed the rotating door and walked into the lobby of Cybro Industries. The receptionist, Amy, a mousey young woman with thick-rimmed glasses, smiled when Mercedes flashed her badge. There wasn't a need these days, since much of the staff knew her, but she figured it best to follow at least some part of the protocol.

She and Ajax had arrived two days ago, and Narissa hadn't wasted any time settling her into a hotel down the street and getting the health screening out of the way. Yesterday, preliminary testing began, and today wouldn't be much different. The two wanted to make sure her body could handle the process before going forward with it tomorrow.

Mercedes hopped into an elevator and pressed the button for the eleventh floor. She sipped her coffee and looked at her phone. *9:05 a.m.* Takashi would be landing in five hours, and the thought sent butterflies fluttering about in her stomach. The prospect of see-ing him excited her more than this project. She never thought that would ever happen to her, and it wasn't like they were dating, either. *Not that I'm all that opposed to the idea anymore...*

She struggled to run from it anymore. Mercedes wanted a close bond with someone, and that someone had been right in front of her the whole time. With everything that happened over the weekend, and how much attention he'd paid her until he had to hop on that plane, it was hard to deny they had potential. She just wasn't sure she was good enough.

The elevator came to stop at her floor and the door opened. She exited and walked down the long hall of glass-enclosed offices and laboratories. She stopped at a door with a plaque that read *Dr. Narissa Okafor, EVP,* but she didn't enter. The room was occupied by two people who were focused only on each other.

Narissa, a curvaceous woman with umber skin and long dark hair, stood in front of Ajax, who sat in a chair, his artificial limb extended on a tray attached to the chair, in pieces. *Looks like he busted his arm... again.*

Neither Narissa nor she knew what he was doing to bust his arm up so much. He wouldn't tell anyone when asked. It annoyed Narissa, since she had to fix it, but since he paid for such repairs, she couldn't be too mad. Shira theorized it was so he could see Narissa more often. To most in the guild, it wasn't much of a secret he had a thing for her friend. Sadly, their tech-savvy friend either didn't notice, or ignored it, preferring to focus on her one true love, cybernetics.

Narissa appeared to be reprimanding Ajax. *No surprise*

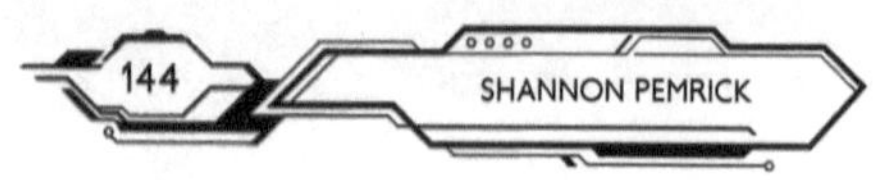

there. Ajax, of course, had a cocky smirk on his lips, and spoke back to her a few times. Mercedes noticed Narissa's cheeks reddening after a while. *Ah, so his tactics do have an effect on her.*

She couldn't understand Narissa's insistence on staying single. She had been married once, and that resulted in one hell of a messy divorce. But Mercedes couldn't see how one failed marriage would cause her friend to bury herself in her work.

Ajax grabbed Narissa's wrist and pulled her closer. He must have tugged bit harder than she expected, because the woman fell into his lap. Ajax grinned at her, making some comment Mercedes couldn't hear, and Narissa's face reddened. A wicked idea formed into Mercedes' mind. Knowing they hadn't spotted her yet, this would work wonderfully.

She whipped out her phone and looked down before pushing open the door and looking up just as she spoke, "Hey, Narissa, I'm h—"

Narissa held up her hands. "It's not what it looks like!"

Mercedes' eyes flicked between the two and then pointed out the door with the hand holding her coffee. "If I'm interrupting something, I can go to the lobby and wait."

The two answered at the same time, both conflicting.

"If you could, that'd be great."

"No, you're fine, there's nothing going on here."

The pair looked at each other, Ajax grinning and Narissa's face reddening more. She smacked him in the chest and stood.

She smoothed out her clothes and addressed Mercedes. "It's not what it looks like. He's just being his usual weird self. Make yourself comfortable. I have to fix his arm… again. Shouldn't take too long."

Mercedes decided to take a seat in Narissa's executive chair behind her computer desk and focused on her phone. She checked in with her father, remotely played a few auctions in Lusara Fates, and even messaged Takashi. She let him know how much she was looking forward to seeing him. To her surprise, he messaged her back. Apparently, even though not an ideal speed for connecting to the game, he paid for the internet access so he could focus on making some money to make up for the time he'd spend in the seminar.

A goofy smile spread across her lips as she messaged with him. Unfortunately for her, the others in the room noticed.

"Talking to loverboy?" Ajax asked.

Mercedes' eyes narrowed, but before she could spit out a reply, Narissa jumped in on the teasing. "If you want, I could show you a room where you'd have more privacy."

Mercedes tossed a pen at her friend, who laughed and went back to fixing up Ajax's arm. She looked to be nearly finished. Though her "patient" wasn't making it easy on her.

Mercedes watched the two, unable to stop herself from finding amusement in their banter. A grin spread across her lips and she snapped a photo when the two were exceptionally close, sending it to Takashi and then deciding to send it to Shira as well.

Takashi got back to her first.

Ha, keep that for blackmail.

Then Shira.

> *Get me more! I need to hang these over*
> *her head. And to distribute to the others*
> *in the guild. I can see my wording now.*
> *"Main healer and tank getting cozy after*
> *raid night."*

Jeez, what great friends I have. But she wouldn't expect anything less from them. *If only I'd thought to get a snap of what I walked in on.* She had more opportunities this week. Ajax made it easy.

Some paperwork caught Mercedes' eye when she spotted Shira's name, and her nosey side kicked in. Narissa didn't leave confidential information lying around, so she knew she wasn't doing anything wrong on the legal end of things.

Her brow rose when she found it to be a formal letter of request and contract—a modeling contract. She looked to Narissa, wanting to ask her about it since Shira refused to allow her photo taken anymore, but noting her friend's concentration while she worked around Ajax's hand, she decided to hold off until Ajax left.

Twenty more minutes passed before Narissa "finished." According to her, she needed to do some more work, but Ajax insisted it would be fine, and hinted that he would potentially return in a day or two with it all busted again. When he refused again to explain what he was doing to put him in this situation, Narissa ragged on him for another five or so minutes about the hazards of these kinds of repeat damages. Mercedes got a snap shot of that, but the two noticed this time.

"What are you doing?" Narissa asked her.

Mercedes grinned. "Making you ask questions."

Ajax used the distraction to his advantage and slipped over to the door. "And allowing me to get out of here. Send me the bill."

Narissa stared at him with a dumbfounded expression as he waved and took off. She crossed her arms and fixed Mercedes with narrowed eyes. "Traitor."

Mercedes held up her hands. "Hey, if I didn't do something, I'd be sitting here for at least another half hour while you lectured him.

Narissa threw up her hands. "Well if he'd just stop destroying that arm, I wouldn't have to."

A sly grin spread across Mercedes' lips. "Maybe this is his way of having an excuse to come visit you."

Mercedes watched Narissa roll her eyes. "If he wants to be a pest, he doesn't have to mangle his prosthetic. My door is always open." She sighed. "I wish he would listen to me. He's putting too much stress on his neuro-mod. At this rate, I'm going to have to replace that, too, and he'll be lucky if he doesn't sustain brain damage."

"Men are willing to do stupid and crazy things to impress women." Mercedes started laughing. "I mean look at how Jasper and Zach act around Shira."

Narissa smirked. "Well, not everyone can be lucky enough to get a smart guy to impress her by doting on her, like you have."

Mercedes turned her gaze away. Narissa knew all about her meet-up with Takashi over the weekend, and knew about the planned lunch date today.

Narissa looked her over, her arms crossed. "You're still not jumping on that, are you?"

She shrugged. "I don't want to ruin my friendship with him because I was dumb and saw something that wasn't really there."

"Please." Narissa sashayed over to her. "He's totally into you. You have nothing to worry about."

Mercedes couldn't shake the doubt. She decided to focus on the paper she found. "So, what's this?"

"Nosey brat." Narissa snatched the papers from her. "It's something I'd like to propose to Shira. We're making some changes that will require models. Since she has the experience and fits what we're looking for, I wanted to offer the opportunity to her."

Mercedes could see the doubt in her friend's eyes. "But we both know how she is with cameras. That's not going to be an easy battle."

Narissa nodded. "I know. I'm hoping I can get some help from Zach and Jasper. They may be able to get her to change her mind."

Mercedes snorted. "They're stubborn enough; it might work."

Narissa snatched up a tablet and gestured for Mercedes to sit down in the chair Ajax had previously occupied. "But enough about that. Let's get to this testing before lunch."

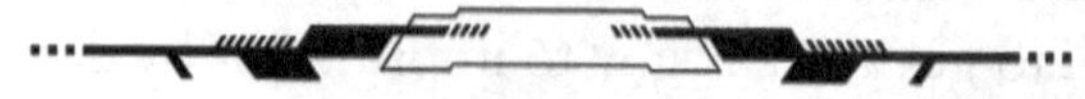

Haphazardly-tossed suitcases moved on the luggage carrousel. Takashi kept an eye out for his, impatient to get out of the airport. He'd coordinated a location to meet up with Mercedes and wanted nothing more than to spend time with her.

He'd grown quite bored on the plane once she had to let him go to focus on her testing. The slow internet made it difficult to focus on his business transactions, and that meant his mind wandered to Mercedes. This taking things slow with her wasn't as easy as he'd expected.

He glanced down at the flowers he'd bought for her from a flower shop at the terminal. Now knowing her mother had been a florist, he was hoping this arrangement would help him gauge her reaction before outright asking.

Takashi spotted his suitcase and was quick to snatch it and maneuver through the crowd. He turned on his phone to find Mercedes had texted him over fifteen minutes ago, indicating she was waiting. He ground his teeth together in frustration. He hadn't wanted to make her wait for him.

Takashi searched for her when he made it to the pickup area. *Where is she?* His pulse skipped when he spotted her standing alone, a thin and wide sign in her hands. *Is that a… rose?*

Mercedes scanned the airport, sometimes going up on her toes to try to look over the crowd. Takashi tucked the flowers away so she wouldn't see them yet and made his way to her. When she spotted him, her eyes lit up, and her smile sent a rush of pleasant emotions through him. She ran over to him, but before she could say anything, he presented her the bouquet, using all the skills he had acquired over the years practicing magic to make it look like he produced it out of thin air.

Mercedes gasped, her beautiful blue eyes going wide. "Takashi…"

He could tell she was taken by surprise and not fear, which made him happy. Mercedes took the flower arrangement and looked at the bundle of white flowers. Takashi made certain to gauge her reaction, especially when she took noticed of the one novelty flower in the center—twelve white, one white with red tips, making thirteen in total.

Mercedes inhaled their sweet scent. "It's beautiful, Takashi." She gazed up at him, her eyes dancing. "Thank you."

He smiled at her. *So far, so good.*

"Though, I don't know how you hid this from me."

A smirk spread across Takashi's lips. "A magician never reveals his secrets."

She peered up at him through her lashes, her teeth catching her bottom lip. "And there's nothing that would persuade him?"

Oh shit. Were they taking public transit or private? It was just going to be the two of them for a while, right? Takashi looked at the sign she carried, using it as a way to divert the question, and his mind, before he said something he'd regret. "Is that your sign?"

Mercedes smirked, seeing her question got to him, and held up the sign. "No, I'm a Libra, actually."

He laughed. "I deserved that answer."

Mercedes continued to smirk. "And yes. I made it Sunday. I figured it'd be hard to miss."

Takashi couldn't stop himself from looking her up and down. "You're hard to miss."

Her face flushed a shade of pink and she glanced

away. He took the sign from her, quite interested in her reaction, and examined her work. She'd painted a white rose on metal, the details positively captivating, and rounded the corners so there were no sharp edges. He ran his fingers across her work. "This is amazing. I thought the images you showed off Saturday was great, but it's nothing compared to seeing this in person."

She stuck her nose into the bouquet of flowers, her cheeks reddening. "Thank you. I tried my hardest to get the details perfect."

Her eyes snapped up to him, the intensity snaring him. *She definitely knows what I'm gauging.*

He decided to ask. "So you're okay with the flowers?"

She bit her lip as she looked down at the flora and then suddenly grabbed his suitcase from him. "We shouldn't keep Narissa waiting. She's eager to try out this new restaurant."

Takashi frowned. He wasn't sure what to think of her changing the subject. She reacted fine to the flowers, but then when the question came up… He'd figure it out later. There was lunch to be had with her and Narissa.

Mercedes had asked him if it was okay for Narissa to join them. He didn't mind, as he like the idea of meeting Narissa in person as well. But a part of him preferred the idea of having lunch with just Mercedes. *Maybe tomorrow.* He had all weekend and then some, as he was staying stateside for at least three weeks. *Plus, this will give me time to figure out why Mercedes avoided my question.*

The pair exited the airport and Mercedes led him to her car. A woman around their age with a dark complexion and curvaceous figure sat on the hood, dark sunglasses obscuring her eyes and protecting them from the L.A. sun.

The woman stood up and smiled bright when she spotted them. "Takashi!"

She held out her arms and Takashi accepted the hug, having to lean down. "It's good to see you, Narissa."

"Sorry for crashing your lunch date," she said she pulled away. "But I figured Mercedes would have you all to herself for the rest of the weekend so it wasn't a huge deal."

Takashi laughed. "I don't mind at all."

Narissa took Takashi's suitcase from Mercedes and went about stowing it in the car. Takashi found it a bit difficult not to be distracted by her. He could see why Ajax wanted her. Mercedes slipping into the driver's seat of the car grabbed his attention. *Mercedes is just far more distracting.*

On top of that, Narissa was intelligent enough to keep up with Ajax. Ajax may look like he should be on some professional sports team, but his intelligence impressed even Takashi. He single-handedly revolutionized the gaming industry by designing the gamepods gamers used today. Of course, not to be outdone by her "baby brother," Ajax's sister designed a mobile version that was both safe and convenient for those always on the go, like professional gamers and other business men and women.

Takashi opened the door of the car to hop into the backseat, but Narissa stopped him. "You'll be too tall to fit back there. I'm smaller, I'll take it."

He knew better than to argue. The moment he sat down in the front seat after letting Narissa in, Tasha's

robotic voice came from the car dash. "Hello, Takashi. It's nice to see you again."

"You as well, Tasha," he replied.

"Where are we off to now, Mercedes?" Tasha asked.

"Chi-Lin Gardens."

Tasha made her calculations and the car pulled out of the space. Takashi glanced at Mercedes when she went about playing with the radio. Narissa complained, saying something about staying on one station finally. He guessed the two had bickered about this earlier today, too. A smile spread across his lips. Spending the day with these two was going to be quite the adventure for him.

The trio followed their hostess to a booth. Mercedes slipped into one side while Narissa slipped into the other, leaving Takashi to choose, though she knew it wasn't really a choice. He sat down next to Mercedes and the hostess set down their ordering devices before leaving.

Mercedes looked over their options. "How was your flight?"

Takashi rubbed his face. "Long and exhausting. You'd think I'd get used to them, but I don't."

Narissa placed her drink order and grinned at him. "If only there was something to convince you to move back stateside so you don't have to deal with the flights."

Mercedes' eyes narrowed at her. She did not appreciate her friend meddling right now. *Especially not after what went down in the airport.*

Takashi chuckled and placed his order. "I've been thinking about it."

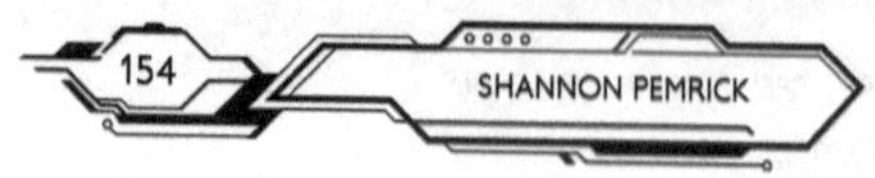

Narissa gave Mercedes a not so subtle "go after him" look. Mercedes' eyes remained narrowed and then she went about ordering her drink and her meal. The exchange didn't go unnoticed by Takashi, though he didn't say anything, making her a bit nervous.

The bouquet he offered at the airport had thrown her. One flower she expected, but what he handed her… White roses, a way to show you care for someone more than friends, but not quite deep enough for the red rose of love. A single novelty rose, white and red, signifying that care is deepening. Thirteen in total, a sign of an admirer. The three together, handed directly to the intended, a proposal for courtship.

When Mercedes looked up at Takashi after noting all of this, she saw the tightness in his jaw, and his pupils appeared dilated. When he asked if she was okay with the flowers, she knew then it was his way of asking—of indicating this "just friends" wasn't working for him anymore. Unfortunately… she wasn't sure she could say yes to such a request, and ended up not answering at all.

She knew it wasn't the best choice to make. "No" would have been kinder than nothing at all, but she felt too conflicted by the situation to give a proper answer. *I need more time.*

"Hello, Mercedes…" Narissa waved, catching her attention. "Earth to Mercedes."

Mercedes blinked and found herself brought out of her head. "Oh, sorry."

Takashi's brow furrowed. "You okay?"

"Yeah, I'm fine. I was just thinking about what I ordered." She found it hard to look at him without feeling guilty. "I wasn't sure if I wanted to go through with what I'd chosen."

She could tell she hadn't fooled anyone, but neither of her friends decided to make a scene about it.

"So, can I know anything about this special cybernetic project you two are working on?" Takashi asked. "Beyond what little Mercedes has told me?"

The two women looked at each other, grinned, and then spoke in unison, "No."

He chuckled. "Well okay, then."

A staff member showed up with their drinks and an appetizer Takashi ordered to split.

"So, did you see PTR is going up for the next Lusara Fates expansion?" Narissa asked between bites.

PTR meant public test realm. It was a mock instance of a game, where developers allowed individuals from outside their company to test new implementations and provide feedback.

Mercedes nodded. "Yeah, if I read correctly, we'll be seeing what this next expansion will be about next month, finally, and then the PTR will be up."

"What are you two theorizing it'll be about?" Takashi asked. "Besides Old Gods, because everyone knows that."

"I think we're going to finally find out how the world was created," Narissa said. "All game texts say there isn't any information on that, and there've been some funny things going on with some old NPC tribes."

"I'm not sure." Mercedes grinned and looked at her intelligent friend. "But I do know, no matter what it is, Narissa and Ajax will be 'questing' late at night."

Narissa gasped and Takashi laughed. "Don't forget

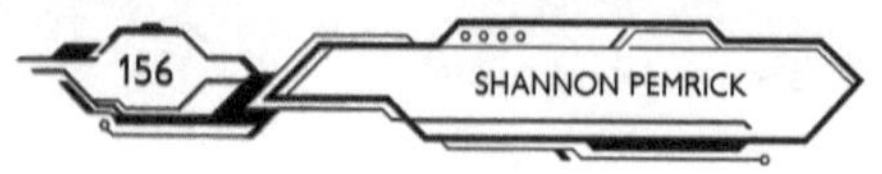

their late night 'raiding.' We all know it's not quite a Dev-team-approved raid style."

Narissa's face reddened. "Oh yeah? And what about you two? Going on all these 'treasure hunts' all the time. We all know what kind of treasure you two are looking at."

Takashi laughed and Mercedes' face warmed. She went to spit out a rebuttal when Tasha interrupted. "My apologies, Miss Mercedes, but I thought you may want to know of this new movie announcement."

Her brow furrowed. "Movie announcement?"

She had her phone set up to get notifications on various geek culture announcements, but there hadn't been a single blip on that radar about possible movies.

Mercedes whipped out her phone and opened the announcement, seeing the name "Lusara Fates" in bold titles. "No way..."

"What?" both Takashi and Narissa said.

"Lusara Fates is getting a movie!"

Takashi immediately looked over her shoulder and Narissa whipped out her phone, her assistant having already pulled up the announcement for her. A mix of comfort and discomfort fell over Mercedes. As much as she liked the closeness with Takashi, it didn't feel right because of what she'd done.

Mercedes focused on the phone, scrolling through the short article. Takashi reached over from time to time to flick the screen in an attempt to get her to speed up her reading. She laughed, the interaction helping her ease out of her awkward mood with him. She really needed to sort out her feelings, sooner rather than later.

"Well, there's not much here so far, but this is exciting," Takashi said.

"I wonder what part of the storyline they'll focus on?" Mercedes queried. "I hope they start from the beginning, and not try to pull what Blizzard did with their Warcraft movies, and start later in the timeline than they should have."

"But they're not bad movies."

"I'm not saying they are. I love them. But they're pretty confusing if you've never played any of the games, or read any of the books. Especially if you watch them in the order the movies came out."

"That's a fair point."

Mercedes looked to Narissa to see why she wasn't engaging in the conversation, only to find her resting her chin on her palm, a goofy grin on her face. "What is wrong with you?"

"You two are adorable."

Mercedes childishly stuck her tongue out at her friend just as a staff member came out with their meals.

Lunch continued, with more crazy discussions transpiring. Her mind kept wandering on her, though, warranting strange looks from Narissa.

Once they'd all eaten, they agreed to drop Takashi off at his hotel. Mercedes could see the exhaustion taking hold.

Not two minutes after they dropped him off at his hotel did Narissa face Mercedes, with clear intent in her eyes. "Okay, spill it."

Mercedes furrowed her brow. "Spill what?"

"You've been acting all out of sorts since we met up with Takashi." Narissa pointed to the bouquet of

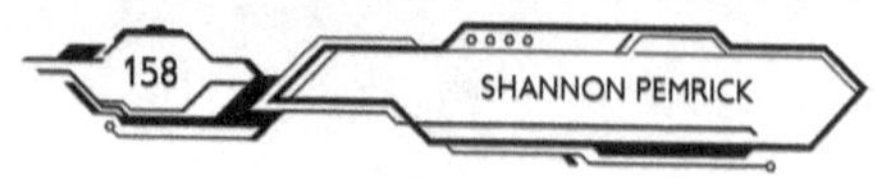

flowers. "And I'm willing to bet ten thousand dollars it has something to do with that."

Mercedes looked away. *Too bad she's right; I could have used that kind of cash.*

"Tell me, girl, what happened? What's so important about the arrangement he gave you?"

She sighed. She knew Narissa. Her friend wouldn't give up until she talked. "Thirteen white roses is a proposal for courtship."

"What?" Narissa screeched. "This is fantastic! Why are you—Oh, no. What did you do?"

Mercedes chewed on her lower lip. "I… I didn't give him an answer."

"Cede." Narissa threw her head back and groaned. "Why would you do that?"

Mercedes rubbed her false arm. "I don't really want to talk about this right now, Narissa."

Narissa crossed her arms. "And I do. I'm not about to let you turn into Shira. Now tell me why you couldn't say yes to dating a guy who is perfect for you?"

Mercedes slumped down in her seat, pain pulsing in her chest. "Because why would he want to?"

"Oh, I don't know, maybe because you're amazing?"

"No, I'm not. I spend my days working at a car shop and playing games. My social life consists of talking to my robot assistant, my fish, and my few friends, only one of whom actually lives in the same town as me. I don't volunteer; my charity work happening once or twice a year for Make-A-Wish or some special restoration case. I—"

"I swear, if you say one more thing that screams 'I'm comparing myself to his ex,' I'm going to slap you."

Mercedes stared at her friend.

"You really think Takashi wants someone like his ex? There's a reason she's an ex!" Narissa took a deep breath to calm herself. "You're not boring, Cede. You're funny, and talented, and you're a lot of fun to be around. I don't know why you can't see that. He certainly does."

Mercedes shrank down in her seat some more and pulled her knees up to her chest. "Five years, and I can't get a single date to work out. For five years, I've tried to be careful who I choose for dates, and yet, they all have an issue with me having a cybernetic arm, as if just one robotic part makes me some android and no longer human."

Narissa opened her mouth to speak, but Mercedes continued. "Even my boyfriend at the time of my accident left me because of this stupid arm. I thought I could rationalize it as him being an asshole and me not seeing it, since many of the guys at the shop kept telling me they didn't trust him. I tried to not think like Shira and hold out and find someone who really did care about me, but now, even with someone claiming they do, it doesn't feel real. It feels like one big sick joke."

Mercedes hid her face in her arms. All sorts of negative emotions bounced around in her head.

"You never told me you had a boyfriend who left you after your accident," Narissa said in a quiet voice. "Not even during your psych evaluations."

"Because I didn't want to think about it. I didn't want to remind myself what kind of failure I am. But every date that I can't get to work out, it reminds me I'm the issue. So why would Takashi see me as more than a friend?"

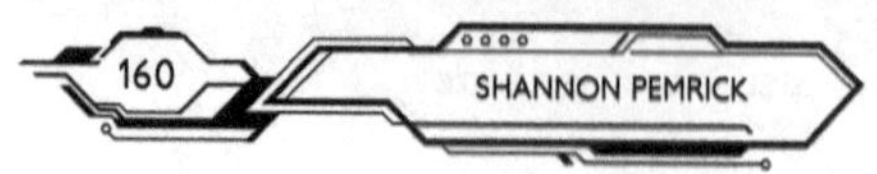

Narissa reached out and grabbed her hand. "Because he sees you. And I mean *really* sees you. He's different from those other men."

Mercedes wanted to agree. Her friend made sense, and it fit the person she knew Takashi to be. And she couldn't deny she wanted to be with him. She just struggled to find it in her to jump on the opportunity. *I need more time.*

CHAPTER 10

Muffled sounds teased Mercedes' ears, and pain pulsed in the back of her head. She opened her eyes, the world around her bright and blurry. A bright light flashed over her eyes, and she heard more muffled sounds. She closed her eyes, not liking the brightness. Something touched her in the arm, sending an unusual pulse through her brain. *That didn't come from my left arm…*

Then everything came back to her. She'd come in to get her new neuro-mod implanted for the arm upgrade experiment. Narissa had hoped she could avoid an extra surgery for this upgrade method, but found it unavoidable.

Mercedes did her best to wake up, but discovered it to be difficult. Her head hurt so much, and the more she tried to be aware of her surroundings, the more strange her body felt.

Then finally, a voice pierced the hazy bubble. "Mercedes."

Narissa was talking to her. Mercedes tried to speak back, but it was nearly impossible.

"Mercedes," Narissa said again. "Oh, good you can finally hear me. Don't panic, and don't try to force yourself to speak. Your mind is trying to readjust, and it's overwhelming your senses."

Something light whisked by her arm. *Wait, was that wind on my false arm?* Her head started to pound all of a sudden and she didn't like it.

"Scanners are picking up that you can feel that, though it looks to be adding extra stress to your brain. Not as much as we predicted, so that's a good sign."

Mercedes tried to speak, and this time found herself successful. "Narissa…"

"Ah, there we go." Narissa hovered over Mercedes' face, but she couldn't make out her features yet. "How are you feeling?"

"My head… hurts…" she admitted. She knew it best not to lie about anything, else it'd ruin the testing. "Can't see well… yet."

"Don't strain your eyes, that will come back as your body adjusts." Narissa moved away. "I've got your arm suspended to reduce the amount of pressure on the artificial nerves I installed while you were out. Based on the computer scans, today is going to get rough for you once I end the suspension."

"I wasn't… expecting… an easy transition." Even with all the testing and poking and prodding, Mercedes knew this wouldn't be a walk in the park. But she had to do it. This would help so many people beyond just her. The pain and stress of testing would be worth it in the end.

Mercedes heard Narissa pick up a device. "Based on this first awaken, even with a non-transition piece, patient will need to go through an adjustment period. Prediction: those with cybernetic limbs for an extended durations, prediction three years or more, will require a longer adjustment period."

Mercedes blinked her eyes, her eyes finally focusing. Glancing at her arm, she found it suspended by thin wire. She couldn't feel the wire, but Mercedes suspected Narissa had intended that. She found her tech-savvy friend had added her notes into a nearby computer, swiping the data to the left side of the screen when done, and transferring it to the computer on her desk. "I can see better now."

Narissa looked back at her, smiled, and then went back to her notes. "Excellent. At first glance, visual stimuli not causing extra harm once patient regains sight. More testing soon."

Mercedes smiled. She liked listening to Narissa speak while testing. Her friend's intelligence, while hard to keep up with a lot of times, fascinated her.

"Mercedes, I'd like for you to look around, and tell me how you feel when you do," Narissa instructed.

She did as asked. Mercedes found moving her head difficult and sometimes disorienting. Bright lights bothered her and made the pain in her head worse. She reported this to Narissa, who added the information to her notes.

Narissa approached her and looked her over. "How much are you feeling with the arm?"

"I'm not sure," Mercedes admitted. "My head feels so

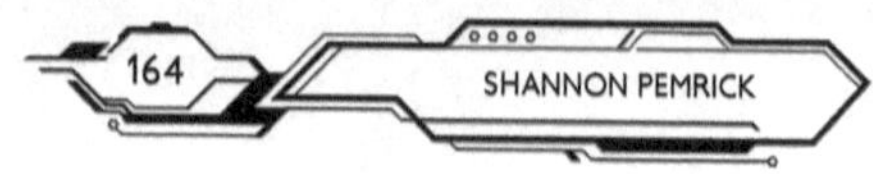

funny right now, I'm not sure what is from the implant install, or what's from the new sensation."

Narissa nodded. "Okay. Have you been able to feel anything specific since waking up?"

"I felt when something passed by it, like wind, but then my head hurt from the sensation. And I don't think I feel these wires."

Narissa picked up a data pad and digital pen, and went to writing. "Okay. Is it okay for me to start doing some testing? I'd like to move your arm up and down to see what your mod does."

Mercedes nodded. "Let's give it a whirl."

Her tech friend put down her device and touched the mechanism suspending Mercedes' arm. Her arm twitched, and something in her mind pinged. Mercedes' eye twitched in sync.

"I saw that," Narissa said. "Involuntary action?"

"Yeah. Just that little movement set off the implant."

"Good to know. I'm going to move it more."

Narissa lowered Mercedes' arm, sending a million sensations through her: pain, euphoria, confusion. Her heart began to race. "Stop!"

Her friend listened and let Mercedes take a minute. "Tell me what you felt. The scanners are picking up a lot of activity in your brain."

"There was… so much going on I don't know how to describe it. But none of it felt like it should. It doesn't feel like when I move my real arm." Mercedes went to show her friend, only for her brain to fire off just like it had with the artificial arm. Mercedes blinked, unable to take in the sensation. "Okay, maybe I was wrong."

Narissa cocked her head. "If I remember correctly,

you had a similar reaction when we originally implanted your prosthetic."

"Yeah, I think you're right." Mercedes looked up at her friend. "Is this a good thing or a bad thing?"

Narissa pursed her lips. "Hard to say. We'll need more tests to be sure."

Mercedes nodded. "Let's keep going, then."

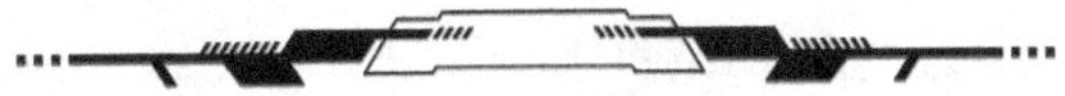

Several hours passed before Mercedes allowed herself a break. Narissa insisted she take more time, but she wasn't a quitter, and as long as she wasn't hurting herself, she didn't see a reason to stop. This of course exhausted her, but it was worth it.

The longer Mercedes had the implant and altered arm, the more accustomed she became to it. But it wasn't perfect. With the way Narissa had planned this, the sensors were added and changed in a three-step process. This was the safest method Narissa could create that wouldn't overload the body, and this also made it a sensible option for people who couldn't afford the upfront cost of the full-feeling tech.

Currently, Mercedes could only feel pressure of a certain amount. The moving-air feeling had been a fluke. Testing proved this, as the longer it continued, her ability to feel that light pressure dissipated. Narissa concluded it to be a side effect of her sensitivity to the implant, and as she adjusted, it resolved itself.

Mercedes' phone rang on a small table beside her and Tasha's voice came from her phone. "Miss Mercedes, Takashi is calling you. Should I answer it?"

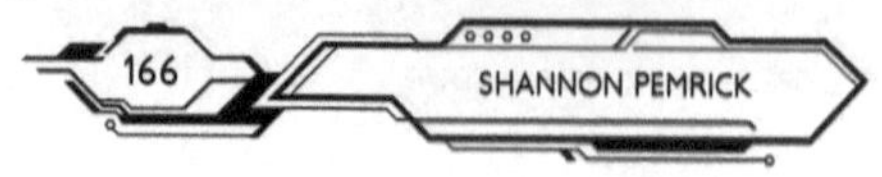

She looked to Narissa who nodded. "Please answer that call on speaker."

"Of course, Miss Mercedes."

The phone stopped ringing and then a voice came through, "Hello?"

"Hey, Takashi," Mercedes greeted. "You're on speakerphone."

"Tasha warned me." She couldn't help but laugh at his wording. "You must be tired if you're answering on speaker."

Mercedes relaxed in her chair. "Exhausted."

"I'm putting her through her paces!" Narissa shouted.

Takashi laughed. "I hope you're not being too rough on our girl. We need her DPS for raids."

Narissa's brow rose. "That's the only reason?"

Takashi chuckled. "Only reason we share."

"And what reason do you need her for?" Mercedes noticed the change in tone and wished she had the strength to smack her forehead. She should have known the conversation would go this way.

"Lunch buddy." His tone was so simple and matter-of-fact, as if it were obvious. "That is, if you're up for it, Mercedes. I don't want you to push yourself."

"Well…" She didn't want to turn him down. She liked the prospect of having lunch with him, but she was tired.

"I only have three hours before I have to get back to the seminar, so if it's not good for you, it's okay," he added.

"I think you should go," Narissa encouraged. "You need a break, and this will give me time to compile my data."

"I'm not sure if I'll have the energy," Mercedes

admitted. "That's a lot for this arm to have to handle. We've barely managed to make it so I can rest it on this chair without my neuro-mod going crazy."

Narissa held up a finger. "And I've set up the arm so I can tell it to stop transmitting when directed. This will give you a chance to let your mind rest. It'll give us a refresh when you return, and see how your mind reacts to the modification turning on and off."

"That won't hurt her, will it?" Takashi sounded alarmed.

"Oh, don't be silly," Narissa said. "I'm not going to do something that will intentionally hurt her. I've done the calculations, and it should only startle her a bit. How much, I don't know. But it'll help me gauge if the on-and-off functions would be best done while she's asleep or awake."

"Are you okay with this, Mercedes?" Takashi asked. "I don't want you pushing yourself."

Mercedes loved the care he was putting into this. He never pushed her more than she wanted to be. "Can I have an hour before I meet with you? That should give me enough time to rest and be good for a meetup."

"I'll give you whatever time you need." His response made her heart flutter. "I'll message you the address to the diner. See you in an hour."

The call ended, and Narissa wiggled her eyebrows at Mercedes. "Don't worry, I won't invite myself to this lunch and cock-block you this time."

Mercedes' face flushed and she had to look away.

Narissa approached. "Now let's turn this off so you can rest enough to meet up with loverboy."

Mercedes rolled her eyes and let her friend work,

thinking of a way to get back at her for the comment while she did.

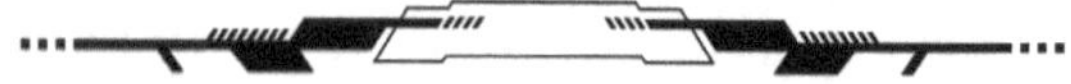

The white sports car pulled into a parallel parking spot and Mercedes cut the engine. Tasha switched her connection from the car to the phone, and Mercedes slipped out of the vehicle. The hot L.A. sun bore down on her as she looked around the busy street. She wasn't able to park close to the diner, so now she had to locate it.

"My apologies, Miss Mercedes," Tasha said. "The destination is two blocks south of here."

Mercedes paid the meter and then headed south. "It's okay, Tasha. That's close for such a busy time of day. I got enough rest where I can manage."

Narissa's rest suggestion had been a good one. Deactivating the sensors had been disorienting, to say the least, and not something she wanted to experience again when awake if she could help it. It took her an hour to readjust, and even still, her head hurt from the new implant. That pain would take some time to go away, but at least she wasn't being hammered with wonky signals from her arm.

Mercedes reflected on the testing and what was to come, passing the walk quickly. When the diner came into view, she spotted Takashi, but he wasn't alone. Emi stood with him, chatting. Irritation flared up in her chest. She didn't hate Emi, actually she quite liked the woman, but Takashi hadn't said anything about others joining them. She had wanted to spend time with just him. *Well, I don't really have a right to think that if I can't even decide what I want…*

A bell jingled, and a well-dressed man exited the diner. Takashi and Emi both looked at him, the latter smiling and greeting him with a kiss. *Oh, maybe I'm wrong.*

She really needed to not jump to conclusions, but doubt clawed at her.

Emi noticed her approach and waved. "Mercedes!"

Mercedes waved back and joined the small group. "It's good to see you, Emi. Sorry I'm late, Takashi. Parking sucks this time of day."

Emi gasped. "You didn't do street parking, did you?"

Mercedes' brow rose. "Uh, yeah?"

Emi dug through her purse, her beautiful ebon hair spilling over her shoulders, and then pulled out a card. She handed it to Mercedes. "Take this. A token of thanks for that referral. It's good for a lot of the garages around here, with security. That pretty car of yours shouldn't be on the street where it can get damaged."

Mercedes chuckled. "At least I could fix it easy enough if it was. And you're welcome. I hope it worked out in your favor."

Emi's eyes squinted as she smiled. "You bet! I have a meeting in a few weeks to show off a few of my designs to Anita and Flynn. Even if they don't like them, at least I had this opportunity. It's more than I could ask for." She gasped and then placed her hands on the man next to her. "I'm being so rude. I haven't introduced you two."

The man patted Emi's hand. "It's okay. I didn't want to interrupt your excitement." He held a hand out to Mercedes. "Name's Jason Atilon, head of the technical

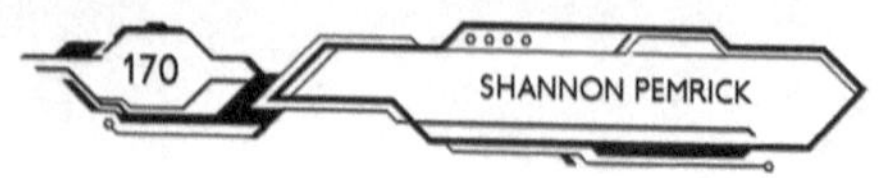

department for Emi's father's law firm. I'm her boy-friend."

Her focus now on him, Mercedes got the chance to take in his features—tall with dark hair, light skin, and brilliant blue eyes. But as she looked at him, a sense of unease washed over her.

Mercedes grabbed his hand with her cybernetic one. "Mercedes Gail, manager at Gail's Restorations."

"Ah, so you're the famous restorer Emi gushed about. She says you've worked on an impressive number of cars in your life."

Mercedes nodded, shoving her hands in her back pocket. "Yeah, but not as many as my father. I don't think there's a car he hasn't worked on at this point."

Jason dug through his pockets and pulled out a folded piece of cardstock and handed it to her. "Are you sure?"

Mercedes unfolded the paper to find it an old pho-tograph. On it was a man in his early thirties standing next to an antique sports car. Mercedes whistled. "It's been a while since I've seen one of those. 1969 Pontiac GTO. We've restored a few of those."

Emi giggled. "Told you."

Jason shook his head. "I'm impressed. You're the first in a while to know what that car is. The man in that photo is my grandfather. He loved those old cars. Was one hell of a hobby for him." The watch on his wrist beeped and he took a look. "My report for my meeting later is done. We'll have to get going so I can look it over beforehand."

Jason took back the photograph when Mercedes offered it, and he smiled. "It's been a pleasure meeting you, Mercedes." He looked to Takashi and extended his hand. "It's been good seeing you again too, Takashi. Glad things are going well for you."

Takashi shook Jason's hand and nodded, though he didn't say anything, perplexing Mercedes. He was unusually quiet.

The pair left, Takashi watching them, and Mercedes decided to address the issue. "You okay?"

"I'm not a fan of Jason," he admitted. "As much as I'm glad she's happy with him, there's always been something about him that rubbed me the wrong way." He gave her a sidelong glance. "And before you say it, no, I'm not jealous she has a boyfriend. I have no feelings for her beyond a friend."

"I wasn't going to accuse you of that." Mercedes smiled at him, but she couldn't help but hate the nagging of the tiny lie. A part of her did not believe his claim. *Great, there's that doubt again.*

But she couldn't exactly blame Takashi for his unease. She'd also felt something off with Jason, though she couldn't place it.

Takashi produced a white and red novelty rose, and handed it to Mercedes before placing a hand on her lower back. "But enough about them. I promised you lunch."

She smiled and let him usher her to the door of the diner. In doing so, she noticed his attire. While a casual business look, he looked good. *He looks good in a tie. Really good.* The untucked white shirt he wore fit his frame well. Mercedes had the urge to tell Tasha to take them for a drive and find out just what that shirt was hiding. *Whoa, that thought escalated quickly.* "You look nice."

Takashi grinned. "You look nicer."

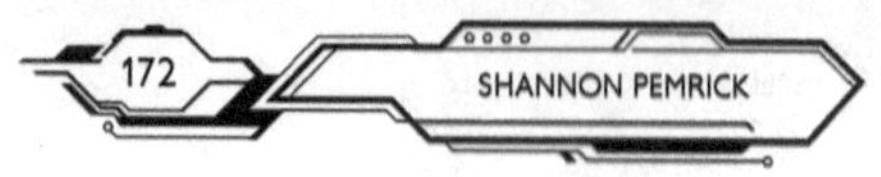

"I'm just in casual attire."

His brow rose, a grin still on his lips. "And? You could wear a burlap sack and make it look fashionable."

She elbowed him. "Stop it."

He chuckled and then spoke to the hostess, getting them a table for two. Mercedes slipped into one side of the booth while Takashi faced her on the other side, and the hostess left them with ordering devices.

Mercedes perused the digital menu. "How's the seminar going?"

"It's about as exciting as watching paint dry."

She laughed. "Are you sure you want to go back, then?"

Takashi eyed her. "As tempting as that is, the information they're giving is solid, so I should return when the break is over." He looked at her artificial arm as it rested on the table. "How's the testing going?"

Mercedes dramatically rested herself on the table. "Exhausting!" He laughed and she sat back up. "But it's going to be worth it."

"Can you tell me more about the project?" Takashi flipped the digital page of his menu. "Or are you sworn to secrecy?"

A smirk spread across Mercedes' lips. "Well, I'm not supposed to talk about it with most people, but the clause excludes Shira, Ajax, and you."

"Me? I can see why the other two, but why me?"

"Because Narissa knew I'd tell you anyway."

Takashi chuckled, and then waited to hear more.

Mercedes filled him in on the details he didn't have yet, only pausing when they needed to order their meals and appetizer so they wouldn't be accused of loitering.

Takashi nodded after she completed her overview.

"The testing you've been doing, what kind of information have you gathered?"

"Well, today is the first day of the actual physical testing. I had to do all sorts of other tests to make sure we had the right data to work with. Because of that preliminary data collection, Narissa realized she couldn't use the old neuro-mods, so she had to redesign the upgrades. She also decided that a three-stage process would be best."

Their drinks and appetizer were delivered, forcing Mercedes to pause for a moment.

"She installed the new chip, and at the same time installed the first-stage sensors. Stage one is heavy-pressure sensors; stage two is light; and stage three is temperature. Based on what happened in the last five hours, she's predicting it'll be best for people to get the sensors in quick succession, but may be okay to get them installed over the course of one year. More testing will have to happen around that before it goes to market."

Takashi looked her over. "You said you had a new neuro-mod installed. Doesn't that involve surgery?"

Mercedes pulled back some of her hair to reveal the small patch of shaved head. "Narissa has been doing this a long time. The chip is so tiny, only a small area of my head needs to be cut into, and she knows how to position the incision area where I can hide it with my hair."

Takashi leaned back in his seat and sighed. "So much involved; it's exhausting just to listen about. I can only imagine the stress that's on you."

"It's worth it. Not only am I going to get a complete

system after this is all over and the product is perfected, but this testing is going to help so many people."

He smiled at her. "You're amazing, you know that?"

Mercedes' face warmed and she looked down at her drink. "Thanks…"

Takashi reached out and touched her false hand. "So you can't feel this right now, right?"

She shook her head. "No, we turned it off to give my poor brain a break. Even if it were on, I wouldn't be able to tell it's a hand touching me without looking, because this mod would just be going nuts with unidentifiable signals. We're not sure if this is because of the new sensation to my brain, or if it's a fault in the prototype. The more I test, the more we'll know."

"You'll figure it out." Takashi smiled at her. "I'm confident of that."

The waitstaff returned with their meals, and the two dug in. Or that was the plan for Mercedes, until she saw Takashi staring at her as she went to take a bite of her hash browns. She paused and then put her fork down. "Something the matter, Takashi?"

He pursed his lips. "I thought you were right dominant."

"Uh, I am."

"How come you're using your left to eat? Today, I'd think it was because you were tired, even with the nerve system shut off, but I noticed this as well the other times we've eaten together. You rarely use your right, unless you need to cut something."

Mercedes lowered her gaze to the breakfast meal she'd ordered. "Yeah… about that…"

Takashi tilted his head. "What's wrong?"

Mercedes stared at her food, struggling about how to answer him. This wasn't something she talked about with others freely. *It's—*

Mercedes' eyes widened when he reached out across the table and grabbed her hand—but her prosthetic one. She looked at him, to find him gazing right at her, unflinching. Very few had ever done that to her. *They always avoid…*

She sighed. "Cybernetics have been around for decades, though only in the last decade or so have they advanced by these leaps and bounds. Even still, you'd think people would be used to them, but they're not. When I use my arm, people stare. Sometimes, it's curiosity, others…"

She sighed again. "I've learned, if I don't bring any attention to it, those looks go away. I don't feel like some weird freak."

"Freak isn't what I'd call you."

Her brow rose at him.

"I think it's pretty badass-looking." He smirked. "And badass is sexy."

He… does? Heat rose in her face. She dropped her gaze to her lunch. A shy smile spread across her lips. "Thanks."

"Ah, there's the beautiful smile I love." He pulled away. "Let's get to better topics, so it stays."

She nodded and started eating her meal. *He's quite the charmer. Or I'm that pathetic to fall for just a few words.*

The next hour and a half passed by quickly. The two joked and laughed. They shared stories and discussed plans for the next few days. Throughout this time, Mercedes found her energy draining, and did her best to hide it, but Takashi noticed. She was able to keep the lunch date from ending for a while, but to her disappointment, Takashi wasn't having it.

"Mercedes, you really need to rest."

She sighed. "I know… I just want to hang out with you, ya know?"

Takashi reached out and placed his hand on her artificial one again. "We have tomorrow, and even tonight, if you're feeling up to hopping on the game. Pushing yourself like this isn't good for you."

She nodded, understanding his point. She pulled up her tab, but before she could pay, Takashi reached over and added it to his bill.

"Takashi, what—"

"Today is my treat. No arguing."

She tried to find the words to argue, but before they could form, he paid for the meals and smiled at her. She huffed, making him laugh, but it was short-lived when she pulled some cash from her pocket and put it on the table for the tip.

"I got that too, Mercy."

Her heart fluttered at the sound of the nickname again. "Nope. I'm covering that, and there's nothing you can do about it."

His lips spread into a thin line and she smiled triumphantly.

The two of them slipped out of the booth, and just as she was stepping away, she caught him trying to tuck some cash into her back pocket. She slapped his hand away and wagged her finger at him. "Oh, no you don't."

He held up his hands, the money disappearing before her very eyes. "Can't blame me for trying."

"More like trying to disguise your attempt to cop a feel."

He grinned. "Maybe."

She pursed her lips and then walked off. Takashi insisted on walking with her to her car. The building hosting the seminar wasn't too far from the diner, so he wasn't worried about a late return. Mercedes remote-started the vehicle when it came into view, to cool it down a bit before she got in.

Takashi opened the door for her and she slipped in. He rested his arms on the door and the frame, leaning in. "Thank you for having lunch with me."

She smiled at him. "Thanks for the invite. I enjoyed the time spent with you."

Takashi leaned closer, pecking her on the cheek. "Me too."

Mercedes' face heated as Takashi pulled away.

"Get some rest. I'll talk to you later."

Takashi shut the door and walked away. Mercedes reached up and touched her cheek.

"Miss Mercedes," Tasha's voice came from her dash. "My sensors indicate a chemical change in you. Are you okay?"

He hadn't flinched away when he touched her cyber-netic. And he'd said it made her sexy. *And that small peck…* A smile spread across her lips. "Yeah, I am."

She then instructed Tasha to take her back to the hotel, calling Narissa to let her know she needed some more rest before testing again today.

The woman presenting droned on and on. Takashi found himself struggling to stay awake. It wasn't her fault, this topic on currency exchange just didn't interest him. He'd much rather be plugging numbers or swapping marketing strategies with the others here. *Or spending time with Mercedes.*

After yesterday's seminar ended, he'd checked in with her. She'd gotten a few hours of sleep and then went right back into testing, making progress. Her excitement made him happy. He didn't like the stress she put herself under for this project, but he understood why she did it.

This morning was no different, though she sounded rather tired. He worried she was pushing herself too much in such a short time. She did that with work too, and he wished she'd just take things easy for once.

The woman at the front of the room concluded her presentation and dismissed them for lunch. Takashi immediately pulled his phone from his pocket and

checked his messages. Mercedes had left him one fifteen minutes ago. Tapping the icon, he opened it.

I'm taking a break from testing. This is exhausting.

His brow furrowed and he left the room to find a quiet place to call her. The call rang twice before Tasha's voice picked up. "Hello, Takashi. If you don't mind holding, Mercedes is just finishing up a conversation with Narissa."

"I don't mind at all."

"You will be placed on speakerphone again."

He suspected that may happen. "I'm fine with that."

About two minutes passed before he was patched through to Mercedes. "Hey, Takashi."

She sounded like she should be asleep. "Hey, Mercy. How are you holding up?"

"This is hard," she said. "I'm so tired. I can't do lunch with you, I'm sorry."

Disappointment fell over him, but he kept it hidden from her in his voice; he didn't want her feeling guilty when she shouldn't. "Don't be. You're putting yourself under a lot of stress."

"We're making progress, though. So that's something."

He smiled. "I'm glad it's working."

"Convince her to take a nap!" Narissa shouted in the background. "She won't listen to me."

"I don't want to sleep," Mercedes grumbled.

The two bickered for a moment before Takashi interjected. "Mercy, you really should rest. You won't be able to keep this pace up unless you do."

"I know, but—"

"No, don't do that." He thought for a moment. "Okay, how about this? You get some rest and don't push yourself too hard today, and I'll stop by your hotel room tonight with dinner and a movie."

"Oh, maybe I'll send her home so she gets *plenty* of rest before you show up," Narissa teased.

"Narissa!" Mercedes shouted.

Takashi chuckled. He definitely liked the idea of getting intimate with Mercedes. Even if she'd acted strange to the flowers at the airport, how she acted around him yesterday gave him a bit of hope for there to be something between them. He just had to figure out how to approach the situation that wasn't going to get her to run. "Do we have a deal, Mercy?"

"Yeah, we do." Her sleepy voice gave her away. "I think I should go take my nap now."

"Sleep well."

"Have fun at your seminar. Sorry this was all about me."

Her thoughtfulness made him smile. "Stop it. I'll text you later."

"'Kay, bye."

"Bye." He disconnected and stored away his phone. He had to admit, he was disappointed they wouldn't be meeting for lunch, but as long as she took it easy— *doubtful*—he'd get to spend an even longer time with her tonight.

"Hey, Takashi!"

Takashi spun around to find an older gentleman around his father's age standing in a small group of other seminar attendees, waving him over. Takashi

complied, thoughts running through his head. *That's… Allen… right?* He'd met so many people that he was struggling to keep names straight.

Allen smirked at him when Takashi approached. "You done talking to your girlfriend?"

"I don't have a girlfriend." As much as he wished that weren't true, it was his reality.

"Yeah, all right, then that girl you talk to all the time. Are you going out to see her again today?"

Takashi shook his head. "No, she's busy until tonight."

One of the women with Allen, Emily, smiled at him. "How about having lunch with us, then? We're going to eat here at the café on the first floor, so nothing fancy, but we were going to swap auction house strategies."

He nodded. "That sounds like an excellent idea."

Takashi followed the group, talk immediately swapping to strategies, giving him a renewed vigor he'd use to get him through the day.

The late evening sun shone through the sunroof of the rental as Takashi pulled up to the hotel Mercedes was staying at. A valet approached Takashi when he hopped out of the car. While self-driving cars were allowed to park themselves without their owners present as long as they were in parking lots, hotels preferred to reduce any liabilities. The young woman took his keys, and Takashi made his way inside the hotel, dinner in hand.

He'd talked to Mercedes after the seminar ended for the day. She sounded far better than when they'd last spoke, but still exhausted. The two discussed what they wanted for a meal, and she insisted on providing the movie since she couldn't convince him to split the dinner bill. An old-fashioned way of handling dates, maybe, but he wanted it that way. Though Miss Stubborn and Independent didn't make it easy on him.

Takashi took in the ritzy hotel lobby. It was definitely a place Narissa would hook Mercedes up with. Hopping into the elevator, he sent it to the fifth and top floor. When the box came to a halt and the doors opened, a familiar blue-eyed, golden-haired smiling face greeted him, throwing him.

Mercedes' smile grew wider. "Surprise."

Takashi left the elevator and couldn't hide his confusion. "How did you know I was here?"

She giggled. "Ochi told me."

Takashi's lips spread into a thin line. "That traitor. I was supposed to surprise you."

"Too bad." Mercedes took one of the bags he carried and then headed for her room.

Takashi noticed she'd taken the bag with her real hand and her false limb hung loosely at her side. "How did the rest of your testing go?"

"Interesting," she said as they reached the hotel room. He watched her lift up her cybernetic arm, her face twitching, and swipe her key card before opening the door. "We're still unable to determine if the prototype isn't working right, or if I need more time for adjusting. Personally, I feel like it's a bit of both."

The two entered the hotel room, for him to discover it was a beautiful suite. There was a full kitchen to their right, a small gathering area, and a bedroom off to the side. The gathering area resided in front of a large

sliding glass door, leading out to a balcony overlooking the ocean.

"Narissa knows how to treat a guest," Takashi mumbled as he looked around.

Mercedes snickered. "Trust me, no matter how many times I've tried to tell her I don't need a room like this, she doesn't listen."

He wandered in and noticed the king size bed in the bedroom. "Not even I need a bed that big." He looked back at her. "For two people that'd be nice, but for one person… that's a bit overkill, don't you think?"

She laughed and put the food down on a counter. "I'm a major bed hog. It won't matter what size bed you give me, I'm taking it all." She tucked a stray hair behind her ear. "And really, I'm going to need the space. With this stupid thing, I'll need to sprawl out to help me sleep. Of course I doubt I'll get much."

She glanced over at him, a playful smile on her lips. "Though, not the reason Narissa hoped I'd have sleep issues."

"The disappointment is going to all be on her. I'm here to hang out and spend time with you. Not for just a Netflix and chill." Takashi held up his hands as he spoke, trying to keep himself from entertaining the idea of throwing her on that bed and seeing how little sleep either of them would get.

Mercedes laughed. It was an old phrase, one that rarely was used anymore, but he knew she'd enjoy his choice to use it.

A grin spread across those tempting lips of her when she calmed herself. "So that's not your end game?"

"Well, if you're offering it to be, I wouldn't exactly say no."

Her cheeks flushed a shade. For a moment, he worried his boldness had pushed that line too quickly, but when she laughed and went about pulling food out of the bag, he calmed his nerves.

Takashi observed her, aware he still carried the other dinner bag. He liked watching her, even if she was doing something mundane such as this.

He caught her favoring her real arm, and her face would twitch any time she used the cybernetic. "Is your mod still active? You're favoring your left side, and physically reacting when you use your right."

Mercedes nodded. "Yep. After my much-needed nap, testing continued, and Narissa determined I wasn't adapting as well to the neuro change as she'd hoped. She wants me to do a full day without turning the mod off, to see if that will help with adjusting."

Takashi approached, his brow furrowed. "That's a bit soon to push, don't you think? This is only the second day of testing."

She looked up at him. "It makes it hard to get normal things done, but I agree with her choice. It's the only way we'll know for sure whether turning the mod off hinders or helps the transition. And it'll help us figure out whether these artificial nerves really are working right or not."

He frowned. "I don't like the idea of you struggling through the night because of this."

"This is what I signed up for, Takashi. I'm willing to try whatever test I need to."

Takashi sighed and entered the kitchen, setting the

last bag of food down on the counter. What else could he do? He didn't have any power in all this, and even if he did, Mercedes' stubbornness outmatched his. It was a trait he loved to hate.

"So what movie did you pick out for us?" He figured it best to change the subject. It wouldn't do either of them any good to focus on anything negative tonight.

"Bros and Beasties."

His face contorted as he looked at her. "Bros and what?"

Her brow rose. "You've never heard of it?" She laughed when his expression didn't change. "Man, I'm glad I picked it, then. My mom and I used to watch it all the time when I was little. It's an over the top, cheesy, b-rated fantasy comedy made way back in 2015 that takes all the typical fantasy tropes and ramps them up to an absurd amount, making a ridiculous number of satirical references to some old classic fantasies including Lord of the Rings and Dungeons and Dragons." She laughed some more. "It's super bad, but oh so entertaining."

Takashi started to pile some food on a plate. "I'll have to see for myself. Do you want anything in particular, or just free-for-all this food?"

The two had settled for Chinese. Mercedes said it'd be a good pick while they sat on the couch, and she was having a craving.

Mercedes snatched up the box with the crab rangoons, a wide grin on her face. "This is all I need."

"Oh, no you don't!" He dropped his plate on the counter and reached out for her as she tried to run off with the treat. She squealed when he wrapped both his arms around her waist and pulled her into him. "You have to share those."

"No, they're mine!"

Takashi laughed as he wrestled with her and she began laughing as well. She tried to struggle away from him, but try as she might, he proved stronger. Mercedes huffed and pouted when she realized she wasn't going to win. Takashi inwardly groaned. She made it hard to resist. "You're not going to win that way."

"Yes I can."

She's right, but only if she's the only one to play dirty. He grinned, getting her brow to twist, and then leaned closer. Her face reddened and before she could say anything, his lips met hers. The kiss didn't last long, the aim to get her to cooperate and not to drink in her taste, as tempting as it was.

When he pulled away, Mercedes' eyes fluttered, her cheeks flushed darker than before. A good sign for him. It was a bold move from him, considering how she'd been acting these past two days, but he had to try.

Takashi pulled the box of rangoons from her hands without any resistance from her, and opened the box as he turned away. "I win."

Mercedes shook herself and narrowed her eyes. "Not fair."

He gave her a sidelong glance, a grin on his face. "And pouting is?"

She reached for the box. "Give it back!"

Takashi tried to keep it out of her reach, but in the process, bumped her prosthetic. Mercedes gasped and her eyes dilated. He jumped back, panic flooding over him. "Did I hurt you?"

She took a deep breath. "No, it was just startling."

Curiosity took hold and he approached, reaching out for her arm. "May I?"

She swallowed and then nodded. Takashi lightly touched her arm, but she didn't react. He remembered she said light touches wouldn't trigger the sensors yet, so he put a little pressure on her arm. Mercedes gasped, but didn't pull away this time. Her eyes remained wide and dilated, so Takashi knew she was trying to adjust.

He then let go so she could stabilize her mind. "Is that what you do all day when testing?"

She shook her head and took another deep breath. "We do more rigorous stuff. But now I'm wondering if we should tone it back."

Takashi tilted his head. "What do you mean?"

His lovely mechanic pushed past him and grabbed the container of lo mein. "When you did that, it was startling, but far easier for me to comprehend. I thought going at this full force was the key to make it work, and Narissa thought so, too, due to her statistics, but I think we were wrong. Smaller steps would be better."

Takashi came up behind her, the sweet smell of her perfume teasing his senses. "Do you have any ideas as to how to go about doing that?"

She put her food down and faced him, undeterred by their closeness. "Well, I'm hoping you could help me. Maybe fifteen minutes to an hour, not more. I want to give it a try before telling Narissa anything."

Takashi's lips pressed into a thin line. "I don't know. I don't want to cause you any unnecessary stress, especially after the grueling day you had today."

She placed her real hand on his arm, looking up at him with big blue eyes. "Please."

He wanted to say no. He wanted to look at this logically and find a way to convince her to give this a rest and test the new theory tomorrow. But those eyes made him say, "Okay. Just a few minutes, though."

She smiled wide and went up on her toes, pecking him on the cheek and sending a rush of elation through him. "Thank you. We can set up on the balcony, and eat and work at the same time. The ocean is really pretty, especially with the sun setting soon."

Watch the sun set with her? Cheesy romantic kind of situation, but he wasn't going to say no. Takashi nodded. "Deal."

The two piled food onto their plates, Takashi noting how she still favored her real side, and she led them outside. The warm ocean stained air slammed them the moment they opened the sliding door, sticking on the lungs.

Mercedes sat down on one of the chairs and Takashi pulled up the other, right beside her. He watched her lick her lips, teasing him just a bit more, before taking a deep breath and nodding to him.

Takashi smiled. "Eat a bit first."

"It would be better to give this a shot for a few minutes and then for me to eat," she advised. "I'd be more likely to throw up if I ate first."

Takashi didn't want that, so he agreed to hold off eating as well so as not to be rude. He first reached out for her real hand, holding it with his. He wanted to get her used to his touch so she knew what to expect. It also allowed him to hold her hand without him pushing too many more boundaries that would go too far for the night. He was pressing his luck as it was. She smiled at him, appreciative of the gesture.

When he determined she had enough time, and was satisfied with the length of time he'd gotten to hold her hand unchallenged, he reached for her cybernetic. "If it gets to be too much, tell me immediately. If you can't put it into words, squeeze my hand."

She nodded to acknowledge, and took a deep breath to prepare herself. Takashi wrapped his hand around her artificial arm and applied a generous amount of pressure. He didn't want to harm her, but knew he couldn't keep the pressure light.

Mercedes gasped, her eyes going wide and dilating. Her breath labored, even though he hadn't increased the pressure, and it concerned him. Just when he thought she may pass out, she squeezed his hand and he reacted, pulling away as quickly as possible.

She took several breaths and her eyes focused after a moment. "Okay, try again."

Takashi did as she asked, and she reacted in the same way as before. After a few moments, she asked him to ease up so she could take a break. This repeated five more times before the two took a break and ate dinner. He wasn't sure how much this was helping her, and he didn't particularly enjoy causing her discomfort, but Mercedes said it was helping, so he had to take her word for it.

While the pair ate, they chatted, joked, and laughed. He told her of his day at the seminar, what he'd learned from other attendees on marketing and auction house strategies. Some were great, while others were so

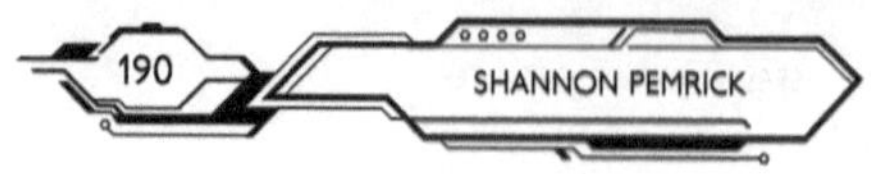

embarrassingly bad he couldn't see how someone could think they were smart choices. As a businesswoman herself, Mercedes gave input of her own, some points he hadn't thought of.

After dinner and chatting, and letting her rest a bit to ensure she didn't lose her stomach, the pair went back to testing. Mercedes had the same reactions as before, but as each test passed, Takashi noticed she was able to handle the touch longer. *Maybe she was right about this.*

Thirty minutes passed before the two agreed to call it for the night. Their hanging out tonight wasn't supposed to be just testing her arm.

Mercedes went into the hotel room to message Narissa about their unofficial testing, and the conclusion they came to. Shock. Her body's reaction to the changes was shock.

Takashi cleaned up their meal. It didn't take him long, and by the time he finished, Mercedes stood out on the balcony again, gazing out at the ocean and setting sun. He came up behind her, slipping his arms around and pulling her into him. Her breath hitched, but she didn't protest. He was pushing his luck again, but he couldn't help it.

He pressed his face into her hair, inhaling her intoxicating perfume. "Is this okay?"

To his delight, Mercedes leaned back into him, her body molding perfectly with his. "Yeah."

The two of them stood like this, watching the sun set, though Takashi's mind only centered on Mercedes. Her scent—her body pressed up against him—it all overwhelmed him, driving him crazy.

He wanted to explore—hear all the wonderful sounds

he could make her create. A throbbing need pulsed in his groin. But as much as he wanted it, he had to wait a little longer. He couldn't screw this up. Even with her acting okay with his actions today, he needed to stay focused, make sure he was pushing the right boundaries and then talk to her. But he also knew he couldn't wait too long. *I'll get through tonight and then come up with a plan for tomorrow.*

When the sun became a mere sliver on the horizon, and he was sure he'd struggled to keep himself in check anymore, he spoke quietly to her. "So, how about that movie?"

She sighed. "I guess we could go watch it now."

"We don't have to. We could stay here, or do something else."

She turned to face him, a twinkle in her eye. "No, you need to see the cheesiness of this movie."

Mercedes grabbed him by the hand and pulled him into the hotel room. He willingly followed, admittedly enjoying the view. She had him sit down on the couch while she set up the movie.

She had to hook up an old laptop to the TV system, and did so with ease, impressing him. *She must do it a lot to get it done without any sort of hassle.* Though, as he thought about it, it made sense. Mercedes prided herself on her knowledge of old tech. It went right alongside of her pride in old car knowledge.

She plopped down next to him when she finished her setup and started the movie.

The credits rolled, and Takashi wasn't sure what he had just watched. Mercedes told him it'd be stupid and over the top, but that really didn't cut it in his mind. Mercedes, of course, laughed through most of the movie. He wasn't sure if it was because she found the cheesiness funny, or his reaction to it all. *Knowing her, both.*

Takashi looked down at her as she rested her head on his shoulder. Mercedes showed to be feeling the effects of her day halfway into the movie, but pushed through.

"Mercy, I should get going so you can sleep." He desperately wished to stay with her, but knew it would be best to head back to his hotel.

"Do you have to go?" she mumbled.

His mind buzzed, but he pushed it away. "Well, no. If you want me to stay, I'll stay."

She remained quiet for a moment, and then sucked in a tight breath as she sat up. "No, I should let you go."

He couldn't deny he was disappointed, but if she didn't want him to stay, he wasn't going to push it. Takashi helped her off the couch, her weariness now far more apparent, and offered to bring her to bed, but she insisted seeing him off, at least to the door.

He now stood in the doorway, reluctant to leave her. "I'll see you tomorrow?"

She smiled. "I hope so."

He understood. This testing took more out of her than she originally thought it would. He didn't want her to push herself in order to fit both testing and spending time with him into her scheduling.

Takashi looked out into the hall and turned back to face her, only for his lips to meet hers. The warmth of her mouth flooded heat through him.

She pulled away and gave him a demure smile. "Goodnight, Takashi."

He couldn't tell if she'd done it on purpose, or on accident and ran with it, but he didn't care. He wanted another. Two in one night made him crave her all that much more. Knowing he'd be pushing his luck, he backed away, a grin on his lips. "Goodnight, Mercy."

Her eyes lingered on his for a moment longer, and then she shut the door. He continued to back away down the hall before spinning on his heels, a new energy to his steps. He hoped tomorrow would be just as promising.

Text flew across the phone screen as Mercedes finished up her conversation with her father while she sat in a chair in Narissa's office. The discussion and testing she'd done with Takashi last night had been a complete game changer. Narissa wanted all the details of their unofficial testing, and details on her night as a whole—*no surprise there*—and determined they'd have to tackle their testing differently. Narissa wasn't sure if this was going to be the way for everyone who went this route with the upgrade, but the more she tested with volunteers, the more data she'd have to be sure.

This change did mean there'd be a possibility Mercedes would have to extend her stay in L.A. Her father understood and supported her, and she knew things would be okay there with them, even with the ongoing investigation. It was Takashi she had to factor in. Mercedes knew he was only down for a few weeks, and planned to go back to San Francisco to be with family during that time back. Even though she'd yet to make a decision where she stood, she did want to spend time with him. It'd be difficult to get that in if he went back to San Francisco and she stayed here. It wasn't like she could ask him to stay. *I need to sort things out and give him a real answer.* But how was she supposed to figure it all out?

The memory of him kissing her in the kitchen, and then her kissing him goodbye last night came to her. His taste—the feel of his evening stubble scraping her skin—his strong smell. Her body warmed and she tried to bury it. The first was him just messing with her. The second… had been an accident. She'd only intended to kiss him on the cheek, like he'd done to her after lunch the prior afternoon. But he turned back to face her, and…

"Mercedes," Narissa's voice slipped into her head. "Your face is getting red."

Mercedes snapped out her trance and looked at her tech-savvy friend sitting at her desk going over notes. Mercedes hadn't told Narissa much about her dinner date. Not even about him holding her on the balcony. She really didn't want any teasing. All of this was hard for her to deal with as it was. She still struggled to wrap her head around some guy actually wanting her, cybernetics and all.

A wide grin spread across Narissa's lips. "What are you thinking about?"

She tried to play everything off. "My dad made me think of something embarrassing that happened when I was a teen."

Narissa's brow rose. "Uh huh, right. The last text you

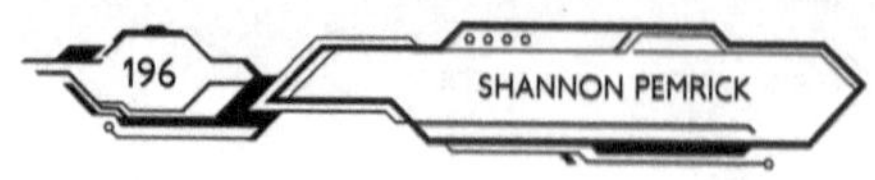

received was over five minutes ago. That's one heck of a delayed response time."

Shit. Narissa's intelligence far exceeded hers. She couldn't think up well-crafted lies on the fly that would outfox that brain. Her friend pulled herself up from the chair and made her way over to Mercedes, her movements fluid as always. Sexy with brains and a personality—Ajax really knew how to pick a woman to follow around like a puppy.

He'd been here this morning, though not because he busted his arm again… surprisingly. He dropped off breakfast for the two of them and chatted, going into deep analytical conversation with Narissa on occasions. Mercedes stayed out of those and watched the two interact instead. Ajax zeroed in on their cybernetic genius and followed her every movement. It made her wonder when he'd make his move on Narissa.

Narissa pulled a chair up and sat down in front of Mercedes. "Spill it. You've avoided telling me what happened last night and now you're actively lying to me. I want details."

Mercedes threw her head back. "Why can't you leave this alone?"

Narissa grinned. "Because I'm your friend, and I'm nosey. So tell me, what happened last night?"

"Chinese for dinner, testing, and we watched a corny movie."

Narissa's eyes narrowed. "C'mon, Cede. That wouldn't get you all embarrassed. What happened between all that?"

Mercedes sighed and leaned back. She wasn't going to get away from this. "After we did the spontaneous testing with my arm, we watched the sun set on the balcony."

A wide grin spread across her friend's lips. "He held you, didn't he?"

Mercedes' face flushed and she looked away as she nodded, unable to keep eye contact with her friend. "No prompting needed. It was… nice."

Narissa leaned forward. "What else happened? That's tame. You wouldn't avoid that answer unless something else happened."

A tight exhale escaped Mercedes' lips. *She would push this.* "There… there may have been some kissing…"

Narissa threw her hands in the air. "Hallelujah, there is a god!"

Mercedes couldn't stop the chuckle from her throat. Narissa's mother was a rather religious woman, whereas Narissa had her own opinions on the matter. It made such outbursts so funny.

Narissa calmed down. "Now, tell me more."

Mercedes' gaze fell on the desk and she rubbed her arm, sending all sort of signals to her brain. *Shit, forgot.* "It wasn't anything major. I was trying to keep the box of crab rangoons to myself and he kissed me quickly to get me to stop long enough to take them from me."

"Did he now?" Narissa leaned in closer. "And what did you do about it?"

She continued to avert her gaze. "I… was too shocked to do anything. I didn't expect him to anything like that."

"So, you didn't kick him out, and I have a feeling that wasn't the only kiss thrown around, either."

"I… went to kiss him goodbye on the cheek and he turned to look at me, and…" Mercedes didn't want to say it, but Narissa's eyes showed she was going to have to. "And I accidentally kissed him for real."

Narissa's eyes lit up and she slapped Mercedes on the leg and stood up. "Look at you taking charge!"

"I just said it was an accident. A pleasant one, but that doesn't change that it was still an accident."

Narissa looked back at her as she walked away. "And? You still took charge and made a move, Cede. Your love life is the only thing you don't take by the horns enough. You wait for 'Mister Right' and run away when he shows up bearing gifts."

Her friend wasn't wrong, but Narissa had flawed thinking too. Mercedes tilted her head down as she stared at her friend. "Like you're one to talk."

Narissa sat down in her chair. "I'm not ready to go back out there yet, Cede. I thought I had a happy marriage. I thought everything was going great. You know exactly how messy that ended." She glanced at her computer. "I'd rather crunch data, install cybernetics, and help people than try to see if someone else will do that to me again or not. I'm just… not ready."

Mercedes frowned. She knew that divorce had shaken her friend's confidence, but she didn't realize it had shaken her that badly. She never met Narissa's ex—Mercedes came along after the divorce happened—but from what she knew, he sounded like a great guy to start, and seemed that way up until all the secrets were discovered. Then everything went downhill quickly. *Ajax will have a better chance at seducing a non-interactive NPC at this rate if Narissa doesn't let go.* It wasn't fair to assume everyone would turn out like her ex, but that fear set deep, and really, Mercedes couldn't blame her friend. *She nearly lost her life in all that mess.*

Mercedes' phone started to ring and Tasha spoke, "Miss Mercedes, Takashi is calling you."

"Of course he is," Narissa teased, her eyebrow rising up and down. "He wants that goodbye to turn into a hello." Mercedes flipped her friend the middle finger and Narissa chuckled, turning back to her computer work. "Save that for him."

Mercedes rolled her eyes. "Go ahead and answer his call, Tasha."

"On speaker!"

The phone stopped ringing and Takashi's voice rang through on speaking. "Hello?"

"Hey, Takashi," Mercedes said.

"I'm on speaker again. Are you not feeling well?"

Mercedes laughed. "No, that was Narissa's doing. She actually got Tasha to answer on speaker without me having to approve or deny."

"My apologies, Miss Mercedes," Tasha said. "I assumed, due to the number of times you spoke to Takashi on speaker in the last few days, Narissa was reminding me."

All three friends laughed and Mercedes spoke to her assistant. "It's okay, Tasha. I don't mind that he's on speaker."

"Very well."

"So, I have to make this quick," Takashi said. "Our lunch is short as they need to cram in a few extra things before the seminar ends today, but I wanted to ask you something. Since today is the last day, there is a dinner party tonight, and I found out I can bring a guest. I was wondering if you'd be interested in going."

Narissa's eyes snapped to Mercedes and she nodded, mouthing, "Say yes. I've got you."

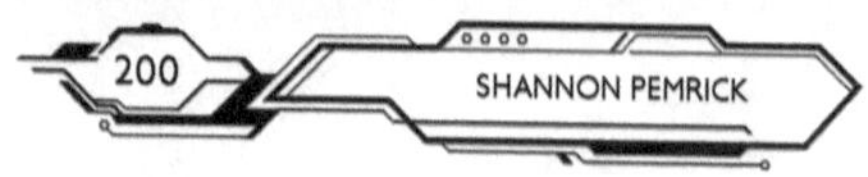

Mercedes smiled. "Yeah, I'd love to."

"Great."

"I'll make sure she looks nice and sexy for you," Narissa shouted out. "You won't be able to keep your eyes or *hands* off her when I'm done."

Mercedes' mouth dropped. She couldn't believe her friend right now.

To her surprise, Takashi chuckled. "You won't have to do anything, then."

Narissa grinned and Mercedes was speechless.

"I'll pick you up at six thirty, Mercedes. I have to go now."

Before she could formulate a response, the call ended. Mercedes found Narissa staring at her, her face resting on the palm of her hand. "You two are adorable."

She needed to get back at her friend. She was getting too many legs up on her today with all these comments. A wicked grin spread across Mercedes' lips when a thought came to her. "Coming from the woman who likes to sit on the lap of a particular hunky patient and then deny everything when caught in the act."

Her friend's cheeks reddened and she sat up straight. "Because it's the truth."

"Uh huh, sure." Mercedes stood up. "Or maybe you just don't want to admit you are ready to move on."

Narissa crossed her arms. "Keep that craziness up and I won't take you shopping."

She shrugged. "Fine, I have my own money. And I'm capable of shopping for something nice all on my own."

A long sigh came from Narissa, and then she stood up. "Brat. You're not going without me. No way am I going to not help you with your big date."

Mercedes' eyes darted away. "I wouldn't call it a date. There will be other people there that we'll have to interact with."

"Doesn't mean it won't be just the two of you later." Narissa winked. "Unless, of course, you're into that kind of thing."

Mercedes laughed. "Now you sound like Shira."

She bowed. "Pleased to be of service."

The two laughed some more and then left to shop.

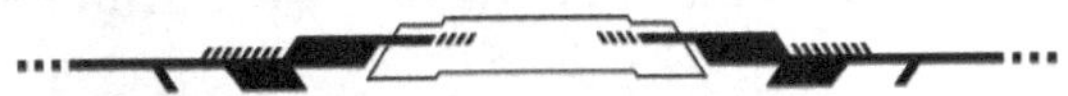

Narissa fussed with Mercedes' golden hair, curled and waved, while Mercedes applied her lipstick. She had to get her friend to stop when her makeup application ended, and then she fussed with her tight, sapphire blue, low-cut cowl cocktail dress Narissa bought for her. The back had a criss-cross back comprised of several strips, and the dress was overall a little short for what she'd think best for a dinner party, but Narissa insisted it was perfect for the occasion.

Mercedes wiggled her toes in her heeled sandals and then faced her gorgeous friend. "I think I'm ready."

A large grin spread across Narissa's lips. "To go to a party or seduce your date?"

Mercedes smacked her friend on the arm. "Stop it."

Narissa chuckled and left the bedroom. Mercedes looked herself over in the mirror one last time and then followed.

"Miss Mercedes," Tasha said from the room infrastructure. "Takashi sent you a text message. He will be here in five minutes."

"Thank you, Tasha." Mercedes took a deep breath. "Here we go."

Narissa handed her a clutch and her phone. Tasha auto transferred to the phone and the two left the hotel room. Mercedes tapped her fingers on her clutch as they stood in the elevator. She didn't know how Takashi would react to seeing her. As much as she liked the dress, a part of her thought it was more club material, rather than dinner party wear.

Narissa nudged her. "Calm down. He's going to love what he sees."

"Yeah… maybe…"

Her friend sighed but didn't push. It'd been a long day for them. Between shopping, dealing with the arm testing, and trying to determine if this move with Takashi was the right one, Mercedes' nerves were all out of whack. Nothing Narissa could say would help her calm down.

The box came to a halt and the two headed for the large entrance doors. The lobby was busy, and Mercedes found herself hyper aware of any attention she received—some positive, some not so much. Nothing she hadn't dealt with before.

Mercedes took a deep, calming breath before leaving the building, the hot and humid California night air slamming into her. *Good thing I know how to use hairspray.* A white 2106 Nissan Altima sat out front, Takashi leaning against the front fender, his nose in his phone as he texted someone. He had one of his hands shoved in one of his pant suit pockets, oblivious of their approach. Mercedes visually assessed him. He looked good in a suit and tie. A primal want simmered in her. *He'd look good without it, too.*

"I hope you're not texting some other woman," Narissa called out. "You got a good one right in front of you."

Takashi's head snapped up and the moment he laid eyes on Mercedes his jaw dropped. *Well... he likes it... I think...*

Takashi composed himself. "You look amazing, Mercedes."

Mercedes looked herself over. "Not too over the top?"

"Definitely not."

She smiled and then squeaked when Narissa latched onto her. "I made her irresistible, didn't I?"

Takashi grinned. "I told you, you didn't have to do anything to get her to that point."

Mercedes' face warmed. She knew he liked her, but hearing him be so open about his opinion of her in front of others, it was a new feeling for her. Not even her last boyfriend had been this way. *Is Narissa right? Were all of them the problem and not me? Or is Takashi just an oddity?*

Takashi flicked his wrist, and a bouquet of white roses with red tips appeared in his hands. Takashi held them out to her, a smile on his face.

Narissa let her go, and Mercedes accepted the gift. "Thank you, Takashi. They're beautiful."

He smiled, but didn't say anything, his eyes never leaving her.

More white and red. He hasn't given up yet. She should give him an answer, but the right one lodged in her throat. She needed more time.

Mercedes smelled the flowers and a coy smile spread across her lips. "You're going to have to teach me one of these days how you manage to do this."

Takashi's smile spread into a grin, his eyes smoldering. "One of these days, I might." He held out his hand to her. "We should get going. We don't want to be late."

Narissa took the roses from Mercedes. "I'll get these into a vase in your hotel room." She winked. "I'll fetch you two some water, too, if you'd like."

Mercedes smacked her in the arm. "Stop it."

Narissa laughed and then excused herself to allow the pair to leave. Takashi took her by the hand and opened the passenger door for her. She smiled and then slipped in. He shut the door and jogged to the driver's side.

"Good evening, Mercedes," Ochi's computer voice said from the car dash.

"Hello, Ochi."

"I am pleased you could make it. Your acceptance of Takashi's invitation made him quite happy."

She smiled. "I'm glad he invited me. I just hope I'm dressed properly for this."

"I'm sure you look perfect."

Takashi hopped into the car. The action caused the necklace he always wore to move from under his tie. She shouldn't have been surprised he still wore it, as he did say he rarely took it off, but there was a part of her that had thought he would have for such a formal event. *I wonder if there's more significance to it than I once thought.* "Ochi, we're all set to leave."

"Please buckle up, you two. We will arrive at our destination in seventeen minutes."

The two snapped their seatbelts into place and the car pulled away, merging into the busy evening traffic.

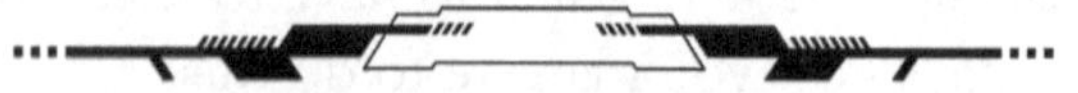

Loud chatter filled the large room. Takashi conversed with a young woman by the name of Amy, who also specialized in auction house trade in Lusara Fates, and discussed the upcoming changes to business coming in the new expansion. The expansion would include improved store fronts that could now be manned by NPCs with custom dialogue, personalities, and reactions. Many, including Takashi, were quite excited for this change, but several were a little less enthusiastic.

A tall man with a physique similar to Ajax approached, though his dark eyes pinned on Mercedes, who stood next to Takashi, listening in on his and Amy's conversation. *Here we go again.* He did his best not to react as the newcomer pushed his way in between Mercedes and another man by the name of Jack, who had been contributing to the conversation every now and then. This had been a common occurrence all night.

The gentleman extended his hand to Mercedes. "Name's Aaron."

Mercedes responded with a pleasant smile and shook his hand, though Takashi noticed the well-hidden twitch of her eye. He worried all this hand shaking was causing her too much trouble with that prosthetic. "Mercedes Gail."

A muscle in Aaron's neck twitched. *Strike one.* To not give a full name in an introduction for a setting such as this, even if he were trying to impress Mercedes on a non-business level, was the most basic mistake.

Aaron was determined to try again. "Can you believe all this talk about the new NPC change? It's not a good thing to get excited over."

Mercedes sipped some wine. "I disagree. This change has a great deal of potential."

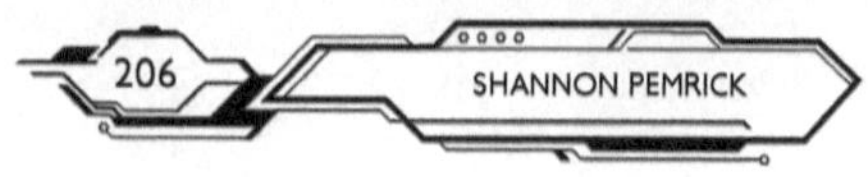

Strike two.

Aaron frowned. "It removes the human element to our business, and will ruin what we have going on now."

Mercedes tucked her hand under her elbow and swirled her wine. The way she held herself told Takashi she was going to invest in the conversation, but not in this man. "I can tell you're not an auction-based businessman, so I'm going to assume you focus on the current style of business fronts. Your way of doing business won't change. This new NPC change will, however, allow for people like Amy and Takashi here to not only focus on auctions, but have a storefront for players to interact with directly, instead of having to visit an auction house. It adds an element to the game that is missing, but it doesn't take away from what you do already."

Aaron's eyes narrowed. Takashi liked that he wasn't getting his way. Aaron assumed Mercedes was eye candy and easy to impress with a few words, but he was going to find out just how intelligent she really was. And how much she didn't like arrogant pricks.

"You can't expect an NPC to act like a human," Aaron argued.

Mercedes smiled. "You're right, and no one is. These NPCs will be NPCs. They will never be PCs. But by having unique NPCs manning a store, it improves PCs interactions with your business and increases the chance of their return. It also benefits someone like yourself if you need to step away from your store front for any amount of time. You are ensured your customer won't receive a static, sub-quality experience in your absence."

Takashi was impressed. He knew she could hold her own around someone like this, but he never expected this kind of insight from her. It also proved valuable for those in this business, as she was technically a potential customer. He could tell Amy and Jack were also taking mental note of her responses.

Aaron's mood soured more, amusing Takashi. He liked that this arrogant businessman wasn't getting his way. "You act like you know the statistics for this supposed win."

"Ochi," Mercedes said, not taking her eyes off Aaron.

"Yes, Mercedes?" Ochi responded from Takashi's pocket.

"Can you tell me the result of the player satisfaction rate increase I had you run ten minutes ago?"

Takashi's brow furrowed. "How did I miss that request?"

She glance him an alluring sidelong glance with a grin. "You were busy talking with Amy."

Cheeky. He loved it, too.

"Without knowing all data factors, my analysis indicates that there will be a minimum of a forty percent increase in player satisfaction with this new non-player character store front change. Did you finish your own analysis?"

"Yes. I came up with a thirty-eight percent increase, give or take five percent error threshold."

Jack adjusted his glasses. "You did all of that calculating yourself in your head?"

Mercedes smiled at him. "Of course. What do you think I was doing while the three of you were talking? Standing here looking pretty?"

Takashi and Amy laughed. Jack looked amused by her words, but also embarrassed for asking. Aaron, on the other hand, didn't seem to find any amusement in the conversation.

Mercedes and he went back and forth some more. Takashi tried to continue his conversation with Amy, but Aaron's increasing irritation tempted Takashi to step in. *No, this is Mercedes. She can handle it.* She was a manager in a male dominated field and knew how Lusara Fates worked. She also proved she was more than capable of handling this guy.

Amy leaned in and kept her voice low. "Your date is handling that guy really well."

"With her line of work, I'm sure she's dealt with worse," Takashi said, finding himself looking at Mercedes again.

He thought Narissa had been joking when she claimed to plan on making Mercedes somehow even more irresistible than she already was. Takashi didn't think it were possible for Mercedes to be any more distracting. He was proven quite wrong when she met him at the car. The way her dress clung to her frame—and the short style—teased his imagination; he found a primal desire demanding he forget about the party and escort her back up to her hotel room and lock the door behind them.

Watching her now go toe-to-toe with this business entrepreneur in the same sexy dress, that need returned.

Amy turned to Mercedes. "Excuse me, Mercedes?"

Mercedes looked her way. "Yes?"

Takashi wondered what this woman was up to. Aaron did not look pleased to be interrupted, but neither woman appeared to care.

"Takashi here mentioned you're a businesswoman

yourself, though not in the gaming industry. May I know what you do for a living?"

Mercedes smiled in a way that gave Takashi the impression that she understood something he was missing. "I'm a manager at my father's car restoration shop. It's a family business."

"Fascinating. So you're probably well-versed in industry changes, yes?"

Takashi now understood. She was aiming to give Mercedes a credibility boost, even if her field wasn't the same.

Mercedes nodded. "You have to be. The technology in vehicles changes at a rapid pace. On top of that, we have to be flexible due to the popularity of cars older than sixty years."

Jack spoke up. "Since it's a family business, as you claim, how long have you been involved in the industry?"

Mercedes laughed. "When other girls were playing with dolls, I was learning the differences between a socket wrench and a hex wrench."

"And how much of the game industry do you know?" Aaron asked.

Mercedes smirked. "When other girls were setting up for tea parties, I was getting frustrated at the dog in Duck Hunt for making fun of me."

Jack's brow rose. "That's quite the retro game."

Mercedes smiled at him. "My mother taught me to appreciate where games came from. I've got a vast collection of systems and games ranging from the 1980's to the most recent console systems that are still hanging on, even with the increased popularity of virtual reality."

Jack's interest in Mercedes grew. Takashi had seen this

happen several times throughout the night. He'd seen very few men deterred by her cybernetic, and most found greater interest in her when they learned more of her professional background, as well as her gaming hobby and contributions to the gaming community. He wasn't sure where she got the idea that her cybernetic put her at odds in the dating scene. He did know, though, she made it clear she was with him, and that made him feel like the luckiest man here.

The conversation continued, Aaron eventually backing out and going off somewhere else. When an hour passed, the party concluded.

Takashi rested his hand on Mercedes' lower back as the pair said their farewells and left. He found himself doing this several times during the party, but she never minded. One thing Narissa had right, he struggled to keep his hands off Mercedes tonight. Every time the space between them increased, he yearned to bring her back to him. He enjoyed the contact—the subtle claim she allowed.

His rental car pulled up in front of the hotel and he opened the passenger door for Mercedes. She smiled her thanks and slipped in. He swallowed hard when the movement gave him a brief glance down her dress, and quickly shut the door. *This dress will be the death of me.*

He got himself situated in the driver's seat and had Ochi drive them back to Mercedes' hotel. As they merged into the late evening traffic, Takashi reached out and grasped Mercedes' hand, lacing his hands in with hers. She looked at him and smiled. The expression elated him, as did her acceptance. "Did you enjoy yourself?"

She nodded. "I did. The dinner was nice, and most

of the conversation was pleasant. I learned a lot, too. I didn't realize there were so many different ways to do business in the game."

A wide grin spread across his face. "Considering changing professions?"

She laughed. "No, I'm happy doing what I do."

"Plenty of people were impressed with your line of work. Made you quite popular."

"I'm used to that kind of attention. People for some reason find it fascinating women like that field of work, even in this day and age. It was the other kind of attention that threw me." She grinned, her eyes glowing. "But, unfortunately for them, I'm happy with the date I picked for the party."

He couldn't help but smile back. "I'm glad."

"So, this was the last day of the seminar. Did you get out of it what you wanted?"

"As boring as some of the topics were, I did, and then some."

She smiled. "That's great."

He noticed her smile didn't reach the full width of her face, which wasn't like her when she was happy. "What's wrong?"

"Nothing is wrong." She pursed her lips. "Just thinking. What are your plans now that the seminar is over? You hopping on a plane tomorrow to see your family?"

He studied her before speaking. "Well, I thought I'd stay a few more days. Spend more time with you and help you out with testing."

She chewed her lower lip and her gaze lowered. Normally that'd be a hard tease for him, but he didn't get a good feeling from it this time. "Narissa thought a week's

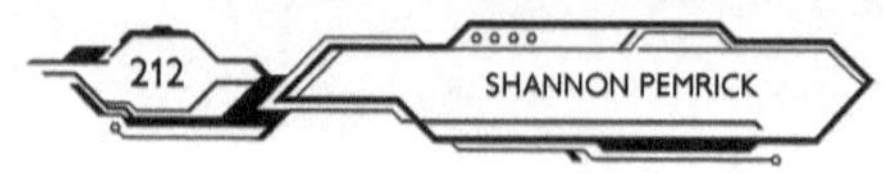

worth of testing would be good to start with this. But as of this morning we're thinking I'll have to stay for another week, if not more."

That was the reason for her distress? "Mercedes, I'll stay as long as needed. If you need to stay here for three weeks, then I'll help you."

Her brow creased. "But your family deserves to have you home. They don't get to see you often."

Takashi squeezed her hand. "Trust me, it'll be fine. They'll understand, and that doesn't mean I won't have time to see them. I haven't booked my return ticket, and I can work just about anywhere."

"But what about your cat?"

"My neighbor is watching her, and told me I can take an extended time away if needed. I just have to let her know in advance, and wire some money to her."

Mercedes sucked in a tight breath, her eyes showing the conflict raging in her. "Okay, if that's what you want."

He didn't understand. Did she not want him to stay?

"I just don't want to get in the way of your life."

What? She thought she was an issue for him? Why would she think that? Mercedes was everything to him at this point. He didn't want to ever have to say goodbye to her.

Wait. Emi said something about her self-esteem. Was this all related to why she didn't react the way he'd hoped to the flowers? He'd given her another bouquet to gauge her reaction again, and nothing had changed since the first time.

Takashi took a quick breath, eyes flicking to their entwined fingers. He needed to put his question into words, and this was as good a time as any. "Mercy, can we talk about something?"

Her brow furrowed. "Uh, sure."

He realized he should have assured her she wasn't getting in the way, but this conversation would clear that up. "I've tried to make this clear without pushing too many boundaries too quickly, but there's been a lot of dodging. So I need this to be out there for us to just talk about now."

Takashi squeezed her hand and then looked into her eyes. "I want there to be an 'us.' If you don't, that's fine. We can stay friends and we'll forget I brought this up. But I don't want to continue to wonder where things stand, and guess what is and isn't okay for boundaries."

Mercedes' gaze dropped, her teeth catching her bottom lips. He would have gotten a bit nervous, had it not been for the fact she wasn't trying to pull away from him. "I… I do want there to be an us. I…" She sighed and leaned back in her seat. "I've just been having a hard time telling you. With everything I've had to deal with, it just hasn't felt real. Like... it's some dream I'm going to wake up from and none of this ever happened."

Takashi tugged her closer, and she complied, her brow furrowed. He reached out, cupping her cheek, and pulled her in until her lips crashed into his. They both inhaled in unison, and he didn't pull away until he saw white.

Her eyes fluttered and her mouth remained partially open as she processed everything. He grinned. "Did that feel like a dream?"

It took her a moment to respond. "Felt pretty real to me." A smile spread across her tempting lips. "But if this is a dream, I don't want to wake up."

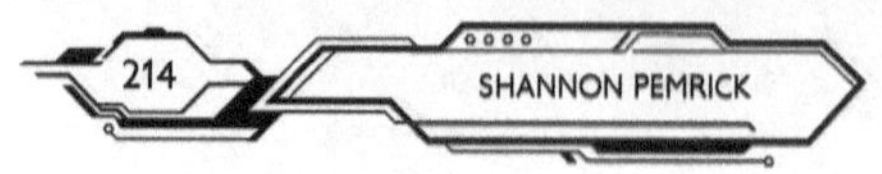

"Me either." Takashi went to lean in for another kiss, but Ochi interrupted, frustrating him.

"Takashi, if you'd like me to 'accidentally' miss the turn for the hotel, you may want to tell me now, else we will be there in less than a minute."

Takashi sighed as Mercedes laughed. "No, continue the course."

He would have liked to say something else, but based on the most recent conversation, and how hard it was for him to get this to be official, he was better off not pushing his luck right now.

The car pulled up to her hotel and he let go of Mercedes' hand to exit. Miss Independent didn't wait for him to open her door. She'd done this when they arrived for the party, too. He wished she'd allow him to dote on her for more than a few minutes.

Takashi managed to get around the vehicle in time to offer his hand to help her out, which she was more than willing to accept.

"Thank you for inviting me to the party," Mercedes said, smiling at him. "I really did enjoy myself."

His hand still holding hers, he smiled back. "I'm glad you accepted. I know short notice isn't ideal, especially since you've been testing all day, but—"

She placed a finger on his lips and hushed him. "Stop. If it was an issue, I would have told you. You know that."

Takashi pulled her finger off and pressed her hand against his chest. "I'll take your word for it."

She glanced back at the hotel entrance. "It's late. I shouldn't hold you up anymore."

Disappointment pricked in him, but if she didn't want

to invite him to stay, he wasn't going to force it on her. *Small steps with her.* He was just glad he'd gotten this far.

Takashi reached out and cupped her cheek, making her look at him. Her blue eyes widened and her mouth opened, but he captured her lips with his before she had the chance to speak. She sucked in a deep breath, and didn't push him away.

Her tantalizing scent and taste numbed all his other senses. He drank it up while resisting the urge to deepen the kiss and push this farther.

Takashi pulled away, Mercedes' eyes fluttering back open. He noted her flushed face and relaxed posture. He grinned, pleased. "Goodnight, Mercedes."

He headed for the car, and Mercedes called out to him. "Takashi, wait." He stopped and looked back, interested in what she had to say. He found her grinning. "Treasure hunt, I pick. I'll give you one hour to meet me in-game."

He had to admit, he was a bit disappointed she specified in-game, but he liked that this date wasn't exactly over yet. He smiled. "Meeting location, my shop."

Her grin remained as she turned away and headed into the hotel. Takashi watched her leave, her hips swaying back and forth, hypnotizing him. The moment she left his sight, he came back to his senses and hopped into the car. He needed to get back to his hotel ASAP.

CHAPTER 13

An arrow whizzed past Takashi's head, sinking deep in the target's chest—a jungle orc, gray-skinned beastly humanoids with sloping foreheads and large tusks. They weren't particularly smart creatures, but they were brutes, and Takashi had riled up a whole tribe of them by accident.

Their treasure hunt had gone smoothly until that point, unless Takashi counted the number of times he had to refocus himself on the task instead of on Mercedes. Even behind an avatar that didn't have many similarities to her, he couldn't help but be distracted. He saw past the rendered façade; the way she narrowed her eyes as she thought hard, the broad smile that reached her ears when she smiled, the way her stride made her hips sway just right. This woman would be the death of him. *If these orcs aren't first.*

An arrow from the enemy orc landed in a tree next to him with a *thunk*, telling Takashi he needed to focus. He conjured up a fireball and lobbed it in the direction of a few clustered enemies. Several jumped out of the way, reducing the damage they took, but a handful weren't so lucky. They screamed and roared as the smell of their burning flesh filled the air.

Three more arrows came at him—two he managed to dodge, the other sinking deep into his shoulder. He clenched his teeth as he stumbled. The one downside to this advanced virtual reality was the pain simulation. The game didn't simulate damage to the full extent, making raiding and PvP doable, but that didn't mean it didn't hurt.

Three battle-weary orcs nearby rushed for him, but Mercedes had his back. A volley of arrows rained down on the orcs, taking two out, and her precious pet, Lo'quena, lunged for a killing blow on the last. The assault gave him a chance to move back and unleash a crackle of lightning. The electric charge zapped another three clustered orcs, sparks arcing between the creatures. It didn't do as much damage as he hoped, but all three hunched over, temporarily paralyzed.

Mercedes took the opportunity to pierce them with more arrows until they collapsed into a heap of flesh. There were only a few enemies remaining, but Takashi was running low on mana, the energy source sorcerers used to cast spells, and he suspected Mercedes may be running low on arrows, though he didn't know how prepared she'd come. On raid days, she'd been known to fill several quivers and bags so she wouldn't have to port in and out of the raid to restock.

"Takashi, I'm going to have Lo'quena corral them for you," Mercedes called out as she let another arrow fly. "Please don't hit her."

He nodded and gathered up the last of his mana reserve for a final fire attack while the glowing feline beast ran on Mercedes' order. The rare elemental-infused creature was Mercedes' newest pet as of approximately thirty minutes ago. The NPC spawned only three times a week in this jungle, and since there was a treasure hunt challenge active here this time around, Takashi suggested they check the spawn locations while they were here. To her luck, Lo'quena prowled near one of two spawn points, and now Mercedes had a new companion, opting to keep the NPC name for novelty's sake.

Lo'quena zig-zagged around, taking quick strikes with claws and electrical shocks to draw the attention of all remaining orcs. As hoped, all but the archers closed in on the pet. Mercedes called the elemental beast back as she unleashed a volley of arrows on the cluster, and Takashi took that as a cue to release his final attack. Fire flew into the sky and then fell from the heavens in a large radius, incinerating the enemy.

The two remaining orcs roared in rage and knocked arrows, but weren't as fast as Mercedes and her pet. She unleashed a flurry of arrows on one, and Lo'quena took out the remaining enemy. Then the jungle grew still. The stench of burning flesh, hair, and plant matter permeated the air.

Mercedes jumped in excitement. "Yahoo! We did it!"

Takashi threw an exhausted fist into the air and then fell back onto the ground. Mercedes gasped and rushed to his side. That last attack had taken the remaining energy from him, and it'd be a few minutes before his mana meter started to recover.

"Are you okay?" she asked as she fussed.

He chuckled and got her to stop. "I'll be fine. I took a bit of damage, but this is from my depleted mana pool. I'm all tapped out."

Her face creased with concern. "Are you sure you're going to be okay? Caster mana withdrawals are a pain."

"Even if I wasn't, it was my fault for walking face-first into that band of orcs."

"Okay, if you say so." She looked to the piles of bodies. "I'm going to search for loot, and retrieve what arrows I can while you rest."

He nodded and she ran off, searching each body that had anything left to them. Takashi suspected she wouldn't find much, since he'd incinerated a good portion of the orcs. It was one of the other aspects of this game people liked. Players liked the realism of the attacks, even if it caused issues from time to time, like fire and loot.

Lo'quena dragged bodies to her master, and Mercedes rifled through their pockets, checking their gear and weapons, too. Thunder rumbled in the distance, concerning him. The jungle terrains were known for their unpredictable weather, and weather conditions did affect players, similarly to how they'd affect people in real life.

Takashi had regained his strength by the time Mercedes returned, a large grin on her face. His brow twisted. "What are you happy about?"

"Your little *accident* led us to a tool needed for this hunt. They had a key that's described in our quest log needed to open a sealed tomb." She leaned in and pecked him on the lips, his heart skipping a beat. "And for that, you deserve a small reward."

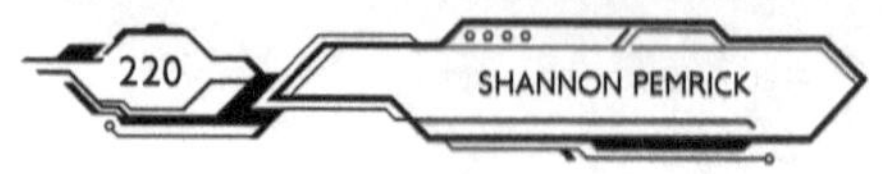

He smirked. "Looks like I need to make those kinds of accidents more often."

Her eyes narrowed as an alluring smile appeared on those irresistible lips of hers and she turned away. "Maybe you do. We still have more of this hunt to go, and I can smell the rain coming, so we shouldn't wait around too long."

Takashi agreed. Getting caught up in the rainstorms in this region wasn't fun. The pair continued on their way, based on the last clue they had been following before the battle. Unfortunately, no more than ten minutes in, the sky opened up on them. Even with the thick canopy above, they found this shower turning into a storm faster than they would have liked. Not even their cloaks saved them from this torrential downpour. They needed shelter.

Mercedes pointed up at some elevated ground, using her free hand to hold her quiver over her head to protect her some from the falling water. "Let's go back to those ruins to get out of this rain. We can figure out what to do next from there."

Takashi nodded and the two rushed to the ancient building. Once there, they shook off their soaked cloaks and shielded themselves when Lo'quena shook the water from her coat. She then went to grooming herself while Takashi and Mercedes tried to figure out what to do.

"These storms are pretty unpredictable," Takashi said. "It's hard to tell whether it'll stop in five minutes or three hours. What would you rather do? I know it's getting late, and you do have testing tomorrow."

"Well, I sorta do," Mercedes said, sitting down somewhere dry. The ruins weren't the best place to stay dry, as the water leaked in many places, but it was better than taking shelter under some tree roots. "With the new testing Narissa is having me do, thanks to the shock theory the two of us figured out, she wants to do three full days of more casual testing. She believes this will reduce the body's shock reaction to the change. I have to keep the neuro-mod active all the time, but I'm able to do whatever I want, even come in to the office late, or not at all. She just wants me to let her know if that's my plan."

"If you're okay with waiting, I guess we could try." Takashi looked out into the jungle, the rain making it hard to see far. "We could always do something else, too. Old raids, achievement runs, a stroll through a big city in the park while the enemy guards hurl spears at us…"

Mercedes burst with laughter, holding her sides. "I think you just described one of Shira's PvP fantasies."

"Yeah? I'm pretty sure that's Jasper's and Zach's too." Takashi grinned. "We also can't forget Ajax. He'd be more than happy to take Narissa as loot from a boss."

Mercedes continued to laugh. Takashi smiled, happy to hear the sound. He pulled out some tinder and wood he'd collected earlier, and started a fire to keep them both warm while they waited the storm out.

Just as he went to light the dry tinder with a spell, an unusual buzzing entered his ear, and then the scenery around them sputtered. Mercedes sat up straight and looked around, her fear evident. The area around them sputtered more, and before they knew it, their avatars glitched and disappeared, leaving their real selves.

The sound of gear clattered on the ground. Mercedes gasped, her eyes snapping to where her right arm should be, only for nothing to be there. *Well, nothing isn't correct.* There was a three- or four-inch nub of what was left of an arm, all scarred up at the bottom where the skin had been forced together and healed. Her bracer and archer's glove she'd worn on that arm lay at her feet where it'd fallen.

The pair exchanged glances, their concern growing. These kind of glitches were rare, but never good.

"We need to leave," Takashi said. "We'll make up for the loss later."

Mercedes swallowed and nodded, her panic barely held back in from the look in her eyes. Takashi activated his game menu and went to log off, to find the option gone. Mercedes' eyes met his, and he could tell she was dealing with the same issue. He jumped into the guild chat channel. "Hey, is anyone else unable to log out?"

"It's a game-wide deal," Zach said. "Some people can't even use abilities. Our match was just canceled because of it."

Takashi watched Mercedes activate her menu with her only arm. "Where is Shira? I see she's offline."

"Yeah, she got off about thirty minutes ago," Jasper said. "Said she wasn't feeling good."

Mercedes sighed with relief. "Oh, good."

"Is there a reason you're concerned?" he asked. "Besides this avatah issue?"

Mercedes chewed her lip and placed her good hand over the nub on her shoulder where her other arm should be. "These glitches are bad for those like us with prosthetics. The game isn't able to simulate an artificial limb, so when we lose our avatars, we also lose the in-game limbs we've gained over our real bodies.

Someone like Shira wouldn't be able to stand or hold herself up well when sitting, since she lost so much of her body on one side."

Sitting would be the least of her worries, with how many cybernetic components she has on that side. Takashi didn't know the full extent to Shira's cybernetics, but had heard enough to make a guess. He'd also heard about a number of the hospital visits Shira had gone through to have real bone and tissue created to reduce the cybernetic count in her body, but such measures took time, and it'd be many years before Shira would have more body than machine on that side.

"Wait, so you're missing an arm right now?" Zach asked.

Mercedes nodded, even though they couldn't see her. "Yeah…"

Takashi's chest tightened. He could see the pain in her eyes. This was not a kind reminder of whatever caused her to lose that limb. *With all this testing with that new prosthetic… how much of it is affecting her mental state?* He never thought to question it. She'd been so adamant and excited to test, he never stopped to think about whether she was covering up her real feelings—ones she could easily forget if no one brought attention to her false limb.

"Mercedes, I didn't upset you with my question, did I?" Zach asked.

"No, you're fine," she replied. Takashi couldn't tell whether she was telling the truth or not. His question was a well-intended and seemingly harmless inquiry, but for someone in her situation, it may not be taken as such. Or it could just be the situation as a whole that was affecting her.

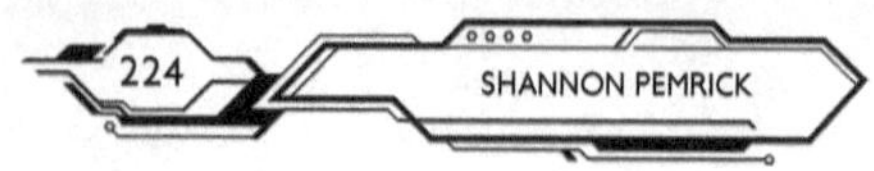

Takashi disconnected from guild chat as he came over to her, placing a hand over the one resting on the nub of her arm. She looked up at him, and he peered back with understanding eyes. Mercedes tried to smile, but it didn't go very far up her face.

"Sorry." Her gaze fell. "I wasn't expecting I'd have to subject you to my condition so soon into our relationship."

His brow creased. "Subject me?" Takashi tucked his finger under her chin and made her look at him. "Subject me to what? All I see is the most perfect woman in front of me."

A demure smile spread across her face as she tried to look away, but he wasn't having it. Takashi leaned in and captured her lips with his. Startled, she placed her hand on his chest, but didn't push him away, not that he expected her to.

Takashi pulled away and her eyes fluttered open. He grinned. "Now, let's get this fire started. Your lips are turning blue and you're starting to shiver."

She nodded, and he went about getting the fire situated. Mercedes sat down nearby and searched her inventory. "It'd be nice if our gear glitched out, too, so I wouldn't be wearing all this wet leather. Even my tunic underneath is soaked."

Takashi nodded. "It is strange. In the past everything would vanish. Even our nerve connectors would go on the fritz."

"They fixed that two years ago, remember?" Mercedes continued to search. "It was causing health concerns, so they made a failsafe. Actually, now that I think about it, I think the gear is another one."

Takashi laughed and warmed his hands. "With how some people dress, or lack thereof, while they play, I could see why the game devs do that."

He had to admit, thinking about the failsafe made him wonder what Mercedes was wearing in her hotel room. Was she still in that dress, or did she change into something more comfortable? *Or maybe nothing at all...* That thought excited him, though he suspected it was the least-case scenario.

Mercedes stopped her searching and looked at him. "You don't have any spare clothes, do you? It looks like I removed all mine from my bag."

Takashi's brow creased as he thought. "I might have an extra robe. Give me a second to check."

He searched his inventory for gear or common clothes that wouldn't be bound to him specifically. His search resulted in one find, a robe tailored to fit a man of his figure.

Takashi removed it from his inventory, the item materializing in his hands. "I have this. It's tailored to fit me, but it's all I have."

Mercedes finished taking her leather boots off and held her hand out. "It's better than nothing."

He handed it over and proceeded to also take out a bedroll. It'd make sitting a bit more comfortable. Mercedes fussed with the belts and buckles of her leather jerkin, managing quite well with one arm. Not wanting to offend her, Takashi resisted the urge to offer unsolicited help.

Her damp jerkin flopped on the ground, her leather bracer next after some work with her teeth and feet. Her ability to adapt impressed Takashi. He knew she didn't want some arbitrary pat on the back for doing something most would struggle with unless they were forced to adapt, and he didn't blame her, but it didn't stop his admiration. She took a tough situation and made the most of it. He adored her tenacity. It was a quality he never wanted her to lose.

Mercedes wrung out her saturated tunic, substituting her body in as the other hand. The fabric pulled against her cold breasts and nipples. Takashi stopped mid-attempt to pull a blanket out of his inventory and stared. He knew he shouldn't; it was rude, but the sight was too pleasing to look away.

She glanced his way when she finished, and chuckled. "Someone has no shame."

Her words snapped him out of his daze and he looked away, going about retrieving the blanket. "Sorry."

Mercedes chuckled again, and the sound of her tunic hitting the ground shot into his ears. Her feet padded on the ground and she knelt down behind him, draping her arms over his shoulders and pressing her now-exposed breasts against his back.

She leaned in close to his ear. "What's there to be sorry about? Unless you're ashamed to look at me."

"Of course not." He reached around with one arm, aiming to lay his hand on her lower back, but instead his hand found purchase on her ass. It felt nicer than he imagined. "But I don't know how well I'd be able to control myself if I were allowed to continue to stare."

"Who said you had to behave?" She chuckled when he visibly swallowed, and then kissed him on the temple. "You're a peach."

He was so confused—and aroused. *Not a fun combo right now.* Was she teasing him or giving an invitation?

"Now…" Her fingers slipped into the collar of his robe, and in one swift and impressive motion, she pulled the robe off his shoulders, the cloth falling to his sides. "You need to get into dry clothes, too."

He lifted his arms as he looked down at himself, the loose clothing bunching up around his hips and torso. *What has gotten into her?* Her giggling drew his attention—and eyes—to her. She'd moved away and pulled her borrowed robe over her body, but it rested loosely over her smaller frame. The neckline fell wide over her shoulders and plunged deep on her chest, drawing his eyes right to her perfectly-sized breasts.

Mercedes' eyes danced as he stared at her. This side of her was new to him. She could be playful, but there had always been that "just friends" barrier.

With no signs of care about his leering gaze, she slipped her wet pants off in a way that didn't open the robe and give him a view of her lower body, though his lower body begged for such a sight. She went about laying out her wet armor to dry by the fire. Takashi refocused his mind and used this moment to swap out his wet robe for a robe with lesser stats, but was most definitely dry.

He found the mechanics of wet and dry items strange for the game. As long as objects were in his inventory, they were fine, but the moment they came out, regular laws were applied to them. He'd never found an answer in any forums or game panels.

By the time he finished, Mercedes had settled down on the bed roll, her feet keeping warm near the fire. He sat down next to her and pulled a blanket over them. "This should help us keep warm."

She smiled at him, her eyes still glowing. "Thanks. I hope you're not mad about all the teasing."

He chuckled. "No, it just surprised me is all."

The two went to staring at the fire, a comfortable silence falling between them. He would have liked to have some sort of conversation, but nothing came to him—well, not one he thought appropriate to ask. He'd like to know the answer eventually, but right now didn't feel like the right time.

Mercedes looked at him. "You know, you're allowed to ask."

Her forwardness took him for a second. "W—what do you mean?"

"I know when people stare at my missing arm." She stared into the fire. "It's one of those things you become hyperaware of, and sensitive to. This is the first time anyone has seen me without my cybernetic in a very long time. It ain't pretty, but it's the truth of the life I live. I'd rather people ask questions than stare and stay silent, afraid of upsetting or offending me."

Her honesty moved him. "Okay, then I will ask— how often do you have to remove your cybernetic? You're currently testing out new ones with nerves, which would indicate not often, but I would think there are some health risks involved with prolonged use without removal."

She rocked her head side to side. "That's true for when you first get them, due to how the body needs to adjust and the healing process for the surgery site. But as time goes on, you don't need to have it removed as often."

She looked at him with warm blue eyes. "Mine has to come off once a year. Narissa says after ten years, I can start going in five-year spans without having to remove it. Unless of course I feel something is off, then it most definitely needs to be removed to check for any health issues. I'll be glad when that happens. I'd prefer the thing to just stay on."

Takashi couldn't help but chuckle. The fire burning in her frustration amused him a bit. When she shivered, a wide grin spread across his lips. He reached out and pulled her into his lap, Mercedes letting out an adorable squeak.

"Here, I'll keep you warm." He smiled near her ear. "This is okay, right?"

"Uh, y–yeah," she managed. He couldn't stop the grin from spreading across his face. The change in her demeanor was interesting.

The two sat there, staring at the fire. Takashi rested his chin on her shoulder and she didn't refuse him. As he held her close, his hand found the shoulder of her amputated arm, and stroked her exposed skin. She glanced down at his hand, but then went back to watching the fire. He decided to finally ask his question. She did want him to be open with his curiosity.

"Mercedes, I'd like to ask you something personal. You're welcome to say no."

"I'm listening." She didn't look at him, but he caught her jaw tightening as if she knew the question coming up.

His fingers grazed her skin as he dragged them toward her amputation scars. She gasped, but didn't stop him. "What happened?"

Mercedes sucked in a tight breath and chewed her lip

briefly. "Do you remember the terrorist attack five years ago at the convention center in Anaheim?"

"Of course." Who didn't remember that? Some religious extremist decided that people's love for gaming deemed them unworthy of living, and he bombed the place. Thousands of people died, and even more were injured and had their lives irreparably altered. "I was supposed to go to the convention happening that day, but missed my flight because my family needed me to help them out with something."

"Shira, my father, and I were there that day."

Takashi's blood ran cold.

"She was actually in the convention center, whereas my father and I were driving near it. I wanted to show him the area before we found a place to park and go inside to see all the cool things going on." She frowned. "We'd just passed the main entrance of the convention center when everything happened. I… don't remember much… just bits and pieces. A loud *bang* sound; and flash and smoke; things flying everywhere; a lot of pain on my right side; someone flashing a light in my eyes…"

Takashi pulled her in close, holding her tight. Every tiny piece of information he caught from various conversations now made sense. The fact both Mercedes and her father had cybernetic arms of the opposite side now made sense. She had to have been in the driver's seat, showing him around.

"I remember my hospital visit the most, even with the heavy sedation. A few hours into my stay at the hospital, my arm was removed. There wasn't much left of it. I was lucky that was the only thing I'd lost."

She took an unsteady breath. "I met Narissa soon

after. She gave my father and me the opportunity to have cybernetics at no cost. Her company wanted to help where they could, but they didn't believe in forcing the cybernetics on people unless it was absolutely necessary… like with Shira. I met her three days later. The woman she'd shared a room with didn't make it, and the hospital thought it best if I were moved in."

Takashi's grip on her tightened, pulling her even closer to him, and he buried his face into her neck. Tightness gripped his chest. What a horrible thing for her to go through. He thought maybe her arm would have been work accident-related or even illness-related. "I'm sorry…"

Mercedes reached up and rested her hand on his head. "Why are you sorry?"

"Because you had to go through that. Because I brought it up."

"I don't want you to be sorry." Takashi looked at her, but her eyes focused on the fire. "Sorrow and pity don't change the past. In real life, time can't be rewound, so we can only push on and make the most of what we have." She smiled. "I'm grateful for the life I have. It's not an easy one, and not one I would have picked for myself had I been given a choice, but it's a quality one. And I can't say it's been dull or lonely."

She frowned. "Testing this new arm is hard. On an emotional level, not just a physical one."

He waited for more, curious what she planned to say alongside those words.

"It reminds me what I lost. This game does, too, because it's a perfect replica, but I know it's not real. It's like a treat for getting through the day without killing anyone at work."

Takashi chuckled. He'd listened to a number of her frustration-induced rants.

"This new arm… it's not perfect, but it's also real. It's a frustrating reminder that when I leave this game, I won't have the same perfection." Takashi frowned when a tear streaked down her cheek. "I got used to not feeling there. I got used to the occasional phantom limb issues. I got used to having this game give me the perfect alternative. Having to test this arm, it takes a lot out of me."

She wiped the tear away with her knuckle. "Sorry, that probably doesn't make much sense."

"No, it does," he said. "It tells me you're human. It tells me you're trying as hard as you can to run with anything thrown at you, but sometimes it's difficult, even for someone as strong as you. But even though it's difficult, where some may even find it impossible, you still keep going. I love that about you."

She glanced back at him. "Is that the only thing you love about me?"

Takashi held her gaze, unsure if that was her teasing him or an actual inquiry. But the longer their eyes connected, the greater the heat smoldered between them, and he realized it didn't matter.

He reached out and cupped her cheek. "Of course not."

Before he could process what he was doing, Takashi pulled her close and captured her lips with his. Searing heat flooded over him, and Mercedes' hand flew up to his.

Takashi was the first to pull away and stare into her beautiful eyes. "I love everything about you." His hand migrated to her right shoulder. "And I mean everything."

The corner of her eyes crinkled as she smiled, her cheeks tinted red. "There's an endless list of qualities I love about you."

He wrapped his arms around her and pulled her close and stared at the fire. "Nah, there's only two lines on that list. We both know it."

Mercedes laughed. "No, there's more. Maybe five or even six lines, but definitely more than two."

The two laughed and stared at the fire. At this very moment, Takashi didn't care if the game went back to normal. He didn't want this to end.

The hand he had on her shoulder migrated to her back, his fingers caressing her through the thin fabric. The longer he did, the more he wished to pull this robe off her shoulders. When he caught a hitch in Mercedes' breathing, he became more aware of her state.

She stared at the fire, acting as if only it interested her, but her breathing had most definitely changed. He could see it in the way her chest rose and fell, and the way she set her jaw. Her attempt to hide it brought a grin to his lips.

Takashi leaned in and kissed her on the neck. She gasped. He pressed both his thumbs into her back and dragged them down, kissing her again. She sucked in a labored breath and he grinned. "Tell me to stop if you don't want this."

"N–no…"

His brow rose. "No, what?"

"N–no… d–don't…" she gasped again when he

reached around and grazed her exposed collarbone with his finger. "...s–stop."

He did stop, though his fingers hovered over her skin, knowing that wasn't what she was asking. "Stop?"

"No."

Takashi grinned, grazing her collarbone again, this time allowing his fingers to dip lower toward her breasts. She gasped. He was having too much fun with this. "So... stop or don't stop?"

She looked at him through the corner of her narrowed eyes. "Don't be an asshole."

Takashi kissed her on the neck again, this time his teeth grazing her skin. "That's the Mercedes I know."

He reached out with both hands and tucked his fingers into the opening of her robe, tugging enough for it to fall loose to her side. Mercedes gasped as the cool air hit her breasts and taut nipples. Takashi's hands slid across her soft skin, cupping a breast in each one. Another gasp escaped her lips as she leaned back into him, giving a better view of her.

He grinned in her ear. "Perfect, like the rest of you."

Takashi nipped the side of her neck as he squeezed and played with her. He rolled her rosy buds between his thumbs and index fingers, enticing a quiet moan. Need flared up in him, but he couldn't sate the desire just yet.

He pinched and lightly tugged on her sensitive peaks. Mercedes leaned back into him more, her hand finding his, but she had no intention of stopping him. Hooded eyes and mouth slightly agape, allowing tiny moans to slip out, the bliss on her face pleased him. Takashi captured her lips with his, drinking in her intoxicating taste. She deepened the kiss, her tongue meeting his, eager for more.

One of Takashi's hands released her and slowly slid down her smooth stomach, down the side of one hip, and found her inner thigh. Mercedes sucked in a deep breath of anticipation, but he wasn't ready to give it to her *just* yet. He teased her, lightly caressing her skin. She moaned, and then broke their kiss as she groaned in frustration.

"Must you tease me?" her words came out at a near whisper as desire wrapped around her plea.

Takashi grinned. "I have to get something out of this, don't I?"

Her hand grazed his inner thigh, her eyes now dark with lust snaring him, sending a jolt of desire to his brain. "Who said you wouldn't? It's just not your turn yet."

Takashi's blood simmered at the promise, and he couldn't find it in him to tease her any longer. His hand slid between her thighs and found her wet heat. Mercedes gasped and then moaned as he found rhythm in his strokes.

He chuckled. "I really did tease you."

"Yes…" she barely managed. Her head rolled back and her breath changed as her body moved with the rhythm he set.

The chosen pace continbued, Takashi listening to her sounds of pleasure. She moaned out his name, fanning his flames of desire. He wanted nothing more than to push her further—hear her cry out with pleasure. He wanted her to know what he'd be willing to give her, as long as she allowed him to call her his.

Takashi slipped a finger inside her, then another,

pushing in deep, increasing her pleasure. Mercedes moaned, deep and heavy. She reached behind her and grabbed a fistful of his hair, pulling him closer. He trailed kisses down her neck to her shoulder, nipping her skin.

Her grip tightened and her breath labored a bit more. Her hips bucked and he held her close, increasing his rhythm. Mercedes whispered out his name and then screamed with pleasure as ecstasy flooded over her.

Takashi eased up when she came down from her high, taking great pleasure in every gasp she'd let out each time he'd tease her sensitivity.

"Asshole…" she mumbled.

He chuckled, ceasing his teasing, and kissed her temple. "Good?"

She nodded, a relaxed smile on her lips, a flushed tint to her cheeks. Need throbbed between his legs but he waited, enjoying the feeling of her relaxing in his arms after what he'd done for her.

"Hey, Takashi?" she said, her voice quiet.

"Yes?"

She was silent for a moment. "Actually, never mind."

His brow furrowed. "No, tell me what you wanted to say."

Mercedes shook her head. "It was stupid to think about. Don't worry about it."

His lips spread into a thin line. He didn't like this. What did she want to say? She didn't need to hide things from him. "Mercedes…"

She pulled away from him, sending concern flooding over him, but when she faced him on her knees, that disappeared. The full frontal view she presented him kicked his desire and want back into high gear. Mercedes came closer, slipping herself onto his lap, her exposed femininity pressing against his prominent erection, his robes the only wall between them. She hung her arm over his shoulder, holding his gaze with those captivating blue eyes. "I said it's nothing. The stupid thought shouldn't even have surfaced."

Was she feeling insecure? His brow knitted. Did she think he was going to leave after this? With their history, did her poor past experiences really convince her that even he'd just up and leave her hanging?

Mercedes' hand slid down his chest. "Don't make that face."

His face relaxed, except his one raised brow. "And if I don't stop making it?"

She looked down at his chest as she pressed a finger into his skin a little harder and then looked up at him through her lashes. "Then I won't be nice and give you what you want."

Takashi rested his hands on her hips as he grinned. "I have what I want."

Those pouty lips of her smiled as her eyes squinted, her devious intent clear. Her hips ground into him, rubbing against his throbbing member hidden barely behind his robe, and he stifled a hiss. "Are you sure you have *all* that you want?"

He tried to keep himself composed as she kept up her teasing. "And if I do behave?"

She bit her bottom lip and hooked her finger into his robe, pulling one side open and off his shoulder, the fabric falling to his side. "I'll only torture you a little bit."

Great. He wasn't sure how much of her kind of

"torture" he could handle. But he did deserve it for teasing and "torturing" her so much.

Mercedes flicked the other side of his robe off him and slowly dragged two fingers down his chest. Her hips stopped rocking, giving him some relief, though what she was doing with her fingers kept the pressure up.

Her fingers dragged down his stomach and she bit her lip again, her eyes hooding. He could only imagine the tantalizing, dirty things running through her mind. The thought made his lower need harder. He needed to bite those tempting lips of hers—now.

Takashi leaned in, but Mercedes pulled back, his teeth forced to snap at thin air. She forced two fingers onto his chest and scolded him. "No, no. Not yet."

He tried to use his grip on her hips to his advantage and pulled her closer. "Yes, now."

Mercedes flattened her hand against his chest, forcing him back. "Be good."

A frustrated hiss escaped his throat. "I don't want to be."

Mercedes' eyes squinted as a grin spread across her lips and she ground hard into him. He sucked in a tight breath, not wanting to give her the satisfaction of winning—yet. But it back fired on him. She found great amusement in his resistance and soon and found himself leaning back as she placed more pressure on his chest. She was going to win, and he honestly liked it.

Takashi leaned on his elbows, keeping himself propped up to take in the view. Mercedes, pleased with his compliance, went back to dragging a finger down his chest in a side-winding pattern, past his navel, toward his pelvic region. The anticipation simmered his blood.

Mercedes used the motion of her grinding to pull back, allowing her fingers to find the bit of his robe still covering him, and the one place he desperately wanted to free. The devious, lust-filled smile on her lips, mixed with her special kind of torture, was almost enough to send him over the edge.

Her finger twitched and his body responded, enticing a chuckle from her. He huffed. This new side of her was exciting, interesting, and a bit frustrating. Mercedes slowly licked her bottom lip, toying with him, before flicking his robe open, releasing him from the material confines. Cold air hit his skin, his full erection on display for her.

Mercedes looked down at him, and then into his eyes through her lashes, a wide grin on her lips. Her fingers circled the base of his shaft, occasionally reaching out to graze the hardened appendage. He gritted his teeth. This teasing was agonizingly pleasant.

She ran her fingers up the length of his shaft, pulling herself up on her knees to hover her femininity in front of him, as if to size him up for a moment. She then wrapped her hand around him and stroked. Takashi threw his head back, relishing the feeling of pleasure. "Mercedes…"

Mercedes continued, stoking the flame of his desire until he moaned. And then she continued, increasing her speed and then slowing.

He wasn't sure how much more he could handle but he needed more. He reached for her with one hand but she let him go and pushed him away, a scolding look on her face. "Mercedes, please…"

She half smiled. "Please what?"

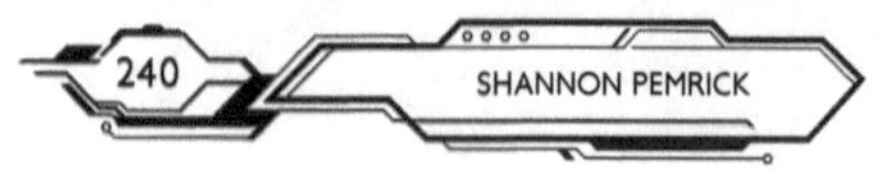

He took a deep breath and tried to request again, but stopped when she slipped a finger between her thighs, her eyes hooding as a rush of pleasure surged through her.

His blood boiled—watching her pleasure herself was more of a turn-on than he could have hoped. He wanted more. "Please."

Mercedes pulled her fingers away, touching the tip of his shaft, and rubbing it against the mouth of her arousal. He hissed and she grinned. "Please what? Do that?" She slipped her fingers between her legs again, her breath hitching. "Or that?"

He swallowed. "Both."

She grinned, glancing at her missing arm. "Sorry, right now you can only choose one."

He cursed mentally. Her and her dark humor were so well-placed in this moment. But he wanted what he wanted. "Both."

She tilted her head, trying to understand what he wanted, still stroking his erection. She grinned suddenly and pulled herself higher on her knees. She settled over him and then rubbed the tip of his shaft against her burning desire. The two sucked in tight, pleased gasps. This wasn't what he'd asked for, but he wasn't complaining.

The sensation of this action, her and him nearly whole together, set his wants ablaze. He couldn't keep up with this teasing. He needed her—now. Sitting up quick, he grabbed her ass with one hand, and her face with the other. He pulled her against him, crashing her lips into his. She didn't fight him this time, her want clear. The teasing had the reverse effect, too, and now he was going to get what he wanted. *Her.*

Takashi nipped and sucked her bottom lip, his hand cupping her rear, reaching underneath her and sliding across her wet heat. She moaned, her lower body quivering with need, and a hungry growl came from him. He kissed her chin, then her neck, then trailed nips down her collar bone to her swollen breasts.

He flicked his tongue across her erect nipples and then captured them, taking his time with each; sucking, licking, and nipping. His fingers continued to massage her pool of velvet moisture, assaulting her with pleasure on two fronts.

"Takashi…" she begged, her words airy. "More…"

With her taut peaks still being sucked between his lips, he grinned. He sucked a little longer before releasing her, settling her over his shaft. She swallowed, her lust-filled eyes eager with anticipation.

Takashi eased her over his swollen member and penetrated deep. His breath hitched, the new sensation rocking him to the core. Mercedes' back arched, her eyes going wide. Her breathing ceased for a moment and her mouth fell agape, as she accepted him inside.

Regaining her breath, Mercedes rocked her hips, quiet moans coming from her lips. Takashi's pulse hammered in his ears. He met her movements, thrusting hard, and she moaned louder. Their breaths came heavier as they continued, syncing.

Mercedes' hand wrapped around the back of his neck, her fingers lacing into his hair and pulling him in for a rough, demanding kiss. A hungry growl reverberated in his core and he captured her face with his hand.

Takashi's body tensed, teetering on the line. "Mercedes…"

She grinned, kissing him a few more times. "Good."

Her permission tore down the rest of his walls. Takashi leaned back, pulling her with him, thrusting harder, and pushing him over the edge. He groaned, abandoning himself into release.

His movements slowed until he stilled, taking deep breaths. Mercedes grinned and then leaned in, kissing him lightly on the lips. Takashi smiled and wrapped his arms around her. She rested her head against his chest, and the two lay there, listening to the beat of each other's heart. No words were needed. All of it had been perfect.

Well, almost perfect. Takashi just wished she were really here with him, not miles away in another hotel.

The tangled-up pair lifted their heads when a voice projected into the area. "Players. We are pleased to announce the character playability and logout issues have been resolved. Avatars will be restored upon logging out and back in. We apologize for the disruption and inconveniences."

Takashi couldn't stop the disappointed sigh from coming out. Mercedes giggled and pulled away, his hands gliding over her soft form. "I guess this means our treasure timer has resumed."

Takashi stared at her, taking in the view. He couldn't care less about the hunt anymore. With the special nature of the game, "down time" wasn't an issue like in real life.

Mercedes grinned, understanding his silent words, and rested her hand on his. She guided his hand along her hip and thigh as she got to her feet in one fluid motion.

Tease. He swiped a hand for her even though he knew she was out of reach. "Come back."

Her eyes narrowed as she grinned and then sashayed away for her leather armor. Her hips swayed, enticing him to stop her from going anywhere. "After we finish the hunt, we'll review the *reward.*"

Takashi sat up. He liked the idea she presented.

"I need to re-log so I can get my avatar back."

"I prefer you like this."

She chuckled. "That may be, but"—she pointed to her missing arm—"I'm no use with a bow without that."

He sighed. "Fine."

Armor collected, Mercedes logged out and he went about gearing back up and formulating a way for them to get this hunt done quickly and efficiently. The better he managed that, the more likely he'd get more time with Mercedes without interruption.

The coin flipped three times in the air, letting out a small whistling noise, and then landed in Mercedes' hand. She clamped her hand into a fist around the small piece of metal, and her eye twitched as the touch sensation signaled her neuro-mod to react. Today the new nerves were doing better. She didn't wake up in pain or overwhelmed with sensations.

But it may have something to do with her distracted state. She couldn't get her time with Takashi last night out of her head. It had been so… amazing. His attentiveness to her—his way of drawing attention away from areas she'd rather forget existed—the way he brought out that side of her after so long.

Mercedes flipped the coin again. Why had she waited so long to do this with him, again?

"Mercedes," Narissa said, extending out her name in a sweet tone.

Mercedes caught the coin and looked at her friend,

well, friends. Shira was video chatting with them today for a bit before going into the game. Narissa had wanted to reveal the new cybernetic plans and Shira received it with great enthusiasm as they'd both hoped.

Narissa chuckled. "About time you heard me."

Mercedes frowned. "Sorry. Lost in thought."

Shira rested her hand under her chin. "Yeah? What's on your mind? You've been awful quiet today."

Narissa's brow furrowed. "Did something go wrong with your date?"

Mercedes' eyes widened. "What? No. It was nice."

Shira looked between the two. "Date? What date?"

Narissa grinned. *Ah shit.* "Mercedes went to a dinner party with Takashi. She got all dolled up and his eyes nearly fell out of his head."

Shira leaned closer to her camera. "Details, details!"

Warmth flooded over Mercedes. She didn't want to go into all the details. "It was a nice party. I learned about more of what Takashi does, as well as many of the other seminar attendees." She grinned. "I even got to prove I know my shit with some of the changes coming to game businesses soon. Didn't make those people happy since they were trying to show off, but I felt good."

Her friends laughed.

"So, what happened after?" Narissa asked.

"After?"

She leaned on her elbows. "Yeah, after the party."

"He brought me back to my hotel."

"Oh c'mon, Cede," Narissa said. "It's obvious you're trying to hide something. You'd be more forward if you weren't. You can tell us. We're your friends. We share all kinds of personal stories with you." She chuckled.

"God knows we've listened to enough of Shira's hook-up stories."

"Hey!" Shira shouted. "You wanted to know those stories."

Mercedes laughed. She knew she should be more forward, but it was a little weird talking about her personal… escapades. "It's nothing big. He just kissed me goodnight."

Narissa slammed her hand down on the desk. "Just kissed you? *Just?* Girl, don't play that off like it's nothing. You let him kiss you and you didn't go running for the hills! You can't be hiding that stuff from us."

Heat rushed to Mercedes' cheeks. If this is how she was reacting to a kiss, how would she react to finding out that's not where it stopped later that night? *Or the fact that Takashi and I are—*

She swallowed and took a quiet, calming breath. "It was just a kiss goodnight. He went back to his hotel after that. I didn't think it was such a shocking thing for a guy to kiss me."

Narissa's excited reaction dropped. "That's not what I'm saying and you know it."

"Wait, that can't be *all* that happened," Shira said. *Shit…* "I know for a fact you two were in-game playing. I was on when you both logged in and went on your weird treasure hunting. And, after I got off because I wasn't feeling well, Jasper sent me a text saying the game glitched and everyone got stuck for about an hour, many people without access to their character skills. So what are you hiding?"

Mercedes held up her hands. "Business transactions?"

Narissa sputtered a laugh. "I should have seen that one coming."

Shira narrowed her eyes. "Don't play coy. He said something about the avatars getting all jacked up."

Mercedes' eyes squinted as she grinned. "Has anyone ever told you, you've started to talk a lot like them?"

Before Shira could spit out a reply, Narissa held up her hands. "Wait, back up. What about the avatar situation?"

Mercedes took a deep breath. "The game glitched last night and the avatars everyone used disappeared, leaving players with their real selves out for viewing."

Narissa's eyes widened, and Shira's hands flew up to her mouth when she gasped. "He saw you…"

Mercedes nodded and looked down at her cybernetic arm. "Without this, since the game can't simulate it."

Narissa reached for her computer. "Do I need to worry about this?"

"No, it's fine actually." Mercedes smiled. "He reacted better than I could have ever hoped for. It… was amazing."

"It was amazing?" Shira's eyes narrowed as she scrutinized Mercedes. "Did I hear you right? You could have said it was 'a nice relief' or 'he took it well,' but 'amazing'?" She sat up, something dawning on her. "Oh my god, you didn't."

Narissa glanced between them as Shira freaked out, and Mercedes swallowed. *She figured it out.*

"Oh my god you did! You fucked him. You fucked him and weren't telling us. You bitch."

Narissa stared at Mercedes wide-eyed, and she hid her face in her artificial hand. Jig was up. "You did what?" Narissa's phone rang and she clicked the speak button, her demeanor changing. "Yes?"

Mercedes and Shira snickered.

"Doctor Narissa." It was Amy from the front desk. "I just sent Kiara up to see you. She has a delivery."

"Oh good, right on time. Thank you, Amy."

"What? You get Kiara's delicious cupcakes?" Shira groaned. "Not fair."

Kiara was yet another guild member of theirs and ran a business from her home in Santa Monica. She sold some of the best cakes in the area. The new shop she and Takashi went to, *Those Buns Dough*, came close, but even they couldn't compete, especially with some of her specialty cupcake flavors.

"Well, if you were here, you could have them," Mercedes teased.

Shira's eyes narrowed. "If I were there I would be smacking you upside the head for keeping this huge secret from us. You can't fuck a guy, especially not one who is your friend that you're considering having a serious relationship with, and not tell your best friends! That's Girl-Code Ethics 101."

Before Mercedes could say anything, Narissa held up her hand to tell them to hold off on the conversation and looked out her glass walls. Mercedes turned to see a short, fair-skinned woman in her mid-twenties garbed in shorts and a tank top approaching. Her curvaceous hips swayed back and forth, and her long red hair bounced about her shoulders and large breasts.

A full-sleeve tattoo covered her right arm, depicting a dice set, symbols from World of Warcraft, Dungeons and Dragons, and Lusara Fates, a Rathalos head from Monster Hunter, and other varied nerdy imagery, and a small hoop ring pierced the side of her nose. She also had a number of piercings in her ear. In her hands she carried a small white box and a cup of hot coffee.

Narissa got up from her chair and opened the door for her, greeting her with a smile. "It's good to see you, Kiara."

Kiara smiled back. "You too, Narissa."

Her words held a trace of a Scottish accent. While she hadn't been born there, her mother was, and immigrated over when she married. Kiara picked it up that way, but tried to keep it tempered. She didn't like the attention that came with it. But she had no control when she got heated.

Kiara turned her gaze to Mercedes and then Shira. "Hey, girls."

The two waved, Shira excited to see her. Mercedes found it interesting that Shira didn't have a problem meeting Kiara in person or over video chats. It was just certain people, mostly men, she tried to avoid the situation with.

She wished her friend would handle this better. If she could handle women seeing her, or people seeing her in public, then she should be able to handle guys seeing her without freaking out. The memory of Shira sending over that photo of her reluctantly the other week when Mercedes had that failed date came to her mind. *I understand her fear, though...*

"Kiara, please tell me you can ship some cupcakes out to me too," Shira said.

Kiara chuckled. "I just need to know what you're after and I can get them over the next day."

Shira's hands shot up in the air. "Yes!"

Kiara handed the box she carried to Narissa. "Here

are those experimental flavors I wanted you to try out. Darius loves them, but he's a guy and eats everything I make."

The four ladies laughed. Darius was their guildmaster, one of Kiara's best friends, and her roommate. He'd rave about her cooking when he had the time to get on, and bragged about how often he got to eat her sweets since he was her guinea pig.

"I'm not sure whether he's smitten with you, or your cooking," Narissa teased as she took the box.

Kiara laughed. "Most definitely my cooking."

"Uh huh." Narissa headed back for her desk, and Kiara followed. "I have another story plot for you, by the way."

Kiara rubbed her hands together. "Oh, tell me more. You give me all sorts of fun ideas."

"One orc, one human, and a long night in the Alavera Woods."

On top of being an amazing pastry chef, Kiara also wrote novels—fantasy and romance, though lately she'd been on a romance and erotica kick.

Mercedes snickered. "Are you talking about Shira's little escapade with that orc last week?"

Shira gasped. "You tell her those? You traitor!"

Narissa laughed. "Well I wasn't giving names or anything. Just situational prompts."

"You're breaking Girl-Code!"

Kiara laughed. "I already figured they may be coming from you, Shira. You're not shy about your in-game sex life."

"Yeah, so?"

Mercedes laughed, realizing why this was such a big

deal. "This orc one, don't tell me, Jasper and Zach were upset you went with this guy instead of teaming up with them for matches, weren't they?"

Shira's face reddened. "Yeah, so what? Like I told them, I can do as I please, and if I want to have sex with some random guy instead of beating the snot out of people in a match, then I can."

Kiara's lips spread into a sly grin and she tapped them with a finger. "Are you sure that's how it went down? Or were they more upset they weren't invited to join?"

Mercedes' eyes widened. She hadn't thought of that. And by the way Shira's cheeks were reddening, it may have been true. "That most definitely didn't happen."

Kiara chuckled. "I think I have a great story now. One orc, one sexy human woman, and two elves. Maybe they'll just watch, or maybe they'll join in. Who knows?"

Mercedes and Narissa laughed, while Shira's face flushed more. "Stop it, all of you. It's not like that."

Mercedes looked at her friend. "How can you say that? They openly flirt with you all the time."

Shira's gaze faltered. "They're just being them. They act like that with other women, too."

"Oh, please. Then explain why they try so hard to get you to go to tournaments?" A smirk spread across Mercedes' lips. "No better place to tag team a sexy woman like you than in a hotel room."

Kiara and Narissa laughed, and Shira's face, neck, and shoulders turned scarlet. "Even… if it were true, I don't screw guildmates like you do."

"Shira!" Narissa shouted. "Now you're breaking this Girl-Code you keep talking about."

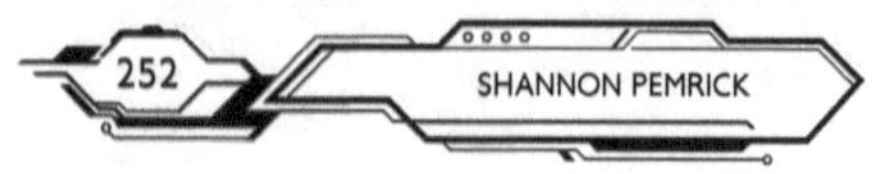

"Wait, hold up." Kiara looked at Mercedes. "You slept with Takashi? About time, girl, jeez."

Mercedes threw her head back and groaned. "Can we stop making a big deal out of this? Yes, I had sex with Takashi. And yes, it was amazing."

"Well don't hog all the details, share, share!" Shira urged.

Mercedes recoiled, her face heating. "I'm not sharing details."

Shira winked. "I'll share some of mine."

"Oh, please do," Kiara said. "I need story material."

Narissa held up her hands. "No, no, no. We're not going into details about all that."

Shira grinned. "Aw, does someone feel lonely?"

Kiara crossed her arms. "I don't know. I'm still convinced she's getting shagged by my best buddy Ajax after hours."

Kiara, along with Darius, had been best friends with Ajax since childhood. She apparently was the reason he even called himself Ajax, and no one would tell how it came about. She learned to hold her own against them as kids, and when they got older, learned she could bribe them with food quite efficiently.

"We are not," Narissa said. "I swear to all of you, that's not going on."

Kiara shifted her weight to one side. "Then why is he always here?"

"Because—"

Her door flew open, and Ajax suddenly entered the room. "Narissa, I need your handiwork."

All four women looked at his mangled cybernetic. Narissa's eyes darkened and her upper lip pulled back. "Because he keeps blowing up his damn arm!"

"Ajax," Mercedes warned.

He nodded. "Yeah, running."

Ajax pivoted and rushed down the hall. Narissa, eyes locked on her target, jumped to her feet, but Kiara held her back. "Easy. As fun as it would be to see you tear him apart, I think it may be best if I talked to him. Maybe I can get some answers."

Narissa let out a long frustrated sigh and sat back down. "If you can, I'd be more than appreciative. I'm tempted to ban him from repairs until he tells me. He's going to blow his neuro-mod and seriously harm himself at this rate!"

Kiara gave her a thumbs up. "I got this."

Taking a sip of her coffee she left on her mission, her back now to them, allowing Mercedes to notice she'd gotten a full back tattoo since the last time she'd seen Kiara. *Darius must have loved that.* From what Ajax told her once, Darius liked a creative woman with "artistic" skin. Kiara fit that bill quite well.

When the door shut, Narissa and Shira focused on Mercedes. She swallowed a lump in her throat. "What?"

"You and Takashi," Narissa started. "Where do you stand?"

Mercedes took a deep breath. She wasn't ashamed to say. She was just not convinced this wasn't some long, drawn-out dream. "We're... we're a thing."

Narissa let out a sigh of relief as she sat back in her chair, and Shira threw her arms in the air. "Hallelujah, finally!"

Mercedes' face warmed. "No need to make such a big deal out of it."

Narissa pointed at her. "This is you we're dealing with. Miss 'I haven't gotten very far with a guy in years.' Miss

'I think I'm going to give up dating.' Miss 'I'm not good enough even though I am.'"

Mercedes threw her hands out at Shira. "And what about her? She's just as bad, if not worse."

"Don't go shifting the attention." Shira wagged her finger. "You're our current topic, so we're going to get excited for you."

Mercedes crossed her arms. "I don't want you to. I don't even know if this is going to work out."

Narissa frowned. "Don't be like that, Cede. This is Takashi we're talking about. He's not like the others you've dealt with."

Mercedes' phone rang and Tasha's voice spoke, "Miss Mercedes, Takashi is calling you."

Mercedes smiled and then answered the phone, this time not on speaker. "Hello?"

"Mercedes," Takashi said.

Her brow furrowed. It sounded like he was in a crowded place. "What's up?"

"I need to cancel plans today. And, well, the rest of the week," he said. "I'm really sorry. I have to take an emergency flight out to San Francisco. Something came up with the family I need to help out with. I can't talk about it now, but when things calm down, I'll call you and tell you everything."

Her shoulders sagged. "Oh, okay…"

Narissa and Shira became concerned, honing in on Mercedes' mood shift.

A woman's voice projected over an intercom, mentioning flight boarding.

"That's my flight. I have to go. Again, I'm sorry, but I *will* explain everything. I promise."

Mercedes tried to smile, but failed. "Okay. Good luck."

She pulled the phone away from her ear when the call ended. Narissa's brow creased. "What's going on?"

"Some sort of emergency happened with his family. He had to hop on a plane just now to help out."

"Oh, that's not too terrible. Well, the emergency part is, but it sounds like it's a legit reason," Narissa said.

"Or he's bailing," Shira said.

"Shira!" Narissa shouted. "Don't act like that."

"You honestly expect me to believe after he says he wants a relationship with Mercedes and then sleeps with her in the same night, he gotta leave town for some emergency the next day?"

"I expect you to not jump to conclusions and make this situation any worse."

Mercedes stared at her phone as the two bickered, doubt gnawing on her very being. She struggled to disagree with Shira. It was far too convenient. *Maybe I was too hopeful about this…* She couldn't have expected her bad luck with men to just up and disappear.

She got to her feet. "I'm… going to go for a walk."

"Mercedes, don't," Narissa begged. "Try to be positive."

She left the room without saying anything. She couldn't be positive. She was always doing something wrong with her choices in men. She was always doing something to make them change their mind about her. *I'm always the common denominator…*

CHAPTER 15

Steam rose up from Mercedes' cup of coffee, the strong maple and honey aromas wafting into her nose, as she sat at a window table in a small coffee shop. She tried to keep herself calm, reminding herself Takashi was different, and this really was an emergency. She'd get an answer in a few hours, at most a day or two. But the doubt of past experience wouldn't let it go.

A bell *tinged* when the front door of the coffee shop. Mercedes' eyes darted over in that direction for no reason but for a temporary distraction. To her surprise, Emi strolled in, her boyfriend, Jason, right behind her. Mercedes went back to looking out the window, taking a sip of her coffee, the sweetness of the flavors mixed with the nippy nature of the coffee beans, tantalizing her tongue.

"Mercedes?"

Mercedes turned her gaze to find Emi looking right at her. She smiled. "Hey, Emi."

Emi bee-lined it to her. "Talk about a happy coincidence."

Mercedes' brow furrowed. "Is… something wrong?"

"Not exactly." Emi sat down in the empty chair on the opposite side of the table. Mercedes noticed Jason hadn't followed, and instead had gone to the counter to order. "Have you heard from Takashi at all today? I tried to call Rei earlier to make sure we were still on for this weekend, but my call went straight to voicemail. Same with Takashi. It's not like either of them. I'm hoping you might know, since you probably have more contact with Takashi than I do these days."

Mercedes nodded. "I do… sort of. I last talked to Takashi"—she looked at her phone—"almost forty-five minutes ago right before he hopped onto a plane unexpectedly. I guess there's some sort of family emergency going on."

Emi's brow knitted. "I hope everything is okay."

Mercedes looked down at her cooling coffee. "Me too…"

"Are you okay?"

Mercedes looked up at Emi to find her brow creased and her eyes giving away her concern. Mercedes smiled. "Yeah. I've just had a long week. Trouble with my cybernetic."

Emi pursed her lips. "That's weird. Cybro Industries technology is top in the world."

Mercedes chuckled. "Trust me, it's not your run-of-the-mill issue. How it happened has stumped everyone, so we're doing a bunch of testing to see if we can recreate it and then learn how to prevent it in the future."

"Well, I'm sure with Narissa on the case, you'll figure it out in no time." Emi turned her attention to Jason when he approached, two cups of coffee in his hands. "Mercedes said Takashi and Rei are dealing with a family emergency."

Jason frowned, his posture shifting a little. "I hope everything is okay."

Was his response delayed? He was only a moment or two longer than she'd expect from anyone else, but it was enough to make her feel like he was lying. Mercedes couldn't shake the uncomfortable feeling she got from this guy.

Emi nodded as she stood up. "Me too."

Something on Jason's person beeped and he pulled out his phone. Emi gave him a quizzical glance, and he smiled at her in a way that sent a chill down Mercedes' spine. "Just a confirmation on a report I asked for."

Emi shook her head. "You need to learn to relax on your breaks." She shifted her attention back to Mercedes. "Thanks for the information. Sorry to have interrupted your alone time."

Mercedes smiled back at her. "Don't worry about it. It was nice to see you again."

The pair left and Mercedes pulled out her phone.

> *Takashi, I don't want to look clingy, but I'm worried. Please let me know what's going on as soon as you can.*

She sent the message and then went back to thinking, her thoughts going back down the dark rabbit hole.

The airport terminal bustled with the usual foot traffic Takashi would expect for an international airport. He watched the luggage claim carrousel for his suitcase, his fingers twitching on his leg. *C'mon, move faster!*

When his bag came into view, he rushed over and yanked it off the conveyor, not caring if anyone thought him rude. He whipped out his phone as he rushed to the exit.

No new messages.

Doesn't matter. Even though he was supposed to get one from his father, Takashi guessed he got held up. He sent off a text to his sister.

Getting a cab now. Meet you all at the shop?

A moment later, a reply came in.

Yes. See you soon.

Takashi wasted no time calling the cab company to make sure his ride would be there to pick him up soon, as he'd arranged before his flight. He needed to get to the shop. Nothing else mattered right now.

CHAPTER 16

Mercedes looked down at her phone as she paced in her hotel room, reviewing the line of texts she'd sent Takashi over the past three days. None answered. She'd called numerous times, each time no answer and a quick voicemail left. He promised to contact her when that "emergency" was taken care of, yet nothing. Pain flared in her chest. What emergency would prevent him from contacting her in the slightest? The only reason she hadn't completely given up was because no one in the guild had seen him online. Of course, that didn't help her settle down.

Mercedes rotated the phone in her false hand, paying attention to how the artificial nerves fired off. Today, Narissa had implemented the next stage of nerves, and this time things had gone a bit smoother than the first stage, though Mercedes did require a few hours of adjusting. After that period, Mercedes found her neuro-mod acting better, even though the sensations had caused her some issues. Narissa jotted down notes, theorizing her mod wasn't overreacting, but instead it was confused. More testing would be required, and Mercedes aimed to do just that. This stage two didn't quite feel real yet, but it was only a matter of time, and that thought excited her to no end.

"Miss Mercedes," Tasha's voice came from the hotel room structure. "Narissa has arrived, and she's messaged to say you have a delivery at the front desk."

"A delivery?" Mercedes' brow furrowed in thought. "Please tell her to bring it up with her."

"Of course."

Before Mercedes had decided to come back to her room to rest a bit, she and Narissa agreed to hang out tonight. Mercedes knew it was because Narissa didn't want her thinking too much about Takashi and stressing over the situation, and she appreciated her friend's gesture.

It didn't take Narissa more than three minutes to make it to her door, and Mercedes greeted her with a smile—until she saw the bouquet of flowers in her friend's hands.

Before Mercedes could say anything, Narissa spoke in a cheery voice. "I guess someone finally reconciled with her boyfriend."

Mercedes' brow rose. "Huh?"

Her friend handed the flowers over. "These are from Takashi."

Mercedes took the gift and looked at the tag, her eyes darkening at the sight of the neat handwriting scrawled on a tag.

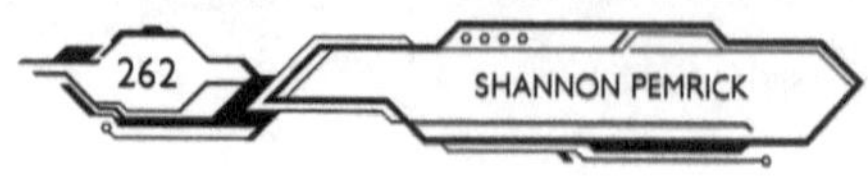

Missing you <3

Takashi

Narissa pursed her lips. "Based on that scowl, I've missed something."

"I haven't heard from Takashi at all."

Narissa pushed her way into the room. "Well, maybe he's still busy with that issue?"

Mercedes glowered at her friend. "Too busy to answer a text or phone call, but can set up flowers to be delivered?" She tossed the flowers on the counter in the kitchen. "Yeah right."

Narissa frowned. "Have you tried contacting him again?"

Mercedes sighed, her shoulders sagging. "Yes. I tried about ten minutes ago with a text. Still nothing."

"I could send him a message." Narissa whipped out her phone. "It's not an issue."

Mercedes shook her head and went to go sit on the couch. "What's the point? He can't be bothered to contact me directly, why would I want a response through a friend?"

Narissa sat down next to her and placed a hand on Mercedes' shoulder. "I'm sure there's a reasonable explanation. Don't let it get to you. This is Takashi. He didn't bail. Hell, he sent flowers, so he's thinking of you."

"Or it's just some elaborate joke."

"Don't," Narissa warned in a dark tone. "Don't you dare start going there. I won't have it."

"Well if you have any legitimate reasons for him to

act this way, be my guest to enlighten me, because I can't think of any."

Her friend's lips spread into a line as even her keen brain struggled with this. None of it made sense, but she could see the pieces in front of her. He was screwing with her, and she didn't appreciate it one bit. *He's just like the others and I was a fool to believe otherwise.*

Takashi frowned, pulling the phone away from his ear when Mercedes' voicemail answered after five rings. He ended the call and looked at his phone history. Several calls and more than a dozen text messages unanswered over the course of four days. He even sent her flowers yesterday and received no response.

He didn't get it. Why wasn't she answering him?

He promised to let her know what was going on the moment he had the chance. The day after the fire at his mother's shop, he tried to call her to explain everything. He hadn't wanted to bail on her like that. He knew it wouldn't be good for their budding relationship, especially with the poor timing, but it couldn't be helped. He wouldn't let his family handle this problem without him.

It made his thoughts narrow and single-focused, causing him to forget anything else, but once things calmed down, he realized how he shouldn't have gone to that extreme. *I should have told her what happened right then on the phone. Maybe she'd be talking to me now...*

Small feet scampered up the stairs from the first floor and Mia burst into his room. "*Niisan!* You have a delivery."

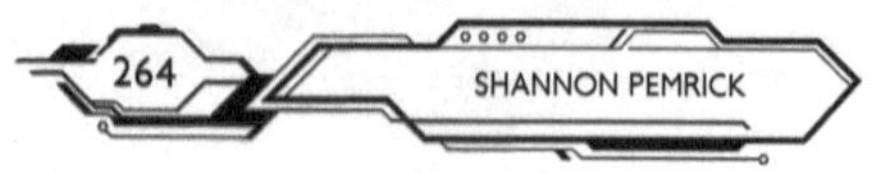

Slipping his phone into his pocket, Takashi's brow knitted. "I didn't order anything."

"I know. It was a florist delivery."

Mercedes? Takashi jogged past his sister, patting her on the head, and headed downstairs. He searched the foyer for the delivered package, but found nothing. Brow furrowed, he called up to his little sister. "Mi-chan, are you pulling my leg?"

She appeared at the top of the stairs. "Not this time. *Okaasan* took it into the kitchen."

Shit. In all the craziness, he'd neglected to inform his mother, of all people, about his new relationship with Mercedes. He braced for an earful as he entered the kitchen.

Takashi found his mother hovering over a white box on the kitchen table. Her eyes snapped up to him and he stopped dead, swallowing hard. She looked beyond livid.

"What did you do?" she asked.

His fear changed to confusion. "What?"

His mother gestured to the flowers. "What did you do to her?"

Takashi walked over, and peered into the box. He found a bouquet comprised of geraniums, foxglove, meadowsweet, yellow carnations, and orange lilies. He swallowed and picked up the tag.

M

Confused, he flipped it over but found it blank. Why such an angry arrangement but only sign it with her initial?

His mother stared him down. "What did you do, Takashi?"

"I…" He looked down at the arrangement again. "I don't know."

"Don't you give me that. She's a nice woman and I know I taught you to treat women respectfully. What did you do to get such an angry message from her?"

Takashi's shoulders sagged. "I don't know, *Okaasan*."

His mother's face reddened and she went to say something, but the door connecting the kitchen to the backyard opened, and his father walked in. "That's enough, dear. Yelling at him won't help the situation."

His father tossed him a leather baseball glove. "C'mon. We'll play some catch like we used to."

"You're going to reward him?" His mother's voice rose an octave. "He's done something wrong—"

His father walked up to her and stroked her cheek, stopping her rant. She gazed up at him, her eyes warm and her cheeks slightly flushed, as she clutched her beaded necklace. Takashi never knew a time when that type of caress didn't get his mother. He never got tired of seeing the two show their affection for each other so openly. "Trust me, *Passarinho*. It's not a reward."

Takashi winced. His father had a mean arm. He fully expected his hand to go numb by the end of their "game."

"Mia," his father called out as he pulled away.

His little sister scurried into the kitchen. "Yes, *Otousan*?"

"There was a mix-up in the delivery, and the florist said to keep the flowers at no charge. Why don't you take them for a craft project?"

Mia blinked. "Are you sure that's the reason?"

Their father smiled. "Go have fun."

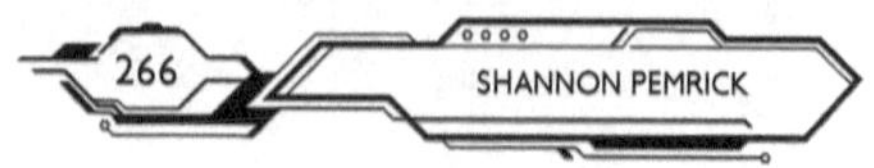

Mia stood there for a moment, shrugged, and snatched the box of flowers. "Okay."

When she left, his father waved him to follow. Takashi took a deep breath and complied, slipping the baseball glove over his hand. His father was the easier of the two parents to talk to, so this wouldn't be horrible, but he wasn't looking forward to the punishment to his hand.

When the two picked a good spot in the small backyard, his father tossed the ball to him. "So you and Mercedes?"

Takashi took a deep breath and threw the ball back. "I asked her the night before I had to run back here."

"Thought you might have been planning to ask her. It's not like you to be *that* eager to go to a seminar. Did you tell her why you had to leave?"

"I was so focused on the issue, I didn't go into details with her on the phone."

Nodding, his father tossed back the ball. "Not hard to see where this is going. Did you keep in contact with her?"

"I tried to. But all my texts and phone calls have gone unanswered. I even sent her flowers yesterday."

"Do you think she'll be the one you give your necklace to?"

Takashi had told Mercedes how he got the necklace, but he never told her of the tradition from his father's side. The men were expected to make a necklace when they came of age, and wear it until they met the one person they were sure they wanted to spend their life with. They'd then present the jewelry as a gift. In some instances, like his, the men could be given the necklace as an heirloom from someone in the family they were close with and had a successful marriage. It was a great honor to be offered this token; one he didn't take lightly when his grandmother handed over her necklace to him. "I want her to be."

His father grinned. "Have a name for her yet?"

"She's not a pet."

His father threw the ball extra hard, the impact stinging. *Disapproval throw.* "You know that's not what I mean."

Takashi chuckled as he threw the ball back. "I don't have one like you do for *Okaasan,* but I've been calling her just Mercy."

His father snickered. "Fitting, though more so for you than her. At this rate, that's what you'll be begging from her."

Takashi laughed, missing the ball when his father threw it. "You have a point."

His father watched him as he retrieved the wayward ball. "Sounds like we're missing something. It's been years since we've seen her, but if Mercedes is anything like her mother, she wouldn't ignore you unless you really screwed up. Having to run home for an emergency wouldn't be grounds to automatically ignore you."

Takashi tossed the ball back. It wasn't that simple, but he wasn't into disclosing the details of the night he'd had with Mercedes. Sleeping with her and then running off the next day was grounds to be pissed off enough for the silent treatment. *Though, factoring in the flowers she sent, it is out of character for Mercedes to act so harshly, even when mad.*

His father smirked. "Ah, so that's it. That is a bigger issue than just bailing." *Perceptive as always.* "Don't worry, I've no input on the matter. The pace you two take is your business. And I'm not going to be like your mother and ask when the two of you are giving us grandchildren."

Takashi shook his head. "I'd like to not think about how eager she'd be for that news."

His father tossed him the ball. "Don't be too hard on her. She comes from a traditional family, after all."

"The interesting mix of raising technique you two used on us kids is burned into my mind." Takashi snickered. "And I'm not the only one getting the brunt of *Okaasan*'s antics. I've overheard her get on Rei's case a number of times."

His father flinched when Takashi threw the ball extra hard. "This all being said, it's obvious your normal tactics to contact her and clear things up aren't working. Have you tried to contact her through Lusara Fates?"

"No, not yet."

"Why?"

"Because I know if I get on, and there is some sort of problem that I'm not aware of, Shira is going to rip me apart."

The ball landed hard in Takashi's glove. *Another disapproval throw.* "So, what you're saying is, she's not worth dying for?"

Takashi frowned and tossed back. "I'm not saying that at all."

His father threw the ball harder than before and grinned when Takashi winced upon catching it. "Yes you are. You won't face a devil's wrath for perceived wrongdoings and fight for what you want. Or, in this case, who you want."

You and your metaphors, Otousan. He shouldn't have

known this was what his father was getting at. Takashi threw back the ball. "As usual, you're right. I'm being an idiot."

His father lowered his arm, the game of catch now over, and chuckled. "In the wise words of your mother, all men are."

Takashi shook his head as his father approached and pat him on the back. "You'll win her back. Now go get on the game and face the wrath of your girl's fiercest *champion*."

Takashi snorted. "Champion? More like an attack dog."

His father's brow rose for a moment. "I'd take on a champion over an attack-dog friend any day."

"My situation exactly."

His father laughed at his expense and then held out his hand. "If you don't mind, while you're taming the attack dog, I'd like to take a look at your phone."

Brow furrowed, Takashi pulled the device out of his pocket. "Okay, though I don't know why."

"I've been thinking. You said she hasn't responded to you after you were vague in your reason for having a family emergency to attend to. This means she doesn't know about your mother's business. Now, if she wanted to send you flowers locally and really drive a point home that she's angry with you—"

Takashi's eyes widened. "Then why didn't she call mother's shop?"

His father nodded. "Exactly. No better way to get you into trouble than to make your mother immediately aware. No flower arrangement has any fury like hers. But had she called, she'd know what was going on, since we set up the voicemail."

"And that means she would have known why I had to bail and shouldn't have been so mad."

"Right. So then she would have contacted you. So, I believe we're not dealing with Mercedes here. Someone else is causing you issues. Why, I can't say, but it's also possible if they're sending you these flowers, there's the potential that the ignored calls and texts go deeper than just being ignored."

That's a good point. His father ran a security firm, so it shouldn't surprise Takashi that there were some red flags in all this. And if there was some sort of tampering, his father would find it.

His father tucked Takashi's phone in a back pocket. "Good luck on your end. If I see a new face at the door seething in rage, I'll start planning the funeral."

Takashi gave his father an unamused look, triggering his father to laugh. *Thanks, Otousan.* His father walked back into the house, and Takashi wasn't far behind, taking deep preparing breaths.

CHAPTER 17

A disorienting sensation fell over Takashi as his mind found itself in his shop. Before he hopped into the game, he checked his friends' list for a status on Shira, only to find her, Zach, and Jasper in a brawl match, instead of the usual arena fight. Brawls took far longer to complete due to the randomized objectives, so Takashi would have to wait it out.

He went about checking on his shop funds and the NPC he'd set up to work in his stead on his flight back to San Francisco. The NPC appeared to be working as well as it could with the current available settings. He wasn't making as much as he would had he been doing the leg work, but it brought in enough to keep his funds from drying up.

Takashi exited his shop and summoned a mount, an elemental cat he and Mercedes worked together to earn through some in-game achievements. Takashi stroked the feline's head, remembering Mercedes' excitement the moment they got it. She wouldn't use any other mount for two weeks unless they had to fly somewhere, and even then she tried to convince others to take the long way to destinations.

Takashi's chest tightened. He really hoped he could fix things between them. He didn't want to lose her. He hopped up on his mount and rode through the city in the direction of their guild hall. When he made it to the large building, he entered through the open front doors and looked around the large gathering hall. The place didn't have a whole lot of individuals hanging around. Didn't surprise him. During usual work hours state-side, the hall was usually quiet.

Takashi ordered a mug of ale from the NPC bartender and found a corner to sit in and wait. Shira should be done with her match soon. He'd deliberately ridden a ground mount here to waste time. He took a few gulps of ale. While his physical body couldn't get drunk, the VR simulated the sensation to the nerves and brain to make players think they were if they consumed too much. Unfortunately, the drinking cracked his walls.

The fear of losing Mercedes crept into his mind. He started to wish he hadn't initiated anything romantic with her. He'd rather have her only as a friend than to lose her completely.

Takashi stopped drinking when a familiar angry female voice bellowed through the main hall. "Where the hell is he?"

Takashi took a deep breath and looked to the entrance to find a short, buxom woman with dark brown hair garbed in half-plate storming into the building, with two tall elven men of muscular builds garbed in leather and plate armor respectively, close behind. *Here comes the party.*

"Shira, cool yah jets," Jasper said. "I get thatcha mad, but you seriously need to handle this a bit bettah."

Shira whirled on him. "And you can keep your mouth shut. I don't need a lecture from you."

"It's not a lecture," Zach said. "Takashi sent you that message because he wanted a civil conversation. You can't go and have a field day because you're mad at him."

"Yeah? Watch me."

This wasn't going to be pleasant. Takashi rose to his feet. "I'm over here, Shira."

Her livid eyes snapped to him and he did his best not to flinch. "You."

"Shira, stay calm," Zach warned.

She didn't listen. Their enraged friend charged him, but before Shira could reach Takashi, Jasper grabbed her from behind and held her back. She struggled against him and shouted. "Let me go! Let me go right now! That jackass needs to pay."

The commotion drew attention from the other guild-mates. Takashi would rather they not overhear all this.

"You need to calm down," Jasper said. "You're acting like a lunatic. Just cool yah jets and talk things out with him. You're makin' a scene, Shira!"

Shira raged and struggled. When she started shouting again, it was in a language Takashi wasn't familiar with. It sounded Germanic, and it made sense if it were German, as he knew her father was from there, but he couldn't be certain.

"That's it." Jasper lifted Shira up and threw her over his shoulder. "Now you can't get at him."

"And we can now move to somewhere more secluded to talk," Zach said.

Takashi couldn't stop himself from snickering. "You sure you want me in that room, then?"

Bemused smiles spread across the two men's faces, but Shira wasn't taking the bait. "Don't you dare start cracking jokes, you *arschloch.*"

"Gesundheit," Jasper teased.

She smacked him in the back of the head. "And you put me down this instant."

"Nope." He started walking off with her. "We're gonna get to the bottom of everything in a calm mannah, away from pryin' eyes."

Shira wasn't going to give up so easily. She continued to rave like a mad woman, in German of course, and make attempts to throw spells and weapons at Takashi, though the game stopped that since he wasn't marked for PvP. This of course only increased her anger.

Jasper stopped suddenly and opened his menu. "Shit. Serenity woke up from her nap."

Serenity was Jasper's daughter.

"I'll handle her," Zach offered. "She'll be more than willing to comply with me if she knows you're doing something with Shira."

Shira's face reddened a bit and she shut up. The soft spot Shira had for Jasper's daughter was well-known, and Takashi found it adorable. Jasper thanked Zach and continued on, Takashi close behind while Zach logged off.

Shira didn't start up her shouting again, but she wore the darkest look Takashi had ever seen before. He really hoped she would let him talk and explain his side. He wasn't an idiot. This lack of communication between Mercedes and him had brought on their friend's rage.

Jasper led them to the chapel. No players were in here at the moment, so it worked well. He set Shira down and kept a close eye on her as he closed the doors to keep curious eyes out. Shira was too set on staring Takashi down to pay attention to anything else.

Takashi held up his hands. "Before you shout at me some more in that Germanic language, let me explain."

Shira's eyes narrowed. "What's there to explain about you bailing on Mercedes?"

"I didn't bail on her. Not intentionally, at least." He took a deep breath. "My mother's flower shop was vandalized. Arson, to be specific."

Shira's expression softened a bit, showing her surprise, but she wasn't letting her guard down or allowing the information he revealed to placate her anger.

Takashi continued. "I should have told Mercedes this when I called her before hopping on the plane. I screwed up there. I admit that—"

Shira's eye's narrowed. "So what? That doesn't mean you can ignore her for days!"

"I didn't. I tried to contact her—several times—by text and phone. She hadn't answered me."

"You really expect me to believe that?" Shira snorted. "I know for a fact Mercedes texted you while you were on the plane, and had tried to contact you a number of times since you bailed. No response, at all."

Takashi's brow furrowed. His father might be onto something. "I never got any of those."

"And she never got your messages. So who do you expect me to believe? My best friend, or the guy who

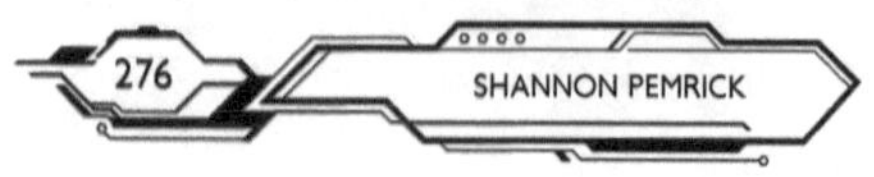

promised her the world, got what he wanted from her, and then disappeared the next day?"

Takashi sighed. He knew she'd word it that way, and hated it, because it really did look that way. "I can prove it."

Shira crossed her arms. "You're not getting away."

"I'm not running. I will send you proof. It'll take me two minutes."

Her eyes narrowed and her upper lip started to curl, but she nodded. "Starting now."

Takashi activated his menu and logged off. The moment he was released from the system, he bolted out of his gaming station and out of his room. "*Otousan*, I need my phone real quick."

"I'm in my office," came back a reply down the hall.

Takashi rushed down to the far end of the hall, into a neatly kept office. His father sat at the desk, moving objects around on the computer screen, Takashi's phone plugged into it.

"I just need to get a screen grab of my recent phone call and text attempts to Mercedes."

His father didn't look at him as he spoke. "I'm too far deep into this analysis for you to be able to do so manually, but Ochi can do it."

"I've already obtained them," Ochi said. "Takashi, please tell me where to send."

"My Lusara Fates account. I need to forward them to Shira so she believes me."

"They will be in your inbox when you log back in."

Takashi rushed back to his room and logged back into the game in record time. Once the disorienting feeling eased out of his head, he opened his eyes to find Shira and Jasper still waiting, the former leaning against a pew with her arms crossed.

"It took you longer than two minutes," Shira said through gritted teeth.

"By thirty seconds," Jasper corrected. "You're being wicked unreasonable. Give him a break, Shira."

Her eyes darted over to him, but she didn't say anything.

Opening his menu, Takashi found the messages Ochi promised, along with a link to the news article about his mother's shop—*Thank you, Ochi*—and he forwarded them to Shira. "Here, take a look at these."

Shira's eyes narrowed at Takashi before she activated her menu to look at the message. While she was doing that, Jasper got his attention and made a motion for Takashi to send the proof to him as well, so he did.

Shira let out a long sigh. "How do I know you didn't doctor this?"

Jasper's brow rose. "Really? It took him two minutes to get these to us. No way could he make this up in that short a time."

"He could have had it all ready."

Jasper sighed. "If he were that sheisty, then he wouldn't need to log off. He woulda already had this."

"That's what he wants us to think."

"Stop being so stubborn about this."

Takashi suspected this would happen. He didn't expect Shira to let this go so easily, but he did wish she'd be a little less stubborn. "Shira, I understand you're mad at me. But I'm not making this up. Those are real screen grabs from my phone. I didn't create them in some program to convince you."

She opened her mouth to speak, but he cut her off. "And I'm not trying to use this as some sort of convoluted way to cover any tracks of intentionally bailing on Mercedes because I regretted it later."

Shira shut her mouth and blinked. Jasper laughed so hard he fell over.

Takashi grinned. "I've heard enough of your bizarre conspiracy theories to know you'd come up with one for this situation."

Just then, Zach logged back into the room. He looked between the three of them. "I missed something."

Takashi nodded, a smirk on his lips. "Yes. I think I've finally placated Mercedes' attack dog."

Zach chuckled and Jasper's laughter worsened. Shira pressed her lips together as she crossed her arms, her nose scrunching, clearly trying not to be suckered into laughing as well. Takashi waited, knowing if he were patient enough, he'd win. He did.

Shira threw her arms up into the air. "Okay, okay, I believe you."

Takashi relaxed. "Thank you."

She went back to crossing her arms and muttered, "Now I feel like a traitor."

Jasper calmed himself. "You can't be a traitor if it's the truth you're seeing. We just gotta get Mercedes to believe it."

Shira sighed. "I guess you're right." She looked to Zach. "Is Serenity okay now?"

He nodded. "I set her up with a snack and coloring supplies. She's making you a picture because she convinced herself Jasper is the one who made you mad and wants to cheer you up."

Shira placed her hand on her chest and her eyes softened, showing how touched she was by the gesture, even if for slightly inaccurate reasons.

"Well shit," Jasper said as he stood up. "Make me the skeezy one."

"I did try to convince her, but she's wicked stubborn, like you."

Jasper glanced Shira's way. "I think she's pickin' it up from Shira."

She gave a flourished bow. "Pleased to be of service." Then her posture straightened. "Wait, why isn't she in school?"

"Teachers' workshop day."

"Ah."

Takashi didn't want this to get too far off track. He was glad Shira wasn't trying to kill him anymore, but there was still the matter of Mercedes. "Shira, do you know if Mercedes got the flowers I sent her?"

She nodded. "She did. Narissa mentioned it when the three of us were talking earlier. Cede killed that topic pretty quick, though."

"Do you know what she planned to do in response?"

Her brow furrowed as she thought for a moment. "As far as I know, she was just going to ignore you. Safe to guess you were hoping it'd placate her?"

He nodded. "I worried she was mad, but because I couldn't get a hold of her, I thought flowers would still show her I hadn't forgotten about her. Then I received some flowers today that were supposedly from her. The arrangement translated to 'fuck you,' but I'm skeptical it's from her."

"Yeah, that doesn't sound like Mercedes." Jasper said.

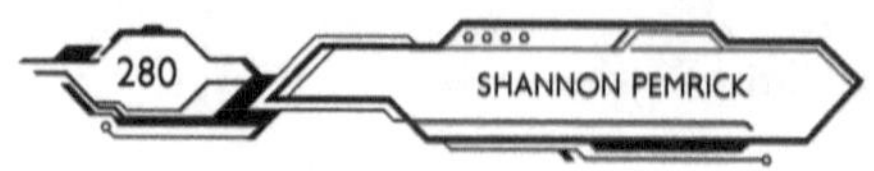

Shira snorted. "No, that sounds exactly like her when she's mad. What makes you skeptical, Takashi?"

"Besides the fact it was only signed 'M' instead of her name, I know that if she was that mad at me, she would have tried to send the flowers through my mother's business. Her fury would be worse than any floral arrangement. But if she tried, she would have gotten an automated message explaining the issue with the arson."

Shira nodded. "And then she'd know what was going on. Partially. This messaging conundrum is weird, too."

"I do have my father looking into that. He speculates some sort of phone tampering." Takashi took a deep breath. "But could you do me a favor and talk to Mercedes for me? I can live with an answer on the flowers for now, if that's all you're willing to do."

Shira opened her game menu. "No, I'm willing to do more than that. She needs to know the truth of all this. I want her to be happy again. Give me a few minutes to privately call her."

She leaned against the pew again and made her call. Takashi made himself comfortable, and Jasper and Zach stayed where they were, both intently watching her.

Takashi wondered what was holding the two back from convincing Shira their interest in her was genuine. Even though the two of them had gotten together after Jasper lost his wife unexpectedly, they hadn't been all that subtle with their interest in their mutual friend.

Shira started to pace, her mouth moving, but not in a way anyone could lip-read, and no sound came out. It was the way the game had been coded, to show someone was having a conversation with either guildmates or privately, while keeping those from outside the conversation from thinking the person was ignoring them.

Takashi leaned forward when Shira's arm movements started to show how poorly the conversation was going. Dread sat in the pit of his stomach.

Shira sighed aloud, signifying the conversation had ended.

"That sounds wicked bad," Zach said.

Shira shook her head. "She's more stubborn than me. I even sent her the proof, but she didn't believe a word of it. I'm going to have to work with her more." She looked to Takashi. "But I did manage to confirm, she didn't send you those flowers."

Takashi nodded, unable to smile. "That's something, at least."

She gave him a sympathetic glance. "I'll work with her. There's only so long she'll be able to fight me. You'll get your chance to talk to her face-to-face to prove your side."

"Thank you. I'll also try to send her a game message. Maybe she'll reply to those eventually. In the meantime"—he grinned and looked to Jasper and Zach—"I think Mercedes' personal attack dog should be praised for doing such a good job."

Zach's bow rose, Takashi's meaning not quite registering yet, but Jasper grinned. He walked up to Shira and literally swept her off her feet. "That's a sick idea. She deserves a rewahd for all her hahd work."

"Put me down, you lumbering warthog."

Takashi and Zach laughed while Jasper gave her a look that says he wasn't sure if he should be confused or offended. "Ma'am, I am a rogue, we don't lumbah."

"One, I am not a *ma'am*, and two, then you need a better rogue instructor."

Jasper put her feet down on the ground, but made sure she stayed nice and close as he spoke closer to her ear. "Bettah yet, I can show you just how roguish I can be."

Takashi clamped his mouth shut so he wouldn't laugh at the sight of Shira's reddening face. She swatted Jasper away. "Stop acting so weird."

Jasper, cocky as ever, held up his hands. "Who said I'm being wicked weird?"

Shira held her hands out at him as she looked to Zach. "He's your boyfriend. Aren't you going to stop this?"

Zach leaned against the chapel doors. "This is a wicked good show, actually."

Shira's jaw went slack for a moment before she turned to Takashi for help, but he was already in the process of pulling up his game menu. "And I'm logging off. Have fun."

"Traitor" was the only thing he heard from her before logging out. It was fun messing with her. But he also needed to give his father a hand with the phone situation.

He was now sure there was some foul play involved. Between the business hacking and now this, how could he ignore that? He didn't know who would do this to him, but he wasn't going to sit idly by while it continued to happen.

He also needed to craft a good message for Mercedes to read. He'd keep trying until she finally allowed him to speak to her face-to-face.

CHAPTER 18

Flakes of fish food snowed down onto the water's surface of the fish tank in Mercedes' living room. The little creatures darted about, gobbling them up. She'd returned home two days ago and was honestly surprised they were still alive. She loved her father, but entrusting him to stop by and feed her fish even once after the two week self-feeding provisions ran out, was a bit of a risk.

Mercedes plopped down on the couch and looked at her cybernetic. She'd spent a total of three weeks in L.A. testing with Narissa. The last stage didn't take as long to adjust to and test as they thought, so they had gone about setting her up with a brand new full unit to test out. This allowed them to figure out any potential differences in the rushed style of testing they'd been doing.

Mercedes' phone went off, a cheesy battle horn sound, indicating Shira wanted to chat. Picking the phone up from the coffee table, she relished the feeling of the device in her false hand. It wasn't exactly like having a real arm, but it was damned close. Narissa had a lot of work to do for her press release on the product, along with more tests with the stepped version, and checking in with those who were testing out the full versions. It wasn't expected to see approval for large-scale human testing and then market for at least another year or two, but Narissa was hopeful, and Mercedes was happy to have helped her friend. It gave her another leg up on the competition, and it was going to help so many people like Mercedes get back into having a life they would have believed they'd lost.

Mercedes looked at the new text, this one like all the others, and again, begging her to talk to Takashi. She frowned. Well, almost have their lives back. They couldn't make others accept them for not being fully human anymore. *And this topic with Shira is getting old.*

When Shira had called her, trying to learn more about what she didn't do with the flowers Takashi sent her, and then went about trying to explain things on Takashi's behalf, she couldn't believe what she was hearing. But mostly she couldn't believe her friend had so easily believed such a story.

Yes, Mercedes had confirmed that his mother's shop had been burned down, and that made her pity the family for their loss, but that didn't mean she was going to outright forgive Takashi, or believe there was some phone issue conveniently happening at the same time as this emergency. Especially since he started sending her in-game messages shortly after Shira tried to convince

her. *Why couldn't he have done that before, if this phone thing was such an issue?*

She typed out a reply.

> *There's nothing for the two of us to discuss.*

A moment later a reply came in.

> *Cede, please just hear him out. That's all I'm asking. Stop being stubborn about this.*

Mercedes wondered when her friend would finally give up. There was nothing to be gained from this. She just wanted to move on now. Pain seeped into her chest. *I shouldn't have gotten my hopes up.*

Text flew across the screen as Mercedes typed back to Shira, but just as she hit "send," her screen locked up and Tasha's voice came from the condo infrastructure. "Miss Mercedes, before I allow that to be sent, may I speak candidly with you?"

Her interest piqued, Mercedes placed the phone down on her lap. "Of course, Tasha."

"You're an idiot."

Mercedes' face twisted as she tried to figure out how to react to such a statement. Tasha had never been so callous before.

"I apologize if my words offend you, but even though I am only an AI assistant, I am glad you are my owner. And because I am so grateful, I wish to see you happy. Therefore I need you to see that your stubbornness is getting in the way of your happiness."

Mercedes went to speak, but Tasha continued. "I understand you're hurt. I sense your pain daily, and analyze the meaning behind the words you send to your friends. But as humans, you make mistakes—even AIs aren't perfect."

Mercedes leaned back into the couch. Tasha had a point.

"I think you should give Mister Takashi at least the chance to explain everything to you himself, face to face. Even if you don't believe him, and the two of you go your separate ways, you both deserve that much. And if I may continue to be candid, I would like to say I hope you don't separate. I have never seen you happier than when you are with him. And my scanners, and his personal assistant, told me Mister Takashi was the same way."

A tiny smile spread across Mercedes' lips and conflicting emotions turned in her stomach. Tasha was right... again. She was being stubborn about this. *No, it's more than that. I'm being a bitch.*

She sighed. "I'll talk to him."

"Thank you."

Tasha released the phone freeze, allowing Mercedes to erase her message and write out a new one.

Fine. I'll talk to him.

It didn't take long for Shira to respond back.

Oh thank god. I thought I was going to have to keep doing this with you forever. I'll tell him to contact you with a meeting spot.

Fine.

As much as this did need to happen, she wasn't going to pretend she was happy about the idea. Even if she was being a bitch with how stubborn she'd been acting, it didn't invalidate how she felt.

Her phone beeped and a notification from Lusara Fates popped up. She had a message from Takashi.

> *Thank you for being willing to talk to me. Can we meet at my business? It'll be quiet there.*

She should have figured that'd be his request. His reasoning was sound, but it wasn't neutral ground, either. Still, she agreed to it and put the phone down.

Mercedes took a deep breath and headed for her gaming station. Doubt clawed at her, whispering into her ear several reasons not to go through with this, but she knew she had to. At the very least, so she could get proper closure.

She sat down in her gaming chair and loaded up the game and her characters, choosing the human city of Balgara as her port-in location. Mercedes took another a deep breath, and then let the system take her into the game.

She shook her head when she finished loading in moments later, shaking the slight disorienting feeling she always got when hopping in. Once oriented, Mercedes left the inn, summoning a ground mount, a flaming horse she got during a raid in the last expansion. She trotted through the street, weaving around NPCs and PCs alike.

Buildings of wood and stone with shingled roofs lined the road on either side, the occasional business marked with a sign. Most cities had a designated business section, but Balgara didn't. It's what made the place unique.

Mercedes rode past the courtyard of the cathedral and followed the canal past a large stone-and-wood building with a large mahogany double-door entrance. An ornate sign hung over the entrance, reading *Baten's Auctions*. It was the local auction house Takashi used when he wasn't doing direct player trades.

Several more minutes passed before she came to a line of businesses and homes. One in particular had a sign with a rose, but no name. This was Takashi's place. Mercedes swiftly dismounted and dismissed her mount. She took a controlled breath and headed inside, only to hear two people talking. One was Takashi, and the other sounded like… *Emi*.

Irritation flared up in her, but she swiftly pushed it down. She didn't have any right to be mad. He was allowed to talk to her. Mercedes chose to not enter, allowing the pair to talk uninterrupted, but that didn't stop her from eavesdropping.

"Are you sure you don't want to talk to me about it?" Emi asked.

Takashi sighed. "Yes. I'm more than capable of handling this. I just need to talk to Mercedes, who should be here any moment."

"Sorry." She sounded sad. "I'm not trying to be a bother, I'm just worried. Rei had been all too happy to tell me you and Mercedes were having some problems, and I know how important it is to you for this to work out." Her feet shuffled. "And I know I make her uncomfortable—"

She noticed that? Mercedes thought she'd hidden it from her well.

"—but I don't want her thinking I'm trying to get between you two or anything. Because I'm not. If I wanted that, I would have asked you to stop being friends with her when we were together."

Mercedes' brow rose. What did she mean by that?

Takashi didn't sound any more clued in than her. "What do you mean?"

"She made me uncomfortable. She's beautiful, talented, and smart. She shares more hobbies with you than I do. She came into your life before me, and you had this deep connection with her that I struggled to create with you…"

Mercedes quietly backed away until she was outside the building and leaned against the structure. It was better if she stopped listening in. *I shouldn't have started in the first place.*

It was weird for her, knowing Emi had an issue with Mercedes long ago, and seeing how friendly she was to her now. She'd always assumed her close relationship with Takashi was problematic for the pair. It's why she still felt guilty about their break up. Even if Takashi told her she wasn't responsible, she didn't believe it fully. And now, this confirmed some of her suspicion. *If she was so uncomfortable with me, why is she so friendly now?*

"Mercedes?" Mercedes looked up to see Emi standing in the entrance way of the shop. "Why are you standing out here?"

"You and Takashi were having a conversation." Mercedes shrugged. "It'd be rude to interrupt, so I thought it best to wait."

Emi frowned. "I'm sorry. Had I known, I wouldn't have kept him so long."

Mercedes shook her head. "There's nothing to apologize for. You're allowed to talk to him."

Emi looked to want to say something, and Mercedes thought for a second she'd be asked what she overheard, but instead, Emi gestured to the shop. "Well, he's all yours now."

She rushed off, and Mercedes entered the building. She found Takashi pacing in front of his cluttered desk, several different emotions playing across his face.

When he noticed her, he stopped, and all the emotions except excitement melted away. "Mercedes!"

She managed a weak smile and his expression dropped. "Well, I'm here so we can talk."

"You can come in. I'm not going to bite you."

If she weren't so mad at him, she would have liked the idea. Mercedes took a few steps in, but refused to get too close to him. She could see it bothered him, though she didn't let it concern her.

Takashi frowned. "Mercedes, I'm sorry. I really am. I didn't mean for it to get to this. I really did have a family emergency."

Mercedes held her arms close to her. "I know. I saw the news article."

"And I did try to contact you when things calmed down—many times. I can even prove it."

Her gaze on him faltered and she feigned interest in the floor. "Shira showed me the screen captures."

He stared at her, confused. "Then… why are you mad at me? You have the proof that I tried, and I really did, Mercedes. I'm trying hard right now. I really am."

Mercedes let out a short sigh and looked at him. "Do you really not understand how much you hurt me? Are you seriously struggling to comprehend just how much this affects me after I finally opened up to you?"

The pain and anger in her boiled up. "After I was intimate with you and then had to watch you run off with a convenient excuse like every other guy I've dealt with for the last five years? As I watched you treat me like my ex did after I had an arm replacement because of an accident that wasn't my fault."

"That was never my intent." Takashi took two steps closer, his face twisted with concern and fear. "Mercy, please believe me. I tried. I really did."

Euphoric sensations fluttered through Mercedes when he used that nickname. It added confusion into the mix of emotions raging inside her. This talk was going worse than she expected.

Takashi came up to her and placed his hands on her arms. "I screwed up. I know that. I should have logged into the game and tried messaging you that way when I didn't hear back after a day of trying through my phone. That would have stopped all of this from going down. If I didn't mean any of this, I wouldn't be trying so hard. I'd have just let everything die. But I didn't. I can't."

She didn't look at him, but his presence overwhelmed her. As mad as she was—hurt as she was—she still craved closeness from him. A part of her desperately begged her to just forgive him so she could sate that desire.

Takashi sighed. "I don't know what else to say to get you to believe me. Only that I can't bear the thought of losing you, and that I lo—"

Boots clomping on the ground pulled the pair's attention, and a man Mercedes vaguely recognized as Game Master Ashton entered the room.

Takashi pulled away from her. "Game Master."

"I apologize for interrupting, but I must speak with you on an urgent matter, Takashi." Game Master Ashton said.

Takashi's brow furrowed. "Please don't tell me this has to do with another hacking incident."

Ashton frowned. "I'm afraid so."

"Are you kidding me?"

Mercedes backed up. Of course this would happen. It was so convenient. "I'll go so you can deal with this."

Takashi grabbed her hand. "No." He looked at the Game Master. "We're in the middle of sorting out something important. Do whatever checks you need to, but I can't focus on it right now."

"I'm sorry, but I need to discuss several things with you directly, and it cannot wait."

"Mercedes!" Zach shouted over guild chat. "Mercedes, please tell me you can hear me right now. It's an emergency."

She would have rolled her eyes at the word "emergency" if it weren't for the panic in his voice. She connected to chat. "What's wrong?"

"Please tell me you're in a position to get to Shira's parent's workplace."

Dread tightened in her stomach. "It's a ten-minute drive from my house. Why?"

"She just texted me to say she wouldn't be on for matches because the place is on fire."

The dread flipped to panic. "Oh my god. I'll go over right now."

She looked to Takashi and he nodded. This new issue was more important, and they both knew it.

"I'll be there as soon as I can," he promised.

She glanced at the Game Master as she pulled up her game menu. "You need to handle this."

Takashi grabbed her hand and locked eyes with her. "I will be there. And I will want to finish this conversation when things calm down."

Mercedes wasn't sure how to feel about that. But she could focus on it later. For now, Shira needed her.

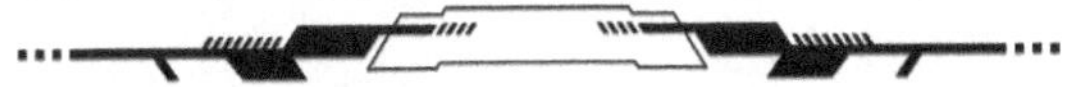

Cars zoomed by as Takashi had his drive a little faster than he should. But seeing as it was an emergency, he had no qualms about it. Rei sat in the passenger seat, trying to get a hold of Emi.

After he'd sped through the issues with Game Master Ashton, he'd logged off, and tried to get to the car as quick as possible, though his family didn't make that easy. His mother wanted to know if he patched things up with Mercedes yet, and Mia wanted him to play a game with her. He managed to get them to calm down enough to explain why he needed to run, and that's when Rei announced she'd be going with him. Apparently Emi was supposed to have a meeting with Shira's parents and she was worried.

Takashi wasn't concerned at first, since he'd only seen

Emi fifteen or so minutes before Mercedes and he had found out about the incident, but when she didn't respond to several phone calls from either Rei or him, he started to worry.

His worry, of course, compounded his concern over Mercedes. She had not reacted in the way he'd hoped. He would have rather been screamed at in anger than watch her keep her distance while so calmly comparing him to the other men that'd let her down. *And then that bit about her ex...*

He'd never pried into her personal life like that, something she also didn't do. They'd only ever discussed such a topic if they brought it up themselves. But now he was starting to wish he had. It was obviously an issue that deeply affected how she handled relationships.

"*Niisan,*" Rei said.

He glanced at her, noting she wasn't looking up from her phone. It was unusual for her to call him that. "Yes?"

"Are you concerned about Emi at all?"

"Of course I am."

She looked up at him. "But she's not the one at the front of your mind, is she?"

He knew where this was going, and didn't like it. "I have a lot of things on my mind."

"But Mercedes comes first."

"Of course she does. She's my girlfriend."

Rei's eyes tightened, though he could see the surprise as well. "Since when?"

"Since right before I had to come home."

"But you two are fighting."

Takashi sighed. "That doesn't mean we're not together. Even mother and father fight from time to time." He frowned. "Besides, it's my fault we're fighting to begin with. I made a mistake that hurt her, so I have to figure out how to fix it. Else we won't be together."

Rei stared at him for a moment. "Do you love her?"

He nodded without hesitation. He'd tried to tell Mercedes this before the Game Master showed up.

His sister's lips spread into a tight line and then she went about trying to call Emi again. No luck.

The car pulled off the highway, and before he knew it, they'd arrived. Or at least, as close as they could get. Cars and people blocked the road, red and blue lights flashed, sirens blared, and in the distance, black smoke billowed up into the sky. Takashi's seatbelt slammed against the back of his seat and he jumped out, Rei not far behind.

The pair rushed down the sidewalk, pushing through clusters of bystanders when they couldn't run around. They continued until they came to a barrier, guarded by police. Just beyond them, Takashi could take in the all-too-familiar scene. No fire raged, but the blackened and partially collapsed right side of the building showed where the inferno had been.

Takashi scanned the area for familiar faces, and found just the two he wanted standing together talking. "Shira. Mercedes!"

The two looked his way, Shira waving to him. She spoke to a man in blue who then let the ones in front of him and Rei to allow them through. Both thanked the officers and rushed over to the two women. Shira's service dog sniffed the air at their approach, but otherwise remained sitting at Shira's feet. Had the dog not moved, Takashi wouldn't have realized he was there. *I can see why his name is Snake.*

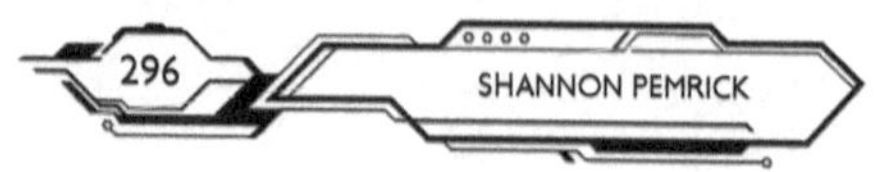

"Are you all right?" Takashi asked Shira.

She nodded. "Yes. My parents, too. Unfortunately there were several people who weren't so lucky and have been rushed to the hospital."

"Did Emi make it out okay?" Rei asked.

Shira shook her head. "She hasn't shown up yet. I tried to call her to let her know about the issue and to stay home, but it went straight to voicemail."

Rei's brow creased. "That happened to us, too. I'm still worried about her, but at least I know she wasn't affected by this."

"Me too."

"Any clues to how this happened?" Takashi asked.

Shira shook her head again. "Not yet. I did overhear one of the officers speaking with my parents about them suspecting arson. While they can't rule out other possibilities, it's been rampant these past few weeks, along with other types of vandalism."

Takashi and Rei looked at each other, understanding this all too well. The incident at their mother's shop had been ruled arson as well, though the motive was unclear, and the investigation was ongoing to determine whether it was related to the others.

Shira peered beyond them. "Well, we can now be a bit more at ease. I can see Emi."

Everyone turned to find her and Jason standing at the blockade. Shira once again asked the officers to allow the two through, though they weren't as okay with it this time and tried to persuade her to just join them over there instead. Stubborn as usual, she held her ground enough for them to give in.

Emi ran over to them. "Is everyone okay?"

Shira nodded and gave her the same rundown she'd given Takashi and Rei.

Emi smiled. "I'm glad it's not as bad as the local news made it out to be."

"I tried to tell you myself, but you didn't pick up your phone," Shira said.

Rei crossed her arms. "Same here. Takashi and I both tried to contact you."

"Sorry. My phone is on the fritz today," Emi explained. "Jason is having a look at it to see what's going on."

"My dad could do that, too," Rei offered. "It's his specialty, after all."

Emi looked at Jason, who was watching the smoldering building, piquing Takashi's interest. Jason was acting odd.

When he didn't look at her, Emi turned back to Rei. "If Jason isn't able to, then I'll be happy to talk to your dad. It's possible the phone is just showing its age and needs to be replaced. I've had it for three years now."

"I've held onto phones longer than that," Mercedes said. "Never heard of any of them not getting phone calls ever."

Emi shrugged. "It was just an assumption. Could really be anything at this point."

Jason placed his hand on Emi's lower back suddenly. "Let's get going."

Emi looked confused, but before she could say something, Mercedes did. "Why?"

Everyone's attention turned to her. She looked irritated.

Jason half-smiled as a light chuckle came out of his mouth. He seemed confused by her question. "Because there's nothing keeping us here at this point. Her meeting is canceled, and the police are going to have to do their investigations before another one is rescheduled."

Shira's eyes narrowed as she crossed her arms. "Says who? We can set up meetings outside of the building proper."

"Besides, she's here with friends. Actively talking to them, on top of that," Mercedes said. "And did you think to ask her what she wanted before deciding for her?"

Takashi noticed Rei's interest in Mercedes' shift.

Emi held up her hands. "Girls, it's okay. Jason and I had plans after the meeting, so it's no big deal."

Takashi frowned. He didn't like how Emi jumped to defend that behavior. Mercedes and Shira were right, he should have asked Emi if she wanted to leave. The Emi he knew wouldn't have been okay with such a decision being made for her. Something wasn't right.

A potbellied man with light hair and eyes and a woman of lithe form and dark complexion approached them. Shira greeted them with a large smile that reached her ears. "*Mutti. Vati.* Are you all done talking to the police?"

The man chuckled and spoke with a light accent. "For now, ja. I see your friends have come to make sure you're okay. It's a pleasure to meet you all."

Everyone greeted him.

He turned to Emi. "Emi, I'm sorry you come out all zis way for nossing. I know it's a bit rough on you for travel. I promise we will make it up to you once sings calm down."

Emi smiled at him. "It's okay. I can use this time to visit my mother." She patted Jason's hand. "And it gets him out and about every now and then."

"Well at least you can see a positive side of it all." He chuckled and took in their surroundings. "Now, I shouldn't keep you. I'm sure you all have important sings to get to today. Shira, dear, go de-stress. We'll handle everysing from here."

Shira managed a weak smile. "If you say so, Vati."

The small family said their goodbyes, and then Shira faced everyone. Emi spoke up first. "I think Jason and I will leave now. Once things calm down, Shira, I'll be happy to reschedule."

"Of course. Expect a request in the next day or two. Even with this going on, my father never stops, and he's eager to see the designs you planned for this meeting. And I hope you get your phone fixed."

"Me too." Emi waved to everyone and the pair left, Jason not saying a word.

"I don't like him," Shira said when they were out of earshot.

Mercedes nodded. "Each time I meet him, I like him less and less. I mean, who does he think he is?"

"A control freak." Shira looked to Takashi and Rei. "Sorry if you like him."

Rei glanced at Takashi who nodded before she spoke. "We don't. He's given us a weird feeling from the start. And him choosing what Emi does doesn't sit well with me at all."

Mercedes looked back at the smoldering building. "He was way too interested in that."

Shira's brow rose. "Do you think he's involved some-how?"

Mercedes pursed her lips. "I think he's creepy, yes. But I don't think he's a psychopath. I just think it's weird

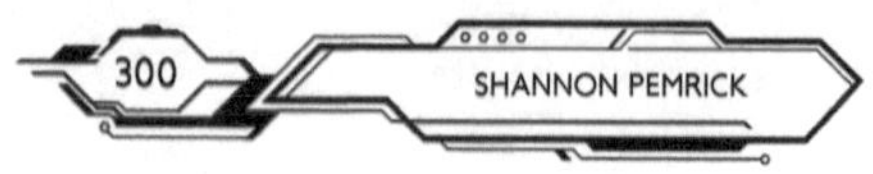

how fixated he was, and then he jumped right into telling Emi they should leave."

Takashi agreed with her. It was a strange behavior.

The sound of a rumbling stomach hit his ears and Shira touched hers. "I think it's lunchtime."

Mercedes laughed, sending an ache through Takashi's chest. He missed being the source of that. Would things go back to normal for them? This whole time, she'd actively avoided any eye contact with him. It felt like he was punched in the gut every time. What he wouldn't give for some extra alone time with her right now to show her how much he wanted—needed her.

"Do you two want to join us?" Shira asked. Takashi realized in his focus on Mercedes, he may have missed a bit of the ongoing conversation.

Rei looked up at him, and spoke before he could invite himself and make Mercedes uncomfortable. "We'll have to pass. The family wanted us for a few things today."

Shira nodded. "That's fine. Thank you both for stopping by. Wasn't necessary, but it's appreciated."

Mercedes nudged her. "No need to be so formal."

"Sorry. I'm just trying not to think about how much I want to find this asshole and shove my shoe up his ass."

Takashi pressed his lips together as Rei and Mercedes laughed.

They all said their goodbyes, Takashi's eyes lingering on Mercedes a moment longer. He wanted to talk to her—finish the conversation they'd started earlier—but she was making it clear she was uncomfortable with him still. Takashi and Rei made their way back to the car. Things were quiet between the two as he set up the GPS to send them home.

"*Niisan*," Rei said when the car pulled away. "What did you do to make her so mad at you? It had to be bad with the way she was actively avoiding looking at you."

Takashi wrestled with the answer. Why did Rei want to know? "It's complicated."

"We have a long enough drive home where you have time to tell me."

He turned in his seat to look at her. "Why do you want to know? You hate Mercedes. Emi even told me how happy you were that she and I weren't communicating well."

His sister's lips twisted as if she were struggling with the right words. "I want you to give me her number."

Not what he expected to hear. "No."

"Ochi, please send me Mercedes' number so I can talk to her."

"Contact sent," Ochi said through the car dash.

Takashi's eyes widened. "I didn't give the okay for such a request."

"I sense no malicious intent from your sister."

Takashi's gaze shifted to his sister, who was now sending a text. "What is going on here?"

"I'm telling her I want to meet tomorrow to talk."

He rubbed his face. His sister's cryptic actions were making his head hurt. "Why? You keep avoiding that answer."

Rei sent the text and sighed. "Because she stuck up for Emi." Takashi watched his sister, waiting for her answer. "Emi is my best friend. She's your ex and yet Mercedes stuck up for her without hesitation. She showed real irritation for Jason's actions."

His sister sighed again. "I thought the two of them

were putting on an act when they were both over for dinner. Getting along and acting like it didn't matter that Emi was the ex and Mercedes was the soon-to-be new girlfriend."

Rei pursed her lips for a moment. "Mercedes has shown she is so much more mature than me. And she makes you happy. More than Emi ever could." She looked at him. "I shouldn't have acted the way I have, and I'm sorry. Let me help convince her to give you one more chance."

He couldn't believe what he was hearing. Rei was one of the most stubborn people he knew. She hated being wrong, and loathed to admit she had been. Takashi reached out and pulled her in for a tight hug. "Thank you."

She let him hug her for a moment, but when it lasted too long, she struggled against him. "Okay, okay. Enough with the love-fest."

Takashi chuckled and released her. "Whatever you say, Rei-chan."

"Don't call me that," she whined.

When Takashi laughed at her expense, she punched him in the shoulder. She then huffed and crossed her arms, pouting.

Takashi found himself amused by his sister's antics. *Why are all the women in my life adorable?* "Ochi, please add a stop before our destination."

"Of course. Where you would like to go, Takashi?"

"Those Buns Dough."

Rei's eyes narrowed. "Trying to butter me up?"

He did his best to not laugh at her unintentional pun. "To placate a woman's anger, give her sweets. It's father's motto, and one I fully agree with. Not even Mercedes is able to resist."

His sister's mouth twisted and she sighed with defeat. "You'd better be prepared to spend a lot."

"I've got a car ride's worth of time to explain to you what went down between Mercedes and me, and prepare for my crying wallet."

Rei rested her arms on the console. "Okay, let me hear it."

CHAPTER 19

The white sports car pulled into a free parking spot, and Mercedes took a deep breath. Rei had contacted her yesterday asking to meet with her for lunch at The Mill. Apparently she wanted to talk, though Mercedes wasn't sure what about.

She couldn't shake her unease as she climbed out of the car and headed inside. She couldn't, for the life of her, understand what would compel Rei to reach out to talk, not after she'd made it quite clear she didn't like Mercedes. She even refused to join her and Shira for lunch yesterday, though of course she couldn't be sure if that was because Shira had invited Takashi too. *Bitch.*

She hadn't been pleased Shira would pull that on her. Yes, Mercedes agreed to talk to Takashi, but she wasn't convinced about anything with him right now. *But it's hard to stay mad.* He'd made a rather convincing argument, and her heart said not to give up on someone like him yet, even though her brain argued to be smarter. It made this all the more confusing for her.

The rich scent of roasted beans surrounded Mercedes as she entered the small coffee shop. She looked around, finding Rei at a corner table by a large window. Two cups of steaming coffee and two pastries sat on the table before her.

Rei lifted her gaze when Mercedes approached and smiled. "Mercedes, you're here."

Mercedes smiled back, finding the friendly warmth from Rei nice, but as awkward as she expected. "I am."

"I'm glad you came." Rei pushed one cup and one pastry toward her. "I got something for you."

Mercedes sat down across from her, noting the coffee was a cappuccino with a cocoa-powdered heart design in the center of the cream. "As much as my mother would tell me pastries do not make a proper meal, I approve. And thank you for buying this for me. You didn't have to."

Rei looked down at her own cup, touching it with her hands but not enough to lift it. "Yes, I do."

Rei continued to hold the cup without picking it up, and Mercedes realized this was a sign of nervousness. Rei's lips twisted. "I'm sorry for how I've treated you. I was wrong to do so, and I hope you can forgive me in time."

That's why she wanted me to come here? She never expected an apology from the young woman. Not anytime soon anyway—or unprompted. *Or is it?*

Mercedes brought her hot drink up to her lips and sipped, taking in the mix of bold and sweet tastes. "You have a great choice in coffee. This is quite delicious."

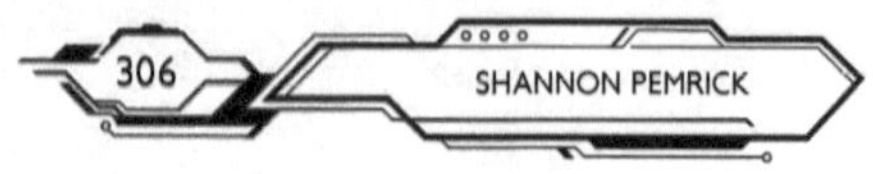

Rei watched her, both concern and confusion crossing her face. Mercedes then smiled. "I appreciate your apology, and accept it."

Rei visibly relaxed. "Thank you."

Mercedes took another sip of her cappuccino. "I am curious what brought it on, though." The look of embarrassment she received tipped Mercedes off. "Does it have to do with your brother?"

"Partially. He's a reason I wanted to talk you, but he's not the reason for my apology." Rei took a quick sip of her hot drink. "After seeing you defend Emi with Jason's ridiculous actions, it made me think about how I'd be acting and how immature I've been. I let it consume me, and put a strain on my friendships and my kinship with my own brother. I've been a major fool."

Mercedes smiled and took a bite of her pastry, finding it had a blackberry-apple cinnamon filling. *Delicious.* "Even though we're adults, we're all prone to immature and stupid actions." She brought her cappuccino up to her lips, and the memories her fight with Takashi surfaced. "Even me."

"Will you give my brother another chance?" Mercedes looked at her to find Rei's attention full on her now. "I got him to tell me what happened, or at least his side of what happened. And yeah, he was an idiot—well I called him a dumbass, but that's beside the point."

Mercedes chuckled but allowed her continue. "My point is, he was stupid, but he didn't mean to hurt you. He's not that kind of guy who would do something to hurt his girl on purpose. And it's eating him up that he did."

Rei reached out and grabbed her hand. "Please give

him another chance." She smirked. "And he's not making or bribing me to do all this begging. In case you were wondering."

Mercedes couldn't help but chuckle. "I appreciate the disclosure there." She then frowned. "This has been very difficult for me. I have not had the greatest luck with men. I have a hard time letting go of that pain that has haunted me for years. This has made it hard for me to up and forgive your brother, as much as a part of me wants to."

Mercedes' shoulders sagged. Which pain was worth it, though? Losing him, or being reminded of the past because of an accident?

Rei nodded. "I get it. I have a cybernetic myself."

This surprised Mercedes. Takashi never mentioned that before.

"It's just one of my feet, making it easier to hide, but I'm no stranger to the judgment. I don't wear sandals or open-toe shoes, and I rarely go barefoot, even at home. It's enough to keep the judgment to a minimum, so much so that not even Takashi would have known I had trouble fitting in at times."

Rei took a deep breath. "It's one reason I'm so passionate about the field. Even with medical advancements for replacing limbs with real tissue and bone, I don't see cybernetics going away anytime soon. And because of that, I want to help improve them, and remove the stigma. I've got several improvements I've been working on in the lab at school. Nothing is quite right yet, but I know I'm close. And If I can get these figured out, that stigma can be next."

Rei looked her in the eyes. "My brother would never

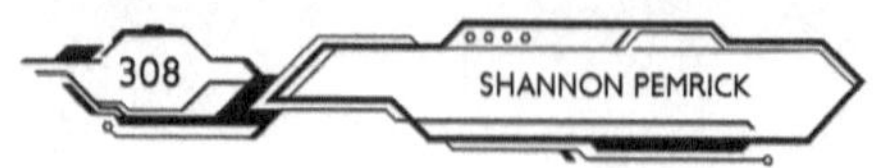

fall into this stigma belief. I promise you, if you took him back, he'd make this all up to you. Please give him a chance to prove that."

Mercedes' lips curved up the side of her face. Rei was a persistent and passionate woman. Mercedes could admire that. Mercedes dug through her purse, pulling out a business card. She slid it across the table. "Take this."

Rei picked up the card and her mouth fell open. "Is this…"

"Someone with passion like you is needed in the cybernetic field. And while I don't know how far along you are in your studies, Cybro Industries is always taking on passionate interns. Tell Narissa I sent you her way, and she'll review your portfolio personally."

"I… I don't know what to say."

A chuckle escaped Mercedes' throat and she pulled out her phone. "While you figure that out, I need to send a message to your brother."

A meek smile appeared on Rei's face. "Thank you."

Mercedes typed out a message through the remote game chat.

Sorry I've been such a bitch.

No more than ten seconds later did she get a response back.

Don't say that. You weren't. You had every right to be mad at me. It's my fault for hurting you. I'm sorry.

Me too.

Dinner tonight? My treat?

Mercedes snorted.

You don't have to pay for everything, you know.

Watch me.

Mercedes shook her head. He was something else.

Then maybe I don't want to go to dinner with you now.

Don't be a bitch ;)

A grin spread across Mercedes' face.

At least this bitch knows how to drive a stick ;)

Promise?

Only if I get to pick where we go.

Nope. I'm already working up reservations.

Jerk.

You love me <3

Maybe :P

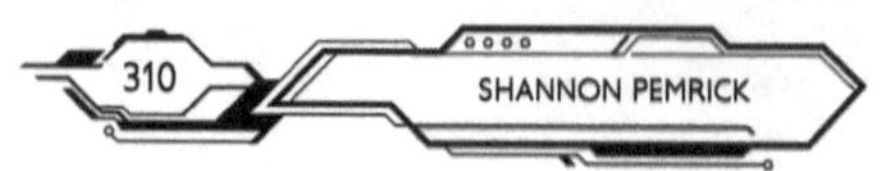

The ease of the interaction sent a flutter of pleasant emotions through her. She missed this. And as much as what happened hurt, losing him would hurt even more.

> *Reservation is at seven, I'll pick you up.*
> *And no, you can't know where until we*
> *get there.*

She shook her head and teased him a bit before sending her address so he'd be able to pick her up.

"Let me guess, my brother set up a date for tonight and he's insisting on paying," Rei said as Mercedes put her phone down.

Mercedes picked up her cooling cup of coffee. "You know him well."

"He gets it from Dad. Both are predictable."

An amused smile appeared on Mercedes' face as she consumed her hot drink. "Most men are. Now, enough about him. I want to know more about you." She placed her cup down. "If that's okay."

Rei's eyes squinted as she smiled. "I'd like that."

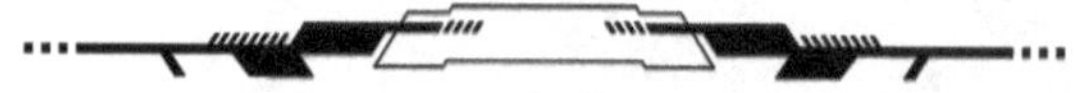

A tickle came to Mercedes' nose as she applied foundation to her face. She did her best to resist the urge that came with it, but ultimately she failed. She sneezed loud, barely managing to angle herself away from all her makeup spread across her bathroom sink.

"Gesundheit," Tasha said.

Mercedes smiled. "Thank you."

"As a reminder, Mister Takashi will be here in five minutes."

"Yes, I know I'm falling behind. Hopefully I can finish getting my face on before he shows up."

"But, Miss Mercedes, your face is already on. Otherwise you'd need to go to the hospital."

Mercedes laughed. "It's an expression, Tasha."

"Oh, I shall research this expression, then."

An amused smile on her lips, Mercedes went back to getting herself ready. Butterflies fluttered like crazy in her stomach. Now that she wasn't being stubborn, the prospect of seeing him had her all giddy.

Mercedes applied her lipstick, the focus reminding her of the last time her lips touched his. She wouldn't mind getting a few more by the time the night was over.

After her talk with Rei, which had turned out to be a wonderful lunch date, Mercedes relayed everything to her two best friends. Neither were subtle with their relief, especially Shira. She'd actually made another one of her treasure-hunting sexual jokes, just to get a small rise out of Mercedes.

"Miss Mercedes," Tasha said. "Mister Takashi has pulled into the driveway."

"Please let him know he's welcome to come right in since I'm still getting ready."

"Of course, Miss Mercedes."

A moment later, someone knocked on her door and then it opened. "Mercedes? Tasha said I could come in."

"Yep, I'm still putting on my face."

He chuckled. "I'm not sure if anyone told you, but that's supposed to stay on."

"Miss Mercedes, is this reaction part of the expression?"

Mercedes smiled. "In a way, yes."

"I will add it to my database so I do not second-guess the expression."

Takashi laughed but refrained any comment.

"You're welcome to wander around and make yourself at home. Just don't go through my drawers."

Takashi chuckled. "I've already done that."

Her eyeliner application halted for a moment. "Well, not technically as I wasn't wearing any that time."

"Are you now?"

She snickered. "Maybe."

"Tasha, you're not adding this to your database, are you?"

She smiled at his change. She guessed it got him a little riled up, as she'd hoped.

"I already have this expression logged," Tasha responded. "Miss Shira is a rather vulgar young woman."

Mercedes sputtered a laugh. She wasn't entirely wrong. Shira hadn't grown up in a prim and proper lifestyle, and had since struggled to adapt to such when it was introduced to her in her teen years.

"Hey, did you get that hacking issue figured out?" she called out to Takashi.

"For now, yeah. Who knows when it'll happen again."

She didn't like the sound of that, but she also understood. It'd happened too often lately, she could see why he wouldn't be confident about the security in the long run.

Eye shadow finally done, Mercedes tidied up her sink and then left her master bath for the full-length mirror in the bedroom to check herself over. Shira and Narissa had helped her pick out a tight black, one-shouldered maxi dress with a thigh split from her closet and helped her decide on some heeled open-toed shoes. Narissa convinced her to style her hair like she had at the party, and Shira told her the exact makeup she'd want to decorate her face with, along with the jewelry adorning her.

While she fussed, making sure everything looked right, she realized how quiet Takashi had been. "You're being awfully patient."

"I have a mother, two sisters, and dated a fashion designer," he replied. "I've learned."

She chuckled and finished with her fussing, noting she'd have to thank her friends for their help. She looked good. *Now, hopefully Takashi will think the same.*

Mercedes emerged from her room to find Takashi leaning against the back of her couch, a bouquet of red roses in his hands. He wore a suit again, flaring up inappropriate thoughts in her brain, reminding her how much she craved his touch. *So many things I could do with that tie…* She needed her hormones to simmer down again. Craving or not, they needed to make it through dinner, at least. *Maybe the car can take the long way home…*

Takashi looked her way and stared. She smoothed out her dress the longer he did and became self-conscious. "Well… say something."

He chewed his lower lip, reminding her of when he'd done that to her. How she wished for him to do that to her again. "I'm trying to rationalize blowing the favor I cashed in for our dinner reservations."

Mercedes' face warmed. *Well, he likes it.* She continued to fuss with her dress. "I know it's not the other dress, but I thought this one might be better for a date for two."

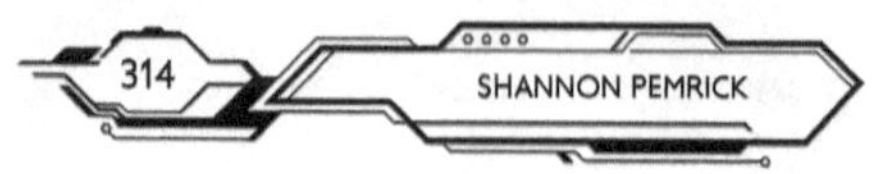

"You could wear whatever you want and still look amazing, and I'd do what I could to adjust plans for it."

A sly grin spread across her lips. "So if I wore nothing?"

He visibly swallowed and then presented the bouquet of flowers. "I have these for you."

Mercedes continued to smile. She enjoyed getting a reaction out of him. She accepted the gift and inhaled the sweet aroma, noting again the color. It made her smile. "Thank you. Let me get it in a vase or two and then we can go. If that's okay."

He smiled. "Our reservation isn't until seven. We have time."

Mercedes entered the kitchen. "Where are we eating?"

"I told you, it's a secret."

She let out a long sigh. "Can I know what kind of food we're eating?"

"Italian."

"Nice. I get to utilize my gym membership tomorrow."

Takashi laughed. "While you won't gain any weight in one night, I'd be more than happy to accompany you on that excursion."

She didn't hate the idea, that was for sure. Shira never worked out with her. That woman rarely ever left her house these days.

Mercedes pulled out two vases and filled them with water. "So what's this favor you cashed in?"

"I helped out a family friend last year and he gave me a free VIP seating at his restaurant whenever I needed to cash in."

"I see." There weren't many restaurants in the area that had VIP seating. None of the more expensive places she'd ever gone to had them.

"Stop thinking now," Takashi said. "No ruining the surprise."

She glanced back at him, her lower lip sticking out. "Don't be mean."

Takashi shoved his hands in his pocket and ran his tongue over his teeth. "Don't be a tease."

Mercedes winked and split up the bouquet of flowers so it'd fit in both vases. "You love it."

He came up behind her, wrapping his arms around her waist, and pressed his face into her hair near the nape of her neck. "You're right, I do."

Her whole body quivered. How she ached for his touch. That one night wasn't enough for her.

"Takashi," Ochi's computer voice said from Takashi's phone, making them both jump. "If you wish to be on time for your reservation, I would highly suggest the two of you leave now. Unless you'd rather cancel."

Takashi sucked in a tight breath and pulled away, sending a pang of disappointment through her. "No, I don't want to cancel. I need to make up for the past two weeks."

"There's more than one way to do that." Mercedes couldn't stop the words from tumbling out of her mouth. *Damn, desperate much, Mercedes?*

Takashi grabbed her hand and pulled her toward the door. "That may be, but dinner with a perfect view is how I'd like to start it off." He winked. "Especially when I have to make it up to a smart, beautiful woman."

She smiled, finding his words corny as hell, but she appreciated them nonetheless.

Takashi helped her into the car and then they drove off.

Soft music played while Takashi and Mercedes sipped wine on the patio overlooking the San Francisco bay. He'd kept the destination a secret up until the restaurant came into view. *Petalo Di Rosa*, one of the best five-star restaurants in the bay area. Mercedes had heard of it, but it was always too fancy, and frankly, too expensive for her. Now here she was, sharing a bottle of wine with *the* most perfect man she could ever ask for.

The waiter approached their table with the caprese kabobs and prosciutto-and-basil-wrapped shrimp appetizers they ordered. The pair thanked him before he left to check on other tables. Mercedes nibbled on her snack, watching Takashi pop a shrimp in his mouth.

"So, Takashi," she began. "Is your family doing okay with what happened to the floral shop?"

He smiled at her. "Yes. Upset, but it can be replaced. My mother is looking up the benefits of rebuilding since she owned the building, or just moving elsewhere and renting. How are you doing about it? Your mom was my mother's business partner there, after all."

Mercedes looked down. "It's been so long since I've been there, I don't have any attachment to that place anymore."

"If it's okay to ask, how long has it been?"

She thought for a moment. "About thirteen years now."

"I'm sorry…"

Mercedes smiled at him. "It's okay. It's taken a long time, but slowly I've come to terms with the loss. There are days it's difficult, but I manage."

"Have I told you how much I admire your tenacity?" He took a sip of wine, not taking his eyes off her.

Mercedes pulled the tomato on her kabob off with her teeth. "Once or twice."

Takashi ate a shrimp. "How is the investigation going for your father's place? It's been a number of weeks."

"Fixing-up-wise, great. The insurance took care of most of the damage, and we didn't have to delay any projects." Mercedes' lips twisted. "Investigation-wise, not so great. They don't have any leads. It's out of our hands now, so all we can do is wait."

"Sounds like us."

Mercedes glanced down at their phones that lay on the table. When they'd arrived and made their order, he'd unlocked it and offered to show her he hadn't been lying about the text attempts. In response she'd done the same, but never touched his phone.

She had no reason to look. Her insecurities may nag her to snoop, just to be sure of... well everything, but she needed to trust him. She needed to shove her insecurities in a dark box where they belonged, and view Takashi as she always had—honest. She'd never second-guessed him in the past when they were "just friends," so this hadn't been the time to do it now.

Eating a fresh mozzarella ball, she looked at him. "Do you have any idea what's going on with your phone?"

"Not yet, but my father is working hard on his analysis."

Mercedes' brow twisted as she lifted her glass of wine. "Analysis?"

Takashi's head tilted. "Did I ever tell you my father runs a security firm?"

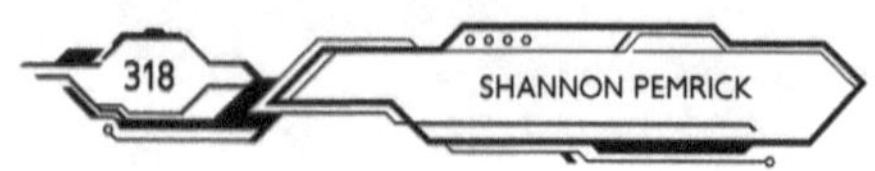

She stared at him, her lips pursed and brow furrowed. "No, you seemed to have forgotten to mention that. Last I knew, he worked in the game industry."

He ducked his head and retrieved his wine glass. "Oops. Well, yeah, that's what he does now. He's been hired out to check security for large companies, software, and even games. If we're having issues like this, he'd be the one to find it."

Mercedes tipped her glass toward him. "Well, here's to him finding out the answers."

Takashi smiled and lifted his glass toward her. "And to us overcoming it without them yet."

A smile spread across her lips and she clinked her glass with his. The two sipped their drinks and then gazed out at the bay, the Golden Gate Bridge stretching across it.

"It's interesting to think how old that bridge is," Takashi said. "That we humans get attached to things like landmarks, and do our best to preserve them. And yeah, that bridge is important for transportation, but it's still a huge tourist attraction." He looked at Mercedes. "Does that make any sense at all? I might just be rambling out loud for no reason."

Mercedes giggled and ate a piece of shrimp. "My mom loved to travel. She had gone to every state and several countries before I was even born. And even then after, she'd take me to so many places, even if my dad couldn't go. One state she loved was New Hampshire. You could go from bustling city to pristine forest in less than thirty minutes. But one thing about them she admired was their love for a lost landmark."

Mercedes took another sip of her wine. "*The Old Man of the Mountain*, they called it. It was a face of a man on the side of the White Mountains. The most amazing part about it, it wasn't man made. It attracted people of all types just so they could see this strange natural wonder. But per the laws of nature, the weather took its toll. They tried for years to preserve it, hold it up there, mixing man's creative ingenuity and nature's random gifts. But ultimately the landmark crumbled under the weight of time. These people loved their landmark so much, that even to this day, their license plates depict it."

She smiled. "I don't know if my answer makes sense or if I'm just rambling out words."

Takashi chuckled, and then she did as well. She was glad he appreciated her little joke.

The waiter returned with their meals, ricetta pansotti alla Genovese for Mercedes, and Ciceri e Tria for Takashi. The pair thanked him and dug into their meals.

"You know, after all these years of knowing you, I never found out what got you into gaming." Takashi laughed. "I do remember how you chewed us out the first time you played Lusara and we treated you like you'd never played a game before. But after that, I just accepted your nerdy side and never thought to ask what got you into it all."

Mercedes laughed at the memory. She'd been annoyed, but it was Shira who had torn into them. "My mom got me into it. As you could guess, my dad is all about cars. But it was my mom who loved both, so when they had me, she insisted on raising a wheel-loving, retro-button smashing, cosplaying nerd. I didn't get into the cosplay in the end, but the rest happened."

Her eyes squinted as she laughed. "But my mom was

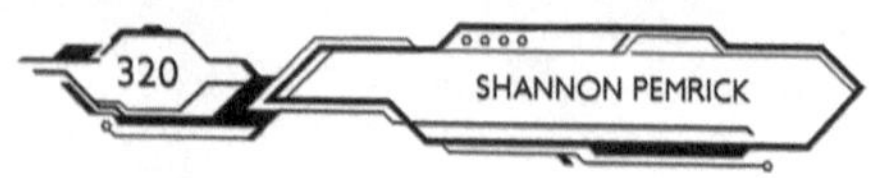

resourceful and just continued to force my dad to cosplay with her. That was always a riot to me."

Takashi chuckled. "I do remember her a bit. She was an… interesting woman."

"That's one way to put it." Mercedes took another bite of her meal. "You got into games because of your parents, right?"

He nodded. "My mother enjoyed gaming as a hobby, and my father tried to make his love for it into a job in the same way I do now. That's what brought them together. Even though they ended up going into vastly different careers in the end, I was still brought up with that same gaming passion."

Mercedes smiled. "That's cool."

The casual conversation continued; their phones lay out on the table untouched. They would buzz a few times, but neither paid them any mind. Over an hour passed, the pair losing track of time, even after ordering dessert. Mercedes chose the tartufo and Takashi selected the budino on the menu.

When they realized they couldn't continue to stay, Takashi paid for the meal, unwilling to allow Mercedes to cover anything, much to her annoyance, and they left. The drive home continued to consist of casual chatter, and a little of her complaining she could have handled at least the tip.

Takashi's strong hand laced into hers and he held her gaze. His eyes were soft and warm. "So, is there still an us?"

Hearing the question made her heart swell. A demure smile spread across her lips. "Yes."

The car pulled into her driveway and the pair remained

there, looking at each other. Several questions played across her mind. Was he expecting her to say something? Should she ask him inside? *Would that be too fast and desperate after clearing things up between us?*

Takashi smiled, letting go of her hand, and slipped out of the car. She couldn't hide the prick of disappointment that she didn't get the chance to sort out her thoughts.

He walked around the car and opened her door, extending his hand. She accepted his offer and slipped out of the vehicle. Takashi tucked her hand into his arm and led her up the front walk. Once under the overhang of the front entrance, Mercedes turned to place her back to the door and gazed up at him. Her focus found his dark eyes, but soon wandered to his strong jaw, recently shaven for the date, his tempting lips, and strong neck and shoulders. *What was I just thinking about?*

Takashi smiled at her, her heart skipping. "Thank you—for accepting my dinner invitation."

"Well, I wasn't given much of a chance to say no." She hoped he caught the teasing tone to her words.

He reached out and brushed her cheek with the back of his fingers. "You sound *so* miserable. I'm sure all the laughter during dinner was a clear sign to others how tortured you were."

She leaned into his touch. "Well, thanks to the kind man who rescued me, I made it home safe."

A half-smile spread across his face. Desire for those lips to touch her skin burned deep in her. "Yes, I saved you from my evil twin. I'm so glad to see you safe, M'lady."

Mercedes leaned closer, fanning her fingers across his muscular chest. This little play excited her more than she thought it would when she ran with the idea. "Is there anything I can do to repay your kindness?" She bit her lips and looked up at him. He visibly swallowed. "Anything at all?"

Takashi's hand cupped her face, and before she had a moment to think, his lips crashed into hers. She inhaled deeply, and desired gripped her. Mercedes leaned in, her body meeting his, and felt his free arms snake around her.

But all too soon, he pulled away. Mercedes' eyes fluttered open, her focus lazily trailing up from his jawline until her eyes met his; the darkness of his eyes snaring her.

A grin spread across his handsome face. "I believe that will be compensation enough." He took a step back, turning away. "Have a good night, Mercy. I'll talk to you tomorrow."

She frowned. This wasn't how she wanted tonight to end. Takashi acted too much of a gentleman for his own good sometimes. She knew he wouldn't do anything that could possibly jeopardize their recently mended relationship. *He's dumb if he thinks this would.*

Mercedes reached out and grabbed his tie, being sure not to snag his necklace, forcing him to face her. "Don't go."

Takashi's eyes darkened and he came closer, forcing her back into the door. He placed both hands on either side of her, and looked deep into her eyes. "I'll stay as long as you want me to."

Her hand continued to grip his tie, all those dirty things she wanted to use it for pushing to the front of her mind. "How long do you want to stay?"

"Forever."

"Me too." She claimed his lips with hers, and her insides melted as he let go of the door and pulled her close to him.

She dug her fingers into his chest. His taste and intoxicating smell—his *real* taste and smell—drove her crazy. The game had done well replicating it, but nothing compared to the real thing.

Need built inside her as her stomach pressed against his *very* prominent erection. Takashi's hand slid down her back, to her rear, and squeezed once before finding the slit in her dress. He slipped his hand under the material and growled when he found out she was in fact wearing something underneath, though it was rather lacking in material.

Takashi broke the kiss. "I'm glad you didn't tease me with this or anything."

A hearty chuckle came from Mercedes. "I was smart enough to tease you with something even stronger instead."

"And had you kept going, dinner would have never happened."

"I wouldn't have been heartbroken in the least. Tasha, please unlock the door. I don't remember where I hid my key."

"Already done, Miss Mercedes," Tasha said from her phone. "Please do be safe with your actions tonight, you two."

The pair chuckled and Mercedes opened the door, pulling Takashi inside by his tie. By the end of tonight, it was the only thing he'd be allowed to wear.

The moment the door shut, his lips found hers again

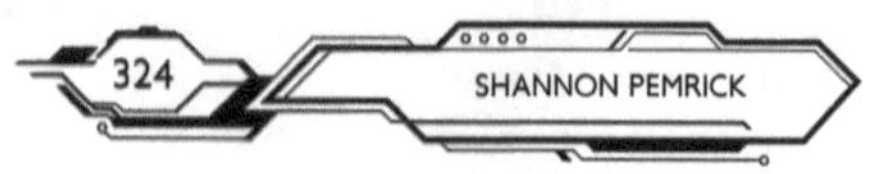

and he tried to pull her back to him by her hips, but she was determined to get him a little farther into the house. Mercedes tugged a little more, and he complied. The pair continued their slow, lust-driven pace into her home. *How big is my living room again?*

She found out a moment later when she bumped into the back of her couch. With nowhere left to go, Takashi pressed against her and his kiss became more demanding, stealing her breath. Her pulse pounded in her ears as his strong presence enveloped her.

Mercedes dug her fingers into his suit jacket and then dragged them across his chest. This needed to go. Her fingers found the buttons and she nearly ripped them off in her haste. She slipped the jacket over his shoulders, forcing him to let her go for a moment, and it fell to the floor. Takashi cared little, and his hands pulled her hips against his.

Mercedes raked her fingers against his chest again, feeling his muscles flex and ripple under her touch this time. Takashi growled and his teeth nipped her bottom lip, one of his hands slipping through the slit in her dress and finding purchase on her ass. A quiet whimper escaped her lips and she pressed harder against him.

Takashi nibbled and sucked on her lower lip, kissing her intermittently, his hands gliding across her lithe form. She needed more. Her fingers fumbled with the buttons on his dress shirt. With each success, Takashi made it more difficult for her. One of his hands migrated up the back of her neck and grabbed a fistful of hair, pulling her head back and exposing her neck to him. Mercedes gasped and then moaned and he trailed kisses down her neck, nipping her skin now and then.

His free hand tugged on her dress by her shoulder, pulling it down a bit. She groaned and went back to fumbling with his shirt. Takashi continued his kissing, pulling her dress lower and lower, until her breast threatened to spill out. Takashi's teeth grazed her collarbone, his hand in her hair letting her go, and then nipped the top of her exposed breast, drawing out a satisfactory hiss from her. He grinned against her skin and then, with both hands, and pulled her dress down, her breast spilling out.

His eyes glanced down at them, noticing the pale silicone discs covering her nipples, and then he looked up at her with a raised brow. "Pasties?"

She grinned. "I'd say it's for a kink factor, but I'd be lying. Bra lines are unsightly in a dress like this, and nipples poking through during dinner is deemed unlady-like."

Takashi slipped his fingers under the silicone. "Well, we're not at dinner now, are we, *M'lady?*"

The pasties popped off with little effort, exposing her taut nipples. Mercedes had made sure to use a pair that didn't have much adhesive life to them left. She wasn't positive this would happen, but she didn't want a new pair to be problematic if it were the end result.

Takashi grinned, making her breath catch, and he kissed her, cupping her supple breasts with his hands and rolling her sensitive buds between his thumbs and index fingers. She groaned as pleasure crept over her. Desire throbbed between her legs, but it wasn't time to give into that. Not yet.

The kissing ended as Takashi dipped his head and slipped one of her taut nipples between his lips.

Mercedes gasped and then groaned as he sucked them, lightly nipping them on occasions. The need and desire in her core grew as she laced her fingers into his hair, ensuring he didn't pull away before she wanted him to be done.

Takashi's now free hand traced her skin, heading up, until it reached her sleeve, still halfway pulled off her arm. With gentle tugs, and switching from one breast to another with his mouth, he distracted her enough to let go of him and he removed the sleeve. His hands glided over her skin again, and slipped between her and her dress, tugging just a bit. At the same time he sucked on her aching bud a little harder, eliciting a moan from her. She couldn't handle it anymore. She needed more.

Letting his hair go, she slipped her fingers into her dress and tugged it down, forcing Takashi to pull away. He tried to stop her. "You're not allowed to rush this."

She nipped his chin. "Who said helping you was rushing?"

He dragged a light touch against the back of her cybernetic arm and she gasped, new sensations rushing to her brain. It felt near identical to her real arm.

Takashi's brow rose. "You felt that?"

She bit her lip. "Forgot to mention, I have a fully functioning one now. It works"—she hissed when he repeated the touch—"beautifully."

Takashi chuckled and snapped his teeth near her cheek. "You've just added a whole new level of fun for me—and you."

Her heart raced and her breath hitched at the promise. She'd always liked subtlety, but she was now seeing why Narissa and Shira found forwardness appealing.

At this rate, he'd get her to pass out from anticipation. She needed to have her own fun to ensure that didn't happen.

Mercedes hooked her thumbs into her dress that now sat at her hips, making sure to loop them into her thong. Now was as good a time as any to try it herself. "If you get to add to this game, then so do I. And I say clothes make this dreadfully boring."

In one swift motion, her clothes fell to the floor. She stepped out of the pile and used one foot to toss her clothes aside. Takashi stared, taking in every exposed inch of her. Mercedes crossed her legs as she sat on the back of the couch and realized she still had her shoes on. She decided they could stay. "Well?"

He licked his lips. "I wish you'd come out dressed like this when I arrived."

She grinned. "Maybe one of these days I will." She pushed off from the furniture and latched onto his shirt, fussing with his buttons again. "Now, this needs to go."

Takashi looped his finger into his tie. "Just the shirt?"

"Tie stays."

His brow rose but he let the tie go and chose to use the opportunity to push her back up against the couch. He came with her, so as to not hinder her task, but the action intrigued her.

The last button dealt with, she slowly slid his shirt over his shoulders, her hands gliding over his skin. His muscles flexed with each touch and his eyes closed a bit, his lips parting just so slightly, giving away his enjoyment of the touch.

When his shirt hit the floor she grinned. "Better."

Takashi chuckled. "Good. Now I can get back to what I was doing."

His reached out, grasping the back of her head, and crashed his lips into hers, devouring her. Her heart pounded in her chest and she attempted to press herself against him, craving the feel of his flesh against hers, but he kept them separate. His free hand roamed her body—her sides—her breasts—her hip—nowhere was safe. She whimpered, pleading for more than just a tease.

Takashi pulled her head back, exposing her neck and kissed her skin. The kisses migrated down—to her collarbone, to her breasts, over each aching bud. His hand continued to tease her with its trailing, and she let out a soft moan. "Takashi…"

He chuckled, his hot breath on her exposed skin sending goosebumps all across her skin. "Patience."

When his trailing stopped at her thigh, she whimpered. She needed some relief, just a little. "Please…"

He grinned and slipped his fingers between her thighs. She gasped, her back arching as pleasure coursed through her, and placed both her hands on the couch for leverage. Takashi continued to pleasure her at those two locations, flooding her with so much desire she thought she may explode.

Then, his lip action shifted, trailing down her stomach, his knees bending and sinking him lower. Her breathing labored, knowing his intent. On his knees now, Takashi's tongue darted into her slick heat, enticing a moan from her. He continued, his action building to a full licking and sucking of her desire. Mercedes threw her head back, letting out a deep moan, and laced her cybernetic hand into his hair.

"Takashi…" she moaned. "Taka…shi…"

Takashi spread her farther apart and plunged his fingers inside her. She moaned more, her words catching in her throat. Her legs wobbled, the desire building in her core becoming too much for her, and she let go of him to grab hold of the couch. Takashi never faltered, continuing his intense pleasuring, setting her whole body on fire.

When she thought she couldn't handle much more, ecstasy burst through her. Mercedes screamed, her hips bucking and her back arching, her whole body consumed with ultimate pleasure. Takashi pulled away as she shuddered out the last of her orgasm and kissed her stomach. She hissed from the sensitive nature of her body.

He touched her between her thighs again with a finger and she sucked in a tight breath. "Takashi, don't."

He didn't pull away, but did stand to look her in the eye. The intensity kept her desire simmering. "Why not?"

She took a controlled breath, trying to find the strength in her legs again to stand upright. "This isn't in-game. I do need a moment's rest before round two."

He pulled his hand away, resting it on her hips and kissed her. "At least I'll get a round two out of you. I want to hear those beautiful sounds from you again."

She chuckled, kissing him back as she placed her hand on his chest and then nipped his chin. "No one said there can't be more than a round one. We do have all night."

He groaned when she nipped his collar bone and slid her hands across his chest. Mercedes' attention migrated south, her barely functional legs lowering her to her knees. She fussed with his trouser button and worked them off his hips. His boxers were next, though she took her time, kissing his navel to tease him. Takashi sucked in a deep breath of anticipation and rested both hands on the back of her neck, but didn't apply any pressure.

She worked him free, his manhood eager for attention. She dragged it out for a moment more with quick, feather-light touches with her fingers, and kissing just below his navel. Takashi's hands twitched and Mercedes grinned. She wrapped her hand around his member and stroked, nipping the soft skin below his navel. Takashi hissed and his hands balled up in her hair. She grinned and then eased her lips over his throbbing manhood.

"Mercy…" he groaned.

She was tempted to pull away, to tease him for picking such a name for her if he complained, but decided what she was doing was more fun. Mercedes sucked and slid his shaft in and out of her mouth with rhythm.

"Mercy…"

The sound of him moaning her name, or plea, she couldn't be sure, a renewed hungry desire flared inside her. Her rhythm picked up speed. Takashi groaned out her name more, his breath laboring. He rocked his hips, his hard member swelled more.

Then suddenly, he jerked away. "Not yet."

Mercedes grinned. "Well, if I knew you were begging, I would have been more mindful."

Takashi rested his fingers under her chin and encouraged her to stand. He pulled her close, his erection pressing into her stomach, and kissed her hard, searing her blood and making her see white. When he pulled away and let go, she took a step back, fanning herself.

"Well then…" Mercedes grabbed a hold of his tie

and took steps toward her bedroom. "I do believe that means this needs to be finished elsewhere."

Takashi's hungry gaze locked onto her, a half-smile spreading across his tempting face, and followed her into the other room. Mercedes led him over to the bed and encouraged him to sit down while she opened a drawer to her nightstand, but he insisted on coming up behind her and trying to distract her. His hands dragged along her sides and arms, and he kissed the back of her neck. His hands migrated down and slipped between her thighs again.

She sucked in a tight breath. "You know, if you keep doing this, you're not going to get to finish your round one."

Takashi chuckled in her ear. "I count my rounds differently, since I need longer breaks. Let's just say, I've gotten my round one, so we're on an even playing field."

Mercedes pulled out the condom from the box she had been searching for. "Well, then I say we need to have a friendly one-v-one match to find out who the winner of round two is."

"Does it have to be a competition? I'm more of a fan of collaboration." He nipped her neck and continued to pleasure her. "It's more rewarding."

She hissed and held up the condom. "Then you're going to need this."

While Mercedes was on birth control, and the medication had an unbeatable effectiveness rate for what was available on the market for women, she liked having the extra peace of mind a condom brought. Once they were together longer, she'd be okay ditching it.

"Prepared, were you?" He chuckled. "Not that I'm

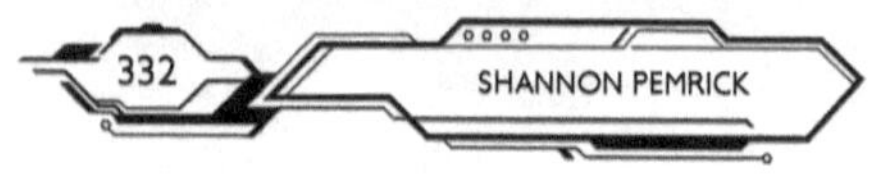

complaining. Means I don't have to run back and grab mine from my wallet."

She glanced back at him. "I'd say you came into this expecting more than me."

"No"—he spread her legs apart, forcing her to brace herself on her nightstand—"but I'd rather be prepared. It's why I have a pair of spare clothes in my car. The only thing I haven't done is jump on male birth control."

Mercedes bit back a moan when Takashi bent her forward and bit her shoulder blade, his fingers still stoking the fan of her slick heat, though stopping in time to keep her from going over the edge. "We can talk about that later."

Takashi chuckled and nipped her other shoulder. "Just so you know, I've wanted to bend you over my desk for some time. I'll take this as a suitable replacement situation for now, though."

She swallowed, her brain getting overloaded. This forward side of him really turned her on far more than she thought it would. "Lamp will be in the way in the long run. Bed would be better."

Takashi angled her over the bed and bent her over, her knees pressing into the edge of the mattress. "As you wish."

"Also…" She took a concentrated breath, heat pulsing through her. "I'd also like that to happen."

He grinned and reached around to play with her breast. "Good."

She took a deep frustrated breath and held up the condom again. "Dammit, Takashi, are you going to use this or not?"

"In a moment." He stared rummaging through the

nightstand drawer. "Possibly. You did say you wanted to try a one-v-one."

She bit her lip. "You said you were into collaboration."

He slipped a finger inside her, making her moan. "I'm not too good at listening, and your idea sounded fun after thinking about it; even more so when I decided not to tell you." He pulled out a bottle of lube she had stored in the drawer. "Besides, we're going to need that."

Takashi went about removing his tie and hung it on her bed post. This left his beaded necklace around his neck, and as she glanced back at him, she was enjoying it on him more than the tie now. "And we'll need that later."

Mercedes bit her lip, dirty thoughts playing in the front of her mind, turning her on more. He rummaged through the nightstand again and pulled out her vibrator. Her face flushed hotter. It wasn't wrong for her to have it… *The fact he took it out specifically—*

Takashi placed it down on the dresser. "And we'll need that later as well."

She swallowed, excitement tingling through her spine into her toes. Takashi leaned over her and took the condom finally. He tore the package with his teeth as he removed his fingers from her to help him easily roll the rubber on. Mercedes heart pounded in her ears as she spread her legs more to make it easier to accept him.

Takashi kissed her back three times before penetrating her, his breath hitching. Mercedes moaned into her comforter and clutched it with her hands, embracing the feeling of him filling her. Takashi thrust hard, and she couldn't stop the moans of pleasure. He continued, finding a rhythm and digging his fingers into her hips.

Mercedes' moaning continued, any words she attempted coming out as incoherent gibberish.

Her time with him in the game two weeks ago felt amazing, but this was different. Even beyond the fact that this was real life, this night with him was far more amazing and pleasurable than before.

Takashi reached around her, slipping his fingers between her legs and teased her sensitive pleasure point. She moaned louder, need building into her core, demanding more. She rocked her body, meeting his thrusts and touches, increasing both their pleasure as skin hit skin. Mercedes' blood simmered and her pulse beat in her ears. Her breathing labored as she came to the cusp of climax.

"Taka…shi…" she managed before ecstasy rolled over her. Her screams of pleasure deafened her and her mind swam as her climax rolled through her entire being.

So overcome by her own release, she barely heard Takashi groan out his. His thrusting slowed as her screams died down. He bent over and rested his forehead on her back, and then he grew still. The only sound that could be heard was their heavy breathing, both nearly in sync with each other.

Once Takashi finally caught his breath, he pulled out of her, allowing her to roll over and sprawl out on her bed, embracing the sensation. He kept an appreciative eye on her as he disposed of the condom and its wrapper in a nearby waste bin before climbing on the bed with her. She snuggled into him, enjoying the feeling of his warmth and strong embrace around her.

"You're the most amazing woman I've been allowed

to have," he mumbled into her hair. "I don't know what I've done to deserve you."

She gazed up at him with a sleepy smile. "You're just saying that because I let you screw me."

Takashi chuckled and dragged the back of a finger up her false arm, sending a million sensations through to her brain. "That helps, but it's not the major contributing factor."

Mercedes watched as he gave her artificial arm more attention. "You really don't mind that I have this?"

"Of course not."

Her brow rose as she looked up at him. "What, do you have some sort of fetish or something?"

A grin spread across his kissable lips. "If being enthralled by everything about you is a fetish, then yes." His gaze shifted down to her arm. "So, you have a fully upgraded model now?"

Mercedes nodded. "This is the full replacement model. After testing, Narissa removed the upgrade model and installed this one. I feel everything like I would a real arm." She chuckled. "Correction, not everything, as it's fiberglass vs. skin at that point, but close enough."

"How are you feeling about it all?"

"More whole than I have in a long time." She kissed him lightly on the lips. "And you... you add to that greatly as well."

He caressed her cheek and kissed her deeply. "I love you."

Her heart leapt at the words and she kissed him back. "I love you too."

Takashi pulled her into a tight embrace, and the pair lay there in bed, naked and listing to the sounds of each other's heartbeat.

CHAPTER 20

Takashi stirred, his head heavy. A muffled pounding on a hard surface pulled him from sleep. He sucked in a deep breath and reached out his arm for the warm body that lay next to him, except he found nothing but warm blankets. His eyes snapped open and he looked around to find Mercedes out of bed fumbling with the buttons of the shirt she threw on—his shirt, he noted—her eyes groggy with sleep. She smiled at him and then left the room, nearly tripping on the shoes she had kicked off sometime last night.

His head still foggy, he looked at the clock, reading *9:03 a.m.* Takashi rubbed his face to wake himself up. *Who could be at the door at this hour?*

The front door opened and Mercedes' groggy voice spoke, "Dad? What are you doing here?"

"Mercedes, why are you not dressed yet?" Jayce asked.

Mercedes sucked in a deep breath; Takashi could only

assume she was trying to wake up. She spoke again, "What are you talking about?"

Takashi rolled out of bed and searched for some pants, an uneasy feeling falling over him.

"What do you mean 'what are you talking about?' Today is the anniversary of your mother's death. We always go to her grave together."

She groaned. "Shit, I forgot. I'm sorry."

"You forgot?"

Takashi threw on some jeans he'd retrieved from his car sometime last night as Jayce's voice rose an octave.

"How could you for—" Jayce's words caught when Takashi emerged from the room, still rubbing his face to wake up more. "What is going on here?"

Mercedes brow furrowed. "You know Takashi, Dad."

"Yes, but why is he here, coming out of your room?"

She crossed her arms. "Besides the fact that I'm an adult and can have whomever I please at *my* house?"

Her father's face reddened. "That doesn't explain why he's coming out of your room, half dressed. You said the two of you were friends."

"We are," she said. "And as of recently, he's now my boyfriend."

If the tension in the room weren't so thick, Takashi would have allowed himself to enjoy those words.

Jayce's eyes darkened. "You forgot about your mother because of him? You'd really put him before—"

"Shut up." Mercedes' fists clenched. "Just shut up. How dare you try to twist Mother's memory into your own twisted prerogative? Have you really forgotten what she told us? Well, have you?"

Seeing the mix of emotions flowing out of her, Takashi

wished to close the distance between them and pull her into a tight embrace; to calm her and reassure her everything was going to be okay. But his feet kept him in the doorway.

"I remember," she said, continuing without allowing her father to speak. "The last thing she said to me… 'It's okay to be sad, it's okay to remember, but please don't let the past get in the way of your future.'"

A mix of emotions played across Jayce's face, and within Takashi himself. Takashi understood her father's position, his grief over his lost wife playing a big role in his actions, but Mercedes had a valid point. Not only was moving on what her mother wanted, but even as hard it was to do, Mercedes was trying, and it wasn't fair that her father was chastising her for it.

Tears welled up in Mercedes' eyes. "She made us *both* promise we wouldn't live in the past!"

Takashi couldn't just stand in the doorway anymore and watch this—not with her like this. He came up behind Mercedes and wrapped her up in his arms. She hid her face in his chest but refused to cry.

Takashi looked to Jayce. "Give us fifteen minutes and we'll meet you outside."

Jayce gave a small nod, his eyes rather distant and his voice coming out hollow. "I'll give you as long as you need. I'll be in my car."

Her father left, closing the door behind him, giving Takashi the opportunity to focus on Mercedes. "Are you all right?"

She nodded, taking a deep breath and wiping a tear from her eyes. "Yes. That was just upsetting. He's never acted like that before."

He tucked a stray hair behind her ear. "Grief is a difficult monster to control. All we can do is help him the best we can, and get him to understand it's not wrong to move on, promise or no promise to your mother."

Mercedes smiled. "Thank you."

Takashi kissed her on the lips. "You don't have to thank me. Now, let's get ready and go together."

"Are you sure?"

"Why wouldn't I be?"

She looked away. "I don't know… I just thought you may want to go home instead."

Takashi made her look at him. "I want to be part of your life, Mercedes. Every aspect of it, even the sad parts. And I did know your mother somewhat. I think it's overdue I go see her too."

She nodded. "Okay. I guess a quick shower is in order so as not to keep my dad waiting."

Takashi grinned and lifted her up in his arms. Mercedes squeaked. "To reduce water usage, and reduce shower time, we should shower together."

She giggled. "I don't think that's how it ends up working out."

He hushed her as he carried her back into the bedroom. "You're not supposed to say that out loud."

Mercedes laughed more but didn't fight him.

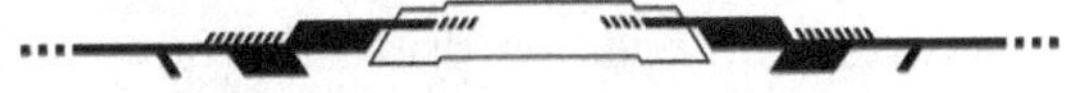

A warm wind blew, bringing the promise of rain, unsurprisingly. Mercedes walked behind her father, flowers in arm. Takashi walked beside her, his hand resting on her lower back. All three remained silent. It'd been like this since they'd climbed into the car with her father.

Last night had been amazing. Takashi had been amazing. And without fail, he'd been there for her this morning. As she figured would happen, the shower they'd taken delayed them more, Takashi taking the time to 'remove all stress' from her, but her father didn't comment on their tardiness. He barely acknowledged them, lost in his own thoughts.

Even now, he showed her words had struck a chord with him. She hoped he was going to be okay. This day, along with a few others during the year, was hard on him, but she'd assumed her father had healed more than he obviously had. She didn't want his heart to be the death of him, and didn't want him dying alone, but if he insisted on holding on, there wasn't much she could do to help him.

The trio came to a dark headstone detailed with flower carvings and gold engravings, reading:

In loving memory
Gail

Jayce T.   *Allyson J.*
2052 -   *2056 - 2094*

Old, dried out flowers from the last time the grave had visitors rested against the headstone. Her father cleaned them up, letting Mercedes set down the new ones. She then knelt down in front of the grave, her father always giving her first chance to talk to her mother. Takashi knelt down beside her.

"Hey, mom, I'm here." It should have felt weird speaking to her in front of Takashi, but it didn't. "I know it's been a while. I've been busy living my life, like you said I should. It's not easy, but I'm trying."

She glanced at Takashi. "And you'll never guess what happened recently…"

Minutes passed as she talked to the gravestone, recapping her testing of the new arm and her and Takashi finally coming together. Neither Takashi nor her father said anything, giving her this moment she needed.

A tear rolled down her cheek when she finished. Remembering hurt; knowing her mother wasn't there when she needed her the most caused the most pain. In the past she'd be bawling her eyes out by now, but having her father, her friends, and now Takashi by her side, it got easier day by day.

Takashi was the next to speak; Mercedes had told him before leaving the house it'd be okay to do. "Hey, Missus Gail, it's me, Takashi. It's been… a *long* time. A lot has happened since I saw you, but the biggest one is what Mercedes told you. You always said I'd like your daughter if we ever met. Surprise, surprise, you were right."

Mercedes couldn't stop the quiet giggle that escaped her lips. Takashi glanced at her, an amused smile on his lips, and then spoke for a bit longer before letting her father have his time. Mercedes pulled Takashi to the side to give her father space. She'd learned over the years he didn't let down his "tough guy" walls unless he felt alone.

"Mercedes," Takashi said in a quiet voice. "Can I ask what happened? My mother wouldn't talk about it to me."

Mercedes frowned. "It was… cancer."

Takashi's eyes widened. Cancer-related deaths weren't common these days. At the rate medical technology had advanced in the last ninety years, most people recovered with little residual health issues. The technology wasn't there to replace the need for cybernetics yet, but at this rate, it was predicted in the next fifty years or so that kind of change would come about. The reminder always made Mercedes wonder how that would affect Narissa and her family.

Mercedes continued so Takashi would understand how it happened, even if it was difficult for her to go through. "It was an aggressive form. The doctors couldn't combat it, no matter how hard they tried. We lost her within six months of finding out about the mass."

Takashi pulled her close and kissed her on the head. "I'm sorry…"

The image of her mother's last moments with her flashed through Mercedes' mind. Her mom had tried so hard to smile and ignore the pain she was in. She'd tried to keep Mercedes on the right path, and teach her to see a light in the darkness.

Tears bubbled in Mercedes' eyes. She buried herself into Takashi's chest and couldn't hold back the pain. She cried and Takashi let her. She tried to be strong; tried to keep moving even when the pain became unbearable. But there were times she couldn't keep up the unbreakable façade. She couldn't keep that wall up. Today wasn't a day she could fight, and Takashi understood.

By the time she'd collected herself, her father had finished at the grave and approached the pair. His eyes appeared a bit red, but she knew better than to say anything.

"Are you ready to head to Sushiki?" he asked.

Mercedes nodded. "My belly is angry I haven't given it breakfast, so it's ready for lunch."

Her father eyed Takashi for a moment. "He can come, too."

Takashi's brow rose. "Huh?"

"We always go for lunch at Sushiki," Mercedes explained. "Goro usually joins us, and we just enjoy each other's company like mom would want us to."

"Miss Mercedes," Tasha said. "I called Goro before you left the house to let him know there'd be an extra body, as I assumed Takashi would be joining you and your father for lunch."

"Thanks, Tasha." She looked to her father when an idea came to her. "Dad, can I invite a few friends to join us? Only one would be there physically if she can go. The others we'd video in."

Her father sighed. "Sure, whatever."

"I'll pay for everything," Takashi offered.

Mercedes gasped. "Stop trying to pay for everything!"

Her father started to walk toward the car. "Careful, kid, I might start to like you with offers like that."

"Oh, well, we can't have that." Takashi laughed.

"Daddy! Don't encourage this," Mercedes complained.

"What, I'm old fashioned."

"More like ancient," she muttered.

Her father pointed at Takashi. "Don't think you'll butter me up enough to ask to marry my daughter. That's never going to happen."

Takashi chuckled. "We'll see."

Mercedes' face flushed hot. She wasn't sure what to make of the situation. *It's a bit early to talk about all that, right?* "Um, Tasha, please call some of my friends so I can invite them to this lunch."

"I've already done so, Miss Mercedes," Tasha replied. "Shira will meet you at the restaurant, and the others are happy to video in. I have notified Goro of the additions. I also made an attempt to invite Takashi's family, but they are all busy. They sent their heartfelt thoughts instead."

"Great, thank you." Her thoughts all jumbled, she followed the two men to the car.

They drove back to her place to retrieve a few tablets for the call-ins, and then headed for Sushiki. Shira was already there waiting outside by the time they arrived, Snake sitting patiently next to her.

Shira waved at them and then her brow rose when she noticed the tablets. "What are those for?"

"For everyone to video chat with us," Mercedes said.

"Every…one?"

Mercedes nodded. "Narissa, Ajax, Kiara and Darius, and Jasper and Zach."

Her expression dropped and she appeared to be struggling not to recoil. Snake nudged her hand, giving away her rising anxiety. "Okay…"

Mercedes' eyes softened. "It's going to be okay, Shira. This will be as good for you as it will be for us."

Her lips twisted and her eyes tightened. "Is this why you wanted me to join you?"

Mercedes *bopped* her friend on the forehead with her palm. "Of course not, don't be silly. Now let's get inside."

Shira huffed but opened the door, Snake getting to his feet and waiting for her to enter after she let the others in. Mercedes looked around, finding Goro approaching from one of the private rooms.

She smiled at him. "*Konnichiwa*, Goro."

The elderly man bowed. "*Konnichiwa*, Mercedes-san."

He turned and bowed to everyone else and greeted them before requesting they follow him to the private room. Mercedes ducked under the cloth half-curtain and gazed around. A long table, set with plates, filled the room to near entirety. Pillows for sitting rested on the floor on all sides, and in the center of the table rested a small shrine, a photograph of her mother standing tall. Mercedes smiled and then found a spot to call hers before setting up the tablets.

She called Narissa first, while Takashi called Ajax, and Shira called Jasper and Zach per Mercedes' request. She didn't look happy about the request, but didn't argue. Mercedes had done it on purpose, hoping it'd force Shira to face her reality. She did too much running. All of their friends helped in ways, those two men especially, but there was only so much any of them could do. Shira had to make the effort to fix her own life.

Narissa and Ajax answered without issue, but the call for the two boys rang a few times before a young girl's voice picked up. "Hello?"

"Hey, Serenity," Shira's chipper voice greeted. The instantaneous change in Shira's demeanor surprised Mercedes. She knew Shira had a soft spot for Jasper's daughter, but she'd never seen her friend interact with the little girl.

"She-ra!" the girl exclaimed. She then coughed and sniffled, indicating she was home from school due to illness.

Mercedes chuckled. Shira had told her of the name the little girl had given her a few years ago. She struggled to say her name correctly, and the one she managed just stuck. It helped that Shira was a fan of a character from an old cartoon with that name.

"Hey, your dad was expecting a call from me and Mercedes. Is he around?" Shira asked as she placed the tablet on the table, giving everyone a good look at the little girl, no older than six, with bright green eyes and dark brown hair.

Serenity shook her head. "No, Daddy went to pick up lunch. Zach is here"—she looked around—"somewhere. Zach! Zach! She-ra is video chatting with me."

Everyone heard something crash to the floor and then someone called out, "She's what?"

"She's video chatting with me. She called for Daddy, but he's not here."

"Keep her on the horn, Serenity," Zach yelled from wherever he was. "I'll be right there."

"'Kay!"

Shira's service dog settled down next to her finally and rested his head on her lap.

Serenity gasped. "Snake! Hi, Snake!" The black dog looked at her, ears alert, but didn't respond audibly, making the young girl huff. "Meanie. You always greet me when I say hi."

Has Shira video chatted with Serenity before? That didn't make sense to Mercedes. If she'd done that, she wouldn't have been so reluctant to make the call.

Shira pointed to Snake's service vest. "That's because he's working. He knows better than to bark unless it's an emergency when he wears his vest. When he's heard you through the game chat, he wasn't working."

That explains it.

"Oh!" Serenity clapped. "Then good boy!"

The room rumbled with laughter. They quieted down just as someone on Serenity's side ran into the room. A tall, athletically built man shot into the feed next to Serenity, almost falling over when his momentum kept him going a little too much. He ran his fingers through his short blonde hair. "Hey… Shira. You're looking wicked good."

She waved at him with her good arm, her body rigid. "Hey, Zach."

Serenity looked at Zach, her nose scrunching. "Why did you run, Zach? She wasn't going anywhere."

His ice-blue eyes darted back and forth between the camera and the little girl. "Um… I… um…"

Mercedes and her friends laughed as he struggled, and Shira's cheeks reddened a bit. *See, Shira?*

Just then, a door opened on their end and Jasper's boomed through their place. "I'm back with the food."

Serenity turned away from the camera. "Daddy, She-ra is video chatting us!"

"Am I that late?" Everyone heard him put some bags down, and far more calmly than Zach, then his face appeared in the feed. Tall, muscular, with tattoos covering his tan skin, he didn't fit the typical look of "father," but anyone who even thought to call him unfit would end up in the hospital, and Serenity… she'd end up with an ice cream out of the deal somehow. His green eyes squinted as he smiled. "Hey, Shira."

"Hey," she also waved to him, but Mercedes noticed her movements were even stiffer this time. Snake was

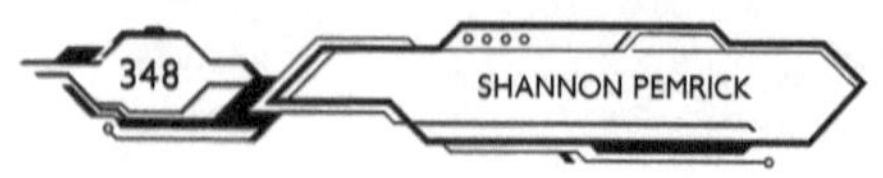

also pressing himself closer to her and nudging her artificial hand. Even with this calmer approach, she was still struggling with this.

Mercedes wasn't sure what to make of it, but she needed to get the attention away from Shira so she could calm down. She went about calling Kiara and Darius as she spoke, "What did you pick up, Jasper?"

"Your assistant said something about Japanese cuisine, so I thought we'd eat the same," Jasper said before ducking out of the display.

"Oh, I'll help you, Daddy." Serenity ran off to assist him. Zach took advantage of the extra space, but Shira turned the tablet so it wasn't as directed on her, clearly disappointing him.

Mercedes finally got a hold of Kiara and Darius, but she wasn't sure it was such a good thing when she was met with the sight of Kiara wrestling with a tall, dark-tan-skinned, man, Kiara telling him to get his own chair. "Um, do you guys want me to call you back?"

"No," Kiara said. "Darius needs to stop bein' a dobber."

Oh boy, he's got her worked up.

"I am not," Darius said, his dark eyes darting toward the camera. "She's insisting on setting up the video where it's hard to squeeze two people in and won't share her seat."

"Because you're over exaggeratin' and can fit neist tae me without issues!" Kiara grabbed a fistful of his dark hair and yanked, getting him to grunt in pain. "Now, get oot o' ma spot!"

Amused smiles spread across the faces of everyone watching. A doorbell rang and Darius stopped. "Food is here."

He let go of Kiara and ran off. The sudden release on his unsuspecting victim left her unbalanced and she fell over, letting out a squeak and then an *oof*. Her hand rose back into the feed, her middle finger extended. "Jackarse!"

"Hey, we have a kid on this end," Zach warned.

"You've said worse around her," Shira chastised.

"And I'm yelled at every time by you and Jasper. So it's not like I get away with it."

"Get away with what?" Serenity asked, popped in next to him, her tiny hands full with a juice box and one takeout box.

"Saying bad words," Zach said.

Serenity giggled. "Nope. She-ra kicks yah butt wicked good when you do."

For the first time since the video feeds started, Shira laughed. It made Mercedes relax a little. She'd started to think she'd done something wrong by doing this.

Goro entered the private room, along with several waitstaff. They all carried food or drink, the drink mostly sake, and set it down on the table. The waitstaff left when there was nothing left to distribute, and Goro sat down next to Mercedes. He and her father poured the sake and offered a toast. Those present grabbed their sake, those not picked up what they could if they were at work, or whatever was available at their home. Even Serenity had her juice box.

Everyone said a few kind words honoring her mother, and then Goro yelled, "*Kanpai!*"

"Kanpai!"

Mercedes, Shira, and her father were the first to finish their sake, consuming the rice alcohol like champs. Takashi's mouth hung open, and Darius whistled.

"Don't count little Serenity out, though," Narissa called. "Look at her."

Everyone watched as she sucked on her juice straw, her face turning red from the single breath attempt she was going for. She finally let go, her lips smacking together and letting out an "ahh…" before shaking her box. No sounds came from inside.

"I did it, Daddy!"

Jasper curled his hand into a fist and held it up to her. "That was sick. Wicked job, sweetie."

She bumped her fist with his and then gave Zach a high-five. Serenity looked to Shira, who put her fist to the camera, allowing the little girl to also virtually "give" her a fist-pound too. *How cute.* It made Mercedes wonder, if she had a daughter, would she be that adorable? Would she be Takashi's? *Whoa, Mercedes, jumping the gun, don't you think?*

She glanced at Takashi when he reached down and squeezed her hand under the table, smiling at her. Was he thinking the same? *Stop jumping the gun!* She smiled back at him and popped a sushi roll in her mouth.

Takashi's phone went off and Ochi's voice came from it. "Takashi, I know you are busy, but this message is an important one."

Takashi, mid-bite into some rice, put his food down and whipped out his phone. His brow creased. "You've got to be kidding me."

Mercedes frowned. "Another hacking issue?"

He nodded and went to typing to the GM. Darius focused on them. "Hacking?"

Takashi was too focused on his messaging to respond, so Mercedes did on his behalf. "Yeah, someone keeps hacking his business. This is like the fourth or fifth time, I think."

"That's peculiar. Takashi isn't the type to make enemies. Which GM is helping you?"

"Ashton," Takashi said. "He's been helpful, but sometimes difficult to deal with."

Darius chuckled. "Sounds like him." He pulled out his phone. "I'll dig around with my contacts to see if I can get any more light on the matter for you. We don't need these types of situations continuing. It presents too big a flaw in the game's security."

Darius worked in the art department for Lion Rage Games, the creators of Lusara Fates. Even though he designed character models and environments, he had good connections with those in other departments. And of course, being friends with him came with some perks, particularly around the time of Gamer Nine and getting discounted tickets, and dealing with annoying in-game matters, like this one.

Takashi placed his phone down and rubbed his face. "Any help would be greatly appreciated. I'd like for this to stop finally."

Lunch resumed; much conversation and laughter with it. It made Mercedes' heart swell. She had such amazing friends, and had her mother not turned her into a nerd, she wouldn't have ever met these people. She wouldn't trade them.

"C'mon, Shira, just one tournament," Zach begged. "It's three months from now."

Shira shoved a roll in her mouth, her cheek resting on her cybernetic hands. "I said I'm not interested."

"Guys, help us."

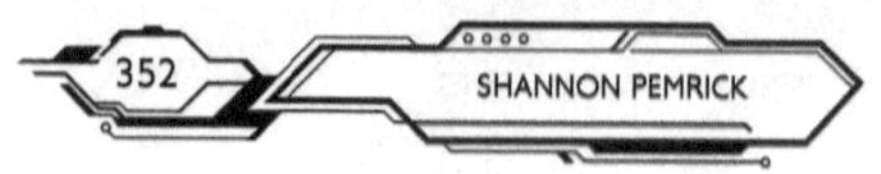

"I don't see why she shouldn't," Darius said.

"I do," Kiara said.

He turned to her, brow furrowed. "Why?"

"Because you think she should."

The two began to wrestle and the others laughed.

"Where is this tournament?" Mercedes asked.

"Anaheim," Zach said. "It's in your neighborhood, so you wouldn't have to go very far."

Mercedes and Narissa exchanged glances, but before they could protest, Jasper jumped in. "I already told you, we're not doing that one."

Zach stared at him. "What? It has a wicked prize pool!"

"We're not doing it." He ate some food, not acknowledging Zach anymore.

I wonder what that's all about. She knew Shira hadn't told them about her accident. Zach would have known not to offer that location if he knew. So why didn't Jasper want to go there specifically?

"Why not the one in L.A. in six months?" Ajax suggested. "That's a big one with a number of different tournaments, right, Darius?"

He stopped wrestling with Kiara. "Well, yeah. It's Gamer Nine. Everyone knows that's the biggest one these days. Your company even does their big reveals, because with big games come big tech changes."

"We couldn't get our sponsahs to jump on that train," Jasper said. "Hahd for us to risk money on those competitions without the backup of the sponsahs."

"You have one now," Ajax said.

Both Jasper and Zach leaned in. "Say what?"

"GameTech is now your sponsor for it. I'll forward you the contract later."

The two boys gave each other a high-five and Serenity cheered, though it was obvious she wasn't exactly sure why the two were excited.

Jasper then focused on Shira. "What do you say? Threes matches happen there, too."

"I'm not going. I will never go. Stop asking."

Jasper's excitement dropped, and he frowned. Zach looked disappointed, but Jasper's reaction was a bit deeper than that. Mercedes didn't like it. Shira needed to overcome this. *But this isn't the time to push it.*

Mercedes clapped her hands together. "We're changing the subject. This is too tense and that's not why we're here."

"Yeah, everybody be wicked happy!" Serenity cheered, holding up the new juice box her father had gotten her.

The chatter continued, going to better topics. Shira's mood improved with the attention off her, sending relief through Mercedes.

Takashi leaned over and whispered in her ear. "We'll work on her."

Mercedes kept her voice low. "I have a feeling they'll wear her down eventually."

"I'm pretty sure it'll be Serenity who gets her. Shira doesn't seem to be able to resist her."

She looked up at him through her lashes. "Can you blame her?"

He grinned. "Not at all." He lowered his voice more. "If we have one, she'll be just as adorable."

Her heart thumped hard in her chest. *He had thought the same...*

Mercedes' father's eyes narrowed. "What are you two whispering about?"

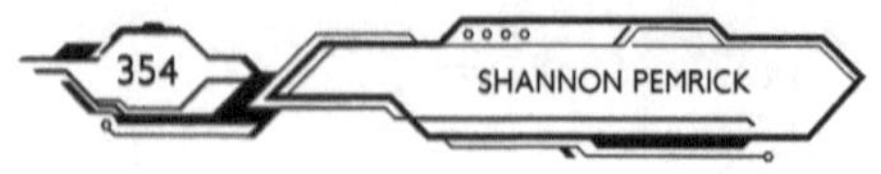

"Daddy, stop." Mercedes poured him more sake. "I'm allowed to date."

"Wait, you two are finally official?" Ajax asked. "About damn time!"

Her friends toasted the two, making her shrink back. She hadn't thought it was such a big deal. Takashi found it amusing, as did Goro, who also toasted them and then winked. Her father looked unamused, but that was to be expected. Ever since she was little, he told her she was going to be shipped off to a convent so she couldn't see any boys.

The party continued, more shenanigans ensuing. Goro slipped away a few times to handle the business, but he allowed them to stay as long as they wished. Mercedes worried about the tab, but Takashi insisted it wouldn't be an issue. They were here to enjoy themselves in her mother's memory, and that's what they'd do. No matter how long that'd take, or inebriated people would get.

CHAPTER 21

The motorcycle engine cut and Takashi climbed off, pulling off his helmet and hanging it on the handlebar. He checked his backpack to make sure the dinner he'd brought for Mercedes hadn't gotten ruined on the ride over and then headed for the shop door. She was working late tonight, trying to get payroll all situated—something about an issue with the computer earlier in the day delaying her. Takashi offered to bring her dinner. He had an update for her on their phone issue, making it a win-win for him.

No lights were on in the main part of the shop, but the office indicated Mercedes' location. Takashi entered, finding her toiling away on the computer. Placing the backpack on the floor as quietly as he could, he tiptoed up behind her.

"I know you're there," she said, not looking up from her work. "The shop echoes."

He hung his head. "Damn."

She chuckled and continued working. "What did you bring me?"

"Soup and sandwiches. Mother made the soup."

She finally turned away from her work, licking those tempting lips of her. "Sounds delicious."

Takashi handed over her dinner and then pulled up a chair. She took several ravenous bites before talking to him. "How was your day?"

"Eventful. My father made a discovery with the phones."

She stopped eating. "Yeah? I hope he's not going too crazy on this. I don't want to inconvenience him."

Takashi waved her off. "Trust me, he likes it. Plus it's given him a nice challenge for his latest interns. With what they found out, a few have just about secured jobs at his firm."

Mercedes' brow rose. "What did they find that could do that for them?"

"Someone tampered with our phones remotely." She put down her sandwich to hear him out. "He's not sure how exactly at the moment, as they covered their tracks well, but the traces indicate short-range connections."

Her brow knitted. "So, we met this person?"

"If we didn't meet them, came in range of them." Takashi pinched his nose. "Of course I can't figure out who would want to do this to us. It'd be one thing if I'd been blocked from anyone on my contact list, then I could see it as some sort of prank. But due to the specifics of the targeting, someone had an end game."

Mercedes nodded. "It is weird… I wonder if this is somehow related to your hacking issue."

His brow rose. "That's an interesting theory. It has

some merit, but, then again, the hacking started first not second. If they were related, the person doing the hacking would also be stalking. And if they're doing that, why only game and phone hacking?"

Mercedes' lips twisted. "Good point. I guess we'll just have to wait on your dad and his interns for more clues. I trust it won't take much longer to get the answers we need."

Takashi leaned closer to her. "True. Though the efficiency of these interns is making me think I need one; one that can work their way up to full business partner."

Mercedes ate some more of the soup, her eyes twinkling. "Oh really? Would there be a no-fraternizing policy with the boss?"

Takashi grinned, leaning in a little more. "Depends on who I pick."

"I might have to dust off my resume."

He traced a finger along her jaw. "Something tells me you'd be plenty qualified."

"Is that so?" Mercedes grinned, poked him in the nose, and then went back to working on payroll. "I'll have to think about it after I get this done."

Takashi couldn't help but sigh, his body rather disappointed. "Tease."

She chuckled. "You can wait another ten minutes."

He moved closer to her and kissed her neck. "You sure about that?"

"You'll have to be or you'll be sent home for gross misconduct." She winked at him and he sighed, sitting back in his seat. *Tease.*

It wasn't like he hated it, but she got a little too much enjoyment out of teasing him like this. Of course, he knew better. She was serious about her work, but that didn't stop him from trying to distract her.

He let her work for about three minutes before resting his chin on her shoulder. "Are you done yet?"

Mercedes chuckled. "No."

He fake grumbled, but remained where he was. Another minute passed and he slid his hand across her thigh. Her muscles tensed but that remained her only reaction. He continued, gliding his hand along her inner thigh.

"Takashi," she warned. "Need I remind you there's a security camera in this office, and my dad would not be too pleased to see any funny business on the recordings."

He continued to tease her inner thigh. "Well, I don't expect him to like me."

She gave him a sidelong glance. "He's actually starting to like you, you know."

Takashi pulled his head back, his brow furrowed. "Come again?"

She nodded and went back to payroll. "With you coming around all the time this past week, and how well you've treated me, he's begrudgingly starting to like you. It also helps you haven't tried to persuade me to move away yet."

"Hmm." He pressed his face against her neck, squeezing her thigh with a firm hand. "That does put me in quite the precarious situation, doesn't it?"

She turned her head and stared deep into his eyes. His heart thumped in his chest and desire crawled through him when she pulled him in for a rough kiss. Unfortunately it didn't last long.

Mercedes pulled away and went back to work on

her employees' payroll. "It's all you get until I'm done. Continue to misbehave and I won't even give you that."

He groaned, this time frustrated by the teasing, but forced himself to sit back in his chair. Her tone had a slight edge to it that screamed, "Don't push your luck, seriously."

The pair froze when something loud crashed outside the shop. They listened, but no more similar sounds came.

"Cat knocking over a trashcan?" Takashi asked.

Brow furrowed, Mercedes went to check the security cameras. "Maybe, but best to check."

Takashi followed her and they looked at the split camera screens on the TV set up for monitoring. Just barely in view was one of the shop trashcans laying on its side. Movement on another camera caught their attention. Mercedes grabbed his hand when someone in dark clothes snuck around the building. "Takashi…"

"I got it." He ran out of the office before she could stop him.

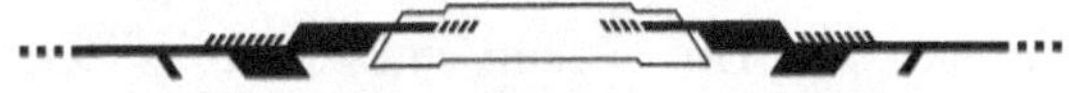

Mercedes' pulse raced and her chest tightened. There was no mistaking this person was planning something devious. Why else sneak around in dark clothes? But Takashi springing into action scared her more. For all they knew this guy had a weapon. "Tasha—"

"I've already contacted the police, Miss Mercedes," Tasha said. "Please get Mister Takashi to cease his pursuit in engaging this individual. He could be dangerous."

She didn't have to be told twice. She bolted after him, catching up quick, and grabbed his arm. "Takashi, wait."

He gave her a reassuring smile. "I'm just going to scare him off."

"What if he has a gun or something?"

"Don't worry, I got this."

But before he could convince her, something smashed through one of the garage door windows, setting off the alarm. She couldn't stop the scream. The figure came in sight, looking right at the pair, and then threw something bright into the building before bolting.

Mercedes gasped at the sound of a breaking bottle and watched in terror as fire roared up from where the bottle impacted.

"Miss Mercedes," Tasha called. "I sense a fire. You must get out of here."

"No." Mercedes steeled herself and yanked off one of the nearby fire extinguishers. No one was taking this business from her.

She smothered the fire in dry chemical powder, as well as the area around it to reduce any extra combustible risks. Mercedes let out a deep sigh of relief when she got it all under control. *That could have been bad.*

She looked around to find Takashi gone. *Shit!* He had to have run after the perpetrator.

"Miss Mercedes," Tasha said. "I've received a transmission from Ochi, Mister Takashi has apprehended the mysterious man. I've relayed the fire and the capture to the police. I have also notified your father of the incident. He will be here as soon as possible."

A wave of mixed emotions fell over her. "That... okay..."

"I've received another transmission. Takashi requests rope to keep this guy still."

Mercedes put down the extinguisher and searched for something to help him. She didn't find rope but did find two tie down straps, and a little bit of duct tape. *I'll just MacGyver this.*

She left the building, grabbing a wrench in case he needed a good thump on the head to make him behave, and searched out this vandal and Takashi. Mercedes found them both by the trashcans the unknown man had knocked down earlier. Takashi appeared to be struggling to keep this guy down, so she went to work.

"Nice work," Takashi said when she finished. The man struggled against her improvised restraint, but wasn't able to get out of it. "Creative, too."

Mercedes placed her hands on her hips. "Thanks. I just hope it holds up until the police get here."

The man looked up at her. "Please, let me go. I can't be taken in. It'll hurt my family even more."

Mercedes' eyes hardened. "Well, you should have thought about that before you tried to burn down my business."

"I didn't have a choice! My wife is sick and unable to work. He would have taken my job from me and made sure I could never work in my field again."

"*He?* Who is he?" Takashi asked.

Before he managed to answer, the blaring sounds of police cars echoed down the street. In seconds, red and blue lights flashed against the building walls.

The man panicked. "Please. Please don't let them take me."

"Who hired you?" Takashi asked again.

"Jason. Jason Atilon."

Mercedes and Takashi looked at each other, Mercedes speaking. "Isn't that Emi's boyfriend?"

The man nodded. "Yes. He forced me to target those who he didn't want having contact with her. He said something about them being a threat and taking her from him."

Takashi turned to Mercedes. "I'm going to call Emi to let her know what's going on. This guy could be lying, but if he's not, she needs to know."

Mercedes nodded. As much as Mercedes didn't want to believe this guy, she couldn't find it in her. Every time she'd met Jason, her skin crawled, and with his controlling actions a few days ago, she could see such crazed, drastic actions. *It also explains the connection between the vandalized businesses.*

Three officers in blue rushed around the corner as Takashi stepped aside to make his phone call—two dealing with the captured man, while another approached Mercedes.

"Are you Mercedes Gail?" he asked.

Mercedes nodded. "Yes, Sir."

"I'd like to talk to you about the incident for our investigation and report."

The captured man struggled against the two officers as they cuffed him and undid the temporary bindings Mercedes had bound him with. He yelled out various things from apologies to repeating Jason's involvement.

"Has he been that loud this whole time?" the officer asked.

"No, but it's what he told us just before you arrived."

The officer nodded and recorded it in a digital notepad device. "Have you met this man before?"

"No, but the two of us know Jason, the man he's accusing of coercing him into this situation. He's dating a friend of ours."

The officer wrote it down. "I was told there was an attempt at arson, but the fire was neutralized. What did he use?"

"A Molotov," Mercedes said. "I saw him throw it into the building and I put out the fire when it broke on the ground."

"That matches some reports in the past month," the officer indicated. "A motor oil mix with a kerosene-dipped rag was used in a few other business-related vandal incidents. We'll be sure to investigate this weapon thoroughly to be sure it's the same method."

Mercedes looked over to the man they were now getting into the police car. "I doubt you'll have a hard time getting anything out of him. He told us a lot as it is."

"This is true, but we must do our investigating as well, to be sure."

The pair gazed out to the parking lot when a car came to a screeching halt and her father climbed out. "That's my father, Jayce Gail. He's the owner."

He tipped his hat to her. "Thank you. I will have to speak with him, but if we need you again I'll come looking for you."

Mercedes nodded. "Okay. I'll stay here until I'm told to leave."

The officer walked away and Takashi approached. "Are you okay, Mercedes?"

She smiled. "I'll be fine. Did you get a hold of Emi?"

He shook his head. "No, similar call situation as when I try to call you. I'm starting to think that guy is telling the truth. I called Rei and she's going to let Emi know for us. She wanted me to tell you she's glad you're not hurt."

Mercedes smiled. "I appreciate the thought."

"I'm glad the two of you are getting along now. I was afraid it'd never happen."

"Same. I look forward to getting to know her more. I like her."

Takashi took in all the officers moving about. "So, what now?"

"The police are going to keep investigating. I need to finish payroll. Hopefully they'll let me do that. Then once things are all cleared up, I think going home is a good idea."

Takashi tucked her arm into his. "Let's get the first item on the list checked off."

The pair strolled into the building, headed toward the office, but as they passed the storage room, Mercedes stopped. She stared at the room filled with miscellaneous parts, tools, and whatever else her father purchased for this place, the lights of the police car bouncing around in the room in a way that made her see it a bit differently.

"Everything okay, Mercedes?" Takashi asked.

She wandered over to the room, turned on a light and peered in. She'd never seen this room empty before. Her mother would complain all the time it needed to be cleaned out so they could make it a waiting room or store front for parts or something, but her father wouldn't listen. *A store front...*

Large windows, a door leading outside, and a counter

somewhere on a back wall, this was big enough and outfitted to work as a reception area, or even fit a small business. "Hey, Takashi. Would your mother be opposed to moving the business to some place smaller?"

Takashi came up behind her. "Huh?"

She pointed to the storage room. "Under all this stuff is a room my mom wanted to use as a lobby or potential storefront to sell parts. I've never seen this room clean, but she once insisted it was before. My guess is that was when my dad first bought this place, but that's beside the point. I'm wondering, instead of using it for a lobby, if your mother could utilize it for her floral shop. It's smaller than the other place, but the location is good, and she can capitalize on our clientele. A lot of them have rather angry partners for their expensive hobby."

Takashi laughed. "That's actually a brilliant idea! She's been talking about not rebuilding, and instead selling the lot, so she may like the opportunity. Once this all settles down, we can work up a time to talk to her about it."

Mercedes smiled at him. "Great. I'll also talk to my dad about the idea." She winked. "I'm sure I can convince him."

"As long as it doesn't result in you having to break up with me."

"Whatever would cause her to do that shouldn't be done." The pair looked at each other and then behind them to find her father approaching.

Mercedes' brow rose. "Dad?"

He slapped Takashi on the back with his artificial hand, getting a silent "ow" from him. "You kept my daughter safe instead of running like some coward. That is what earns my respect."

Mercedes crossed her arms and tilted her head down, looking up at him. "Really, Dad?"

He chuckled. "Really, really."

She threw her head back. "I'm never going to understand you."

Her father ruffled her hair. "I have to keep you on your toes. Now what's this talk of yours about some idea that he doesn't want you to break up with him over?"

Mercedes laughed. "You got that way out context. I thought maybe Missus Asaka could use this spare space we have, since you're not doing anything worthwhile with it, and she needs a new place to put her business."

"Hey, storage is worthwhile."

"Uh huh, keep thinking that. And after you realize I'm right, you'll agree she can rent it out." She smiled wide. "Please, Daddy? It'll benefit you, too."

"I don't know." He rubbed the back of his neck as he looked into the room. "I like having this here."

"Dad, you never take anything out from there. Seriously, in all my years being here, you've never taken more than one percent of this stuff out. You don't need it."

He frowned. "You nag like your mother."

Mercedes giggled. "That's because she was right, and you know it."

"All right, fine. If Asaka likes the opportunity, I'll work up a price for rent and clean this out." Her father pointed at Mercedes. "But you're helping me."

Mercedes threw her arms around her father's neck. "You're the best, Daddy."

He patted her on the back. "Now, go home. You've had a long night, and the police have given us clearance to leave."

"But I need to finish payroll. I've got four people left."

"I'll take care of it."

"Dad…"

He smiled. "Really, it's no trouble. You've earned the time off for the night. And you can come in late tomorrow."

She let out a deep sigh. There wasn't going to be any winning with him. "Okay." She kissed him on the cheek. "Have a good night, Daddy."

"Goodnight, Sweetie."

Mercedes threaded her fingers in with Takashi's, and the pair retrieved his backpack and then left, Mercedes putting back the wrench she borrowed for her "just in case" moment. When they made it to his motorcycle, she sat down on it sideways. "So, what's the game plan?"

He placed his hands on either side over her, leaning close. "I thought I'd go back to your place and we could figure things out from there."

She grinned. "I do owe you, don't I? Especially after how good you were today."

He dragged his finger lightly up her arm. "A little bit."

Her gaze fell to the motorcycle and she ran her hand across the seat. "It's a shame I don't have a helmet. I'd love to take a ride with you."

"We'll work on getting you one soon, how about that?"

Mercedes looked up at him and smiled. "I like that idea. But I guess I have to drive home alone." She got up and pecked him on the lips. "I'll see you at the house."

Takashi pulled her close. "Maybe I could leave the bike here and ride with you."

"Don't want to do the walk of shame?" Her eyes sparkled.

He chuckled. "There's no shame in what we do together."

"Hey!" Mercedes' father's voice carried across the parking lot. "You two cut that out, and get out of here before I stop liking him."

The pair laughed and then parted, promising no pit stops between there and Mercedes' house. Mercedes sat down in the driver's seat, a smile on her face.

Even with what they'd gone through tonight, Mercedes felt good. They'd stopped the vandal, figured out a potential solution for Asaka, and even managed to get her father to accept Takashi, even if for a short time. The next few weeks wouldn't be easy, what with the investigation, but with Takashi by her side, she knew she could handle anything. Even though they lived far apart, she was excited to build this new relationship with him, and figure out how to make it work, no matter what stood between them.

The white sports car pulled into an available parking space and Mercedes climbed out, her arms full of pizza boxes. The boxes teetered and she did her best to right herself, only to overdo it and have to shift the other way.

"Miss Mercedes," Tasha said. "Wouldn't it be easier if I call for help?"

"No, I got it," she managed out as she teetered back and forth due to an unruly box on the top. "Besides, I was told it was busy thanks to the grand opening. I don't need to cause any more issues."

"Very well."

Mercedes finally got her bearings and headed for the shop, noting the new sign next to her father's, half in Kanji and Hiragana, half English; *Hana no Kaze Floral Arrangements*. It roughly translated to Flora Wind Floral Arrangements.

When Takashi and she had proposed the idea to

his mother, they weren't sure she'd go with it. But the first thing out of Asaka's mouth mirrored Mercedes' reasoning. It didn't take long for the arrangements to be made. After three long months of cleaning out the spare room and getting it renovated for a small florist shop, today Asaka had her grand reopening, under a slightly new name.

"Your mother loved this shop almost as much as she loved you. It's only right I add her into the name when you've given me this new chance to start again. You honor us both, Mercedes."

Her words stuck with Mercedes, making her a bit emotional every time she replayed them.

"Hey, I got the food!" Mercedes shouted as she entered the shop.

Metal clanged on the ground, and what sounded like a herd of animals came running for her. Before she had the chance to think, the boxes were taken from her arms in batches, and a jumble of happy "thank you" and "you're the best" praises hit her ears. Her employees dispersed, happy to take their lunch break, leaving her where she stood.

"Bunch of freeloaders, aren't they?" a familiar voice she loved said from behind her.

"That's men for you." She smirked as she turned and faced the handsome dark-haired man behind her. "They think with their stomachs most hours of the day, and with the limp thing between their legs the rest of the time."

Takashi chuckled and presented her a red rose in his usual "magic" fashion. "Limp? Glad I'm not them."

She accepted the customary gift and inhaled the sweet scent. "How's the grand reopening going?"

He smiled wide. "Great. It's been a while since I've

seen my mother this happy. And the customers love the new arrangement. A few of your father's patrons from earlier today were sure to get Mother's 'Don't Kill Me' bouquets."

Mercedes laughed. Miguel had come up with the naming for some of the arrangements as a joke, and Asaka ran with them.

"But I'm due for a break, and thought lunch with you while unpacking would be a great way to spend that."

Mercedes' heart swelled as she nodded, an uncontainable smile on her lips. After some discussion, Takashi had decided to move back to the states, but not in with his parents. He and his adorable cat moved in with her, and she couldn't be happier. Mercedes had offered to move out there with him, but he shot it down almost as quickly as she'd offered.

With his job not requiring him to be in one specific place anymore, and knowing the struggle she'd find starting up a restoration shop of her own in a new, unfamiliar country, Takashi deemed it best he move back. It helped that his family was also in the states, so he saw no reason to take her from her father as well.

Mercedes hadn't expected Takashi to move in so soon after deciding, since he didn't want to leave a neighbor of his alone, as he'd grown quite fond of her during his stay in Korea, but apparently she'd passed away unexpectedly last month.

Takashi laced his fingers in with hers and tugged her to follow. Before they got very far, his mother called out, "Takashi, did you pay for that rose?"

"Of course, *Okaasan*," he called back. "It's in the register."

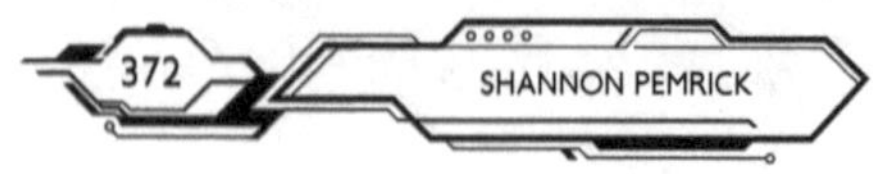

Mercedes giggled when the register drawer slid open. Asaka was something else.

The pair left the building and hopped into the car, Mercedes punching in their home address as Tasha spoke, "Hello, Takashi. It's good to see you've survived the first half of your day."

Takashi laughed. "Thanks, Tasha. I'm happy, too."

The car pulled out and sped down the road, Takashi lacing his fingers again with Mercedes'. She smiled at him.

"How'd your chat with Shira go?" he asked her. "I heard you answer a call from her as you were leaving."

She frowned. "Not as well as I hoped. She's still being stubborn about this convention thing, but now I know the big reason. While she is hesitant to meet Jasper and Zach, it's the idea of going to a convention center that gets her worked up. Any time she passes one, her anxiety goes through the roof and her PTSD gets the better of her."

Mercedes looked down at her lap. "From what she says, until this past year, even going to see Narissa for checkups was a chore. She doesn't even stay at a hotel. She travels from their family vacation home in Manhattan Beach. I didn't realize how much she struggled still."

Takashi squeezed her hand. "She'll get better. Now that we know, we can help, and maybe this convention will be a good way to steer her in the right direction."

"I hope so…" A thought came to her. "Hey, have you gotten the chance to talk to Emi lately to see how she's holding up?"

After the incident at the shop three months ago, an intensive investigation had been conducted, and Jason was in fact found to be responsible for the issues she suffered, along with Takashi's family and others in the community. He had coerced the man caught setting the fire at the shop, as well as a few others, into doing the vandalizing to keep his tracks covered.

Miguel's digging with his interns, along with Darius' own investigation, also uncovered Jason to be the source of the phone tampering and the hacking incidents with Takashi's shop. An arrest was made, and Jason was held without bail until his trial later that month.

Mercedes, her father, and many others were required to attend the trial and testify against him. He was convicted of felony charges and sentenced to twenty-five years in prison. Those who had been forced to work for him were given much lighter sentences, mostly doing mandatory community service working for those affected. The guy Takashi and Mercedes caught, Merlin, worked odd jobs for her father and Asaka at the moment. He didn't cause any fuss, and Asaka used some of her contacts to help his wife with her medical needs, earning his eternal gratitude.

Due to Jason's involvement with Emi's father's company, a public announcement was made, apologizing for the wrong doings and making it known that their own investigation was in the works to ensure their clients weren't affected by any other activities. Jason's father also made an appearance, apologizing for his son's behavior. He assured that the family did not condone such actions and he publicly disowned his son.

Last Mercedes knew, Emi was coping as best she could, considering the circumstances.

Takashi nodded. "I spoke to her earlier today. She's

doing well. With the time that's passed, she realized how controlling he was, and while she was upset when everything went down, she's happier than she has been in a long time."

Mercedes smiled. "I'm glad to hear that. She deserves to be happy."

"I agree. It also helps that Shira's family liked her designs and are getting them into a show in a few months."

Mercedes' eyes lit up. "Really? That's fantastic! I'm so happy for her. I'll have to contact her to let her know. Hopefully she won't mind."

"I'm sure she'd like that." Takashi smiled. "Now another question is, how are you doing?"

Mercedes squeezed his hand and then gazed into his eyes. "Now that you're here, never better."

A wide grin spread across Takashi's face. "With that kind of answer, I think an extra special lunch is in order."

Mercedes' eyes narrowed as a smirk spread across her lips. "I think you're right. But first…" She removed her seatbelt and climbed into his lap. The beaded necklace he used to wear, but gave to her as a gift before his temporary return to Korea, draped low enough from her neck to touch him. Apparently the beads had more meaning than he'd originally revealed prior to giving it to her. "I think Tasha needs to take the long way home, don't you think?"

Takashi pulled her closer and grinned. "I think you're right."

"Miss Mercedes, I don't think you should do that," Tasha objected. "There is a seatbelt law, and to sit on someone like that when a vehicle is moving is incredibly unsafe. It would be wise to wait until the two of you arrive home to engage in any lewd activities."

"I don't care right now." She ground her hips into Takashi. "Please find a long way to take us home."

If an assistant could sigh, Tasha most likely would have. "As you wish, Miss Mercedes."

Mercedes leaned in and captured Takashi's lips with hers. She'd been dying to do this with him for a while now, but the opportunity never came up. Now she was going to take full advantage of the chance. Unpacking, and lunch, could wait a little longer. They had plenty of time for that leg of their journey together.

Shannon Pemrick is a full-time USA Today best-selling author of slow-burn romantic fantasy, fuller-time geek, and dragon obsessed. She also has too many novelty mugs, not enough chocolate, and a forbidden love-affair with all things shiny. When she's not burning her fingers across a keyboard handing out adventures and HEAs, she's rolling dice and getting lost in RPGs or searching for brides for her dragon overlords.

You can learn more about Shannon by visiting her website at:
Shannonpemrick.com